Secrets

Murder Lies and Politics

By

Rob W Davis

Evershine Press, Inc.

Published by Evershine Press, Inc.
1971 W Lumsden Rd #209
Brandon, FL 33511

ISBN: 978-1-7364040-0-3 Hardback
ISBN: 978-1-7364040-1-0 Paperback
eBook ISBN: 978-1-7364040-2-7

First Edition:
First Mass Market edition:

Printed in the United States of America

Dedication

Thank you to my understanding wife, my publisher and all my great friends who helped make this book possible. 'Secrets' has a special place in my heart because of an exceptional friend 'Carolista' who gave great insight into the crux of this story. She helped iron out some of the details. Unfortunately, she passed to a better world before she got to enjoy the final result. I hope everyone enjoys the novel as much as I loved writing this tale.

Chapter One

Rose Finley races her gray Chrysler 300 she nicknamed Bertha across the strip and screeches into a parking spot next to a black van. She notices a G-string hanging from the rearview mirror of the van. Being an FBI agent Rose makes a mental note of that and other things as she races to the dock of the 'Bacalao' party boat. She scrambles across the concrete walk and her four-inch heels clink on the metal gangplank as she scurries up the incline. Her shoulder-length scarlet hair flaps in the gusty wind under her navy blue wide-brim hat that she holds down with one hand. Her low-cut matching blue dress with silver spangles glitters in the ten o'clock sun. The dress seems too tight and too formal for her, but at age twenty-eight Rose wants to look sexy and rich, the two things that seem attractive to political party men. But Rose has little interest in politics or romance. She is intent on gathering evidence against Senator Sancho as she approaches the stern of the boat.

The noticeable wind reminds her that even with the sun bright in the morning sky, Hurricane Jezebel is racing toward Cuba and threatening to swing toward Florida. The forecast for Miami is only a lot of rain and wind gusts from the outer bands of Hurricane Jezebel if she takes the predicted path across Cuba.

Despite the imminent stormy weather, Rose wants to get on the *'Bacalao'*. The party boat is about to motor away with the incumbent Florida Senator Hubert Sancho onboard. She normally would have her .38 Glock handgun with her but not today. Rose knows she may be searched and with tight security there, what could go wrong?

Reaching the top of the ramp, she stops in front of a big man blocking the entrance to the party. She admires his tanned biceps that stretch the sleeves of his black shirt that hangs outside his tight black Chinos. Rose shows her straight white teeth that contrast her girlish freckles as she smiles at the man. She wobbles a little on her stiletto heels focusing her green eyes level with the six-foot burly man's eyes. She pouts at the man and babbles.

"I so hope you will let me onboard. I lost my handwritten invitation to the private party for Senator Sancho but I really want to be at this rally for our man. It's less than three months until the election and he may not have another party like this in Miami." She pleads and flashes a smile but the man still blocks her.

"What is your name, Miss?" The man says admiring the beautiful woman standing in front of him. Even with the wind blowing, he senses her pleasant cinnamon perfume and he forces himself not to smile at her.

"Carter, Rose Carter."

"Your name isn't here." He says after looking at his guest list.

"Yeah, I'm a last-minute addition. What is your name sir?"

"Frank ma'am, but you can't..."

"Well Frank, they probably didn't have time to put me on the list. I'm having a really hectic day. You see, first I had trouble getting into this dress. It seems too tight even with the built-in bra, don't you think?" Rose Finley wriggles adjusting the top of her dress and smiles seeing Frank stare at her and tilt his head.

"Then I had trouble finding my checkbook, and I barely made it through traffic in time to get here. You see, I want to give Hubert another contribution in person. So you tall handsome fella, will you let me on?" Her green eyes fix on his but the man remains silent so Rose wobbles and fakes a stumble. As she starts to fall, Frank grabs her. Rose wraps her arms around his waist feeling the hard butt of his concealed handgun. She leans into him and smiles seeing his annoyed look soften.

"Oh, thank you so much, Frank. I could have fallen overboard."

"Okay, let me look in your purse ma'am." Frank grunts as he helps Rose stand up. He backs her away before releasing her and taking her purse. His eyes stray to her several times, as he opens her purse and examines the contents. Frank sees an MP3 player and earbuds, lipstick, some pills, a hairbrush, a cell phone, a checkbook, and some cash. He checks the fake ID that shows the name, Rose Carter. Nothing looks threatening to him. Frank returns her purse and waves a metal detector over her body and thinks. *Just another* gorgeous *party doll. The boss will love her!* He fakes a smile and waves her onboard.

"Thank you so much, Frank!" Rose smiles at the man and purposely rubs against him as she steps onto the closed-in party deck. She slips through the plastic strips hanging from the entrance to keep the air inside and thinks. *Glad I didn't bring my gun!* Her Glock normally hides in her purse or under her blouse on her waist on any dangerous assignment. She feels even more naked without her bra and her gun, but she laughs and thinks. *I'm hardly at risk here. I have one thing to do and then party! What can happen in a crowd of boozed-up political cronies?*

Rose stands at the edge of the huge dance floor feeling a cool breeze flow across her face from the air-conditioned room. She sees many couples dancing to the rock music blaring from overhead speakers. Some of the guests are sitting on the perimeter or in the bar area sucking on adult beverages. The women range in age from twentyish like Rose to sixty or older and their clothing ranges from a tube top with shorts to a party dress similar to hers. The men are either wearing shorts with loose flowery shirts or suits. She guesses nearly half of the fifty or more people are dancing. The strong bass beat vibrates her insides as she scans the area, but sees no sign of a newsperson and no Federal employees that she knows of. Rose looks at the huge bar on the port side. She wasn't able to check out the boat yesterday when she got word of a secret party for Sancho. She saunters toward the starboard side next to the restrooms and sees a room marked private. *That's where I need to go!* Rose thinks. She corrects her balance as she feels the boat start to move.

Chapter Two

Just after ten o'clock in a brisk wind, the shoremen release the last hawser from the *'Bacalao'*. Florida Senator Hubert Sancho and fifty-plus of his closest political friends adjust to the motion as the boat glides away from the marina. The boat sails toward the East and Hubert Sancho stops dancing and snugs up his tie. He shuffles through the crowd to a platform near the stern and motions to cut off the music that has blared since before his supporters came on board.

Senator Hubert Sancho hates being only five feet tall with his lifter shoes on so he stands on a small wood platform near the tail of the boat to peer over the crowd. His weight matches his age at fifty. Even with the breeze from the air conditioner, he wipes sweat off his face with a handkerchief before waving at his cheering supporters.

"My friends welcome to this secret thank you slash fundraiser party! All of my special guests are here now and we will have a great time despite a little turbulence." Hubert raises his fist to the cheering audience and waits until the people quiet down.

"I must talk politics for a moment. Our campaign is going strong even with this recent dip in the polls. We will crush our opponent and keep the Senate seat thanks to your generous help." Sancho smiles as the crowd cheers. He talks for a few minutes about his team's achievements including the massive crowd at his recent rally in Fort Myers, the new ads set for next week, and his denial of the slanderous claims by his opponent, before wrapping up his speech.

"I know I'm trailing my opponent but we have some great ads airing tomorrow that will put us back on top." Sancho waits until the cheering settles again. "I will give an update on our plans and plea for more funds when we are heading back to shore. I know you are worried about the storm, but the Captain assures me if the storm moves toward us he will head back long before Jezebel could hurt us. In the meantime, have fun! The drinks are on the house and I hope all of you generous and mutually beneficial friends enjoy the party! Start the music!" Hubert Sancho smiles as he eases off the platform. He dances and makes his way into the middle of the cheering crowd loosening his tie in-between shaking hands along his way. Then he sees his prospective new donor Rafael Matuso slink out through the plastic strips.

Rafael Matuso, the six-foot-six muscular man looks garish in his tailored black suit and his tan deck shoes. His short black hair is unruffled by the wind as he eases by his man Frank. After pushing through the plastic strips, he leans on the railing at the stern. He turns and smiles seeing Sancho coming to him. Matuso looks back at the wake and the receding shoreline. He takes out a cigarillo and cuffs his gold Zippo against the wind to puff the small cigar to life.

Hubert Sancho rushes toward the rear of the boat. The party invitations went out before Hurricane Jezebel became a possible threat. He tried to delay the party because some of his worried cronies canceled their invitation, but Matuso insisted he hold it as scheduled and meet with him here today. Sancho grudgingly gave in to this, although he feels resentful for taking orders from the man. He expects to reap a big donation for his concession. As Sancho walks toward the rear deck, he sees his PR man Victor Campbell approach him.

Victor being nearly six feet tall leans over and grabs Sancho. He has to semi-hug the shorter man to talk over the music. "This is wrong to befriend Matuso!" Victor speaks into Sancho's ear careful that no one else is listening. "I told you police arrested him several times for murder, but none of the cases ever made it to trial. Witnesses mysteriously disappear or suddenly die. Just because the public and the media love him for his large charity donations doesn't mean he is a good man. Please, he isn't safe to deal with!" But Victor feels Sancho pry loose and grab his arms.

"You still don't understand politics Victor. We could lose this election! We must do whatever it takes to win, nothing else matters! I don't know why Attorney General Bill Medina is so popular and chose to run against me. With Matuso's money, we can counter blitz his negative ads. I have to do this." Sancho releases Victor and walks toward the stern.

"This is a bad plan!" Victor shouts but Sancho keeps walking.

Senator Hubert Sancho knows his time in office has done wonders for his personal financial gain. Between unethical deals and payoffs, Hubert has amassed a fortune he hides in an offshore bank. He only wants to double his cash stash to feel confident retiring. Hubert must keep the cash rolling in so he can retire in the Cayman Islands. He believes he needs one more term to accomplish his goal.

Because the Senator has done so little for the public good over his years in office, the huge number of smaller contributions has tapered off and he must have big money to run ads against his opponent's allegations of corruption. Hubert has considered other ideas but he likes easy, and Rafael is an easy fix. The man has practically promised Sancho he will be reelected. Hubert dislikes Matuso knowing the man is part of a crime organization that his office should be fighting, but he needs help. The whole purpose of agreeing to have the party now is to get the huge money he needs from Matuso knowing the man is sure to ask for some big favor. At this point, Hubert is willing to do anything to stay in office. He stops and leans against the rail next to Rafael.

Rafael Matuso looks like a giant standing next to Sancho as he nods and extends his massive hand. He smiles at the man as if Sancho were an underling rather than anyone close to his equal. After shaking hands Rafael turns back toward the churning wake, puffs on his cigarillo, and enjoys the warm August breeze. He reaches inside his suit jacket and discretely hands a thick envelope to Sancho. Matuso breaks the silence, confident that Sancho will be his puppet.

"Take this for you."

"Thanks." Sancho peers into the envelope and sees a cashier's check and a large wad of hundred-dollar bills. "Thank you very much!" Sancho says mentally seeing the hundred-dollar bills going into his personal funds.

"The cash is ten thousand. There will be more my friend."

"Your cashier's check is very generous too. It will help fund the ads I have in mind. I'm leery of putting the cash into my campaign account though. The snoops will want to know why I didn't get a traceable check."

"You understand why I give you the cash? You don't want the money?"

"Oh yes, I do! I will handle it!" Sancho stuffs the envelope in his coat pocket.

"Good, I do much more. I have a plan for us." Matuso shouts over the music.

"I doubt if I need..."

"Look out this way." Matuso waves a well-tanned hand pointing toward the shore. "I like to watch the buildings drift out of sight. Once we are in the ocean they will start fading down as if the sea is eating them up."

"You have a plan?" Sancho stares at Matuso, ignoring the comment.

"Yes, the noise is too much here. We go to a quiet room upfront across the dance floor to talk. This morning Frank checked it for bugs. For now, we watch the ocean eat the land, then we go there."

"Sure, anything you say." Sancho tightens his lips, still not used to someone telling him what to do. He stands impatiently with Matuso and stares at the shoreline as he thinks. *I don't need a plan from this thug!* Then he remembers the ten thousand in his suit pocket and waits.

"We will make a good team Sancho. Like a Hurricane Jezebel, my plan will soon stir the political world!"

Chapter Three

As the *'Bacalao'* steers away from its Miami pier with its loud music and noisy people Rose Finley merges unnoticed into the dancers but she and the dancers stop when the music cuts off and Sancho starts to talk to the crowd. Rose invited herself on the party boat to spy on Senator Hubert Sancho against the orders from her superior, Donna Grant. As she hears Sancho talk from the rear of the boat, Rose thinks back.

She recalls Donna telling her. *"If the hurricane shifts course and that party boat goes down, I could lose one of my best agents. This Sancho-Matuso thing is only a rumor. There are other more productive things you can work on. Forget it, Rose!"* Since the 'rumor' about an unannounced Sancho party came from Rose's mole, she had to check it out herself. Donna never told her to back off investigating the politics of Sancho before. *Is Donna really concerned for my safety or what?* In the past, she tried catching Sancho getting kickbacks from overpaid contractors among other things but she always lost the trail. Rose wonders why Grant would say she is one of her best agents.

Her gut tells her she did right coming onboard. She knows Matuso is a honcho involved in drug trafficking and other activities, a bad influence on the incumbent Senator from Florida. This could be a super score for her. Rose wants to be the best FBI agent on the force. Today all she needs to do is plant her micro-camcorder in the private room up front, then relax and enjoy the dancing, free food, and booze. She will send the video to Donna after the boat docks. Rose expects to get a figurative gold star for today, even without approval to crash the party. Her boss will have to like the video she records.

She glances out a window and watches the boat sail past Fisher Island. The music starts and Rose sees Hubert Sancho break away from his PR man and rush onto the stern next to Rafael Matuso. Rose dances in place enjoying the music and staring at the two men. She sees Sancho take something from Matuso, probably a bribe. She begins dancing toward the room marked 'private' when a handsome man dressed in a dark suit and tie steps in front of her. Smiling, and not wanting to draw attention by ignoring the man she starts dancing with him. At political parties, she knows 'suits' like to do things with young women, especially if they are hot and under thirty like Rose is.

"Hello! I'm House Rep. Alan, Alan Duncan. I'm sure you have heard of me."

"The name sounds familiar."

"You're new and cute!" He shouts over the music.

"Yes, I'm new. I'm Rose Carter, nice to meet you, Alan." She feels an attraction to him, noting he is tall, no wedding band, fortyish, dark brown hair, blue eyes, and a movie star smile.

"I'll be replacing Sancho for the Senate seat when he retires."

"That's a bold statement, Alan." Rose says flustered by his perfect smile.

"It takes good looks, guts, and a thick hide to survive in politics and I have all three. I received great press about my bill for a senior citizens program, and I will step in when he steps down."

"That's another bold assumption." Rose shouts. She looks away from his eyes. Rose tries not to get too friendly or think about any kind of romance. She tries to just concentrate on her mission.

"I'm a bold man and I say the man who left a beauty like you alone is a fool. Some bold guy like me might sweep you away from him!" Alan says. Then he sees an angry man approaching from behind her. As he reaches for her hand, he hears Rose mumble.

"Oh um, I um I'm..." Rose feels her face flush. She turns her head not wanting him to see how flustered she is.

"Oh... excuse me." He leaves as the angry man reaches Rose.

Rose gapes at Alan but he just waves a sheepish hand as he dances away. She is stunned and yells at his back. "Hey, I'm not with anyone!" She shouts but the music drowns out her voice and Alan is gyrating with another woman already too far away to hear her. The angry man cackles as he passes in front of Rose and grabs a dancer. Rose starts to go after Alan to explain but she stops. As she stands motionless with the music blasting from the overhead speakers, she snaps back to reality. Rose shakes her head and dances toward the front of the boat. When she reaches the restroom area, she goes to a door marked private. Seeing no one looking her way, she slips inside the private room and closes the door.

All her senses are on alert as she glances around the room. Rose feels an icy cold breeze from the air conditioner vent. With the cabin door shut, the rock music, the shouting, and the laughing all hush. Except for the distant hum of the boat's engine, there is an eerie silence in the soundproof room. Her nose starts to stuff up from a faint odor of mildew. She sees a driftwood coffee table in front of a tan couch on the starboard side of the room next to a giant three feet high window. The window sprays in enough sunlight so Rose leaves the cabin light off. A bookcase, with half-high brown straps to hold in the books, hangs on the wall over the couch.

Rose is sure Matuso will use this room for a private talk. She walks across the gray and blue carpet with fish designs, her shoes crackle, slightly sticking to the rug with each step. Reaching the couch Rose thinks. *No big deal, just plant your camcorder and go explain yourself to Alan Duncan. This could be a great party!*

Easing behind the couch, Rose examines the bookrack and finds a perfect gap between two books for her camcorder. She grabs her hairbrush from her purse, opens the hollow handle, and slides out the micro-camcorder. The unit can capture many hours on its microchip memory but she only needs to record at most an hour or two. She turns it on in proximity mode so it records anytime it senses someone close by. Rose discretely wedges the micro-camcorder in place aiming its lens at the middle of the room. "That will do it. Now I can party!" She whispers, happy the camcorder is out of view and recording.

Rose starts to ease around the couch but she hears Sancho talking as the door starts to swing open. Instinctively she drops to the floor behind the couch. The music, chatter, and laughter blast into the room as she thinks. *This is a mistake! I should leave!* She slips off her hat and lies flat on her back. Rose hears Rafael Matuso start talking while the door is still open.

"As I said, Frank checked this for bugs earlier, so only you hear me talk."

"What do you want to discuss?" Sancho asks closing the door.

"In the polls, you are behind Attorney General Bill Medina. I take action."

"I know I'm behind Medina. We are already taking action. He has no solid proof of corruption in my organization and our new ads deny all his claims and accuse him of making up lies. I will use your campaign money to increase our TV spots."

Rose breathes as quietly as she can. The musty odor from the rug causes her nose to itch so she squeezes it to kill the tingling. Then thinking they may find her, she takes out her MP3 player and earbuds to pretend she is engrossed in music and can't hear them talking.

"Understand there are no maybes, you must win." Matuso says.

"Well, I'm pretty sure the voting will swing my way."

"Not good enough Sancho! I have a better plan."

"I can always use good help. What is your idea?" Sancho tries not to show his contempt. He feels Matuso is telling him what to do again.

"I have a score to settle with Medina and he knows too much about - shall we say your secret deals. He can ruin your chances of winning. He might even put you in jail!"

"How could he? I have been careful to hide things."

"Late last night I created this plan with Don Ruiz to fix things. I will tell you what we think he knows. Then I will explain what we do to fix that."

"Who is Don Ruiz?"

"I must clear plans like this with him, Sancho. I tell you so you can prepare a response. Do you know Medina's girl Friday Sara Troutman is leaving him?"

"Yes, it was on the news last night. Maybe I can use that against him. You know, say he tried to molest her or something."

"Well, she claims she is too sick and can no longer run his campaign. I created this plan when I heard this. We will use the media to our advantage. We make this into a romance gone bad, a lover's spat. It gives him a motive and makes perfect my plan!"

"What motive? What plan?" Sancho is puzzled.

Rose hears a rap on the door. It opens letting air whoosh in the room stirring the carpet dust. Over the noise from the open door, she hears Victor Campbell shout.

"Sorry to disturb you Mister S but the weather is getting worse. The Captain says the sea is getting too rough so he is turning back to the marina."

"Okay, give me a few minutes." Hubert says.

"We are a little over ten miles out. I suggest you give your rally speech now!"

Before Sancho can answer, Matuso shouts.

"Sancho will be a few minutes. I'm talking..."

"Achoo!" Rose sneezes loud enough to exceed all other noises.

"Hey! Who is there?" Matuso shouts and he rushes toward the couch.

Chapter Four

Rose sits up holding her MP3 player with her earbuds in her ears. She looks at Rafael in shock and acts as if she is turning off the MP3 player.

"Who the Hell are you?" Rafael Matuso shouts.

"Who the Hell are you?" Rose asks. She puts her hat on and takes one earbud out.

"Never mind that, what are you doing in here?" Matuso shouts.

"I'm listening to music and hiding from my boyfriend. We had a fight. I thought you were Wayne coming in." Rose stands up and steps from behind the couch.

"This Wayne is your so-called boyfriend?"

She fakes a pout as she stretches her hand out to show Matuso her MP3 player. "Yes, I was just listening to music to avoid him for a while. I will leave now. You guys can have the room." She frowns and starts toward the door, but Matuso blocks her way.

"Where are you going?" Matuso shouts remembering a briefing he had yesterday.

"No need to shout at me, I'm leaving!"

"Miss Finley, is it? I think you are hiding in here to listen to what we say! Is that a recorder?" Matuso swats the player away from Rose. The other earbud snaps out of her ear as the player flies across the room bouncing off the front wall.

"Ow!" Rose shouts. Caught off guard, she feels more pain as Matuso grabs her arm and twists it behind her back.

"Ow! Let go! You're hurting me! Hey, that's an expensive player!"

"No one can hear you honey." Matuso smiles at her.

"What do we do now?" Sancho shouts watching Rose jerk trying to free her arm.

"Let me go. I have enough problems!"

"You have the worst problem now!" Matuso twists her arm higher. He pushes her near the window.

"Open up!" Matuso shouts to Sancho. He struggles with Rose as Sancho rushes to the window and fumbles with the latch to swing open the window.

"This opens to the sea. What are you doing?" Sancho feels his gut wrench as the wind rushes through the open portal and buffets his thin hair. He stares at the girl.

"I toss her through the window!"

"No! You can't just toss her out there!" Sancho shouts. His mind is in shock, not believing what Matuso wants to do.

"Yes, I can!" Matuso shouts pushing Rose closer to the window.

Rose squirms and twists trying to scratch Matuso with her free hand. She tries to elbow him but he forces her away. She stomps at his foot but he twists her arm still higher and she misses. She feels more pain in her shoulder. Her hat caught in the wind floats across the room and falls onto the carpet.

"We're miles from shore. She will drown! We can tie her up until we figure out what to do." Sancho cries. He locks eyes with Rose's wide-eyed stare for a second, feeling her fright.

"Yes, she will drown!" Matuso forces Rose to the edge of the window. The wind whips a stream of mist at him and he hears the muffled noise of the music coming through the opening as the ocean rushes by. He avoids Rose's free hand trying to claw at him as he grabs the bottom of her dress with his other hand and aims her at the window. He smiles feeling her struggle violently but her tight dress restricts her movement, and he is too strong for her. Matuso lifts her off the floor and heaves her out the opening. He hears her scream cut off when Rose plunges headfirst into the ocean.

"How can you do that?" Sancho yells.

"Easy, she weighs maybe a hundred twenty pounds." Matuso chortles.

"You joke? This is terrible! You sealed her fate! She can't survive out there!" Sancho's shaky legs collapse and he melts onto the couch. He pulls out his large handkerchief and mops his face.

"She's going to die!" Victor says standing frozen in place near the door.

"Exactly, and what do you think she was doing here? She is Grant's red-haired agent Rose Finley! Grant described her to me in case she came aboard against orders. She came here to spy on us, Victor! She was recording us but we surprised her before she could get away to tell anyone." Matuso picks up the MP3 player. "This is her recorder!" He picks up her purse and her hat off the floor. With a flick of his wrist, he tosses everything out the window.

"I think that was just an MP3 player." Victor says with a shaky voice.

"These spies, they make innocent-looking things into recorders Victor."

Sancho mops his brow again. "If she really was hiding from her boyfriend, you murdered an innocent woman!"

"I tell you she is Grant's impudent spy and that was her recorder. No matter, problem solved! It's time to forget about this! If anyone asks, we never saw her! Hubert will come out in time for his speech." Matuso latches the window shut.

"I hope no one saw her go!" Sancho mops his forehead, a bundle of nerves. He slides over on the couch for Victor to sit but Victor turns to leave.

"Victor, wait!" Matuso shouts.

"I'm not sure what to do here sir."

"I'll tell you what to do. Just do nothing and say nothing about this to anyone!"

"Someone might have seen her go in the ocean. We should check."

"We would have heard a commotion by now and we are too far away by the time she gets to the surface. She can yell all she wants and no one will hear her. Can you keep this a secret and act normal? Can you do that?" Matuso sees Victor give a nod of resignation. "Good, leave us alone Victor. We will be out in a few minutes." Matuso motions for Victor to leave and waits for the door to close before speaking again.

"I will go over the details of our plan. If you talk too long you can finish your speech while the boat is docking." Matuso steps next to the door after Victor leaves.

"Sara will die from a single headshot. My man will wipe the gun clean using a handkerchief with Medina's initials on it and leave it at the apartment with the gun. He will send a text to Bill Medina using her phone begging him to come to her apartment because she wants to negotiate some dirt she has on him. He will find her dead just as the police arrive due to an anonymous call from a burner phone. I'm sure Medina will get his fingerprints on the gun, but no matter. The police will believe he murdered her and then cleaned the gun."

"This isn't what I want to happen." Sancho stands up still shaken.

"We have no choice. Sit down!" Matuso forces Sancho back on the couch. "You must get yourself back in control! Act natural as if nothing has happened."

"God help us!" Sancho mumbles mopping his face again.

"God won't help us, we aren't angels! We help ourselves. That woman was an agent and agents are expendable! Grant was supposed to keep her off this boat." Matuso says as he dials his FBI contact Donna Grant. He sees Sancho bury his head in his hands leaning forward on the couch. Matuso frowns and thinks. *What a weak man!* He turns away, hearing Donna Grant answer.

"Why are you calling me?" Donna asks.

"Listen Grant, you told me no agent would be at this party!"

"None should be. Finley is the only one who wanted to go but I told her no... I described her to you in case, remember?"

"Yes, she is the redhead?"

"Yes. But I told her not to go on the party boat."

"Well, she disobeyed. I caught her spying on us."

"You will have to change your plan then. I don't know how I can handle this if she tells me anything."

"No worries, I tossed her into the ocean maybe ten miles off shore. Soon the rain and wind will hide her forever. She will not be talking to anyone!"

"Oh no! What the..." Donna pauses to regain her composure. "My boss will have questions about an agent disappearing. I'll have to think up something when I report her missing. What about her recorder, did you find her recorder?"

"Yes, I tossed that and her purse and hat too. There is nothing left of hers."

"Good, but I'm not happy losing her, Rafi."

"What do you mean?"

"She was a good agent, she trusted me. I could send her on false leads. Now I have to pick a new agent to investigate Sancho, but you did what you had to do."

"I did it, for both our sakes." Matuso disconnects and looks at Sancho. "Just so you know, her demise is a hazard of her job Sancho. She was a spy! Now I need to talk to Frank." Matuso says as he walks toward the door.

"You mean your goon by the entrance?" Sancho is despondent as he leans over feeling dizzy thinking. *I'm a witness to a murder and a planned assassination!*

Matuso opens the door but turns back. "Careful Hubert, he's my number one man!"

"Sorry." Sancho says and sees Matuso stare at him.

"I have to see if this Wayne fellow came with that woman. Act like the politician I know you are. Be out in two minutes. You must give a fearless speech! Just hit on the highlights." Matuso steps out of the room and swings the door closed.

Hubert Sancho sits alone on the couch, listens to the hum of the engine, and tries to cope with what happened. He mops his face again still dizzy. "I just need more money, not murders! There is no way out of this!" He sobs and toys with the idea of having the Captain go back to find the girl but believes she is already dead even if they could find her. He could blow the whistle on Matuso but he knows he can't do that. Political suicide and possibly his own death would happen if he did. Sancho feels his heart still racing as he rises to leave the room. He takes a deep breath, straightens his tie, and walks out of the quiet room into the music and noise.

Chapter Five

Matuso makes his way through the crowd giving a fake smile as he shuffles across the dance floor. He feels content. Murdering the girl as a solution to the problem just solidifies his hold over Sancho and Campbell. He hums contented, feeling no remorse. Rafael sees his man Frank standing near the bar, scotch, and water in hand, watching the crowd. As he nears Frank, his man shouts.

"Hey boss, all is good here. Everybody is having fun."

Matuso leans into Frank's ear to overcome the loud music.

"You remember seeing a red head in a tight blue dress with no invitation card?"

"Yes sir, but I checked her. She was clean."

"My mistake, I should have warned you."

"Warned me about what?"

"No matter, who is she with?"

"No one sir. She crashed the party just before we left the marina, and said she lost her invitation. She's a good looker and checked out okay so I let her on."

"You're sure she is with no one?"

"Yes sir, I would have noticed. She came onboard late, mingled with the crowd and then I lost sight of her. She must be on the far side of the dance floor. Do you want me or Craig to find her?"

"Oh yeah, Craig is here for backup. No Frank, just forget you ever saw her."

"Saw who sir?"

"Grazie! I will explain later." Matuso smiles at his number one man and pats Frank's shoulder. He sees Hubert Sancho walk to the platform with Victor trailing behind him. Matuso smiles thinking about how everything is happening correctly. He listens to Sancho talk to the crowd and smiles knowing agent Finley is dead by now. The start of his relationship with Sancho is going better than expected.

Rose plunges head first deep into the Atlantic Ocean tasting its salt before she can close her screaming mouth. She curves her arms and body reversing direction and pops up to the surface. She sucks in air and then the weight of the waterlogged dress drags her beneath the surface again. Rose kicks off her shoes and thrashes her arms and legs violently but can't stop her descent further into the black void. Her tight dress constricts her movement too much as she sinks deeper unable to stop her descent. Flipping on her back she sees the surface receding and concedes defeat to the ocean.

She feels calmness and joy inside that she never felt before as she relaxes her body to the inevitable. She feels her lungs ready to explode as she prepares to exhale and breathe in ocean water. Her final breath will end her short career as an FBI agent. *What a waste!* She thinks as she continues to drift deeper.

Then her mind slaps her back to reality telling her she must not die! She resists the urge to survive but her strong will to live takes over. She grabs the zipper on her dress pulling it down to her waist. Rose starts forcing the dress off her body. The tight dress material drags her panties down too. Her lungs are burning. Rose has no time to grab anything. The dress and the panties tangle into a wad at her feet. She kicks and raises her feet up and down until she finally ejects the dress and her underwear.

She swims with seemingly supernatural strength back to the surface and gasps uncontrollably, sucking air and spray into her starving lungs. Coughing, kicking, and paddling, she manages to keep her head above water. After her lungs calm down Rose flips her tangled hair out of her face. The wind whips a sprinkle of rain against her, and she swallows a gulp of ocean, as a new wave hits her from behind dumping her hair in her face again. Rose swings her head up to assess her surroundings. She struggles to stay on the turbulent surface. She can barely hear the noise from the distant engine and the music of the party boat already several hundred yards away. *I hope someone saw me go overboard.* Rose thinks but then as if to taunt her, she hears the faint blare of a saxophone stop, and the happy crowd cheer, "Tequila!"

"Hey! Oh no! Oh no!" Rose shouts working her legs to keep her head above the choppy surface. The party boat and the music continue to fade away. She becomes aware of a dull continuous ache from her right shoulder, where Matuso twisted her arm so violently. She treads water trying to think of what to do next.

With no bra and her panties and shoes gone, Rose laughs a nervous laugh realizing she is completely nude and has nothing around her to help her stay afloat. She treads water still gasping for air as she looks and listens, hoping to hear or see another boat. Except for a possible cargo ship several miles away, she sees nothing but waves and no sign of land. Even the party boat is now just a speck that shows up between wave crests. The foamy waves seem to be rising in height, cresting and relentlessly trying to force her underwater. She works hard to stay atop the bottomless ocean. Rose panics thinking a shark or other predator may make a meal of her or worse just take a bite and leave her to bleed to death in pain. She can feel her heart pounding much faster than normal.

Then her survival instincts kick in. *I can make it!* Rose asserts, determined to stay alive. She looks toward the blacker clouds she knows are to the south. *That must be an outer band of the hurricane. You aren't dead yet! You must not panic! You can swim to shore.* Her shoulder, arms, and legs are aching but her strong will to survive gives her strength. Rose analyzes her surroundings. She knows she can do the doggy-paddle almost forever so she starts swimming west, in the same direction the boat went.

"You bastards!" She shouts after a cresting wave douses her from behind. *I wonder how long I can survive here.* Rose thinks and once again forces herself to continue paddling. She examines the sky. The sun is straight up still glowing through the scattered dark clouds and waiting for the thicker black clouds to roll over. Rose keeps working at a slow steady doggy paddle. She tries not to think about her struggling motions that may attract sharks and other predators lurking near her. Rose concentrates on her swimming hoping she won't drown in the ocean before she reaches the Miami shore and before she loses strength or something eats her.

Rose tries to think about positive things. She flashes back to watching reruns of John Drake, the "Secret Agent Man" on TV when she grew up in Atlanta, Georgia. He was the best secret agent man on TV. He would foil an assassin's plan or save some place from blowing up. From her early childhood, she always wanted to be like the secret agent man. As she grew up, she recalls taking Karate lessons and Jujitsu and later took courses in police tactics before applying for work as an FBI agent. Her recruiter in Atlanta said she could wait for an opening there, or start work immediately in Miami, Florida. Rose snaps back to the present thinking. *So here I'm, in the middle of the ocean. I have absolutely no chance of saving lives and capturing bad guys as Patrick McGoohan would do!*

Some birds circling an area ahead of her bring her back to reality. The white fliers seem to work together swooping down perhaps targeting small fish. A strong feeling of loneliness creeps into her thoughts. She feels the inevitable end to her life is near and for a brief moment, Rose feels sadness take over her emotions. Surely if she dies out here her body may never be found. She thinks about her parents forever wondering what happened to her. Once again she has to force her mind to concentrate on surviving.

Rose focuses on paddling, trying to ignore her aching muscles and shoulder. *I must survive! I have to!* She shakes off feeling panicky, although she sees no sign of land. Rose tries to think about what she could have done differently to avoid being tossed off the boat. If she had not ducked behind the couch maybe she could have saved her life. The plan was to get out before Sancho and Matuso came into the room. If she could have used her special police training more effectively, but that didn't happen. Matuso just used his street smarts and brute force to manhandle her.

Her thoughts are interrupted by a wave bashing her backside and pushing her forward. *Keep your head up girl. You can make it!* She mentally blanks out the pain in her shoulder and muscles and keeps paddling. Rose sees the black clouds and the rain wall closing in on her from the south. She struggles to believe she will make it to shore. Then she pauses as a cold chill runs through her. She sees the surface churn ahead of her but this time it isn't any small fish the birds are after. Rose counts six gray fins on the surface rushing toward her. They come straight at her, almost touching her before they veer off and circle around her.

Chapter Six

Max Merchado is living serene and clean on this warm August morning in the luxury housing development of Blue Lake Estates in Fort Lauderdale, Florida. The relaxing ambiance of grass growing, birds chirping, squirrels scurrying about in the oak trees, coconut palm fronds swaying and a few American flags flapping in the gentle breeze, all contribute to his comfortable easy living.

The pristine streets including Lux Lane where he lives are empty except for a blue solid waste truck making a final collection of trash from the curbsides this Thursday morning. Sturdy shutters cover the triple pane windows on the oversized homes along the streets including Max's home at 250 Lux Lane. The community is prepared for any winds and rain in case the hurricane veers north.

Max Merchado isn't happy. He is unable to close a huge order for helicopters. His client wants to wait until after Jezebel passes. Silvan Enterprises has given the dark-haired thirty-year-old man the salesperson of the year award several times and has decided to close early Thursday until Monday to give its employees time to board up in case the hurricane changes course. Even though Jezebel is a mild category one hurricane, with winds barely over 75 miles per hour, his prospective client in Denver, Colorado is waiting to release funds until after Jezebel isn't a threat to the factory in Fort Lauderdale.

The powder blue shutters on his windows block the early morning sunlight, so Max turns on the elegant glass and brass chandelier to light up the living room before moving to his chair. Max and his fiancée Peggy Clarkson ignore the 6:30 morning news on the giant screen TV. Max is thinking of what to say to Peggy. He sits in his swivel rocker with his black cat Hera purring in his lap.

Hera showed up at his old house on Clifton Street after Max came back from a cruise to celebrate the reward money he earned for returning a diamond to an Italian family. She watches everything he does and seems so mysterious to Max that he named her Hera after the woman psychic of the same name he met in Italy. Since then, Hera became a part of his family, even seeming to answer questions for him.

An older weatherman is saying Hurricane Jezebel is moving unexpectedly faster and the eye will pass over Cuba by late today. The outer bands are starting to ruffle Miami with some wind and rain now instead of showing up on Friday morning.

Max looks at his pricey Jaeger-LeCoultre watch expecting a taxi to arrive for Peggy any second. He knows Peggy will fly away for her week-long stay in Las Vegas long before much rain from the hurricane reaches the Fort Lauderdale-Hollywood International Airport.

His bare feet massage the thick tan carpet next to his blue sandals. Max likes to squeeze the thick pile with his toes. He turned thirty last month and feels uneasy about gaining a few extra pounds as he looks at Peggy again and thinks. *Peggy is gorgeous.* He feels out of place. Dressed in blue shorts and a flowery shirt he is in awe of Peggy sitting bolt upright across from him on the sofa.

With her flawless complexion and trim body, he believes Peggy could have been a top-paid model. Max is five feet ten and with heels, Peggy is as tall as he is. She sits with her hands folded across her lap showing her perfectly manicured pink fingernails. Every strand of her dark brown hair is in place, pinned atop her head. Her high cheekbones, her long eyelashes underlined with pale blue, and her glittery blue sapphire earrings highlight her sparkly blue eyes. Tucked into her sharply creased dark pink slacks that partly cover her matching pink stiletto heels is her light pink blouse. She has the buttons undone just far enough to show off her ample cleavage. Peggy remains quiet. She sits straight-backed on the sofa and stares at the news on the TV.

Max is ready for some turbulent wind and rain, but he is having trouble dealing with the turmoil inside his own house. He pets Hera and thinks about all the good times with Peggy that ended yesterday. His mind flips from the fun of the sales deal he is working on, to his formal proposal yesterday to Peggy and her answer. He was still kneeling holding a two-carat diamond ring for her when her words stunned him.

"Let's talk Max. Come sit next to me."

"Is it about the fake snakes in the pool? I'm sorry. I promise no more pranks."

"No, I'm used to your pranks, this is about us."

"What about us?"

"You know Ann and Sam married without any hoopla. I know you want an elaborate wedding, but I don't. Actually, I need you to cancel any plans."

"You think I will spend too much? You're still mad at me?"

"No Max, I love you but we have different goals. I'm sure you want kids and I don't. I don't think it is right to stay with you."

"We have this huge home now. There is plenty of room for children and we have a ton of money to support them. What is wrong with having kids?"

"They will burden us down Max. I want to see new places and new things like we used to do. Kids would just hamper that."

"So, what are you saying? Are you leaving me?"

"Yes, I'm sorry Max. I will rent a small apartment when I return from Las Vegas or maybe rent a place there if I like it. I've thought about this ever since you bought this house, even imagined me having babies, but it isn't what I want Max. I can return the million-dollar reward money if you want. I need to be free and go wherever I want."

"Wow, this hurts Peg. Oh no, I insist you keep the money. You helped us return the diamond. You risked your life just as we all did."

"Oh dear... Okay Max, I do love you. This is hard to do but it is for the best."

"I love you too. I thought we should be married."

"You need to find someone who wants what you want. That unfortunately isn't me. I love you too much to marry you Max."

"So, you love me too much to be with me?"

"Yeah, and you love me too much to take back that million dollars."

"This is the strangest breakup ever! I won't toss out my wedding plans until you get back. At least will you think about kids and us when you are in Vegas?"

"And you think about not having kids while I'm away, okay?"

Max remembers ending their talk still in a daze. He thinks about the happy times they had with the big reward money. He reminisces about being young and in love with Peggy and enjoying everything a wad of money has done for him and his friends. He split a five million dollar reward four ways with his friends Sam, Ann, and Peggy who helped return a rare diamond to its owners in Italy.

Then the big house next to Sam's friend Chet Hatter, lead guitarist for the Danglebatts, became available in Blue Lake Estates. Max bought it and moved with Peggy and his adopted cat Hera from his old frame house on Clifton Street. Max knows the luxurious concrete block five-bedroom house is the perfect place for raising his kids since Chet and his wife Katie will have children too. He had hoped to convince Peggy to fill the extra rooms with children, but when he talked to Peggy about finally having kids, she balked. He thought Peggy would change after having no financial worries and seeing the great big house. He found out she not only hates the house; she still hates the idea of having a bunch of kids too. He stares at Peggy who seems as nervous as he is sitting on the couch waiting for a taxi to arrive.

His gaze is broken when Peggy speaks.

"I hear the garbage truck going by so please remember to roll the empty trash bucket into the garage. We don't want it flying all over the place."

"Yes ma'am." Max says as he stares affectionately at her.

Chapter Seven

"So you and Sam will be alone for a week?" Peggy says.

"I'm not happy separating like this. You and I had a perfect life together, we're set for life financially and all." Max says but thinks. *Maybe Peggy is right. We really do want different things. I want at least a son to teach about fishing and life.*

"We really should have kids Peggy."

"No, you want kids. I don't want any at all. I wish you had not bought this gigantic house. I feel so lost here. It's a waste of space and money."

"Not if we have a lot of kids…"

"It is no secret Max. You knew I didn't want kids soon after you met me. Do you remember all the thrilling things we used to do? I want to do a lot of exciting things and I can't do those things if I have to tend to children. I can't leave kids at a nursery to go to Italy or Africa, and taking them along would be a real burden.

"Yes, I knew you didn't want kids, but I thought you would change. That reward money freed all of us from financial worries. Think about having a little girl to teach things. I thought you would want some kids." Max sees Peggy flush with anger.

"Well, I don't Max! Now that you are free, you should find someone who does want kids! Maybe I'm not your soul mate after all!" Peggy jumps to her feet.

"Maybe you're not! Oh, let's not argue."

"I want both of us to be happy Max." She puts her hands on his shoulders.

"What exactly are you saying?" Max feels Hera tense up and pets her head.

"We should each do what we want."

"You mean find someone else, a lover?"

"I've thought this over a lot Max. I still love you, but you need to look for someone who wants kids and I need to find someone who does not. As soon as I get back, I will move my things out. Thank you for letting me keep that money." Peggy stares into Max's eyes.

"Wow! You couldn't be more frank! Okay, go to Vegas! I know you want to so bad Peggy. I want you to be happy too, but while you are away think about the great kids we could create. I hope you change your mind and bring us together or maybe not."

"Thank you for being you." Then Peggy sings in her best Dolly Parton voice. "Max, I... will always love you! I will always love you!"

"Yeah, somehow I believe you..."

"I'll miss you Max, even while I'm in Vegas."

"Is Ann going to Vegas for the same reason as you?"

"I think she just likes the sewing group. I quit my job at the flower shop and Ann is taking vacation time so we can stay for a week. Being free to explore the world is what I want. Don't you want to tour somewhere or sail somewhere, spend that money while you can enjoy it?"

"I'm having fun right here Peggy, like with my new boat I call 'Journey Too' because it replaced the old boat "Journey".

"I still don't understand the name Max."

"Remember I always say enjoy the 'Journey'? Now I say enjoy the 'Journey Too'."

"Okay whatever, I still don't get it."

"Well I do and enjoy 'Journey 2' wouldn't sound right to me."

"Well, it is your boat. You can name it whatever you want."

"Okay, I guess the Las Vegas thing is exciting for you."

"Yes, doing some R&R in Vegas will help me get refreshed. I saw some previews of shows in Vegas and wow! They have some top entertainers there. I especially want to see the magic shows by Penn and Teller."

"What about the three days of sewing classes?"

"Yeah, that's more for Ann than me. I just want to see Las Vegas. I really wish you and Sam would come with us, but you seem so excited about your latest deal and your new boat. I'm not a boat person. I never have been. I want to do more exciting things."

"I thought we were exciting together."

"We used to be Max but now you want to settle down too much. You want to have kids and that scares me. It's different now because you seem obsessed with your work. It's all you seem to care for. I have thought about what you want. I hope you understand what I want." Peggy sits down again and stares at Max for an awkward time. Then she turns away.

"Please remember to roll in the trash can."

"I will definitely take care of it."

Chapter Eight

Outside the bright azure sky, is blotched with a few dark gray clouds to the south, but Max ignores the fact that Hurricane Jezebel is about to attack Cuba. The sun is well over the edge of the city spewing brilliant rays of orange sunlight on Max's neighborhood. The temperature is already rising from the seventies overnight. A blue trash truck rolls away from Lux Lane. The streets are bare in the gated community. Then a white taxi covered with writing and phone numbers turns onto Lux lane. It rolls up Max's circular driveway and squeaks to a stop under the huge stone canopy by the front door. An older Hispanic man steps out of the taxi and presses the doorbell.

Peggy stands and pulls down on her slacks as she waits for Max to set Hera aside and stand up. She embraces him until the doorbell rings again.

"Be careful what you wish for my love." Max whispers releasing his hug on her.

"I'm sorry Max. I feel like I'm letting you down."

"It's okay Peggy. Maybe we both need to do some thinking. Maybe this is good to see how we feel about not being together."

"Thank you, Max. The weatherman said to expect intermittent bands of rain later today. I wish you wouldn't take out your new boat at all until after the hurricane passes. I worry about what could happen." She kisses Max and goes to the door.

"The yacht club called last night. My 'Journey Too' is ready to go! I want to see how it handles. We may do some fishing too, weather permitting. My cousin Donny says the Mahi-mahi are running strong."

"Please be careful and if you catch a mermaid keep it a secret!"

"Yes, what happens in the Atlantic stays in the Atlantic!"

"Okay smarty, you know what happens in Vegas…"

"You're meeting Ann and the others at the airport?" Max interrupts her comment.

"Yes, we have three days of sewing classes and then a few days and nights of gambling and enjoying some shows with some of the sewing group. We will be back next Thursday. Promise not to get in trouble." Peggy says smiling.

"I can't promise anything but after fishing, I know Sam and I will just relax until Monday. We will probably go to the Danglebatts' hurricane party next door until we go back to work. Try to stay out of trouble, have fun and try not to lose all your money!" Max laughs and stops at the door. The doorbell rings again. He kisses Peggy.

"What happens in Vegas stays in Vegas!" Peggy winks.

"Be careful love. If you must be naughty, don't get caught!"

"I'll try not to be wild and crazy, but after all, I hear Vegas is a wild and crazy place. If I get in trouble, maybe I'll keep that a secret. I think this is my ride." Peggy gives an impish smile for Max. As she opens the door, she sees Max look doubtful. "Max, you know I never keep secrets from you, right?"

"Oh… Yes, of course love, me neither. Let me carry your bag." Max chuckles with Peggy as he grabs the bright green handle of her pink suitcase and rolls it out the door.

Max gives Peggy a long goodbye embrace and several kisses as the driver stashes her suitcase in the trunk. Then Max holds her hand as she slides into the cab. He eases the door shut and waves, feeling sad as the taxi rolls away. The sun is rising bright but Max feels gloomy sensing the wind stir. A lump forms in his throat as he stands under the stone canopy. *Peggy is telling me goodbye.*

Max stares at the departing taxi and wonders if Peggy will change her mind when she returns; if she returns. Then he sees the dark blue Caravan of his best friend Sam Stormen turn onto Lux Lane. Max wants Sam to pull the minivan into the garage to load up some supplies but he remembers he set the new garage door control for Sam on the table stand next to his chair. As he runs back to the door he crams a big toe on the edge of the threshold before limping inside. Max curses as he hobbles inside and taps a control button to open the extra-large garage door. He shuts off the TV and as he slips on his sandals he sees blood ooze from his big toe.

Chapter Nine

Sam Stormen rolls to a stop on the circular driveway and waits for the garage door to fully open. He parks his Dodge Caravan between Max's red Corvette and Peggy's pink Ford F150 truck. Scanning the garage he sees a foldup ladder, a first aid kit, a few storage boxes, and an oversized water heater. The garage is barren of the normal lawn tools for a garage. With a lawn service and automatic sprinklers, Sam knows Max never acquired any gardening skills or tools. As he gets out of the minivan, he sees Max limp through the house door.

"Hello, Max." Sam says as he steps around the minivan.

"Hey Sam, that's a good outfit!" Max sees Sam is wearing a similar shirt, shorts, and sandals. "Come, carry some supplies and vittles from the refrigerator. There is absolutely nothing on my new boat except life preservers."

"Do you have to take it out today with a hurricane just south of us?"

"It's my new toy, Sam. I have to do it!"

"I knew that. I already took some Dramamine."

"Yeah, that's good Sam. I'm excited about my brand new Chris Craft! Here, these are for the boat." Max says handing some new raincoats to Sam.

"Why are you limping?"

"It's your fault!"

"My fault?"

"Yeah, I stubbed my toe rushing back in the house to open the garage door. If you came a little later, I wouldn't have rushed and stubbed my toe. I'd be relaxing in my swivel rocker chair, see you on the monitor, and open the door from a relaxed position."

"Yeah, okay clumsy, you'll need a Band-Aid for that toe." Sam shakes his head.

"It's only a little bloody. Let's load up the Caravan. I can bandage this on the way to the marina. I bought an extra garage door remote to put in the Caravan. You can open the garage yourself next time." Max says as he trots down the driveway to retrieve the trash bucket. He stows the can in the garage, while Sam loads the rest of the supplies in the minivan.

"It looks like we are ready to go." Max says.

"Okay, Captain. Next stop is Bahia Mar. I'm closing the door with my new remote."

Sam drives east into the sun. The sky is gathering patches of dark clouds. He turns onto the beach road and sees tourists wandering along the beach side of the road. Sam smiles at a pair of Bikini-clad women as he steers into the Bahia Mar Yacht Center.

"Is that your boat to the right?" Sam asks.

"Yes, go right and park along the strip by the best-looking boat!"

Sam parks next to Max's bright white Chris Craft Commander 44 boat gently rocking at the dock. He gazes at the custom white poles that strut up on either side near the rear of the boat, and a custom white canvas top that covers all but the very rear deck. Sam is impressed as he looks at the gleaming white stern that displays 'Journey Too' in bold black letters.

"Wow Max, your new toy looks awesome! You always say 'Enjoy the journey', so you called it the 'Journey Too'." Sam asks.

"Well, duh… Yes, Sam. My last boat was just the 'Journey'."

"That's what you mean by enjoy the journey?"

"That's what I mean. I will enjoy this 'Journey Too'."

"Okay, I think I understand that."

"Yeah, I bought it thanks to the reward money for returning that rare diamond, hah! I got a good deal making a big down payment. The marina called last night saying that she is ready, but too late to go then. With Peggy leaving this morning, it would have been bad to take her out last night anyhow. That's why I'm testing it today and hoping the storm holds off and doesn't hit us!"

"Have you ever piloted a Chris Craft?"

"Yes, but not this one. This baby is brand new Sam. They just got it in and finished the detailing last night. It's great that my best friend gets to go on her maiden voyage with me." He pats Sam on the back.

"You're just going to drive it around a little, right?"

"Well no, I called my cousin Donny last night. He said he caught a cooler full of Mahi-mahi. Donny said there's a zillion of them about ten miles offshore and suggests we try a little south of Fort Lauderdale this time of day. There was a new moon last night so the fish will be hungrier this morning. I want some!"

"I heard it's better to fish the morning after a new moon."

"Yeah, the fish bite better the day after a new moon."

"I would still rather wait until a safer day. You know Jezebel is closing in on Cuba as we speak. I heard it is approaching faster than expected. It could swing north and that would be bad news." Sam says but he grabs a case of Michelob and carries it onto the boat.

Max still limps as he hobbles onboard with his box of supplies. After he stows some food in the small refrigerator he proudly shows Sam where everything is on his prize boat. He displays the roomy compartments for tackle and the powered cooler for storing any fish they catch. The helm has a Captain's chair for Max and one for Sam to ride shotgun. With his tour done, Max calls to the shore man.

"Cast off, we're ready to go!"

Chapter Ten

After waving to the dockhand, Max starts the powerhouse engine. The man releases the last line and the 'Journey Too' idles away from the marina. Max maneuvers along the waterway steering behind another fishing boat heading the same way.

"Look Sam, the sky is still blue in spots, there are no sprinkles and it's not too hot. It's a beautiful day for fishing!" Max feels full of glee as he steers the boat onto the open Atlantic Ocean.

"It's your first voyage with an unknown boat Max. If the engine quits out here we could be stuck for hours and get torn up if Jezebel changes direction."

"Relax Sam, forget the what-ifs and enjoy life! We have a ship-to-shore radio, a GPS to guide us, and beer in the icebox. You took your Dramamine so any rough water should be okay for you. Stop your worrying!"

"I think the pills already kicked in. You're right Max. I'll try to relax and as you say I will enjoy the 'Journey Too'."

Max is happy the other boat turns northeast so he aims southeast.

"Well said brother, this will be a pleasantly memorable trip. You will see. Here we go!"

Max pushes the throttle to maximum keeping the bow to the southeast. He feels the lurch of the boat catapulting forward racing up to full speed through the ripples of the Atlantic Ocean. Max loves the sound of the engine roaring and the ocean waves splashing and banging on the hull. His boat seems to glide over the light chop. Scanning ahead, he sees a boat-free ocean. Max is lost in his thoughts enjoying the solitude of the ocean when Sam shouts over the noise.

"I talked with Chet Hatter last night."

"Our Danglebatts friend next door?" Max shouts back.

"Yeah, he reminded me to join the hurricane party at his house today. He's starting it around eleven this morning and it will last until Monday or Tuesday, maybe four days!"

"Yes, he invited me too, but is he nuts? Four days of partying, we'd be wasted!"

"I know but I told him thanks. We'd see him later."

"Perfect! We will be fashionably late with our entrance."

Max keeps the full throttle on until he sees a patch of seaweed about five miles from shore. After trolling around the weeds a few minutes Max steers away and continues until he's ten miles from shore where he sees the water stirring near a large patch of seaweed. There are no other boats around. He slows down and aims the boat toward the edge of the weeds. *I think this is the Mahi-mahi Donny told me about!*

"Look Sam, fish! Get ready!"

Max sets his speed to 5 knots as he approaches the school of Mahi-mahi. He and Sam set out their trolling lines.

The sun is high in the sky by the time Max and Sam reel in their lines for the last time. He watches Sam plop into one of the angler's chairs after stowing his last catch. Max eases into the other swivel chair and exhales noisily as he glances at Sam.

"The sea is getting choppy. It isn't quite noon yet and the cooler is full. I feel a sprinkle and it's getting darker." Max says.

"I say let's head back!" Sam tilts his head back to rest.

"Yes, we need to stay out of that weather."

"How many did we catch?"

"I lost count. This is a great first day of fishing with my new boat. You see Sam, nothing strange has happened." Max smiles as he helps store the fishing tackle. He grabs two beers from the refrigerator and hands one to Sam before twisting off the cap on his and taking a long drink.

"We're not home yet." Sam says and follows Max forward.

Back at the helm, Max steers toward the coastline and moves the throttle to full speed. He feels the pull when the engine revs up. The warm wind swarms over the windshield, ruffling his black hair as he steers northwestward.

Max scans the horizon less than ten miles off the coast of Hollywood, Florida. He glances at the dark clouds that cover the sky to his south. Max smiles at his best friend Sam standing next to him, knees bent to absorb the bouncing of the boat.

Jezebel is the first major hurricane of the season to invade the Caribbean this year waiting until the middle of August to come across the Atlantic. In the rough ocean, the waves are starting to be an issue, and larger swells lift and drop the boat.

"Max, you look dazed." Sam shouts over the noise from the roaring engine and the waves pounding the bow.

"Yeah, I'm thinking about Peggy again."

"Just block her from your mind. She will come around."

"I don't think so Sam."

"You two seemed perfect for each other. I like Peggy a lot Max, and I know Ann does too. Just remember whatever happens with her, we will be here for you. And you know even if you lose her, you're not a grossly ugly man Max. You can find another."

"Yeah, thanks a lot for the ugly comment. Of course, you are right Sam. I know I can find another woman. I just thought we would be together but now I'm not so sure. Oh well, this is truly a fantastic day. Let's not spoil it talking about her!"

"I hope the weather holds until we get back to the house."

"Yeah, the fishing was great. I think we should give some to Chet and Katie. I love this part, going full throttle! I think this boat is faster than my old one. It handles like a dream!" He bends his knees more to absorb the harder jarring of the boat on the waves as he swerves left and right zigzagging to show off how maneuverable the boat is. He smiles but inside he still hurts as he tries to block losing Peggy from his mind.

"We're bouncing pretty high Max."

"This baby can take it. Chris Crafts are rugged. We'll be dockside in ten minutes."

"Good! I'm ready to get off this bucking bronco!" Sam shouts and then is caught off guard.

Chapter Eleven

"Yahoo!" Max shouts speeding straight ahead over the choppy waves. Max is at full throttle on the 'Journey Too' when he sees a waving arm off the port side and throttles back hard, nearly dumping Sam into the ocean.

"What's going on Max? Lucky I grabbed a post. I was watching the wake and almost flew overboard!"

"Sorry, Sam! There is someone in the water off the port side!" Max shouts and steers the boat to his left.

"We're still miles out. Are you sure, where?"

"Yes look, I think it's a woman!" Max stares at the woman, as he steers closer. Some dolphins swim away when he maneuvers the boat closer and reverses thrust to stop. He sees her shoulder-length red hair flipping back and forth across her bare shoulders and flopping in her face as each wave hits her.

"Help! Help me, please!" Rose shouts gasping and treading water struggling to stay above the rising swells. She waves frantically with one hand and treads water with her other hand. As Max drifts the boat next to her she is hit by a large wave. She goes limp and sinks below the surface.

Sam tosses a life preserver toward her and leans over the edge of the boat but he sees her sink below the surface. He dives next to her dips underwater and struggles to pull the woman back to the surface. He wraps one arm under her arms and grabs the life preserver. Sam kicks and paddles to the rear of the boat.

He pushes her legs and Max pulls her arms to hoist her onboard. When she is safely onboard Sam pulls himself onto the stern.

Max lifts her up, and helps her stagger across the deck where she collapses onto one of the angler's chairs. He stares at the naked woman noting freckles are all over her slim body including her ample breasts. Her red hair half flapped across her face is a tangled mess. Even though the water isn't very cold, he sees her shiver as she coughs and gasps for air. Then she leans back, her arms flop down the sides of the chair and she closes her eyes, unconcerned about her nudity. After staring at the panting woman in disbelief Max goes back to the helm and searches the horizon for the boat she must have come from.

Sam sits silently dripping water with her and watches the woman cough and pant. Then he remembers stowing new raincoats in a cabinet onboard. He brings one and wraps it around the woman's shoulders when she sits up. He rests his hand on her shoulder and feels her body shaking. Her bright green eyes stare up at Sam and he sees her trembling lips. He thinks. *Is she cold, or shaking from being alone in the ocean?*

"I would offer you a blanket but we have none onboard."

"I'll be okay. Thank you! Thank you!" She whispers drawing the coat together and panting.

"You're most welcome Miss. In the vastness of this ocean, you are lucky some dolphins found you and stayed with you."

"Oh the dolphins, I wasn't sure why they were hanging around me. They would swim away and then come close to me but they never touched me. It was scary."

"They were protecting you from predators."

"Why would they do that?"

"It's just something dolphins do."

"Then all I know is thank you dolphins! It's great to be alive!"

"You are lucky they were there."

"I'm lucky you rescued me!"

"So tell me, what is your name and how did you end up alone in the ocean miles from shore with no lifejacket or anything else?" Sam asks thinking maybe he saved a hooker. He hears Max shout before she can speak.

"I've scanned all around. There are no other boats here Sam! How can that be?" Max leaves the boat in neutral, and joins Sam on the rear deck. He looks into her bright green eyes as he speaks.

"Hi there." Max utters dazzled by her stare.

"Hi, I'm Rose, Rose Carter. I was thrown overboard." She says still panting and clutching the raincoat.

"What! You mean you're not just skinny-dipping?" Max smiles.

"A man tossed me off the party boat. He tried to kill me!" Rose frowns at him.

"You got naked together and he tossed you in the ocean!"

"No, and yes, I was fully clothed when he threw me overboard. I had to remove my dress to stay afloat. So go ahead and stare at me." Rose fakes a smile and flaps the raincoat a couple of times.

"I apologize. We've never rescued a naked woman before." Max says. Mesmerized, Max keeps staring at her green eyes.

"I certainly believe that. I just feel really uncomfortable."

"I understand, and I apologize for staring at you. So you didn't just fall off a boat and no one noticed? You say you were intentionally tossed overboard!" Max says.

"Who are you guys and what are you doing out here? There's a hurricane lurking that may come this way!" Rose glances at Sam and then stares at Max.

"Oh I'm Max Merchado and he's Sam Stormen. I wanted to test my new boat today of all days. We were fishing. We caught a bunch of Mahi-mahi. Now we're going back to Bahia Mar in Fort Lauderdale. You're lucky we happened along... Miss Carter is it?"

"Yes, I'm so grateful. I think I could have swum all the way to shore but I was getting very tired. Thank you."

"You'd have to be in great shape to swim to shore from here."

"I'm and I think it's possible, but I'm tired and it's sprinkling now. This is much nicer and warmer than being in the ocean."

"Yeah, and the weather is changing." Max says. He looks into her green eyes feeling an attraction for her and also sensing danger.

"There is no boat around. Did someone intentionally leave you out here to drown?" Max asks.

Chapter Twelve

"I was on the party boat 'Bacalao' out of Miami with Hubert Sancho. You know, it was a secret thank you and fundraising party to re-elect Sancho for Senate. I knew he would be planning something because one of my moles told me Rafael Matuso would be there."

"I hate to say this but I'm not a fan of Hubert Sancho." Max says. "Hey you said mole, and the only Rafael Matuso I heard about is a criminal. Do you mean that Matuso?"

"Yes, Rafael Matuso owns several parking lots and runs a legitimate business but he is allegedly part of a crime organization. I too dislike Sancho! I've been trying a long time to nail him for getting cash payoffs. He always manages to elude me. He is a clever man and is good at laundering his money. My boss says he's just lucky or my pursuit is too slow."

"You say Sancho is friends with Rafael Matuso?"

"They are more than just friends now. Sancho was with him when Matuso threw me in the ocean to drown. Matuso will own Senator Sancho! Medina is ahead in most polls this week so Sancho must have asked for help from Matuso. I did some research on Hubert Sancho. He is more corrupt than you think. I know he is stashing his bounty in the Cayman Islands but I can't prove it yet. Sancho is running for another term in office and now Matuso will own him!"

"You said we, who are you? How do you know all this stuff?"

"Oh um, research Max, I'm a freelance writer." Rose fibs.

"But you mentioned you have a boss and won't someone miss you not being on the boat when it docks?"

"Yeah, well I was by myself. I call my editor the boss. She's not really my boss."

"Okay then, welcome aboard Miss Carter! So Matuso threw you overboard way out here? He had to know that was like signing your death warrant!"

"Please just call me Rose. Yes, it was Rafael Matuso in person. Murdering me was an easy fix since he has no conscience."

"What upset him so that he tossed you in the ocean?"

"He caught me spying. He should be in jail for what he did!"

"Yeah, but proving that will be hard to do."

"I recorded the whole incident and more, but the recorder I need is still on that boat in Miami unless he found it. I need to go to the 'Bacalao'. I have to get my camcorder for my proof. If I don't get it I have no evidence." Rose tells Max how Matuso caught her listening and grabbed her. Sancho opened the window and Matuso brutally tossed her through it into the ocean.

"Holy cow! I wouldn't believe you if we hadn't just plucked you out of the ocean. What a horrible thing to do. That man is a monster and Sancho too!" Max blurts.

"I agree." Rose says giving a last uncontrolled shiver.

"So right now you have no proof of anything." Max says.

"True Max, and Matuso has no regard for life. I don't think Sancho knew what he was getting into. And as you can see, I had to strip off everything to stay afloat. I thank you very much for the rescue and the raincoat!"

"You're welcome Miss Rose. So what do we do now?"

"I must know if they found my camcorder. I must go back to the 'Bacalao' in Miami."

"We have to go to Miami Sam. We have to help her." Max shouts. He stares into her eyes and senses truth and danger and a strong need to help Rose.

"Oh no, Max!" Sam exclaims. "That's a dumb ass idea!"

"Yeah dumb ass, I remember that subtle code meaning you're in danger, but we have to help her." Max says and sees Rose stand up crossing her arms.

"Hey, you guys are civilians, I can manage for myself!"

"With no clothes or anything,, how will you do that?" Max says. He sees Rose stare at him with her lips pressed together and no longer shivering.

"My boss, um…my editor friend, she will send someone."

"Fine, call her." Max hands her his cell phone. He watches her stare at the phone, not entering a phone number.

"What's the matter Rose?" Max asks.

"There is something wrong." Rose frowns and fiddles with her hair, brushing it away from her face with her hands.

"What, you can't remember her number or you don't want your editor to know you were tossed in the ocean?"

"That's not why. I just…" Rose stares at Max and then frowns.

"An awkward pause I would say. Here's a new plan Rose from a dumb-ass civilian. I say we take you to my house to put on some clothes. You're about Peggy's size…"

"Wait, who is Peggy?"

"She is my fiancée, well my ex-fiancée, but all her clothes are still at my house."

"Oh, I see." Rose lowers her voice. "Will she be okay if you bring a semi-naked woman home?"

"Peggy is in Las Vegas for a week. She wants to leave me but I'm hoping she will come to her senses out there."

"She is in Vegas and you think she'll come to her senses?"

"Well, she is with a sewing group. Anyway, you can borrow some of her clothes, and then we will decide what to do."

"No Max, I want to get the camcorder immediately. I have to know if they found it and destroyed it. This can't wait. It's already stormy. The 'Bacalao' is an old boat. There is an off chance all the rain and wind may sink her. The evidence would be lost!"

"How will you get the camcorder? You have no clothes. People will stare."

"When I got to the 'Bacalao' this morning I noticed the strip stores were closed for the storm threat. I'm sure the boat is back at the marina by now. No one will still be around that boat. Just this slicker and one minute on board is all I need!"

"You plan to go barefooted?"

"Yes, trust me I need to get that camcorder!" Rose waits but Max is silent. "That's how you can help me one more time. Just get me to that marina. Then you can drop me at my apartment and be rid of me forever."

"We'll see. The rain is starting. It's time to get back to the marina." Max concedes. For a split second, his eyes lock on her eyes. Once again, he senses he must help her.

Rose stares at Max with her green eyes watching him analyze her face. She feels a strong tingle of attraction for Max as he salutes her and heads back to the helm with Sam. Rose stares at his backside. He isn't quite as lean and fit as Sam but she likes his broad shoulders, narrow hips, and hairy legs. She likes his gentle yet baritone voice. Just for fun, she imagines being on a soft bed and having her way with him. Then Max throttles up the boat, forcing her back in her chair. She grabs the armrests and her daydream vanishes.

The engine roars and the boat bashes into the waves bouncing her around as it accelerates to full speed. Rose is alone under the canvas top as the boat slices its way through the waves. Then she wonders how she could be here from the 'Bacalao' out of Miami even though she senses she is safe. She stands up and heads for the helm when Sam comes back knees bent and holding on to a support frame of the canvas top.

"You look so tense. How are you doing?" Sam says.

"Sorry Sam, I learned not to trust anyone no matter how innocent they seem to be. But somehow I trust you guys. I can't figure out how I could be here. That party boat is out of Miami. Why would I be off the coast of Fort Lauderdale?"

"First of all who are you, Rose Carter? You're acting strangely for a writer."

"I feel like I can trust you now. I'm not Rose Carter. I'm FBI agent Rose Finley."

Chapter Thirteen

"You gave us a false name?"

"Yes, Rose Carter is the name I used on the party boat. This is a big thing Sam. Rafael Matuso tried to murder me!"

"I'm trying to make sense of it."

"He is a murderer Sam! He just hasn't been caught yet!"

"If he is so dangerous why were you there?"

"I have been trying to get evidence to take down Sancho for receiving bribes, mainly from drug deals and a few other things we suspect him of being involved in. I knew Sancho and Matuso might be planning something too. Why would Sancho and Matuso meet?"

"That's why you crashed Sancho's meeting."

"It was supposed to be a fundraiser party that Matuso used to bribe Sancho. I saw him hand an envelope to Sancho, probably full of cash. I should have had fun there, just let my recorder work while I had fun partying. I even met an eligible bachelor before I went to the private room and thought I could make friends and maybe pick his brain. He thinks he will be the next Senator when Sancho retires. I didn't expect to be dumped in the ocean. I was too careless."

"Well, you're safe with us now."

"But why would I be off the coast of Fort Lauderdale?"

"First let me say Max has a way of finding unexpected trouble even when I think there is no way anything should go wrong. He's drawn to these situations like a moth to a candle!" Sam turns away from Rose to regain control of his emotions.

"I'm so sorry to be trouble for you Sam."

"It's okay. If it wasn't you, something else would show up."

"I'm truly sorry Sam." Rose squeezes his shoulder to comfort Sam, but she feels him tense up more so she removes her hand.

"Okay, to answer your question, I think you must have drifted north with the Gulf Stream. It's an ocean current that runs northward off the coast all the way up Florida. We were south of Lauderdale, probably due east of Hollywood, now heading northwest back to the Bahia Mar Yacht Basin in Fort Lauderdale. You don't know how long you were in the water?" Sam grabs a cabin edge to keep his balance as the Chris Craft smashes through a large wave.

"Yeah, I don't know Sam. It seems like hours but maybe a half hour or even less. I'm truly sorry I got you drawn into this. Is Max serious about wanting to help me, take me to Miami?"

"Oh yes but like I said, Max has a way of getting us into jams."

"So why do you stay friends?"

"We are more than friends Rose. I think of Max like a blood brother. We've been through a lot of terrifying events together, but somehow we come out okay. Also, when he lured me back to Fort Lauderdale, I met Ann Picard, the love of my life."

"So you are spoken for."

"Absolutely, I married her."

"I wondered why you tensed up when I grabbed you. Men usually grab back!"

"Trust me I was tempted, but I would never forgive myself if I did anything to hurt Ann. For sure you are a beautiful woman... all of you." Sam smiles at Rose standing with her hands holding onto the edge of the canvas top and her slicker flapping open. He watches her close the front with one hand as the boat slows down. "Maybe you should button up the raincoat now." Sam says.

"Ann is a very lucky woman Sam." Rose nods, starts to button up the slicker, and moves back to her chair.

"We are both the lucky ones Rose." Sam says. He watches the scenery go by, taking his eyes off Rose, and is silent as Max steers the boat along the channel and into the marina and the dock.

Max backs the boat into its stall like a pro and shuts down the engine. A dockhand named Charley helps Max with the moorings that secure the boat.

"We had a great day of fishing Charley. We caught more than we imagined." Max says smiling at Rose.

"Should I filet the fish and freeze them Mister M?"

"Yes, and take your share we agreed upon."

"Yes sir. How many did you catch?"

"We lost count! I'll get my filets after the storm."

"I will secure the boat. It looks like rain is coming soon."

"Thanks Charley." Max says and helps Rose off the boat. He sees the nervous face on Sam and wonders what is bothering him.

"You don't look happy Sam."

"Do you realize someone tried to murder agent Finley? I'm sure they will try again! And now we are involved too."

"Sam, be calm. No one else knows she's still alive. That Matuso guy thinks he killed her. Relax, it's Miami time!"

Sam steps from the boat and as he walks to his minivan he thinks. *What kind of mess are we in now?*

Chapter Fourteen

The sky is filling with black clouds and Max feels the denser wind picking up speed as Max leads Sam and Rose away from the 'Journey Too'. His mind is still analyzing this new twist to the day. *Who tosses a woman into the ocean to die? Who fetches a naked woman with freckles out of the ocean?* He shakes his head. When Sam unlocks the Caravan he helps Rose get in.

Sam starts the minivan and asks. "Where is the party boat?"

"I remember the address. You can plug it in your GPS thingy." She sees how depressed Sam seems. "Don't worry Sam, by now the boat will be abandoned. I expect the whole area to be empty. I can zip on and off the boat without any trouble."

Sam nods at Rose but he feels uncomfortable about the whole situation as he loads the address in his GPS. He flips on his headlights and intermittent wipers and works his way onto I-95 South, worrying as he drives along mechanically. *This weekend is supposed to be a fun time at Chet's hurricane party and maybe just guitar jam with the band guys. I know their next concert in Dallas, Texas isn't for several weeks. Now we are hauling around a woman someone tried to kill. I know they will try again! I hate being in the line of fire! I just want this to be over!* He realizes he isn't paying attention to the road and almost runs into an older red Mustang slowing to veer onto an exit ramp.

Although the near accident shocks Sam, he starts thinking about all the weird situations he struggled through with Max. He recalls the close death experiences in Jamaica, the lunatic Jake Crocker who was trying to kill them, the crash into the barrier wall at Silvan Enterprises, and the gunshot wound. Then he remembers the near-fatal events in Italy, and the crazy man on a cruise ship. He feels this is another dangerous situation and the sooner this is over the better! Sam finally gets off I-95. He weaves through two-way roads until he can see the coast. The GPS tells him to turn left to reach his destination.

"Sam, that's the road to the marina." Rose points to her left.

"You want to borrow my sandals?" Max asks.

"No, I can't run in sandals, and I may have to leave in a hurry."

Sam eases the minivan down the narrow tar road and into the parking area. As Rose predicted, all the shops around the marina are closed with boards and plywood covering the windows and doors. The only car Sam sees in the parking lot is a faded gray Chrysler at the far edge of the strip of parking slots. No one is around so he parks next to the 'Bacalao'.

He watches the boat gently rock up and down in the light chop with "Bacalao" in faded green letters printed across the grimy stern. The windows are boarded up and the boat is fifteen feet away from the dock held in place with drooping anchor and dock ropes.

"Wow, they boarded up the whole boat." Rose mumbles.

"How will you get on there?" Sam asks.

"I'll figure it out." Rose says. She slides the door open, jumps out, and slams the door closed.

Rose braces against the gusty wind and feels the cold concrete on her feet as she runs across the wet walkway. Her legs feel a blast of rain as she jogs along. She stops on the 'Bacalao' dock and analyses the situation. The 'Bacalao' is rocking in the turbulent water straining and slacking the ropes mooring it to the dock. She determines the only way on is to climb across one of the ropes. She sighs and grabs a rope attached to the starboard side.

Rose swings her legs up and wraps them over the rope. She feels a cool wind gust up her slicker soaking her backside as she starts her monkey crawl across the rope. The rope keeps going taut and then slack. Near the middle of her crawl, the rope goes slack and her bottom is within a couple of inches of touching the water. She finally swings her feet onto the stern and rolls onto the tail end of the 'Bacalao'.

She pulls down her raincoat, stands on the rear deck under the overhanging roof, and looks at the plywood-covered rear door. Rose tries to turn the doorknob but the door is locked. However, with some jiggling the weak latch gives way. She eases the door open and swings it out of her way, prepared to handle anyone still on board. Rose presses through the plastic strips inside with her senses on full alert.

The room is still cool from the air conditioning that was on during the party only a few hours ago. She smells the stale scent of alcohol and orange juice. The only light is from the gaps in the window coverings. As her eyes adjust to the darkness, she scans across the polished wood floor looking for any movement. Seeing and hearing nothing unusual, she sneaks across the cold dance floor to the front of the 'Bacalao' and slips into the private room.

Rose stops to stare at the big window hastily covered with a cross pattern of one-by-four boards. A cold shiver runs through her thinking about Matuso tossing her through that opening. She thinks about the dark ocean, the dolphins, and her aching shoulder. Rose forces herself to shake off the daunting memories as she walks to the couch.

She can see the tiny lens of her micro-camcorder, still discretely wedged between two books on the bottom shelf of the bookcase, and she silently cheers. Rose grabs the unit, turns it off, and starts to put it in the slicker pocket but shakes her head, afraid it would fall out of a pocket when she climbs onto the rope. Rose glances at the big window one more time and feels her body give an involuntary shiver before she cracks the door open and peeks out. Hearing and seeing nothing, she trots to the bar area to grab a wrinkled hand towel from a table. She wraps the camcorder in the towel and forces it into a pocket on the raincoat. Convinced it can't fall out; she walks across the cold dance floor, slips through the plastic strips, and closes the rear door.

Rose grips the rope exposing her backside again and monkey crawls over the water back to the dock. She runs across the walkway in the rain and jumps into the van. After closing the door she shakes rain from her hair, elated with herself.

"I got it! Let's get out of here!" Rose shouts.

Chapter Fifteen

"We're leaving!" Sam says as he speeds out of the parking area.

"Max, may I borrow your phone? I think I should report all this to Donna!" Rose says shaking off some rain.

"Who is Donna?" Max asks handing her his phone.

"She's my superior, FBI Director Donna Grant."

"FBI, Donna Grant? I thought you were a freelance writer Miss Carter." Max says.

"I'm sorry Max. I guess you didn't hear me tell Sam I'm an FBI agent and my real name is agent Rose Finley. I didn't want to say that at first until I got to know who you were. I do thank you so much for helping me get my camcorder."

"I should call you agent Finley now." Max says.

"Please just call me Rose. Donna is the focal point of all this investigation of Sancho. I don't know why she wouldn't believe me about Matuso. I've missed catching Sancho meeting with other known criminals by a few minutes. This time I got not just a photo of him but a video! I recorded Matuso and Sancho tossing me out the window and I should have video of them talking about some master plan too. This is evidence we have been trying to get for a long time."

"Fantastic Rose!" Max shouts.

"Thanks! Drop me off at my apartment please."

"Not a problem. What's your address?" Sam asks feeling happier.

"Use your GPS thingy again. I'll call Donna on the way there. I need to tell her what happened. This is wonderful!" She shouts and gives Sam her Gatsby Apartments address and dials Donna Grant.

Sam speaks as he loads in her address. "You know who you are dealing with? These people are dangerous! Matuso and Sancho are powerful men. I think they know people too. If we're not careful they can make us all disappear!"

"Hey, they don't know I survived the toss in the ocean and my guys are powerful too. We have an advantage right now. We can catch them in the act because I recorded what they did and what they are planning to do! I have the camcorder!" Rose pats her bulging pocket. "When my boss sees this…" Rose says. The phone is in speaker mode when Donna Grant answers.

"Hello, who is this?" Grant asks.

"It's Finley. I got the…"

"Agent Finley! I thought you were dead!"

"Why would you think that?" Rose asks and listens to Donna's forced laugh.

"I'm joking of course. I thought you would call from the boat."

"Right. Well, I got on the party boat…"

"The one I said not to go on, right?"

"I know but I had to do it. Listen, I just got in the front room when Sancho and Matuso came in. I hid behind a couch and I heard them plotting against Medina, maybe framing him for something. We have to stop them!"

"That's hard to believe Finley that Sancho would team up with Matuso. He hasn't the guts. I didn't know Matuso was dabbling into politics. Was your camcorder on?"

"Yes, my camcorder was on. I was hiding behind the couch but that rug is awful! I had to sneeze and Matuso found me. He called me by name! How would he know my name? Then he threw me overboard."

"Did you save the recorder or did it go in the ocean too? Did you hear any details of how they will frame Medina?"

"No details, but I went back to the boat and got my camcorder…" Rose feels Max grab her shoulder. She pauses, gives a questioning look at Max who makes a hush sign and points to her slicker pocket.

"What?" Rose frowns at Max as she mutes the phone.

"I wish you hadn't told her the camcorder is safe." Max whispers. Before Rose can object, Grant starts talking again.

"Rose, you know I'm in Atlanta, I just finished a meeting with our Chief Walter Langston. I don't know how Matuso would know your name. We must have a leak somewhere. I will be back in Miami after the storm is over but I want Agent Cooper to meet you. I'll have Cooper meet you wherever you are and take you home. Cooper can watch the video with you."

"You know I stripped off everything when I was in the ocean."

"You mean everything?"

"Yeah, everything! I don't want to wait around practically naked for Cooper. I'll meet him at home in an hour. I need some time at home to shower and put on some clothes! I think the salt water ruined my earrings too. The FBI should pay me for my dress and stuff."

"I can arrange that Rose. Someone rescued you?"

"Yes, Max rescued me. I was totally nude!"

"Great luck... Max who?"

"Merchado." Max says seeing the question on Rose's face.

"You were careless to get tossed overboard."

"I'm sorry but Matuso is a very strong man. Just have Cooper meet me at my apartment. I will go there. We can arrest Matuso for attempted murder!"

"Well, let's see the video first. Meet with Cooper, okay?"

"Okay, I will go to my apartment." Rose rings off. When she ends the call, she sees the doubtful face of Max and frowns. "What?"

Chapter Sixteen

"Something is wrong Agent Rose. I heard how shocked she was that you are alive, but not shocked that Matuso tossed you in the ocean. Like maybe she already knew you were tossed into the ocean and already believed you were dead!"

"I know it seems that way, but I feel I can trust her Max. She was being sarcastic not hearing from me after the party boat returned. She's a real trouper!"

"You told me she didn't know you were on that party boat, but she admonished you for that. Her big shock seemed to be that you are alive and not the fact that you were tossed overboard. Also, you said this Matuso knew your name. How is that possible?"

"Oh...We must have a snitch." Rose stares at Max.

"I think your Donna is the snitch and she told Matuso about you. It's just a feeling I get about her, the tone of her voice."

"How can you think that?"

"I get a gut feeling about people and things. I think she thought you were dead until you called her. That means someone told her what happened, someone on the boat in that room with you! I also noticed she seemed anxious to know what's on your camcorder. I think you are worried about her too. That's why you rang off. Since the recorder was on when Matuso pitched you overboard, it must have recorded the attempted murder and whatever plan Matuso explained to Sancho! You have it all!" Max pats her shoulder.

"You may be right Max. My instinct says be careful." She bows her head.

"I think that's wise. Did you tell anyone else you would be on the boat?" Max asks.

"No, and I know Louis is okay."

"Is that Louis Cooper, how?"

"Yes, I dated him for a while. I trust him. We can watch the video together."

"Then just give it to the police."

"No, the FBI will handle this, not the police."

"Do you still want to go to your apartment?"

"Yes, if I get there before Louis I can put on some clothes, and get ready to watch the video with Cooper. You guys can take off and forget about me forever."

"I don't think I can forget you Rose." Max says fondly rubbing her shoulder.

"I won't forget you either Max, but maybe you should try."

"Why should I do that?"

"Well, you live in Fort Lauderdale and I in Miami. And don't you see how dangerous being with me is Max? Imagine if Matuso finds us. You could get killed for being around me. That would be awful if you were hurt... or Sam too. When you drop me off, forget you ever met me!" Rose stares into Max's eyes.

"Okay, we will drop you off so you and um, this Louis guy can watch the videos."

"Right, the videos... what videos?" Rose's mind is foggy.

"You want to watch the videos on your camcorder."

"Oh yeah, I lost my concentration looking at your big brown eyes." She continues to stare at Max, frozen until Sam interrupts her.

"Rose, the sign is broken off. Is this the Gatsby Apartments?"

"Yes, the sign broke off last week. The only entrance is next to that big oak tree."

Sam drives into the brightly lit parking lot. The area is half full of cars and SUVs. He sees a spot near the main door and aims for that when Rose shouts.

"Sam, don't stop!"

"What's the matter?" Sam swerves away from the parking spot.

"I think I saw that black van parked at the marina this morning."

"Why would it be here?" Sam asks as he drives past it.

"I don't know. I don't see agent Cooper's car anywhere either. I think Matuso sent someone here? How could he know where I live?"

Sam says. "Maybe Matuso sent someone to greet you or check for a roommate. What do we do now? Are you sure about the van?"

"I'm not positive yet. Just turn around and drive slowly past it."

Rose watches with her hand partially blocking her face as Sam eases past the van a second time. She sees the same G-string hanging on the van mirror that she saw at the marina and no one is in the van.

"It's the same van! I don't think this is a coincidence. They are waiting for me in my apartment. Do you have a gun I can borrow?"

"Not here, are you going in there?"

"I can't fight without a weapon. Just get away from here!"

Sam drives out of the Gatsby Apartments and heads back to I-95. A wind gust rocks the minivan as Sam drives slower careful of the wet roads.

"Let's go to my house. We can regroup there." Max says.

Hearing no comment from Rose, Sam sighs and drives toward Fort Lauderdale. He wonders. *What happens now?*

Chapter Seventeen

The sky is dark gray and rain is falling in small drifts. The perimeter of Hurricane Jezebel is starting to affect the Miami and Fort Lauderdale coastlines sporadically buffeting the condos and hotels along the beach. Palm tree fronds that normally sway in the gentle warm breeze are flapping back and forth mostly angling to one side. The rain and wind strike in waves almost dangerously strong. Most people are staying indoors to avoid the weather.

Sam eventually drives through the open gates of Blue Lake Estates purposely left open in case of a power failure. He drives onto Lux Lane, swings into Max's driveway, and waits with his headlights shining on Max's garage door as it opens. Once inside, Sam hears the wind and rain calm to an eerie quiet when the garage door touches down on the concrete. Sam kills the engine still wondering why Max would bring a strange woman into his house. Then he feels Rose reach forward and kiss him on the cheek.

"What are you doing?" Sam asks.

"Just overjoyed and thanking you for saving me."

"You're welcome." Sam says. He shakes his head and gets out of the minivan. When he starts to go around the minivan to the house, he sees Rose stop next to Max.

Max is finishing his text that they are home from fishing in answer to Peggy's text that they arrived safe. He is nicely surprised to feel Rose kiss his cheek and wrap her arms around him. He turns his head toward Rose and gently backs away breathing heavier.

"Oh... I just hugged you to thank you for saving my life. Can't I hug you too? What's wrong?"

"Even though you look great tangled hair and all, I still feel guilty hugging you."

"Hey, I think you look great too!" Rose blurts and blushes as she turns away from Max thinking. *Rose Finley, what are you doing? You can't be kissing these men!*

"Thanks." Max says.

"What did you mean you still feel guilty?"

"Even though Peggy said goodbye yesterday and she hates this big house, I still don't feel free to get involved with anyone. I'm free technically but I still want Peggy to sort things out and marry me when she returns."

"This looks like a beautiful ginormous house. Why would she not love it? What kind of things does she have to sort out Max?"

"I'd rather not say."

"I'm sorry. I didn't mean to intrude on your private life. You and Sam are like two peas in a pod, real gentlemen."

"Tell me about you Rose."

"Well, I'm not a promiscuous person as you may think I'm right now. We have been running around so much, this is the first time I thought to physically thank you. I wanted to kiss both of you, on the cheek. After all, you two saved my life.

"Have you ever been married, have any hobbies?"

"No, to both questions. I'm concentrating on my job."

"Did the FBI ever train you for being dumped in the ocean?"

"You know, I'm not absolutely positive I could have swum all the way to shore." Rose folds her arms across her chest. She flinches as the rough raincoat rubs her skin. Feeling awkward, she turns away.

"Even if you could stay absolutely on course, you were at least five miles from shore! With the wind and the rain starting, that would be amazing for a great swimmer."

"Hey, I'm in excellent shape and I know how to swim. I was doggie-paddling and I could do that all day!"

"I agree with the excellent shape part… Okay, I think you are about Peggy's size. Come to the bedroom." Max says and walks across the living room.

"Hey, you just told me no hanky-panky, and really, I'm a great swimmer." Rose says and trots into the hallway behind Max.

"Sure, I'm just showing you where Peggy's clothes are. Okay, if it makes you happy I think you could have made it to shore." Max winks at her, leads her into the master bedroom, and waves at Hera perched in the middle of the king-size bed.

"Wow, nice cat." Rose says seeing the jet-black Hera. Although the cat is purring Rose feels creepy, sensing the cat is analyzing her.

"Her name is Hera in memory of a psychic woman I met in Italy. Hera just showed up around our old house. When I was outside one day, she started rubbing my ankles. Somehow, I knew she belongs with me. When I petted her, I felt an instant bond and took her in. Hera is family now. Sometimes I ask her for advice as if she were a real psychic like that woman. I believe my cat has psychic powers."

"Really, you believe in psychic powers?" Rose says thinking. *I'd like to pet your cat, and you too! There you go again Rose! Why are you thinking like that?*

"I never used to think about psychic powers until I met that woman in Italy. She seemed to do the unexplained. I believe there are forces most of us don't understand. Like, right now I hear her purring. That tells me Hera knows you are okay."

"I think that's you talking Max, not the cat." Rose says as she follows Max into Peggy's walk-in closet.

"Take what you want." Max switches on the closet light.

"Wow, big closet! This whole house is huge Max. Do you have anyone living with you, any kids?" Rose says. She sees Max tense up as if she slapped him.

"I bought this house thinking we would have a bunch of kids, but Peggy doesn't want any." Max drops his head.

"I'm sorry Max. I didn't mean to pry again. I know if I ever get married, I want lots of kids! Why doesn't she want kids?"

"Let's get off that subject Rose."

"Yes sir!" Rose salutes Max and smiles. She sees sorrow in his face and thinks. *Why did you tell him you want lots of kids?*

Chapter Eighteen

Max smiles as he backs away from her. "So just shower off the ocean salt put on some clothes and come to the living room. Then we can decide what to do next."

"Yes, I should shower first. Good grief, look at all these… pink things. Everything in here is pink or has pink trim. Oh, last chance for a look Max!" Rose says as she starts sliding the raincoat off. She grins impishly over her bare shoulder at Max.

"Um… You find what you want… Oh um yeah, shower and come back to the living room." Max stares at her but backs away.

"Peggy and you are split up Max. Come help me shower!" Rose teases still smiling at Max and exposing her upper back. *Have you totally lost your mind!* She thinks then looks away from Max and cringes, shocked by her own words.

"Um… You're on your own Rose." Max turns and struggles to walk away.

Rose drops the slicker on the floor as Max leaves the closet. She thinks how idiotic she is acting. *What in Hell are you doing Rose Finley! Why are you flirting with Max? He is a civilian!* She bows her head, closes her eyes, and exhales loudly. She finally selects a bright pink blouse and shorts. Rose, suddenly shy, peeks into the bedroom to verify Max is gone. Hera is still perched in the center of the bed watching her. Rose leans onto the bed to pet Hera. She hears the cat purring, but the piercing blue eyes intimidate Rose so she backs up.

She stares at Hera trying to turn away but can't resist the urge to talk to the purring cat and she finally speaks.

"Well um… Hera, you and Max have seen a lot of me. Are you in here when Max showers? I wonder what he looks like naked.

You know he like owes me some naked views now, both him and Sam!" Rose closes her eyes for a second. Envisioning Max in the buff just makes her more bothered and frustrated.

"Does Max want me at all?" She blurts. To her surprise, Hera nods. Rose leans over meeting Hera almost eye-to-eye.

"Okay, maybe you are psychic. Hear me out. It seems I have a stupid crush on Max. Tell me is he really interested in me?" Rose sees Hera nod again.

"I hope you really are psychic Miss Hera!" She blows a kiss toward the cat.

Rose sets the clothes on the edge of the bed, strolls into the master bathroom, and turns on the shower. She feels gritty from the salt water. Rose finds a washcloth and an oversized bath towel in the linen closet. She adjusts the water temperature until it suits her outstretched hand and steps under the spray. The water flows onto her head and over her body. "I need this!" She whispers and stands motionless for a moment.

Raw from chaffing inside the rough raincoat she feels her armpits and nipples sting a little in the water. The minor sting reminds her of happy times growing up in Atlanta, Georgia. She loved to wash away dirt and grime at day's end from playing in the mud and clay. The shower always felt good even if she felt a little sting from a cut somewhere. After her shower, Rose would put on clean clothes for dinner. Still feeling the spray rinse over her, Rose reminisces about sitting at the dinner table with her two brothers Ray and Regis, and mom and dad eating her favorite dinner of fried catfish, corn on the cob, and fresh greens. She would rinse down everything with a glass of cold milk. Rose misses her family and her childhood playing with the neighborhood kids.

She thinks about watching 'Secret Agent' on TV, and John Drake foiling some bad guy's plan. *So I'm out of the ocean, showering in this man's bathroom in Fort Lauderdale. I can continue saving lives and capturing bad guys now just like Patrick McGoohan did!*

Rose feels happy to be alive and hums the melody of 'Secret Agent Man'. She grabs a container of cocoa shampoo and washes her hair. Then she takes a container from the shower ledge and pours body wash onto a cloth to bathe away the ocean.

She finishes her shower, towels off, and walks into the bedroom with the towel wrapped around her. Rose opens several drawers before she finds one filled with pink undergarments. Happy that Peggy is about the same size as she is, Rose drops the towel and slips on underwear.

Rose goes back into the bathroom brushes and fluffs her hair into order. She finds some deodorant to roll on and then stares at the full-length mirror checking out her body and hair. Content with her appearance she walks back into the bedroom. Rose slips on the pink blouse and shorts. She removes the camcorder from the towel in the slicker and stuffs it in her bra. Rose wants to talk to Hera again, but the cat is gone.

"Oh well… It's show time!" She whispers and swings open the bedroom door.

Chapter Nineteen

After leaving Rose in the closet, Max walks into the living room in a daze. Flushed after watching her, he sees images of Rose in the buff. He wipes his forehead whisking away imaginary sweat before flopping in his swivel rocker chair and closing his eyes. His mind is whirling and he admonishes himself. *Why did Rose flirt with me? Why is she trying to turn me on when she says she loves her work and can never love me! I need to stay cool and forget about doing anything with her!* After a long pause, he opens his eyes and sees Sam stare at him from the sofa.

"That's a really lovely woman Sam." Max closes his eyes and takes a deep breath. "I wonder if she really wants a lot of kids."

"Max, she is a complete stranger and you just left her alone in your bedroom?" Sam blurts ignoring Max's comment.

"I admit she is strange but not a stranger Sam. I feel like I know her already and she wanted me to shower with her!" Max says smiling and closing his eyes.

"But you left her there alone. How could you do that?"

"So you think I should have showered with her Sam?"

"No, but at least you should have stayed in the bedroom to guard things. You are too trusting Max."

"Yeah, Peggy would kill me if I tried to… oh, why not leave her alone? She's not a crook!"

"She only says she's an FBI agent but no real proof, no ID or anything, and a total stranger! She could be a hooker thrown off a boat by an angry john."

"Yes, but a lovely one. Do you really think she is lying about being an FBI agent?"

"No, actually I think she's telling the truth."

"You know that extra sense I have?"

"Don't tell me you *sense* she is legit."

"Yes, that sense or whatever it is tells me she is okay Sam. I believe she needs our help." Max stares back at Sam.

"I know you're usually right about people but I'm not sure I would trust her that much. Let's not forget that she deals in deception and with dishonest and unsavory people. Does Peggy have a lot of jewelry in there?"

"She does, but I believe Rose is no thief. I hear the shower running. She must be washing down that beautiful body." Max closes his eyes forming a mental image of her.

"You're acting like you want to jump her bones!"

"She started to drop the raincoat Sam! I remember seeing her cute freckles. Her skin is all salty from the ocean. I really did want to shower with her and lather up her freckles! It was tough to back away from her! I may not be able to do that again."

"Wow Max, I think she's getting to you. You need to settle down, think about Peggy. Don't get mixed up with her kind. You might be killed just for being close to her!"

"I understand Sam, but there is something about her. It is more than her just being a beautiful woman. And if you remember Peggy left me." Max smiles when his cat Hera walks out of the bedroom and jumps in his lap purring.

"Does that mean you just throw away your relationship?"

"Peggy already did that. She wants to try other things." Max leans back in his chair realizing for the first time Peggy is gone.

"Does that include other men?"

"Yes Sam."

"Why is she doing this?"

"I can never have children with her. She wants to just do exciting things without kids."

"You can adopt if she can't have children."

"No, she is capable, she just doesn't want any. She wants to find someone of like mind and she says I should do the same." Max pets Hera, and enjoys her purring.

"Well, this is a shocker, Max. I know you two have had some spats usually over a prank you did but I never thought of you two permanently splitting up."

"I think we are both too set in our ways Sam."

"I know she's always been a little wild and crazy Max. She used to get mad at your pranks and leave, but she always came back."

"I'm seriously trying not to do any more pranks. Those were my childish days. I want to raise some kids while I still can and she knows that, so she is leaving me because she loves me. That's why I love her Sam. I'm hoping she will see the light and stay with me. We need to create some kids while we are still young."

"This is crazy in more than one way. Cripes Max, you're only thirty. Do you feel old and decrepit already?"

"No, it's just that..." Max pauses when he hears the bedroom door swing open. He sees Rose come out dressed in pink and smiling. He feels his jaw drop.

Chapter Twenty

Rose poses in front of Max flapping her hands. "I guess Peggy likes pink. That's all I could find to wear. I even have on pink underwear and sneakers!"

"Ahem yes, Peggy has an affinity for pink things. It looks like everything fits."

"The sneakers are too big but much better than nothing, thank you and thank Peggy for me when she gets home."

"It's times like this I like being a man! The videos can wait now that you have it off the boat. Are you ready to party?" Max says. He sees Rose make eye contact for a second and smile at him as if stunned, but then her smile disappears.

"Not quite Max." Rose says. "I want to see the video to verify I have the attempted murder of me on file."

"No problem." Max says and then his phone rings.

"Hello, Chet! What's up?"

"Max, I hope you are close *hiccup* by. We are starting the first movie in twenty minutes. Sam said he wants to see Jurassic Park again. The sky is black now. If you are coming to the party, maybe you ought to come here before the rain gets heavy."

"We have a guest."

"Bring him! Everyone is welcome, the more *hiccup* the merrier! We have extra stuff." Chet slurs his words.

"It's a woman."

"How the... I know Peggy just left for Las Vegas. Did you find another woman already? You and Peggy broke up for good? Well, maybe I interrupted **your** party!"

"We just fished her out of the ocean and..."

"Wow! You caught a mermaid!" Chet manages a horselaugh.

"No Chet, she isn't a mermaid. I will explain when we get there. Sam is here too. We will all come over. Even though she isn't a mermaid Chet, the guys will like her. She's a good looker."

"Oh wow, *hiccup*, a good hooker! I think some of the women here are too. She'll have some hookers to talk to." Chet giggles, his words slurring more.

"Not a good hooker Chet, a good looker. We'll see you soon." Max rings off chuckling. "I think Chet is already tanked!"

"You want to go over there now? Is that a good idea?" Sam asks.

"Rose, do you know the Danglebatts Band?" Max says ignoring Sam.

"I love the Danglebatts! I love their new song *Black Spider Woman*. It is so like what I'm!" Rose sings. "Black Spider Woman, You crawl - all over me..."

"Really? Well, you can meet them in person. Chet Hatter lives next door. He is having a hurricane party and the whole band is there."

"Okay! The whole band! We have to go there!" Rose jumps up and down.

"When you bounce like that all in pink, you look like the Energizer Bunny!" Max kids her as he turns on his laptop he set on the dining room table.

"Be careful, the Energizer Bunny might thump you!" Rose pity pats Max on his arm and bears her teeth at Max.

"I'll sic Hera on you."

"She likes me." Rose says reverting to a smile.

"I know. I like you too. So we watch the video?"

"Please, I want to know what I recorded."

Max plugs in the camcorder and opens the file. He watches Sancho and Matuso enter the room and later the demonic look on Matuso's face when Rose sneezes.

"Stop it!" Rose turns away from the screen suddenly feeling sick. The feeling of treading water while the party boat disappears comes back to her and she shudders.

"Are you okay?" Max asks touching her shoulder.

"I'll watch it later. I want to see the Danglebatts!"

"They aren't going to perform *Black Spider Woman* or anything Rose. They call it the Ultimate Jezebel Hurricane Party, but it's just a regular party since Jezebel isn't visiting Fort Lauderdale."

"I don't care. I want to meet Dan Batts, maybe get his autograph. You know, for the scrapbook I may have someday." Rose forces herself to smile again.

"I think it is wise not to take the camcorder with us. You might drop it, lose it, or damage it there. We need to hide it before we go." Max says as he shuts off the laptop.

"With all this going on you want to celebrate?" Sam says showing his stress.

"Yes, no need to spoil a good party. Rose, the Danglebatts are fun guys. I know you'll have a good time there, maybe even dance with Dan if he isn't too sloshed."

"That's what I need right now Max. Well, let me call Donna." Rose says

"Why call her now?" Max asks.

"I want to let her know why I'm not at my apartment."

"Keep it on speaker. I want to hear her voice." Max says as he gives her his cell phone.

Chapter Twenty One

Rose dials Donna and before she can say hello Donna answers.

"Where are you Rose? Are you okay?"

"Yes, I'm okay. I'm with my new friends."

"You know you should be debriefed and turn in that camcorder before going anywhere. Why aren't you home? Agent Cooper is waiting for you. He just called and said you aren't there."

"I'm with the guys who saved me. I'll ride out the storm here."

"You said guys. I thought Merchado rescued you. Are there others with you?"

"Yes."

"You need to come home now Rose. You need to be debriefed! Bring the recorder and your new friends. We will need to talk to them too. You could all be in danger from Matuso's men. Get with Agent Cooper. He can take you all to a safe place until we figure out our next move."

"I'm in Fort Lauderdale now. I will meet with Cooper and play the video later. Right now I'm okay!"

"Go to Agent Cooper now Rose! You need debriefing!"

"I'm sorry but I'm safe where I'm."

"I'm ordering you! Go to your apartment!"

"I respectfully disobey. I will stay here." Rose rings off. She stares at the phone not believing what she said.

"That was strange!" Max says. He lets Rose lean on him.

"I think I just lost my job. I need some time to sort out things. I need some R&R." She hands the phone back to Max and presses her head to his chest. "Why would Donna insist I meet with agent Cooper? How in Hell is he going to keep us safe?" She closes her eyes and wraps her arms around Max.

"Let's hide this camcorder and then enjoy the party!" Max pats her shoulder. "The attic is a good hiding place." He quickly hugs her and then leads the way to the garage.

"Hide it in the attic?" Rose asks as she trots behind Max.

"Yes, hide it under some insulation. No one will find it there."

"We know about things hidden in the attic." Sam nods his head thinking back to when he found the rare red diamond in Max's old attic.

"Okay Max. Maybe I shouldn't carry it to the party." Rose frets over wanting to watch the rest of the video and wanting to meet the Danglebatts band. Her normally keen judgment is messed up thinking about her plunge into the ocean, the Danglebatts, and her feelings for Max. She wants to do whatever Max wants.

"You can always watch the video. How often do you get to go to a Danglebatts party? You can meet all the band members while they are still almost sober. All the food, drink, and drugs you are into are free. Why not enjoy life for a while."

"Okay Max, why not hide this someplace simple?"

"Robbers know where to look. The attic is too much trouble for them. They won't bother to look under every patch of prickly insulation. It's a much safer place."

Max sets a ladder under the access hole and stares at Rose as she climbs to the ceiling. To Max, she looks even sexier in pink shorts than she did in the nude. As she slides the access cover to one side, Max shouts up to her.

"Just hide it underneath some insulation."

Rose pokes her head through the access hole and looks around the attic. The only illumination comes from the lights in the garage. She sees the mounds of pink fiberglass insulation between the rafters. She carefully lifts up a wad on the right side and stuffs the camcorder under it. Rose steps down and slides the cover back in place. She looks down and sees Max staring at her. Rose backs down the ladder but as she steps off the bottom rung, she loses her balance and Max grabs her.

"Thanks for not letting me fall Max. But maybe you shouldn't hold me."

"I like holding you."

Rose smiles as Max lets go of her. She watches Max store the ladder and then follows him and Sam back to the living room.

"Let's party!" Max raises his arms to celebrate.

"You still want to go with Matuso after us? I believe we are in danger Max." Sam shakes his head.

"What can he do? Matuso doesn't even know Rose is alive. He won't find us here. I want to see the Jurassic Park movies, Rose wants to meet the Danglebatts, and I think we are all hungry and thirsty. I don't think anything is going to happen. We might as well spend some time with friends. Enjoy the journey Sam!"

"Maybe Rose should watch the rest of the video first."

"It can wait, Sam." Max says seeing Rose shake her head. He motions for Sam and Rose to come with him.

Rose follows Max and Sam outside bracing against small gusts of wind as she runs across the manicured grass yards. She sees Chet's tan window shutters are closed just like on Max's house. She feels the wind swirling around in circles as she takes care not to lose her footing on the slippery grass. *Look out Dan Batts!* Rose thinks as she runs feeling strangely happy.

Sam rushes across the yards. He braces against the cool wind gusts as he runs and he thinks. *This is a bad omen, the black clouds and everything boarded up... I hope we get through this alive!*

Chapter Twenty Two

Victor Campbell the campaign assistant to Hubert Sancho paces the living room floor in his 'Lauderdale by the Sea' home. His wife is in the kitchen preparing dinner and he hears his son playing a video game on his tablet in his bedroom, both are out of earshot. Victor stops to stare at his cell phone on the coffee table, concerned about what he witnessed today. He looks outside through the sliding glass doors and sees the wind whipping across his pool enclosure flapping the screens. The gloominess of the day fits Victor's mood. He thinks about the woman twisting and flailing like a rag doll as Matuso tosses her into the ocean. The reality of what Matuso did still haunts him.

Victor had to lower his standards when he hooked up with Hubert Sancho four years ago. He needed a job and this one was available through a friend after the freak death of Sancho's campaign manager. He doesn't mind the alleged drug dealing, even Sancho being with various prostitutes, but murder is too much for him to tolerate. *This isn't like the other things he does. I actually witnessed a murder!*

Victor's mind flip-flops between exposing a murderer and his money gravy train with Sancho. The brief image of the woman staring at him with her wide eyes is still burning in his mind. He relives Matuso spinning her around and tossing her out the window. *Is murder okay, as long as we get the votes?* Victor asks himself. He hesitates but tightens his jaw and dials his boss Hubert Sancho.

"Hello Victor." Sancho says seeing his caller ID.

"Mister S, we need to talk about what happened today."

"There is nothing to talk about Vic."

"You know this isn't like your other deals, this is murder!"

"You shouldn't talk like that over the phone Vic, even though I have my phone checked for bugs regularly, someone could be listening in. We are all home free. Who knows what happened, and you know we had to do it. Our operation would be compromised if we did anything else."

"But we are involved with killing a woman!"

"You and I didn't kill anyone. That woman will wash up on shore someday, or she may never be found. Perhaps the wind will carry her further out to sea. She may float a hundred or a thousand miles away. If they eventually find her, who can figure out what happened. Vic, get it together and stop fretting. It is a gamble FBI agents take and she lost. Just blank it from your mind."

"Our campaign never was to kill anyone, just win the election. I... we could all go to jail or worse!"

"We have to go along now. I hate it but Matuso is the boss now."

"I don't like this. We could lose everything!"

"That's why we must stay the course. If we don't, my Senate race is over, your career is over and we will be charged as accessories to murder. We all go to jail, understand?"

"I understand." Victor sounds depressed.

"Good, just go on with normal things. Since we canceled the Boca Raton and the West Palm rallies due to possible bad weather, see if you can get them back or you can relax for a couple days. It looks like the hurricane isn't a problem." Sancho feels sweat seeping down his cheeks and uses his hanky to mop his face.

"This can ruin my career but I have to get this off my chest."

"You already have Vic. I'm listening to how you feel! Just keep this a secret. You mustn't tell anyone, not even your wife Karen! We need to ride the good life as long as we can. Then we can exit and enjoy the fruits of our labor. Remember you have Karen and your son Benny to think of, and I have Joanna and my daughter Cynthia. You know whom we are dealing with. I hate for anything to happen to them if you get my drift."

"Are you threatening my family?"

"Not me Vic, it's Matuso. He has us by the short hairs."

"So now murder is okay? We could end up on death row!"

"I don't like this either but people die every day. It's kill or be killed. We have to go along with his plan. There is too much at stake like a long prison sentence. I'm leery of this kind of talk on the phone. Settle down and hope Jezebel doesn't change direction and hit here. It could destroy your lovely house."

"This house is the least of my concerns. I will hang okay. I don't want to go to jail! That would be disgraceful!"

"Just keep your mouth shut and you will be fine. Matuso assured me we are going to win the election. It is mutually beneficial Vic."

"I hope you are right." Victor ends the call.

Hubert Sancho leans back in his chair, hoping he convinced Victor to keep quiet. He wipes his forehead again wishing he had never dealt with Matuso, and he is fearful of doing anything now to upset the devil man. Wondering what to do next, he taps his fingers on the oak armrest of his chair and jerks his head in shock when his phone rings. Oddly, he sees it is Rafael Matuso calling.

"Sancho!" Matuso's gruff voice barks at him.

"Yes Mister M, What do you want?"

"We need to talk. Come to my car."

"You are here?"

"Yes, come outside now."

Sancho hears his phone click dead. *The SOB is ordering me around again!* He mumbles to himself. He grabs a raincoat from the rack by the front door. As he starts to leave, his wife asks.

"Where are you going? Dinner is almost ready." His wife says.

"I will just be a minute Joanna."

Peeking through the peephole on the door, Sancho sees a black limo parked at the curb. He rushes out the front door against the wind and sprinkles. When he nears the limo, a motorized side door opens for him. Sancho ducks inside. He sits facing the rear across from Matuso and Frank. He shakes off some rain as the door closes.

"What's this about? Where are we going?" Hubert asks feeling the car start to move.

"We just ride away for a few minutes. We have a problem."

"I know Victor is shaky. He had a meltdown years ago but I can control him."

"That is a separate issue. No, it seems that FBI agent survived her swim in the ocean."

"How can that be?"

"A fisherman called Max Merchado rescued her. We have the worst luck with this. I should have snapped her neck before I tossed her out."

"Kill her! Why... how do you know all this about her and..."

"As I suspected, the woman is FBI agent Rose Finley. Finley disobeyed orders and went on the boat. Fortunately, Finley called Grant to tell her about her near demise. So we found out about her survival. She used this man's cell phone to call and we know he is the man who rescued her. I got phone registration information."

"So more people know what happened, this is too messy! What can we do?"

"I will take care of them. Just continue as usual!"

"How... well, you can call off the hit on Sara Troutman then. We can plan something else. I'm relieved this Finley woman is alive."

"No, it's worse! Think about it Sancho! We have major problems if she talks and I'm sure she already talks to this Max. I thought I threw her recorder into the ocean with her, but I was wrong. She hid a recorder in that room.

"It looks like checking for bugs did no good."

"She is a clever agent. However, we will get rid of her and this man and the recorder. I really should have killed her before I tossed her to make sure she couldn't talk. Who would think with the stormy weather and all, that someone would rescue her? My boss says I was careless Sancho. Mister Ruiz hates carelessness! I must fix everything soon, even with the rain upon us!"

"You still want to kill the girl and an innocent man now too?"

"It has to be done. I will have this fixed before the hurricane is history. Now we discuss what to do about Victor."

"Victor is upset about all this but he knows not to talk about anything."

"I warned you about Victor. He isn't very stable. What is it with Victor?"

"He was okay before." Sancho says and explains the call from Vic.

"Can he prove anything?"

"No, but he could crack under pressure, I know he had a mental issue in the past with panicking. I just need to keep him focused. There is a lot of work he has to do between now and election day."

"I just saw on the news, that Medina is ahead of you on all the polls still. I have a possible replacement for Victor. Maybe we should quiet him now."

"What are you implying?"

"Victor may not have the fortitude to handle what is happening. That is what I'm saying. He may need to be replaced."

"No, I know he will be loyal to the end. I know he can't stand the thought of going to prison. That caused him to panic before. He will hang in there, you will see."

"You be sure he does hang in there. I will take care of Finley and this Max fellow. You must keep Victor under control! Now go, enjoy your family." Matuso motions for Sancho to leave when the limo stops in front of Sancho's house. He presses a button and the side door starts opening.

Sancho stares at the man thinking. *This SOB is telling me what to do again. Victor was right. This was a bad idea and it's too late to back out now!* A little dazed, Sancho gets out and runs back into his house. As he hangs up the raincoat, he mulls over what to do about Victor. Then he hears his daughter calling.

"Daddy!"

"What is it Cynthia?"

"It's dinnertime! Mommy fixed your favorite fish, Mahi-mahi."

Chapter Twenty Three

Craig Benito takes a deep breath as he parks his van at the Gatsby Apartments. He feels bloated from consuming too much food and booze on the 'Bacalao'. A well-tanned Hispanic overweight man in his mid-forties he senses that age is creeping up on him. He finishes applying his disguise for his afternoon job. Craig wears a blonde wig on his shaved head, a temporary tattoo of an anchor on his arm, and a large black mole pasted on his left cheek. The disguise is perfect in case someone is asked to describe him. As much as he wants to relax after all the political talk he got orders from Matuso to gather anything of interest from Finley's apartment.

Working for Rafael Matuso for over ten years and never caught, he is the cause of several unsolved murders. To Craig Benito, killing is just a job that someone has to do. Always very cautious and detailed in his plans, he feels no remorse for snuffing out a life. Victims are like fake soldiers in a video game to him. Killing is fun for Craig Benito, like a game that pays him well for playing.

He gets out of his black van still woozy from all the drinking he did on the party boat just an hour ago. He flips up his nondescript hood on his slicker and stuffs his flashlight in his pocket in case the power goes off. The rain hits him in sheets as he walks across the concrete to the building entrance. Inside, Craig avoids the elevator and climbs the stairs to the third floor. He feels fortunate that no one is around the stairs or in the hallway as he locates Rose's apartment. Not knowing if Rose has a possible roommate inside, Craig readies his gun. He knocks hard and waits hiding his gun behind him. Hearing nothing for a minute, he uses his lock pick kit to open the door. No one is inside. The only light is what cloudy sunlight seeps through the gaps in the shutters covering her windows. He switches on lights searching everywhere. The apartment is empty. Craig gathers papers, file folders, and thumb drives from her desk drawers. He grabs her laptop stuffing it and everything else in a large construction bag. Then his phone rings. It is Rafael Matuso.

"You never call me! I call you when I'm clear! No exceptions!" Craig shouts, more irritated that he carelessly kept his phone with him. If someone calls at a critical time it could be fatal for him. *I'm getting too sloppy!* He thinks easing onto the couch.

"Never mind that, Finley is alive! She may go there. Be prepared!"

"When did you find out that?"

"Just now, Finley called her boss. She is alive and she has a recorder. I want to alert you. You must stay there. Take care of her and anyone with her."

"I understand."

Craig curses as he shuts off the phone that should have been left in his van. However, he knows it was good to get that information from Matuso. He finishes gathering up anything that may be useful before resting in a chair that he turns to face the doorway. Craig watches the door, his Berretta 9 mm with silencer attached resting on his left thigh. Both he and Rafael have incriminating evidence on each other so these two unsavory men have moderate trust in each other.

Originally, he only came to check for a roommate and gather Finley's stuff but now that agent Finley is alive, his order changes. Craig waits patiently. An hour passes. He sits in the dark apartment, waiting and checking his watch often. Around four o'clock the power and thus the air conditioner goes off. Finally, at five o'clock he calls his boss, still watching Rose's front door.

"You are still there?" Matuso asks.

"Yes, I could have left hours ago!" Craig is upset. "There is no activity at all here. I don't think she is coming here. I looked through a slit in the window earlier. A dark blue minivan drove in, started to park, and left without stopping. It could have been her."

"She drives a gray car, it wasn't her. Did you pack all her stuff?"

"Yes, I got her laptop and some thumb drives and papers too, like bank statements, phone bills, anything you could possibly use. I stuffed everything in a bag. It looks like she lives alone, so no cause for alarm from a worried roommate."

"Good work, bring that to me. She is a major problem for us. Too bad she didn't come to you. Now you have to go to her. When she called her boss, Grant got the ID of the phone Finley used. Grant is doing all she can to help us. A few minutes ago, she sent me the owner's name, address, and pictures of him and Finley. The man who owns the phone is named Maximiliano Diego Merchado."

"What a name!"

"He goes by 'Max', and lives in Fort Lauderdale. The GPS on his phone indicates Merchado is at home. Rose is probably still with him at his home for the night. Frank is texting everything to you as we talk. I want you to find them and especially the recorder!"

"So I leave here?"

"Yes, you need to find the recorder and complete your mission."

"You know I'll want an extra fee if I get the recorder?"

"Yes, I give a big bonus when you hand it over."

"Good, I will look at the details and get it done." Craig rings off.

As he leaves Rose's apartment carrying the black bag with Rose's belongings he swings the door but debris on the floor keeps it ajar. Craig ignores the unclosed door and rushes down the stairs and out the exit. He runs to his van through the light rain and wind. Craig tosses the construction bag inside and jumps in, slamming the door shut. He looks at the photos of Max and Rose.

"Good looking broad. I'm going to have fun!"

Chapter Twenty Four

Max leans on Chet's doorbell. Instead of chimes ringing, he hears the opening riffs of the latest Danglebatts hit song *Black Spider Woman*. He waits under the stone canopy listening to the wind whoosh through the opening, and finally Chet's wife Katie answers the door. Max sees her long auburn hair, which normally would be draped down to her waist on her powder blue kimono, flow straight back shoulder high by the wind blowing through the house. Her kimono is pressing against her bare petite breasts and swelling belly. Max rushes inside after Sam and Rose and forces the door shut.

"Hello guys! Chet has the pool door open thus all the wind." Katie says holding an orange drink in her left hand and a question on her face.

"Hello beautiful! You look like it's about time." Max says giving Katie a big hug.

"I'm due in a month." Katie says returning his hug.

Max looks over her shoulder at the enormous living room serving as the dance floor. Through the haze of what smells like Marijuana mixed with cigarette smoke and alcohol, he sees psychedelic and strobe lights flashing about the ceiling and across the dancers forming weird light patterns. He sees maybe thirty strangers undulating to the rock music that blares from multiple speakers. Max smiles as he watches Chet hobble to the foyer. Max extends his hand to shake.

"Hello Max, hello Sam! Who is this lovely lady?" Chet slurs.

"This is Rose Finley. Rose this is Chet Hatter, lead guitarist for the Danglebatts."

"I know who he is!" Rose rolls her eyes. "Hello Chet!" She shakes his hand.

"How many drinks have you had?" Max says smiling.

"Oh, let's see…" Chet starts counting on his fingers but stumbles. He wraps an arm around Rose and then leans on her and hugs her to steady himself. "Sorry Miss! Well Max, I just don't know. Rose, welcome to our Ultimate Jezebel Party!"

"Thank you! Am I really hugging Chet Hatter?" Rose says flustered.

"It's really me. You should meet the rest of the band, honey. Max tells me you're not a hooker." Chet sees her shake her head no. They laugh as his arm reaches over her shoulder and he pulls her toward the crowd swaying to the music.

Max watches Chet and Rose disappear among the dancers, smoke, and flashing lights. He feels a twinge of jealousy watching them go. Then Katie grasps his arm.

"Hey Max, at least I know her name now. You need a drink. Tell me all about your new friend Rose! Come along Sam!" Katie says wrapping her arm around Max's waist, but Sam stands still.

"I just want to take in the view for a while."

"Suit yourself Sam." Katie leads Max through the crowd to the wet bar.

Max waves hello to Dan Batts leaning against the bar counter that is shaped like a guitar. He remembers Chet telling him the bar is specially made by an artisan working with strips of Rosewood. It has embedded pearl inlays and a black bat that appears to be hanging from the main area of the guitar neck. The artist sealed the top with a clear polyurethane coat. Max walks by the custom countertop and Dan before speaking.

"Again, how far along are you Katie, and what about Chet going off with Rose?"

"Eight months Max, and Chet never strays. I trust him. He will only flirt a little."

"Still, I'd keep an eye on him. She's a looker and maybe a hooker."

"Wow, you're a poet and don't know it, Max, you should write a song!"

"Someday I will. It will be a hit about an FBI agent like Rose."

"See now I didn't know she is an FBI agent, but I think Rose is the one in danger from the rest of the band members! A curious mind though wants to know three things. First, why would you go fishing with a hurricane that may come at you? Secondly, where did you pick up this redhead, and why is she wearing all pink like Peggy? What can I get you, whiskey, wine, soda?"

"That's at least um, six questions Katie. Okay, my new boat just got ready today. I had to try it out. I call it the 'Journey Too'. I miss the old 'Journey' but this new one rocks! We went fishing for Mahi-mahi and we caught a bunch of them! Then on the way back in, we saw this woman about to drown in the ocean several miles offshore.

"Did she have a life preserver? What boat was she from?"

"That's the thing. There were no boats in the area and she had no life preserver."

"Really, you must be kidding."

"It's true Katie. She also was completely nude!"

"Really?"

"Yes, as we got to her she went under. Sam dove in and rescued her. We gave her a raincoat to cover up but she couldn't go to her apartment in Miami so we took her to my house. I let her use some of Peggy's clothes, thus the pink outfit. She's a big Danglebatts fan so that's the reason for bringing her here. I like fruit drinks and yours looks good." Max points at her orange glass.

"But why was she out there... Oh, this is orange juice and no booze, the baby you know. What else would you like?"

"Well, maybe I'll just have a beer." Max leans against Katie for a second, closes his eyes, and thinks about all that has happened today. The excitement catches up with him.

"Beer it is. So tell me, why was this naked woman in the ocean?"

"Oh… someone threw her off a party boat. She couldn't swim in her tight party dress so she had to shed it." Max sees Katie frown and shake her head.

"Someone threw her off a boat and left her to drown?"

"That's her story. I believe her."

"That sounds like something that would happen to James Bond, not to a young woman like her. She looks too um, pretty. Are you telling me the truth?"

"Yes, and I can tell you she is strong too. That's all I can say right now."

"Never mind, I can make up my own story about her like maybe she was naked before she dove in the ocean!"

"That's a good one. I don't think so."

"Harrumph! If you or your friends get hungry, you know where the kitchen is. We have all sorts of food there. I prefer the peeled shrimp, but there are lobster tails, King Crab legs, and melted butter, beef stroganoff, hamburgers, all sorts of raw vegetables, and a whole tub full of baked potatoes to mention just the stuff I like. The stuffed green peppers and the creamed spinach are great too. Dan had the caterers bring a ton of food in here this morning in case Jezebel comes this way. We refrigerated a lot of it for later or whenever. The caterer shut down until Monday so Dan went crazy ordering food. Try the Jalapeño poppers if you want your mouth on fire."

"I'll pass on the poppers. Sam and I caught a load of Mahi-mahi today. The dock guy Charley is fileting them. I'll bring you some filets after the party."

"I love fish. Now please tell me more about this woman." Katie hands Max a beer.

"I told you all I can for now. Let's forget about her." Max says.

"Do you want me to make up my own story? I saw the way you looked at Rose. Are you attracted to her? Are you dumping Peggy for the naked girl?"

"Actually Peggy dumped me."

"Oh no! She said she was worrying over that."

"When did she tell you?"

"A few weeks ago, but she said not to talk about it."

"So I'm the last to know."

"I'm sorry Max. The victim is often the last to know. Maybe she'll come to her senses when she gets back."

"I don't know." Max says and accepts a long hug from her.

"Well, maybe this Rose is a new start for you."

"No, as much as I would like that, she says no dice. She says her job is too dangerous so she wants to work alone."

"My God, is she running from the law?"

"No not the law, the bad guys. She is one of the good guys. After the manure hits the fan I will tell you all about her."

"Something exciting is going to happen?"

"I think so. Now let's just mingle and enjoy the party." Max starts dancing and as he moves into the crowd Katie starts dancing with him.

Chapter Twenty Five

Sam stands by the doorway watching his friends merge into the crowd and takes in all the festivities. He starts to weave through the dancers and the smoky haze aiming for the bar where Max and Katie went when a girl waves her hand at his face. He looks down and sees a strange-looking woman slightly shorter than Peggy maybe in her late twenties staring at him with big brown eyes. He mostly notices her orange and blue hair sticking up in two orange and blue pigtails, her silver nose ring, and her orange and blue blouse and short shorts. She has an orange scarf wrapped around her neck. She blocks Sam's path as she sways to the music.

"Hello Sam." She chants.

"Wow, you look Gatorish… do you know me? Who are you?"

"You don't remember me? We dated a few years ago."

"Your face looks familiar but…"

"You must remember our night on the beach and the moonlight and that cabana. Now that was romantic! I was a brunette then. Do you remember me now?"

"Holy cow, you're Charlotte?"

"Yeah, I know I look different. It's weird that you look just the same Sam. You moved to Colorado, so why are you here? Oh yes, I'm hooked up with Dan Batts now, so don't try anything!" Charlotte slurs her words and giggles, obviously not sober.

"No problem, I'm happily married. Hey, you really look the part of a Gator girlfriend. I know Dan is a big University of Florida fan."

"Yeah, I'm his Gator bait! It's fun, Sam. Come with me. I'm sure Dan wants to say hi to you." Charlotte wraps an arm around his waist and directs him toward Dan Batts. She finds Dan the lead singer and leader of the Danglebatts band sitting on a barstool and she holds Sam tight when Dan waves hello.

"Hey Sam, does Max still carry around a fake spider? He came up with a great segue into our new song 'Black Spider Woman', flipping that fake spider on the stage at me. That was a great idea!"

"I was going to say I'm sorry about that Dan. He really didn't flip the spider at... Um, well Max has a talent for stepping in poop and coming out smelling like a rose."

"You sound jealous." Dan laughs and smiles at Sam.

"Maybe I'm a little. In all the messes we got into Max never gets hurt, and he is the one who gets all the praise and attention. You know number one salesperson, big fancy boat, hot red Corvette, and big personality. Everybody loves Max. Sometimes he really does seem to be larger than life." Sam shrugs.

"Do you remember that song 'The Wind beneath My Wings'?"

"Vaguely, I think Bette Midler sang it in the movie 'Beaches', a chick flick."

"Yes Sam, well you are the wind beneath his wings. He would be in deep trouble without you Sam. I think people know that about you. So just give Max a hug for me the next time you see him." Dan Batts tilts left, almost tumbling off his stool.

"Max and I rarely if ever hug. It's just the idea we have that men hugging isn't a manly thing to do. We just high-five or pat each other on the back. And, by the way, I think Max would survive very well without me."

"Okay Sam, if high-five works for you. Just don't put yourself down. Max needs you more than he knows, and you need him too. You guys are like soul brothers. He always tests you. He lights a torch and you keep everyone from burning. You don't know how strong your bond with Max really is. It will surprise you when you realize what brotherly love is. You really are the wind beneath his wings!"

"Yeah and I think your wings are three sheets to the wind, Dan."

"You think? But you two will stick together no matter what."

"We have helped each other out a few times but I think it is more about self-preservation. Maybe you are right. I think of Max more like a big brother than a friend."

"I feel even more fortunate than you Sam. My band guys are my brothers. I would do anything for them and them for me. Not everyone has such a fortune as we do Sam. Guard it with all you have. It is more precious than gold!"

"You are totally schnockered Dan!" Sam laughs and Dan joins in.

"Just a little Sam, I get carried away with thinking after some hard liquor and a few joints." Dan waves as Charlotte drags Sam away from him.

"Come on Sam, Dan does too much thinking when he's loaded! Let's get on the dance floor! Do you smoke weed?" Charlotte asks as she drags him along but sees Sam shake his head no.

"So I'm the wind beneath his wings!" Sam shouts as he slips through the crowd with Charlotte to the opposite side of the living room. He starts to dance with her just as the music stops. He sees Katie tap on a microphone to shush everyone.

"Are you guys having a good time?" She shouts when she has everyone's attention. She hears cheering and waits for the whistling to settle down before she continues.

"I know some of you missed the original Jurassic Park movie and some of you just want to see it again." She hears more cheers.

"We're starting the first of the four by yawl's request in a few minutes in the movie room. After that, we will show The Lost World, Jurassic Park III, and finally Jurassic World. If you want to rest up and watch some good movies, follow me. It's movie time!" Katie turns off the microphone and kicks the music back on. She motions the crowd to follow her.

"Hey Charlotte, I want to see this." Sam says.

He tries to leave but Charlotte follows him into the huge room. Sam sees a giant pull-down screen opposite three rows of armless chairs and sits down in the rear row. A small crowd shuffles into the seats in front of him. Charlotte sits down beside him and he feels her smooth bare leg press against his bare leg and her arm wraps around him. The movie starts, the room darkens, and for a moment Sam stops thinking about Max, Rose, Dan, and everything. His feelings for Charlotte return like a kaleidoscope of fireworks!

"I'm sorry Charlotte, I can't stay here!" Sam rushes out of the room and bumps into Katie. He holds her until she is steady again. "Sorry Katie, I wasn't looking."

"I'm okay Sam. What's the hurry?" Katie asks. Then she sees Charlotte come from the movie room and grab Sam's arm.

"What's the matter Sam?" Charlotte asks.

Sam steps away from Katie and lowers his voice. "We need a quiet place to talk."

"Did I flirt too much?" Charlotte asks as Sam takes her to the foyer area. She sits on the couch near the front door and stares at Sam still standing near her. She reaches for him but he steps away. She bows her head in silence waiting for Sam to speak. "You don't want me Sam?" Charlotte pouts. She stares at him with sad eyes.

"Oh yes, Charlotte! You are as exciting as ever! You may even be more exciting now with those orange and blue pigtails sticking up and all." Sam waves a frustrated hand at her. "Your perfume and everything about you is exciting. If I wasn't married I'd want you but I just can't! Go back to Dan. Please don't taunt me I love my wife madly and I'd regret it if I gave in to you!"

"Wow, you're so serious Sam! I'm just here for a good time, nothing else, and no commitment. I thought I could give you some pleasure and have some pleasure for me too. I guess it won't happen." Charlotte leans forward to touch Sam but he backs away. She sulks as she looks into his hazel eyes.

"I'm sorry Charlotte." Sam turns away to avoid her stare.

"Okay then, it is goodbye again Sam!" Charlotte says.

"I apologize for giving you a wrong signal Charlotte."

"I was thinking we could be just friends flirting with each other."

"We can't be just friends. You are still way too exciting!"

"I'm with Dan now. I wasn't going to do anything with you."

"Are you sure about that?"

"No." Charlotte shakes her head. "What about you?"

"No. I couldn't live with myself if I betrayed Ann, my wife!"

"Perhaps I better go to Dan."

"Yes." Sam looks into her eyes for a moment and then kisses her cheek. "Goodbye Charlotte."

"Goodbye Sam." Charlotte fakes a smile, stands up, and dashes off, leaving him alone in the entranceway.

Chapter Twenty Six

Peggy Clarkson is awestruck as the taxi works its way along Las Vegas Boulevard from the airport to the Stratosphere Hotel in the early afternoon. Her first impression of "The Strip" is fascinating. She stares in amazement at the water displays of the Bellagio, the larger-than-life majestic lion at the MGM Grand Hotel, the hugeness of all the other competing casinos and hotels, and the giant video displays hawking current and future events. She is impressed by the opulence, the fantasy-like splendor, and the gigantism of the gambling mecca. The taxi inches its way into the traffic finally stopping at the hotel.

After checking in, Peggy drops her suitcase inside the room she shares with Sam's wife Ann Stormen. She sees Ann drop her suitcase and flop onto the king-size bed. The room is warm, so Peggy unbuttons her blouse and flaps it to stay cool. She checks the thermostat.

"The air conditioner is set too hot. I'll put it to 70." She says.

The long airplane trip and chatting for five hours with another sewing enthusiast Carol Novak made Peggy's voice slightly hoarse. Locating her luggage, the exhilaration of the taxi ride, and the heat of Vegas all add to her excitement. She is tired but thrilled that her images of Las Vegas were true. Peggy takes a sip from her water bottle and thinks. *This is what I need!* Peggy stands for a moment, blinks her eyes, and smiles.

"Is this place exciting or what? Did you see all the casinos?"

"Yes, but I'm tired." Ann says stretching out on the bed.

"Why don't we go exploring in the bar or the gift shops?"

"I'm going to rest. Why don't you take a nap too?"

"No, Carol Novak may stop by. She has been here before and we can go exploring together. I'm stashing some stuff in the little safe and then I hope Carol comes here so we can tour the town. You might want to come too before you take a nap. The welcome dinner isn't until six. We don't need to be anywhere until then."

"I just want to lie here. I need some rest." Ann says.

"Yeah, you're right. Get some sleep now and howl later!" Peggy looks at Ann resting on the king-size bed. She still feels too warm, so she leaves her blouse open. She picks up her roll-around and places it on top of an ottoman. "I'm going to take the second drawer for my stuff. You can have the other drawers, okay?"

"Okay, but I will unpack later."

Peggy hangs her clothes in the closet and stuffs her other things in the drawers. She exhales noisily. "I hope I cool down soon. Why do we have only one bed? We ordered two queens." Peggy says annoyed.

"It was supposed to be queens, but I don't care. Complain later. It's only two here but I'm exhausted." Ann says lying on her back with her eyes closed.

"Why are you tired? This is an exciting time."

"I've been up since early this morning and with the time change, I'm exhausted. I need to rest."

"Me too then, it will take me a day or so to get used to this time change." Peggy kicks off her shoes, lies down on the bed, and giggles. "Hey, did you ever sleep with another woman?"

"You're a wisecracker! No, I haven't and don't get any ideas!" Ann joins Peggy in laughing about their bed situation.

"You're just not my type Ann."

"I should try calling Sam again. I got his voice mail earlier."

"If I know Max, he and Sam are at Chet's party whooping it up."

"You aren't worried about Max hooking up with some bimbo?"

"No, but are you worried about Sam?"

"No. Sam loves me and is extremely loyal and faithful. Remember, they may be facing a hurricane. I seem more worried about Sam than you are of Max."

"Well, remember we just split up."

"I know but I didn't think you'd actually leave Max forever."

"Yes, we aren't like you and Sam. We sort of twisted each other's arms to stay together. I sure wanted Max to be a party animal, especially with all the cash we got."

"I thought you were set with Max. Why are you leaving him?"

Peggy explains and concludes. "I just want to party and enjoy our wealth, and go to new places like you and I are right now. I think all the extra money changed Max. He is bent on having kids now. I love him too much to keep him from having kids."

"Wow, so you'd like to be a free woman again?"

"Yes! I'm free as a bird and here to party, except for the classes."

"I guess you don't care if Max um, hooks up with someone."

"I know I'll be looking. I'm sure there will be hot women at the Jezebel Party, but Max wants a baby machine, not just a bimbo."

"Okay, so you are fine with him messing around? Why is the party at Chet's house anyway? Dan Batts is the band leader."

"Max says Chet has the only big house. You've seen inside, it's enormous! The other guys have apartments and they said a clubhouse has too many restrictions. Max says it is going to be a super hurricane party. The whole band will be there and according to Katie about thirty or forty of their close friends. Imagine what a zoo that is. You can call him but I bet he can't hear his phone ring. He's having a ball by now. Just send a text that we got here okay."

"I already left a text message that we got here okay and he texted back that all is well there too. I just miss talking to Sam."

"I left a text too and Max answered. Max and Sam are typical men. They won't call, especially since they got our texts that we are okay… unless they need something. Relax, they are fine just like us."

"Yeah, let's get some rest. The group dinner is at six. I'll set an alarm on my phone for 5:30." Ann says. Then she hears a knock on the door and groans as Peggy rolls out of bed to answer the door.

Peggy looks through the peephole. She sees two men and Carol Novak, the woman who sat with her and Ann on the plane. Carol is a tall slim woman maybe in her forties. She is still wearing tan slacks and a white blouse with her arms stretched out onto each of the men's shoulders. The man on her left is maybe thirty, tall and slim with short hair. He fills out his dark blue shirt with muscles and has on white shorts. The other man is tall, handsome, and casual, wearing a floral T-shirt and light brown shorts. To Peggy, both men look like rugged outdoor types and have no wedding bands.

"Just a minute!" Peggy shouts. She buttons her blouse, smiles, and opens the door.

"Hello, Peggy!" Carol says. "This is Barry and Carl. They are going to a private party and we are invited. Put your shoes on and come along! You too Ann!" Carol Novak leans inside the door smiling, her arms still draped over the men's shoulders.

"I'm taking a nap. Aren't you tired from the trip?" Ann shouts.

"A little, but I want to party hardy before the expo starts. We are meeting the rest of their friends at the Luxor Hotel. They say the more the merrier and free food and drinks!"

"I'm in! Give me a minute to freshen up!" Peggy closes the door and runs into the bathroom to smooth her hair. She leaves her blouse un-tucked, looks in the mirror, and smiles as she unbuttons the blouse again down to her cleavage. Happy with her looks, she slips on her shoes and opens the door before looking back at Ann.

"You really aren't coming Ann?"

"I'm not the partying type." Ann is still stretched out on the bed.

"Not interested in free food and drinks? It may be better than the planned dinner."

"Not right now Peggy. Remember I changed phone numbers because of the crank calls, so if you need me to call my new number."

"Yes, I do still have the old number and your new one. I will be sure I call you on your new number if I need to."

"Come on Peg." Carol pleads sticking her head inside again.

"Wait, isn't the Luxor at the other end of the strip? That's a long way to go."

"Barry has a limo waiting, and we can taxi back here from the party. Don't worry; the taxi will take cash or credit card. He is in a hurry to get to the Luxor and tip a few before we go to the party. Let's go!" Carol says tilting toward one of the men.

"Well, okay. Who are these handsome guys?" Peggy asks joining the threesome.

"Oh, Barry says he and Carl are half-brothers but Barry arranged the birthday party. I met them in the lobby. They are collecting people. It is a party for their brother and they want more party animals, especially women!"

"Yeah, why not. You sure you're not going Ann?" Peggy asks.

"I'm napping. You go on. Just stay out of trouble!"

"Okay, but plan on me missing the dinner tonight." Peggy waves goodbye and closes the door. She laughingly says, "Ann is usually more sociable when her husband is with her."

"It's okay. We at least have a foursome. Perhaps we can gather more guests at the Luxor." Barry says and walks to the elevator.

Carol sees Ursula in the lobby, a tall local woman she talked to earlier in the lobby while she waited to check-in. Peggy convinces Ursula to join the group. They climb into the 'limo and trek toward the Luxor Hotel.

Once again, Peggy enjoys looking at all the hotels and casinos along the strip, thinking how great it is to be alive. She feels excited as the limo swings to the front of the Luxor Hotel. A valet opens the door for her and the others. As she walks inside Barry directs everyone to the Aurora Bar. As he escorts Carol and Ursula to his group of friends Carl stays behind with Peggy.

"Hello everyone!" Barry shouts and hears a brief cheer. "These are my new friends Ursula, Carol...Oh, and Peggy and Carl are over there. Help make them welcome!" He hears the crowd cheer. "Listen up folks! I asked everyone to meet here before we all go to Brendan's place at seven. The caterers will be there at six-thirty and all of us will descend on Brendan at seven. Have fun, and then we go!"

Chapter Twenty Seven

Peggy hears the small crowd cheer as she stands still watching Ursula and Carol merge into the group with Barry. She notices Carl is holding her arm. He directs her to a vacant table. Peggy feels a sudden attraction to Carl and tries not to stare at him, focusing on the ceiling. She sees colorful rainbow-like patterns of mostly green light constantly changing and dancing across the ceiling.

"I hope you don't mind. I asked Barry if I could kidnap you from the others." Carl noticed Peggy has brown hair and blue eyes and is just what he is looking for.

"No, that's fine. I like the lighting, it is so pretty."

"Pretty colors," Carl says. "They try to imitate the lights of the Aurora Borealis. This is the only bar I know of that does this."

"It's definitely different from anything I have seen." Peggy manages to say as calmly as she can, wondering why she feels guilty and thrilled at the same time. *Max knows I will be dating. We're split up! I'm here to have some fun!* She reminds herself. She sees a waitress approach their table and speak.

"Hello, what can I get for you two?"

"How about rum and Coke, do you like rum and Coke Peggy?" Carl rests his hand on her shoulder and gives her a slight squeeze.

"I'm not sure. Oh, I guess so, yes that's fine. Shouldn't you be with your friends?"

"They're Barry's friends. He actually lives here in the Luxor. Now tell me about Miss pretty blue eyes."

Peggy feels alive even though she should be tired. She likes Carl's warm hand that gives her shoulder another squeeze. His hazel eyes stare into hers, mesmerizing Peggy. Something inside her is stirring up but she feels guilty too. She takes a deep breath to find the courage to answer.

"Carl, I still feel spoken for." She barely utters wishing she hadn't said that.

"That figures, a beautiful woman like you. Where is your fiancée?"

"Oh, he's in Fort Lauderdale. I flew here this morning and… we are splitting up."

"Well, lucky for me. Tell me about you. You came all the way from Florida just to go to some boring sewing classes. Is that the only reason you came to Las Vegas?" Carl removes his hand from her shoulder accepting drinks from the server. He hands one to Peggy and waits as she takes a sip before answering him.

"This is quite good." Peggy takes another sip of her new favorite drink rum and Coke before continuing. "How did you know about the sewing classes? Oh, Carol. Carl, I'm not sure about anything right now. Life back home is boring compared to Las Vegas. I just decided to be free again." Peggy sips more rum and Coke.

"Is the split a permanent thing?"

"I'm not sure it is yet."

"I'm a good listener. Tell me what's on your mind."

The lights of the bar are pleasantly dim and the occasional loud laugh from another patron seems pleasant to Peggy. She talks about her life and avoids mentioning her relationship with Max again. Peggy makes a bathroom stop and returns to find another drink waiting for her. *I like this handsome sexy man. I'm free, right?* She takes a swallow from the new drink and smiles at Carl.

Carl leans toward Peggy offering his lips to her. To his surprise, she leans forward and meets his lips lingering there for a second before jumping back.

"I'm not sure that is what I want." Peggy says.

"Sorry, I couldn't resist." Carl says thinking she is giving him a green light.

"Things are a little fuzzy. I probably shouldn't have started drinking on an empty stomach. I feel like I need to lie down. It's like these drinks are going right to my head." Peggy's vision is blurring. She has trouble focusing on Carl. "I'm getting tired of pretzels. Can we get a burger or something?"

"We could eat here, but I have a suite available. I can order food and you can rest on the bed while we wait for food."

"You're a naughty boy!"

"I just want you to be comfortable. Do you want steak or pizza?" Carl asks.

"Oh, right now a pepperoni pizza sounds great!"

"Just let me check something." Carl smiles as he walks to the bar.

Peggy sees him tap Barry on the shoulder and talk to him. She sees Barry hand something to him. Carl talks to the bartender but her sight is so blurred she can't tell what he is doing. She lays her head on the table and waits for Carl.

Carl helps Peggy stand up and wraps an arm around her waist to steady her. He walks her out of the bar to the elevator. Carl squeezes her waist during the elevator ride enjoying the smell of Peggy's lavender perfume and the feel of her body leaning on his. He feels her rub legs with his as they walk to the room. After some fumbling, Carl opens the door and leads her inside the suite.

"You can rest while I check on the food." Carl says.

"Oh wow!" Peggy says looking around. "This place is huge! How can you afford this?" She examines the living room, the kitchenette, the wet bar, a giant flat-screen TV, and an open door leading to the bedroom.

"It's nothing." Carl says not revealing he borrowed the suite from Barry and he knows Barry and friends will soon leave for the party."

"It's getting close to seven. Are we going to the party?" Peggy asks. Everything is spinning.

"Yeah, we should go."

"You do look a little like Barry."

"Yes, we are brothers. I'm in a risky business so I stay in a different place. I have an apartment but I decided to keep us here. I will check on the pizza. The bedroom is over there if you want to lie down until pizza time."

"Ah yes, I see it. That's where I'm going." Peggy staggers into the bedroom and flops spread eagle on the bed. The off-white ceiling and wood-framed light seem to rotate making Peggy dizzy so she closes her eyes and wonders. *Why am I so woozy?*

Carl picks up the phone to dial the restaurant but he sees Peggy on her back with her eyes closed. He waits for a moment, hangs up the phone, and walks into the bedroom. Carl sits on the bed next to her, realizing she has passed out. He unbuttons the rest of her blouse and sees that her bra hooks in the front. Carl unhooks the strapless bra. She snorts but offers no resistance as he eases the bra off her breasts.

Carl slips off his shirt and starts caressing her. He kisses her neck and shoulder. He feels her arch her back aroused and hears her moan as she starts to wake up. He reaches down, rubs her stomach, and tries to undo the belt on her slacks. Then he sees Peggy wake up.

Chapter Twenty Eight

"Hey, what are you doing?" Peggy slurs her words as she comes out of her coma. *No, I don't want to do this with him!* She admits to herself. Her adrenalin kicks in and she pushes on his shoulders but is unable to force him away.

"You want it as much as I do!" Carl grunts as he grabs her arms. He kisses her on her neck rolling his body on top of her and pins her arms to her sides. Carl presses his lips on hers. He feels her respond for a second before turning her head.

Peggy is aroused from Carl's body pressing on her. *Yes! I want you! Take me!* Peggy thinks before coming to her senses, then she tries to get free.

She realizes her struggling is doing no good. Carl is too heavy and too strong for her to push away. Peggy relaxes to let it happen. Then she feels him release her right arm and slide his hand down her body clutching her belt buckle again. She reaches out feeling a lamp on the night table. Determined to be free, she grabs the heavy lamp and blindly swings it hitting Carl on the head. She feels him go limp for a second so she pushes him and helps him slide onto the floor.

"You pig!" Peggy cries. Her bra slides off her back and falls to the floor as she jumps to her feet to leave. She hears Carl groan in pain and sees blood seeping from the cut on his forehead running down his face.

"I'm so sorry I hit you Carl! I don't know what to do. I just know I can't do this right now." Peggy sobs. She drops the lamp on the bed and starts to button her blouse.

"Oh no!" She gasps noticing her bra is missing and lying next to the bed. *How did that happen?* She thinks, but then Carl stands up. She tries to pick up her bra but Carl grabs her arm.

"You're a feisty thing." Carl shouts. He grabs her shoulders and tries to toss her on the bed.

"Let me go!" Peggy shouts. She breathes hard afraid of him now.

"Come on girl. Let's have some fun!" Carl tries to pull her closer.

Peggy kicks his shin with the point of her stiletto heel, putting all her strength into the kick, and hears him cry out but he holds on to her. She panics and knees his groin. Carl screams in pain releasing his grip on her. *Forget the bra!* Peggy thinks as she staggers away from Carl. She picks up her purse and hurries into the living room. As Peggy pulls the door open to leave, she looks back and sees Carl come out of the bedroom. Her bleary eyes see him limping toward her, bent over with blood oozing from his head and his shin. She stumbles as she backs out the doorway.

Peggy swings her head back straight and bangs heads with a man standing outside Carl's door hiding one arm behind his back. The impact nearly knocks her out. As she starts to fall, the man catches her with his free hand. For a second she stares into his eyes completely confused seeing the man adjust his dislodged toupee.

"Excuse me sir." Peggy slurs as the man continues to hold her arm to steady her. She feels her head hurt from the bump. Oh, why is this man wearing gloves? What about his chin and his eyes?

"Sorry Miss!" The man says with a cockney accent.

Peggy tries to step away, but the man still holds her arm. Then with seemingly superhuman power she wrenches loose and stumbles down the hallway to the elevator forcing her eyes to stay open. Peggy is in panic mode and thumps the down button several times.

She glances back toward Carl's room hoping he isn't coming after her. Carl and the wig man aren't in sight. The elevator doors open and Peggy jumps in and taps the ground floor button. She leans against the elevator wall as the doors shut and forces her eyes to stay open and to stay awake. Her head spins as she buttons up her blouse. Her stomach growls and she laughs wishing she got to eat some pizza.

The elevator doors open in the lobby, and Peggy nearly falls over. She straightens up, staggers out of the Luxor Hotel, and sees the Barry Limo waiting outside with Carol Novak about to slip inside.

"Wait!" Peggy shouts as she rushes to the limo.

Carol steps back and helps Peggy slide into the back seat before she gets in and sits next to Peggy. "Are you okay?"

"I feel woozy and sleepy." Peggy closes her eyes unable to move.

"Well girls, we are ten minutes away from the big celebration." Barry shouts from the front seat with Ursula sitting next to him. "I guess Carl isn't coming." Barry says and gives Ursula a squeeze. "Wait until you see the fun you're going to have. The Luxor is just a warm-up!"

The limo door shuts and Peggy feels the car start to move. The limo gets off the main strip headed for the outskirts of Las Vegas. With her eyes closed, she listens to the quiet hum from the engine. Peggy drifts into a dream state. She feels like she is in a boat gently rocking along the water's edge on a calm day.

As the limo approaches Mobley Villa it stops and waits for two tall iron gates of the entrance to open before it glides along the tar road and stops under the enormous stone canopy at the door of the large stone house. The limo driver opens the side door and helps the guests get out.

Peggy feels helping hands assist her to walk and lay her on a soft surface. Suddenly Carl is in her dream reaching for her again. She tries to resist but has no strength. Then she thinks he is gently slapping her face and hears Ursula talking.

"Wake up Peggy." Ursula says after avoiding Peggy's swishing hand. She sees Peggy opens her eyes and tries to focus on her. "Hey, it's about time you woke up. I think you've been drugged girl."

"Is that you Ursula?"

"Yeah, I'm Ursula."

"Where am I? Who is that with you?"

"Oh, remember this is Barry." Ursula offers.

"Nice meeting you again Peggy." Barry says.

"Thank you."

"Peggy, what happened? Why aren't you with Carl?"

"Who?"

"Carl, Barry's brother. You were with him until you jumped in the limo with us."

"Is Carl here?"

"No, you came alone," Ursula says.

"He's definitely not here?" Peggy asks again. "I...I don't remember. I kinda remember sitting at the bar with him." She sees Barry give Ursula a gentle squeeze.

"Carl is definitely not here." Ursula says.

"Well, I'm famished, let's eat!" She tries to get up but is still woozy.

"There is lots of food and anything you want at Mobley Villa."

"Really?"

After some coffee and sitting upright Peggy starts to feel normal again. Ursula and Barry are still watching her along with the birthday man Brendan Mobley. As her vision clears she sees all three people but she focuses on Brendan's handsome face. His short dark hair and hazel eyes contrast his lightly tanned face and square jaw. Peggy smiles at the man when he offers his hand.

"Hello, I'm Brendan, I own this place. How do you feel?"

"I've had better days. Who are you now?"

"Brendan Mobley, you are a guest at my Villa."

"How did I get here?"

Brendan explains what happened to her. "I apologize for Carl. Barry told me you were with him earlier. Did you have a row?"

"I don't remember. I think we went to his room because I wasn't feeling well, but everything's a blur after that. Like a dream. I think he may have tried to force himself on me and something about a man with a strange wig. I don't know if it was some sort of dream or what."

"Jeez, are you okay? A man with a wig? Anyway, how do you feel now?"

"I feel better now."

"Well, I'm glad you got away from him. I'm not sure what happened between you two, but I didn't want him here anyhow. I'm glad Carl didn't come to the party. Carl is bad news, Peggy. Should I call the cops?"

"No, I don't really remember much of what happened and anyway, it doesn't much matter. I'm here and I'm okay."

"Are you sure? Do you know what happened to your bra?"

"My bra? Peggy says looking down at her chest and realizing suddenly that her bra is missing. Oh my God! What happened to my bra?"

"I don't know. That's why I asked if you wanted me to call the police. Barry tells me Carl borrowed his room key and the two of you left together. It appears that you seem to have been drugged. And since your bra is missing, I assume he may have attempted to rape you or something."

"Carl is your half-brother? I think I remember him laying on top of me and kissing me, but I honestly can't tell you what actually happened. I don't think I was raped."

"Well, I'm sorry. Yes, unfortunately, Carl is my half-brother. Barry and I have the same father. Carl has the same mother. If you're feeling up to it, let me show you around the place." Brendan gently helps her to her feet.

"Whoa, I'm still a little unsteady." She wobbles as she stands up.

"That's to be expected. Carl must have spiked your drink at the Luxor. Carl is a bad seed and I'm upset with Barry for giving him his room key. Barry should have known better."

"I thought I had jet lag. We just got here this afternoon."

"Well, you are in good company now. Come with us." Brendan waits until Peggy looks stable enough to walk and escorts her to the pool area.

"Thanks! I need some good company right now. You say he drugged me?"

"That would be in character for him but hard to prove…"

"Yeah, but I can't prove anything because my memory is too foggy so he'll probably go unpunished."

"It sounds like you were able to take care of yourself just fine. You got away from him, and that's what matters. Try to forget it, Peggy. This is a happy party!" Brendan tugs at her sleeve and Peggy smiles and walks with him to an open bar. Ursula and Barry follow.

"You have beer here?"

"Does a camel spit? Do you want a Corona, Bud Light, or Michelob?" Brendan says with a smile.

"You know about camels?" Peggy asks.

"Yes, I spent a few days in Cairo last year. I know camels spit!"

Chapter Twenty Nine

Peggy giggles, swigs from the Corona beer he hands her, and scans the pool area. A balloon man is finishing an elaborate elephant figure he hands to a woman. A local four-piece band is playing from a small thirty-foot stage on one side of the giant open pool patio. The stage is surrounded by balloons and streamers and a large "Happy Birthday!" banner is hanging just below the stage ceiling. Multicolored lights bounce around the guests and off the ceiling. Most of the people are seated at small tables near the stage. Others are standing at the open bar or on the dance floor slow dancing to 'Colorado High' a John Denver cover song. Peggy follows Brendan and starts to slow-dance with him. She feels comfortable pressed against him and she rests her head on his shoulder.

"You dance very well." Peggy says stretching her arms around his waist.

"Dancing lessons." Brendan shrugs as the music stops. "Please come sit with me. I'm going to open my birthday presents."

"But I have no present for you." Peggy states.

"I have too many presents already. Come with me."

Peggy follows him to his party table. She watches Brendan open each gift and hears the small crowd cheer occasionally. For a late dinner, Peggy has Pepper Steak and rice from a Chinese buffet, another beer, and finally a slice of Pecan pie for dessert.

By midnight the party is breaking up. Most of Brendan's friends have left. Peggy is very drowsy. She can tell the late hour is affecting Ursula too. Barry announces he is taking anyone back to the Luxor who wants to go in the limo.

"I need to take the Limo back. Are you coming with me?" Barry asks Ursula.

"Ursula, Peggy, please stay." Brendan says holding Peggy's arm.

"I should go back to the Stratosphere."

"I have seven guest bedrooms, why not stay here?"

"We have no clothes or anything with us."

"I have a closet full of expensive new clothes I bought for my ex. You two are about her size. You can use some of those."

"We hardly know you Brendan or each other." Peggy admits looking at Ursula.

"You know each other and Barry and I aren't at all like Carl."

"If Ursula wants to stay, I will too." Peggy says giving a wishful look at Ursula.

Barry says. "I'm coming back to stay the night."

"Because," Brendan adds. "We are flying our private jet to Reno tomorrow to see our friend Harry Suave open tomorrow night at the Grand Theater. I want you two lovely ladies to come with us. We stay at the Grand Sierra Resort Saturday and Sunday night, dine with Harry at the Charlie Palmer Steakhouse and return here on Monday. Think about it. We'll have a blast!"

"Who is Harry Suave?" Peggy asks.

"Harry Suave is a great Elvis impersonator and a personal friend of ours from high school. Trust me; you'll think Elvis is alive and well." Brendan says.

"Why isn't he here in Las Vegas?"

"He got an offer he couldn't refuse."

"This is all so sudden." Ursula says. "What do you think Peggy?"

Peggy thinks about the boring sewing lessons at the Stratosphere versus seeing Harry Suave live. Harry wins. "I vote we stay."

Ursula looks away for a second and then nods. "Let's do it!"

"Great!" Brendan says. "We leave tomorrow morning. You can use the green bedroom. All the clothes are in that closet. Pick whatever you want to wear."

"I will be back later. We'll start early for Reno." Barry says.

"That sounds good to me." Ursula waves goodbye to Barry.

"Okay girls, follow me." Brendan escorts them to a pale green bedroom with a huge walk-in closet and a private bathroom. He knows Peggy and Ursula have decided to stay together for safety reasons. *They're not too sure about me yet.* Brendan thinks as he exits the bedroom.

"I'm sure Ann is asleep by now." Peggy says seeing it is after midnight. "I'll text her that I won't be back. Oh, my battery is at ten percent, I better hurry." Peggy yawns and uses the speech feature to make her message. *I'm going to Reno to see Harry Suave. I won't be back to the Stratosphere for a couple days. Have fun!* Not totally alert, and with her tired eyes she mistakenly selects the wrong Ann and hits send. Seconds later she receives the message. *Okay.*

"That's odd. She must be waiting up for me. I didn't expect to hear from Ann until the morning and then I expected a rash of nagging for not calling her earlier." Her sleepy thoughts are dismissed when Ursula speaks.

"I saw a charger on the nightstand. You can charge your phone."

"Right, I'll turn it off before it goes dead. I just have to remember to call her in the morning. This has been the most exciting day of my life!" Peggy plugs in her phone and lies down on one side of the king-size bed. She is asleep before Ursula stretches out on the other side.

Chapter Thirty

Detective Jack Foster walks into the Luxor Hotel at nine in the morning and enters the twelfth-story suite. He bends down to examine the body that is lying face down in the living room. Jack scans the bedroom and sees the pink bra on the floor and a lamp out of place. The forensic photographer takes one more picture of the victim. He listens to Officer Clark as he waits for the coroner's preliminary word about the victim on the floor.

"The room is charged to a Mister Barry Mobley. The chambermaid discovered the body about 8:15 AM. She said she came in to change sheets and general cleanup when she saw the man deceased on the floor. The victim is Carl Minion according to his ID. He's in the local database for having many arrests, suspected of trafficking young girls for the Middle East market. He had a door key in his pocket."

"Why would he have that?"

"We suspect the owner loaned it to him since Carl Minion is his half-brother according to our database. We talked to the barman from last night. According to him, they were all supposed to go to his brother's birthday party at a Villa. Mister Barry Mobley took some friends to the party but never came back to his suite at the Luxor."

"When did he leave the Luxor?"

"Mobley left at 7:05 PM to go to the party. I met one of his friends who said Mobley was at the party until after midnight when he drove several guests back here."

"I thought you said he didn't return?"

"From what we know, he dropped off some party guests at the hotel before returning the limo."

This is a brutal murder, Officer Clark. It looks like Minion was bludgeoned with that heavy lamp. The lamp didn't even break in two, a real solid lamp. The room isn't messed up so maybe the victim knew his killer." Detective Foster says.

"There is no break-in. We saw that pink bra by the bed. Nothing is disturbed in the room. I found a blue contact lens in the hallway outside the victim's door." Officer Clark waves a plastic bag with the lens inside and Jack nods. The coroner rolls the body onto its back.

"Let's concentrate on the victim for now. Is his wallet missing, empty?" Jack waits while Officer Clark checks his notes.

"No sir, his wallet has over five hundred dollars and was still in his rear pocket."

"Why was a woman here if she wasn't trying to seduce him for money? Let's say for now that the killer is a woman who caught him off guard and hit him. He looks like a strong man." Detective Foster says and watches the coroner approach him.

"Why did she leave her bra behind though?" Officer Clark says.

"What have you found out Pete?" Jack Foster asks the coroner.

Pete Malden shakes his head. "The best guess is the man died between six and eight last night Detective, but the cause of death is a deep wound in his chest, not the whack on the head. The stab went into his heart."

"You found a stab wound and a gash on his head?"

"His hand is cut and he has a cut and bruised shin too."

"So the killer kicked him, hit him with a lamp, and stabbed him?"

"That's about right sir, and everything took place close together time-wise."

"Did you find the murder weapon?"

"No Detective, but my guess is the wound is from a long thin knife or a stiletto. The blade went in horizontally to go between the ribs. A professional killer would stab a person that way."

"What came first?"

"I can't say but I think the whack to the head is first because of the blood flow. The head wound may have been hard enough to stagger him, maybe even knock him out, but the stab wound to the heart caused instant death. It's all determined by the amount of blood seepage and the skin condition. I'll do a complete autopsy."

"This doesn't make sense!" Jack scratches his head. "The killer kicks him on the shin, knocks him out with the lamp, and stabs him. But the man has a defensive cut on his hand so he fought with whoever stabbed him. If the woman did it, why didn't she bother to pick up her bra and steal his money? Why would she leave before doing that? The cut on his hand indicates he tried to defend himself when he was stabbed. And why not just stab him in the first place?" The Detective asks but the coroner just shrugs.

"I know it all sounds weird but 'it is what it is'. The good thing is the victim has some tissue under his fingernails. It looks like skin, as if maybe he scratched someone in the struggle. There may be enough to get a DNA sample." The coroner says. He turns and goes back to the victim as another officer comes into the room and speaks.

"A concierge on duty last night, Mister Shelly Beatty says a woman ran out of the hotel about seven in the evening. All her clothes and even her shoes were pink and she looked scared as Hell. He also says he thinks she left in a limo."

"That's a strong lead since we found a pink bra. Find out if there is a camera on this floor. Maybe we can see a video of her. Are there any surveillance videos outside? Did she take a taxi from here? Maybe we can get lucky and ID her. It's possible she is the killer or saw something that scared her. Officer John, are there any useful prints on the lamp?"

"I didn't expect it to be fruitful but the lamp must have been new. It doesn't appear to have been handled much. We got a full set of one hand and some smudges."

"Are the prints in our database?" Detective Foster asks but sees John frown.

"We're running them now. Nothing so far, but I'd guess it's a small man's or a woman's hand from the size. I will run it through the National database next." He turns back to his laptop.

"Officer Clark, check for a video on this floor. Talk to the other guests, especially those who went in the limo to see if anyone heard something. There had to be an argument or some noise. And check the limo services last night at seven, plus or minus half an hour, for a lady in pink."

"We'll get on it sir."

"Yes, let's find this lady in pink!

Chapter Thirty One

Peggy moans as she wakes up to sunlight in her eyes from a gap in the window drapes. She checks her watch seeing eight in the morning. Her head is aching and her stomach is growling. She is sure her hair and her clothes are a mess. Her mouth feels like it is full of cotton. Peggy sits up on the king-size bed still a little woozy and wonders where she is. Peggy's eyes finally focus. She looks around and realizes she is in a bedroom at Brendan Mobley's Villa. Then she sees Ursula coming from the bathroom talking in a seemingly extra loud voice. She cups her face in her hands.

"I ate too much last night." Ursula says rubbing her stomach.

"Hey, I'm not feeling chipper either." Peggy moans. "We didn't sack out until after one. That's four in the morning Fort Lauderdale time." Peggy says.

"Well, I'm local so one isn't too late for me. I've already showered and found everything I need to look great." Ursula says.

"Is there any aspirin in there?"

"Go look, I'm done and I'll wait for you if you hurry." Ursula says as she zips up the dress she chose from the closet. She poses in the new slate gray dress that still has a price tag on the sleeve. "What do you think?"

"You look great except for the price tag! You found that dress and it fits?"

"Yes! I think you can find one too." Ursula says as she rips off the tag. "I smell bacon and I want some, so make haste!" Ursula says. She turns on the TV to wait for Peggy.

Peggy relieves herself and feels happy in spite of the throbbing in her head. After stripping and adjusting the shower temperature she steps into the stall and washes away any remnants of Mister Carl. Peggy wraps up in a big towel, wraps her hair in a smaller one, and exits the bathroom.

"I did a foolish thing!" Peggy admits.

"I know you lost your bra. Did you have sex with Carl?"

"No, but Carl was so charming and handsome... I remember going to his suite, boy is it big! No, he borrowed it from Barry. I think I flopped onto the bed and the rest is foggy. Like how did he get my bra off? I think I hit him!"

"You went to a hotel room with a stranger?"

"Yes, I thought he was okay. I barely remember meeting at the limo, but everything before that is hazy." Peggy says joining Ursula in the bedroom.

"I helped you into the limo. I think you were drugged. I deal with that type of men all the time. I'll teach you the tricks of Vegas." Ursula steps into the walk-in closet. "Take a look at all these clothes!"

Peggy asks. "Are there any that don't need a bra?"

"Yes, a lot of them will do. So slip into a nice new dress before we go." Ursula says. "Come on Peggy. How often does someone give you a dress?" She says as Peggy reluctantly peers into the closet.

"There is nothing pink in here."

"So what, there is about every other color."

"I always dress in pink."

"Why?"

"I just feel better in pink. All my clothes are pink."

"You need to break outta that pink shell girl! Look at all these fine dresses. I bet Brendan spent a fortune on them."

"Well, this will have to do." Peggy selects a Navy blue dress.

"Put it on and let's go get some food!"

Peggy dresses in a slightly loose Navy blue dress and walks to the kitchen with Ursula. She eats breakfast from a small buffet next to the dining table.

"I guess I need to thank you for rescuing me. I don't remember most of what happened!"

Peggy relates what little she remembers while she eats some bacon and a great-tasting waffle smothered in maple syrup and strawberries. Her stomach thanks her with a burp.

"So, you lost a good bra. Chalk it up to the rum and Coke." Ursula says.

"Yeah, he has a great souvenir to brag about! I hope I never see him again!"

Brendan Mobley comes into the kitchen area wearing a Navy blue suit, dark blue shirt, and white tie. He grabs a plate and fills it with scrambled eggs, some bacon, and a slice of toast. Before he starts eating he looks at Peggy and Ursula and speaks.

"Wow, you two look great! We go to the plane at nine. Are you ready for the ride?"

"One hundred percent!" Peggy says.

"And Ursula?"

"Me too!"

"Okay, as soon as I wolf down some food and find Barry we leave. This is like an extension of my birthday party. I'm excited already!"

Chapter Thirty Two

Ann is worried that Peggy didn't come back Thursday night from the Luxor and isn't back this morning. She is concerned but goes to the first sewing lecture. The main speaker finishes and Ann stands by the exit doors and searches the chatty crowd until everyone is gone. She doesn't find Peggy. She dials Peggy's phone but gets her voice mail. Alone, she walks to the dining room to join her friends in the sewing group for lunch. She takes a seat next to Carol Novak, the woman who enticed Peggy to go to the Luxor last night. As soon as she is seated, she inquires about Peggy.

"Hello, Carol. You and Peggy went to the Luxor last night but Peggy didn't come back to the room. Where is Peggy?"

"Hello, Ann. She must have stayed at the Villa."

"What Villa?"

"Barry's brother Brendan has a Villa south of here. He had a big birthday party last night with about fifty people and Peggy clung to Brendan all night."

"But she would have called me to let me know where she is."

"Maybe, ask Barry if you can find him. He lives at the Luxor."

"Thanks, Carol. I will track Peggy down after the classes."

After lunch, Ann calls Peggy's phone but again gets her recording. As Ann heads for her room to check on Peggy, she stops to talk to another sewing student until time for the next class. The afternoon session on double stitching starts at one thirty and Ann still hasn't seen Peggy.

"Does anyone else need a partner?" The instructor asks. "I want you all to pair up two on each machine."

Ann reluctantly raises her hand and joins with the only lone person at a sewing machine, a blonde-haired man. Ann fakes a smile for the man who looks like a big blonde teddy bear with two rings in his right ear, an afro hairstyle, and a knit green shirt that reveals his muscular frame. Her first impression is the man is more rugged than he should be. However, when he speaks he sounds like a little kid talking. His high-pitched voice reminds her of Mike Tyson being interviewed early in his career after knocking out some brute.

"Hi, my name is Ralph Gale. I love your hair. That ponytail style is so gorgeous and the blonde color is wonderful! My partner's hair is blonde too just as pretty."

"Thank you, I'm Ann Stormen. Where is your partner?"

"He had a death in his family and had to leave. I hope he returns soon, I miss him. So why are you alone? You're too pretty to be alone!" Ralph says waving a hand at Ann and smiling at her.

"My sewing partner is missing."

"Where did she go?"

"I don't know. She left our room yesterday afternoon and I haven't seen nor heard from her since."

"That seems rude."

"I think she especially wanted to learn the tips and tricks about double stitching. She got turned on by this city I suspect. I hope she isn't in with a bad crowd. I will look for her after this class and call the police."

"Well, at least my partner let me know why he abandoned me."

"Peggy isn't rude. I'm worried something happened to her."

"She'll show up, don't worry." Ralph says but makes a mum gesture when he hears the instructor start to talk.

The lecture and sewing event lasts until three forty-five in the afternoon. Listening to the speaker and working with Ralph, she forgets about Peggy for a while. After class, Ann calls Peggy's phone again and hears the familiar voice mail beep. She wants to leave and search for Peggy but Ralph begs her to stay for the next class.

"I hate sitting in these classes by myself. It's only one more hour. I really like you Ann. Please stay. Whatever Peggy is doing, she must be having more fun than this class would be. Leave her alone for now." Ralph pleads his case.

"She said yesterday she wants to party. Maybe you are right, she's having fun somewhere. I came all the way to Las Vegas to go to these lectures. I'm a little upset that she didn't let me know she is skipping classes. Maybe she is hanging with that Barry fellow and went off somewhere although I don't know why she would. I'll look for her after the class." Ann forces a smile for Ralph.

"I could hug you!" Ralph says but only waves his hand at her.

The last class for the day ends right at six. Ann is tired, feeling a headache starting as the attendees clap for the instructor. She vacillates between being mad at Peggy for leaving and not calling her and worrying about her disappearing.

"Well, I guess I will check with the front desk to see if Peggy left a note. She may be still partying from last night with her phone off. I hope she is okay and in our room. Hey, it was fun being with you Ralph." Ann smiles as they step into the elevator.

"Ditto Ann. Listen, if you don't find her and want to be with someone for dinner, I'm in room 602. Call me. I like to dine at eight and I hate to eat alone."

"That's sweet Ralph. Maybe Peggy had a rough time last night. She's probably still crashed out. If I don't find her, I will call you." Ann gives Ralph a small hug before she gets off on her floor.

"Bye Ann. I hope you find her." Ralph calls out as the doors shut.

Chapter Thirty Three

Ann steps into her room, expecting to see Peggy there, but the room is empty. She checks the house phone, no messages. Then she gets a chill up & down her spine. *Did someone abduct Peggy?* She thinks as she sits on the edge of the bed and wonders what to do. She calls Sam on the cell phone but after the voicemail kicks on, she hangs up. She calls Carol Novak's room but no one answers.

"I feel awful!" Ann sobs, feeling alone without Peggy and Sam. She dabs her eyes as she bows her head and says a prayer for Peggy.

After some hesitation and finagling, Ann gets through on the phone to the police. The officer says she should wait at least 24 hours and fill out a missing person report. Her stomach growls so Ann looks at her watch that shows 7:35. She vacillates a moment and then she rings room 602.

"Hello, Ralph I don't know why I called you. Are you busy?"

"No, did you find your friend?"

"No, but her stuff is still here. I got no help from the police either."

"I was hoping you would find her, but I'm glad you called. I bet the police said you should wait a day."

"Yes, but the man said I have to fill out a missing person report."

"You should go there now."

"This is like a nightmare Ralph! How can I go to the police station?"

"Meet me in the lobby. We can go there and I can give you a shoulder to lean on."

"No, I'm a mess."

"What room are you in? I can come there."

"Oh 508, but don't come here. I don't want to see anyone right now. I'm just going to crash tonight. I'll order room service." Ann rings off. She grabs a new tissue to blow her nose. *I hope Peggy is at a party and just forgot to tell me. Maybe she doesn't want to see me because she is embarrassed about missing classes.* Ann thinks. She lies on the bed and closes her eyes to rest. Just after she lies down she hears knocking on her door. She looks through the peephole and sees Ralph smiling at her.

"Room service!" Ralph blurts and knocks again.

Ann cracks open the door. "Ralph, I asked you not to come here."

"What you need is a friend for solace. Here I'm."

"I don't think anything can help."

"I can escort you to dinner or the police station, whatever you want to do. I'm sure you are hungry. Dinner will take your mind off Peggy for a while. That's how I can help." Ralph smiles at her.

"Actually, I would like that very much Ralph if you don't mind looking at a puffy-eyed woman."

"That's okay. You look fine."

"Give me a few minutes to freshen up."

"Go ahead. Should I wait out here?"

"I'd be more comfortable if you did."

Ann closes the door and makes a quick bathroom stop. She runs a brush through her hair, freshens up her runny mascara, grabs her purse from the small table, and steps out of her room. She gives Ralph a quick hug before stepping away.

"I'm sorry you had to wait so long. I..."

"Girl you look fabulous!" Ralph says smiling at Ann.

"How can you say that? I'm all puffed up from crying."

"I can hardly tell. What you need is a great dinner."

"I'm not all that hungry Ralph, but thanks for being here."

"You'll love the Steak House Restaurant, right here in the Stratosphere."

"Maybe I can have an appetizer or something light. I mainly just want to…"

"You want to be with someone who cares." Ralph says.

"Yes, I don't know you that well but I like you a lot."

"All we did today is sewing stuff. We can learn about each other over dinner with a nice wine to loosen us up. What about that Ann?"

"Are you flirting with me now?"

"My only interest is as a friend." Ralph smiles hoping Ann knows he is sincere.

"Okay Ralph. You remind me of a big teddy bear, so okay!" Ann smiles as she follows Ralph to the elevator. She feels surprisingly comfortable with him as she walks.

The restaurant is elegant and Ann enjoys relaxing with Ralph at a table near the edge of the dining area. The lights are low and Ralph's charm fascinates her. She nixes the glass of Zinfandel wine Ralph offers opting for iced tea and filet of sole for dinner. She tells him how she met Sam in a most strange situation and how she fell for Sam the first time she ever touched his hand. Then Sam came to work at the same company and she prayed he would ask her out and he answered her prayers.

She learns about how Ralph felt different as a kid and how he bulked up his muscles mainly to defend himself. Ann talks, listens, and dines and by ten o'clock, she is talked-out and very tired. She leaves the restaurant with Ralph, ready to go to her room.

Ann walks to the elevators with him. She is weary and holds his arm for support feeling a little sorry for Ralph not being able to enjoy sex with a woman. "Thanks for the shoulder to lean on Ralph. I had a great time at dinner."

"My pleasure, I'm ready to sack out." Ralph says when he steps into the elevator with Ann. When the doors open on the fifth floor he watches Ann smile at him.

"Good night Prince Charming. I will go to the police station in the morning."

"If you want me to go with you I will. I know how to get around in Vegas. It may help to have me along."

"Let me think about it. I'll see what happens." Ann says as the elevator doors shut, but she knows she will call him.

When Ann opens the door to her room, she sees the empty bed and no Peggy. The sight makes her feel even more lonesome and sad. "I guess we won't need the single beds tonight." As she prepares to go to bed, she thinks. *I can't believe Peggy hasn't called. If she's not back by morning, I will definitely fill out that report.*

Chapter Thirty Four

Ann tosses and turns all night and is thankful when her alarm rings at six in the morning. She strips and showers before dressing in tan slacks and a white blouse. She grabs the small and only sweater she brought to Las Vegas. She thought summer in Las Vegas would be hot. Outside is hot, but she found the indoors are cold everywhere she goes, including the conference rooms at the Stratosphere and in the main restaurant. She heads straight to the buffet for a quick breakfast. Looking inside the restaurant Ann sees Ralph leaving the buffet line with a heaping plate of food.

"Hello Ralph, will you save a seat for me?"

"Hey Ann, yes I will."

"I'll be right behind you."

After Ann fills a plate with some fruit, toast, and sausages she is ready to find Ralph. Then she satisfies a strange craving by grabbing two sprigs of parsley to eat. She locates Ralph at a table and joins him as she finishes munching on the parsley.

"I was hoping to see you." Ralph says.

"The first class is just on fabric types. That information is all in the workbook, so I can miss that class to go to the police station."

"I volunteer to go with you if you want."

"I should say no, but if it's not too much of a bother for you, I could use the help."

"Normally I wouldn't offer, but I like you a lot Ann. I want to help."

"Thank you, Ralph. I should call Max to tell him Peggy is missing."

"I'd wait. She may be out partying and you'll just upset Max."
"Okay, let's eat and go."

After breakfast, Ann follows Ralph outside the Stratosphere and hails a taxi. She tenses up as the taxi travels down Las Vegas Boulevard and then east to the Police Station on Sierra Vista Drive. She enters the station with Ralph and looks at a billboard with several missing person pictures. The newest one is six months old. By eight o'clock Ann has the report finished and hands it to the officer. The officer takes the report and stuffs it in a pile with many other papers.

"Thank you ma'am, most people show up in a day or two."
"Or it looks like never!"
"I wouldn't worry miss."
"She's not the type to go off for days and not tell me! She may be in trouble."
"Give it another day before you worry too much." The man says.
"I know a detective." Ralph interrupts tapping her shoulder.
"You know a detective?" Ann asks. "Is he any good?"
"You should never think all detectives are men. This is a woman and she is very good!"
"Oh sorry Ralph, who is she?"
"Her name is Carey Lange. She fixed something for me once."
"I hate to keep imposing on you Ralph, but please call her now!"
"I love it when you assert yourself Ann! You sound so manly."
"I'm not manly!"
"See there, another positive assertion." Ralph sees Ann shake her head. "I'm sorry. You are definitely not a man. I was kidding. I know Peggy is a nice lady if she is your friend. We'll find her!"
"I know you mean well but this isn't fun!" Ann closes her eyes for a second, not knowing what to do next.
"I will give Carey a call." Ralph says.

Ann leaves the police station with Ralph as he phones Carey. She takes a taxi with Ralph to the Vista Pointe Plaza on Serene Avenue. Ann observes the scenery along the way seeing how hot and desolate Las Vegas looks. If not for the human interventions, she believes the town would be a dusty wasteland. The taxi comes to a stop in front of a strip store door. She sees a bright red door that shines as if just painted. The overhead sign reads Lange Investigations Inc. Ann pays the cabby and follows Ralph onto the sidewalk and through the door.

After stepping into the cool of the large office Ann looks around. Her first impression is of a successful lawyer's office seeing the plush paisley carpet and leather couch and chairs. She sees ornate lamps on the two end tables and a plethora of certificates on the tan walls. A tan suede jacket is hanging on a wooden coat rack next to the desk. Ann smells a hint of strawberry in the air. A lanky brunette woman sits behind a large mahogany desk wearing a pale blue blouse and tan slacks. Her stocking feet propped on top of her desk drop to the floor as Ann approaches her with Ralph at her side.

"Hello, Carey my love! Thank you so much for seeing us on a Saturday." Ralph says smiling at Carey. He waits to hug her as she slips on her shoes.

"I'm working a case in my office or you would have gotten my answering service when you called. Ralph dear, what brings you here this morning?" Carey Lange asks giving Ralph a long embrace.

"My friend Ann has a problem."

"It's not a divorce job, is it? No divorce jobs for you anymore!"

"It's nothing like that love. This requires real detective work."

Ann explains the situation to her. How Peggy came to Vegas for sewing classes and must have got involved in something where she can't call. Ann tells Carey all about Peggy, concluding that something may have happened to Peggy.

"Did you bring a picture? The police can send it to all their cops to watch for her."

"The police made a copy of this picture this morning. She always dresses in pink." Ann hands a picture of Peggy to Carey and watches her take a phone photo and then go to her copier and make a color copy before returning her picture.

"You say she is missing since Thursday afternoon?"

"Yes, like I said she went with some guys to the Luxor Hotel."

"There is a lot I can do Miss Clarkson, but I can't guarantee anything. That was over twenty-four hours ago. Anything could have happened" Carey admits.

"I need to know where she is and that she is okay."

"I'll need a retainer fee. Who's paying the bill?"

"I will pay whatever it takes!" Ann asserts.

"Good, let me have a check or a credit card and I'll get to work."

Ann digs out her VISA card and hands it to Carey.

"Thanks. I can't guarantee anything but I sympathize with you. That helps motivate me." Carey charges her retainer fee and returns the card to Ann. She continues to question Ann, gleaning whatever information she can to help find Peggy. Carey scribbles more notes as she listens and finally extends her hand to say goodbye.

"Please do your very best." Ann says shaking Carey's hand. She leaves with Ralph. Once outside, even though she is worried about Peggy, she has to ask.

"Okay Ralph, I want to know why she quit doing divorce jobs for you. Is it because she handled your messy divorce?"

"Maybe someone got dumped in the fountain waters of the Bellagio, a long story Ann. Let's go join whatever class is going on. Maybe I will tell you later."

Chapter Thirty Five

After Ann and Ralph leave, Carey mulls over her notes and then thinks about Police Detective Jack Foster and smiles. Happy for any reason to talk to him she dials his personal cell phone.

"Hello, Detective Jack!" Carey sings in her cheeriest voice.

"Hello, Miss Lange. You caught me in the office when I should be home and sleeping in on Saturday morning. What do you want?"

"I knew I would catch you at work, can't stay away can you?"

"Yeah, I'm a glutton for punishment. You know I have a murder case I'm working on."

"I didn't, but I hope it's not at the Luxor Hotel."

"How did you know that?"

"Oh no, is the victim a woman?"

"No. Why?"

"I'm looking for a woman who went to a party at the Luxor on Thursday night. She disappeared just like the other case I'm working on. Seventeen-year-old Janet Winslow disappeared last Monday."

"We are also looking for a person of interest from the Luxor on Thursday night."

"Was she wearing all pink?"

"How... Well, we appear to be looking for the same person. What is her name?"

"Peggy Clarkson, now tell me why are you looking for her?"

"Are you in your office?"

"Yes. Why?"

"I want you to come to the station and tell me all you know about Miss Clarkson. Can you be here in ten minutes."

"I will if you will please tell me what happened at the Luxor."

"Just come here."

Carey moves to her half-bathroom to freshen up before leaving her office. Outside she straddles her small purple Vespa motor scooter and steers toward the police station. An air-conditioned car is nice in the Las Vegas heat, but her Vespa is much more practical for zigzagging around the crowded streets and especially the strip. Within ten minutes she is staring into Police Detective Jack Foster's office. He seems to be preoccupied with some paperwork.

"Hello handsome." She flirts after knocking on the open door.

"How is it you get involved in a lot of our investigations lately?"

"I'm just lucky Jack. Do you have any info on Janet Winslow our other missing girl?" She sees him shake his head smiling.

"No, and call me Detective Foster. An officer may be around."

"We're alone Detective Foster. I'm sorry."

"I'm sorry to Miss Lange. I'm too grumpy today. I haven't had much sleep the past two days. Let's trade information like the professionals we are. You go first."

Carey tells Jack all she knows about Ann and Peggy staying at the Stratosphere for a sewing convention. "Ann hired me because Peggy disappeared. Peggy went with a small group Thursday afternoon to the Luxor Hotel and hasn't been seen or heard from since. The only person Ann knows who went in the group is Carol Novak."

"Well, we did talk to Miss Novak. It seems a Mister Barry Mobley had a small party at the Luxor and then took her and several others to Brendan Mobley's Villa. We tried to find Mister Mobley but he has been unavailable since Thursday night and the hotel doesn't know where he is. We tried to see Mister Mobley, but the Villa staff said they didn't know where he is and no guests are staying there at this time. It's like pulling teeth from a wild hog to get any information out of the Villa workers."

"You said someone was murdered? Who is the victim?"

"The victim is Carl Minion and he was stabbed in the chest while in Barry Mobley's suite. He was a local criminal. We have not been able to locate Barry or Brendan Mobley or this lady in pink. The main party was at Brendan's Villa. Here is a list of addresses."

"Thanks, and did you find anything at Carl Minion's address?"

"We went to the address on his driver's license and met a nice couple who never heard of Carl Minion." Jack says finally handing Carey a scrap of paper.

"Thanks, so he lied for his driver's license."

"Yes."

"You said he was stabbed in the heart?"

"Yes, he was also hit over the head with a heavy lamp found in the room. Do you know why Clarkson would hang with Minion's type?"

"I don't think she would if she knew he was a criminal."

"At first we suspected a woman murdered Minion because we found a pink bra lying near the body, but then we got the floor video of our lady in pink coming out of his suite... I mean Barry Mobley's suite. She bumps heads with a man going in who we suspect is the actual killer. We also found a blue contact lens by the door possibly dislodged from the bump. Does Miss Clarkson wear blue contacts?" Jack asks and waits as Carey looks through her notes.

"I don't know. My client says Peggy has blue eyes but she didn't specify if she wears blue contacts. Now please tell me about the crime scene."

"Nothing much was disturbed and no break in."

"We ruled out that the victim had to know the killer since the lady in pink opened the door for the man. That could have been on purpose, or she didn't know he was waiting at the door. Next to the bed, we found a pink bra like what your lady in pink would wear. We have an eyewitness who saw the pink lady fleeing the Luxor about the time of the murder. I really need to talk to her as a person of interest. Of course, she could be an accomplice but not very likely."

"What about these two guys, are they brothers?"

"Yes, Barry and Brendan are brothers. Our research shows they are the nerdy type. They develop gaming software and have made millions together with their sister Bailey Mobley, also unmarried. Barry likes the hotel life thus the suite at the Luxor, while Brendan likes the Villa lifestyle. Carl Minion is the outcast half-brother, always in some kind of trouble."

"So that's why Barry loaned him his suite. Carl must have promised to be on good behavior. Did you find the knife?"

"No, the man in the video must have taken the weapon with him. It is probably in a dumpster somewhere. I have men searching through the trash and grounds at the Luxor and the Stratosphere for a knife or anything bloody. And no, the man in the video isn't Barry or Brendan Mobley."

"Did the video show any blood on Ms. Clarkson or her clothes?"

"No." Jack admits.

"So the stab to the heart caused the death, not the head wound?"

"Yes."

"You think she hit him with a lamp and then let in her accomplice to stab him?"

"Doubtful. But she obviously lost her bra. Either they engaged in a tryst or things got out of hand and began going too far so she hit him and left. It's all speculative right now until we talk to her, but we can't find which isn't helping the investigation."

"You said the man had over five hundred dollars in his wallet so we know this wasn't a robbery attempt. Do you agree that Ms. Clarkson, who has no criminal record, came across country to go to sewing classes, didn't plan to kill the man? She is a tourist from Fort Lauderdale Jack. She can't be involved in the murder."

"She's just a person of interest Miss Lange. Well Miss Lange, I have a meeting with my divorce lawyer and on Saturday no less. I stayed to chat because you said please."

"I'm trying to be nicer Detective Foster. I'm sorry you have that kind of meeting."

"I have to go now. Let me know if you discover anything."

"Thanks Jack, you're the best!" Carey sighs as she watches Detective Jack Foster leave. She grabs her purse and leaves the police station.

Carey ambles across the parking lot. She hops on her Vespa and eases into traffic heading for the Luxor hoping Barry Mobley will be home now. The Vespa helps her zigzag through traffic along the strip. She weaves her way through the dry heat and parks in an out-of-the-way niche near the Luxor Hotel. Just a short walk takes her into the lobby and to the elevators. As the elevator ascends toward Barry Mobley's suite, she thinks. *I wish Jack were with me.*

Chapter Thirty Six

Carey Lange knocks on the door of suite 1209. She waits for several minutes and is about to try later when the door opens. Carey sees a woman with hazel eyes stare at her. The woman is wearing a red kimono and Carey estimates the girl is thirtyish, tall and muscular, with brown hair partly wrapped in a towel. The woman speaks first.

"Who are you and what do you want?"

"I'm Carey Lange, a private investigator. I'm looking for Barry Mobley."

"I just got here this morning. I was showering. Barry isn't here."

"Who are you?"

"I'm Barry's sister Bailey Mobley."

"It's nice to meet you, Miss Mobley. Has Barry been here since Thursday night?"

"How would I know, I've been in LA until this morning."

"So you didn't go to Brendan's birthday party Thursday night?"

"No, who are you again?"

"I'm a private investigator, Carey Lange." She hands the woman her card. "I'm trying to find a woman who was in here Thursday night."

"Barry had a woman up here?"

"No, the woman was with the deceased, Carl Minion."

"Carl is dead?"

"Yes, I'm sorry, he was murdered. You didn't know?"

"No, I've been out of touch in LA. Barry often keeps me in the dark."

"I'm sorry for your loss Miss Mobley. Actually, I'm not sure if either of your brothers are aware. It seems no one has spoken to them since the party."

"Call me Bailey, and don't be sorry. Whoever killed him did the world a favor. What happened?"

"He was killed here in this room from what I've been told by the police.

"Here? He was killed here and no one told me!"

"Like I said, I don't believe your brothers are aware. I get the impression you didn't like Carl."

"There is nothing about him I liked."

"May I come in for a minute?"

"Come in Miss Lange. Barry was supposed to pick me up at the airport this morning. Do you know what happened to Barry?"

"Thank you. I don't know where Barry is either." Carey says.

"Have a seat. Let me call him." Bailey waves at the couch and sits next to her.

"Please do." Carey takes out her notepad.

Bailey dials Barry and listens to his voice mail. "He must not be answering or he left his phone somewhere. Barry is forgetful sometimes."

"Please tell me anything that might be helpful Miss Mobley."

"Brendan and Barry are my full brothers and we are honest people. We make a ton of money selling video games and programs. It's great competition seeing who comes up with the weirdest ideas. I like staying here at the Luxor with Barry. I like to play the slot machines and love all the other amenities that come with living here year round. Barry likes it here too. Brendan likes living at the Villa away from the strip. He says he can concentrate better there."

"So why would Barry let Carl bring a woman to his room?"

"Carl must have convinced him he wouldn't do anything with her that he shouldn't. Barry was probably too involved with the party and just let Carl use this suite rather than take him to

Brendan's party. Brendan doesn't like Carl either, so Barry probably figured it was an easy way to dump him so he wouldn't have to take him to the party. He should have remembered Carl is a liar and a low individual."

"What do you mean?"

"Carl has been known to associate with unsavory people. I suspect he participates in criminal activities although I can't prove that, but I know he has a record. I just don't know what for and my brothers wouldn't tell me if they knew."

"You know this?"

"Not a hundred percent, but his words sometimes betrayed him. I know enough about him to wish we weren't related by any means and that I don't want to know what he's into because I don't want to be a party directly or indirectly to anything he does!"

"Please tell me all you can about him. I'm trying to locate the woman Carl was with. She has been missing ever since that night. The police say a hotel concierge, Shelly saw her run out of the hotel. The man thinks he saw her get in Barry's limo that was going to Brendan's party. The limo came back after midnight but he couldn't tell if she came back."

"Wow, I know Shelly. He's a good friend. He starts work at three in the afternoon. If you talk to him, tell him I said it is okay to tell you everything he knows. I want to catch the killer as much as you want to find the woman, so I'm going to tell you all I know about Carl. I'm sure you know he lives near the brothel Happy Ranch."

"No, the address I have from his driver's license is phony."

"Let me see." Bailey looks at Carey's paper. "That's a bogus address. Like I said, he's a liar. Barry said he lives in the Oasis Apartments. I wrote down his new address and stashed it somewhere. Let me find it." Bailey picks up a slip of paper from her roll-top desk. "Here it is, 5316 Danville Lane, apartment C."

"Well, thank you! Tell me more." Carey gathers as much information as she can about the three brothers before she thanks Bailey for her help.

"Like I said, Carl is no loss but we all want to catch the killer. Do you know if Carl was the target? I mean, whoever killed Carl didn't think he was killing Barry by chance."

"No, as far as I know, the killer meant to kill Carl. Why would you think Barry might have been the target?"

"Well you know, Barry lives here year-round as I do, but Barry likes to party and everybody knows he has money. I was concerned that whoever killed Carl might have thought he was Barry to get money. Since I live here too, I was sort of trying to find out if I'm safe."

"Oh. Yes, as far as I know, you have nothing to worry about. The police said nothing was taken which ruled out robbery. The only thing that wasn't right was Carl being dead. May I ask, you said you and Barry both live here, but I understood this is only a one-bedroom suite."

"Yes, it is. Barry and I are rarely ever here at the same time so there is no need for two bedrooms. If he should come while I'm here, he sleeps out here."

"Oh okay. Thank you for your time and the information. I have your phone number and I will call you if I need anything else or find out anything." Carey shakes hands and leaves.

Carey bypasses the lobby since Bailey said concierge Shelly Beatty isn't here until three in the afternoon. She checks her notes for Minion's address and verifies the location on her city map before she hops on her Vespa and drives to his apartment. Carey stops next to the front door of apartment C and sees a small gray cat on the windowsill. First, she tries knocking on the door and turning the doorknob. Nothing happens so Carey picks the lock and eases inside the apartment. She knows she should contact the police first, but that will only delay her and they might not let her in afterward. After she checks out the place, she can call Jack later and provide him any information she finds.

She stands still and slides on latex gloves. Carey listens and scans the living room noting all the trash scattered about. She sees the modern décor of the furniture from the chrome lamps to the black and white couch. Then she sees the gray cat eyeing her from across the kitchen floor standing next to the empty water and food bowls. Carey looks through the cabinets, finds a bag of cat food, and dumps some in the food bowl. The cat starts eating ignoring Carey as she picks up the water bowl, rinses it, and fills it with water. After tending to the cat and stroking its back she checks out the small apartment.

Carey notices one ceiling tile in the kitchen is smudged on its edge. She takes a chair to stand on and lifts the tile to probe around. Close to the opening, she finds a small notebook. *He obviously didn't expect anyone to find this.* Carey thinks as she thumbs through the pages.

Chapter Thirty Seven

The notebook reveals various transactions, dates, and amounts dating back over ten years. *Wouldn't Jack like to have had this a long time ago?* She thinks as she stuffs the notebook in her waist-line.

She examines the rest of the apartment. Empty bottles and cans of various alcoholic beverages lie on the floor, mixed with food wrappers and soiled paper napkins, mostly next to the living room couch. She finds nothing else useful in his bedroom including a scan through the contents of a small desk. Carey leaves the apartment and as she gets on her Vespa she sees two men hurrying toward her. She starts the engine and races out of the parking lot.

Carey looks in her rearview mirror and sees the men run to a black car and rush after her. Carey is counting on getting to a more crowded area before they can catch her. She can feel them within a few car lengths when she turns onto Las Vegas Boulevard and wiggles through the slow traffic. She is unaware that one of the men wrote down her tag number before giving up the chase. Feeling relieved and yet excited she stops at her office. Once inside, she dials Detective Foster.

"Hello Miss Lange. What do you want now?"

"Hello Jack. I'm guessing there are other officers around."

"Yes."

"Well, I just had a most exciting experience. By the way, how did the lawyer meeting go?" Carey asks as she turns on her copy machine and starts copying the pages of the notebook.

"I'm a free man again. It just cost a lot in lawyer fees."

"That's great Jack, sorry for the cost. Have you applied for the warrant for Carl Minion's correct apartment address?"

"No, like I said there is a lovely older couple in that house, not an apartment. We have no idea where he was living."

"Jack, I got the correct address from Miss Bailey Mobley an hour ago. She returned from Los Angeles this morning and I was lucky to catch her. She told me Carl's license has a bogus address on it. Carl lived in unit C of the Oasis Apartments. I just came from there. Two men chased after me when I came out but I lost them."

"You should have given the address to me right away instead of going there. Did you go inside his apartment?"

"I saw his starving cat staring at me through a window. Lucky for you I thought he might have a pet. That's my excuse for going there and going in. The cat couldn't get out of the apartment and he looked like he was starving so I went in. I fed and watered his cat."

"So you made an illegal entry. I hope we don't find your fingerprints there?"

"No, I wore gloves. I just fed the cat and I might claim the door was unlocked."

"Okay, what did you find that is so interesting? Why were you chased?"

"Someone must have decided to send these guys to check out Carl's place. I was lucky I got away."

"I'm glad you are safe but you shouldn't have gone in his place." Jack steps away from the group and cups his phone before speaking. "You know that's tampering with evidence! What did you find there little Miss 'Illegal Entry' woman?"

"Jack, sometimes it is better to ask forgiveness than permission. After I fed the cat I did look around and found a notebook hidden in the kitchen ceiling. There wasn't anything else of value so I left. As I was leaving I saw the two goons coming toward me." Carey says as she flips another page to copy from the notebook.

"You truly are lucky Carey."

"You should give me some brownie points. This notebook has names, abduction dates, and..."

"You found his notes!"

"Yes, and from what I see, he procured women for Frank Rizzo and was paid by Frank Rizzo the owner of the Happy Ranch Bordello. Carl must have gotten cross-threaded with Rizzo and got himself terminated. What do you think about that?"

"I think you have illegally obtained evidence, Miss Lange. With a warrant and a search we would have legally found that."

"Or not...The goons would have found the notebook. As I explained, I'm an animal lover. I went inside to feed the cat."

"I want to see what you got Miss Lange." Jack hears a stifled laugh and quickly adds. "The notebook, I want to see the notebook."

"We should do a late lunch, Jack."

"Yes, I forgot to eat lunch, any suggestions?"

Carey thought about several suggestions she wanted to say but just smiled. "I'm starving. What about Diablo's Cantina?"

"Good Mexican food, but I have a half hour of stuff to do, so let's meet at four?"

"Okay, I have something I can do until then."

"Bring the notebook beautiful."

Carey rings off and sighs. "He called me beautiful!"

She takes the copy of the notebook with her and drives to the Luxor to find Shelly Beatty. Carey walks into the lobby just after three in the afternoon and inspects a uniformed short man she guesses is about fifty years old and a little overweight. His shoes are polished and his hair is dyed dark brown. He has a scar on his left cheek from his hair down below his brown eyes. Carey files details without realizing she does it. She asks him how to find Shelly Beatty.

"I'm Shelly. I just came on at three. How may I help you?"

Carey shakes his soft well-manicured hand. "I hope you can. I'm Carey Lange, a private investigator. I'm checking into that murder two nights ago. I spoke with Bailey Mobley a short while ago and she said you would be able to help me. You know, she's worried about her safety living in the suite and hopes you can help. She said she'd be so grateful if you could."

"Oh yes, Miss Bailey is very nice. She's very kind and appreciative of the staff, unlike some guests. How can I help?"

"Do you remember talking to the police about the murder?" She sees Shelly nod when she hands him her business card and a twenty-dollar bill. "Tell me everything that happened before and after the pink lady ran by you. Any details you remember could be helpful."

"Thanks Miss." Shelly accepts the money. He can think of nothing unusual happening just that the woman ran very wobbly and right into Mister Barry Mobley's stretch limo.

"I hired the limo for Mister Mobley so I know it was his and I saw her get in. People come and go all the time, nothing unusual. But I do remember when a nice lady all in pink runs through the lobby."

"Do you remember any other details?"

"Oh yeah, she looked really scared."

"Thank you so much. If you see her again, please call me immediately. I'll make it worth your call." Carey says.

"Thank you Miss um, Lange is it?" He whispers with a smile.

"Yes, and you are welcome. Remember cash money!"

"You must want this woman bad!"

"Yes Mister Beatty, we fear she is in danger and need to find her ASAP!" She shakes his hand before leaving. It's almost four when she straddles her purple Vespa and drives to Diablo's Cantina to meet Detective Jack Foster.

Chapter Thirty Eight

Saturday afternoon Frank Rizzo at the Happy Ranch Bordello orders his men Peter and Zach to go to Carl's apartment and search for his notebook. He is mad over the death of Carl Minion and suspects his Las Vegas rival, Arthur Cannon is the culprit. Carl was working on Frank's current contract for a pair of under-thirty, blue-eyed brunettes, and Carl had the first one, nineteen-year-old Janet Winslow, sedated and ready to go. Frank heard from Carl Thursday evening that he found the second, but Carl never showed up with the woman. Later Frank found out Carl was killed, and the woman is gone. "I will have to use Peter or Zach now to find a second girl." Frank mumbles to himself.

After Peter and Zach lose the woman on the purple Vespa, they return to Carl's apartment. Zach sees the ceiling tile askew and searches in the ceiling for any records Carl kept hidden there. Then he and Zach ransack the rest of the apartment and find nothing. Peter calls Rizzo.

"Hello boss. The girl must have found Carl's notebook."

Frank Rizzo pounds his office desk with a fist. He knows Carl's notebook is incriminating evidence.

"You have to find that woman. I looked up the license tag. It belongs to Carey Lange of Lange Investigations. I sent you a text with her addresses. Split up; watch her office and apartment. Bring her here." Frank rings off. He closes his eyes and leans back in his chair for a moment then he remembers he needs to give his captor Janet Winslow another sedating shot.

Peter pockets his phone and leaves the apartment. He and Zach drive to the office of Lange Investigations but the purple

Vespa isn't there. Peter stops next to a bus stop bench and lets Zach get out.

"You watch her office. I'll go to her apartment. Look for that purple motor scooter. Call if she shows and I'll come help take her down." Peter leaves for the apartment.

Carey parks her Vespa near Diablo's Cantina and fast walks inside. She smiles seeing Police Detective Jack Foster already seated at a table, his suit jacket off and his tie loose. She sits next to him and fans herself to cool down before she speaks.

"Hello Jack I hope you haven't waited long."

"No and I'm glad you are okay. So off the record, let's see the notebook."

"Get right to it huh?" Carey exclaims. She slides the copy of the ledger from her waistband and hands it to Jack. She smiles seeing Jack thumb through the records but then is somber realizing all the women are victims of an unwanted lifestyle or horrible death.

"This is awful Carey! Look at all these names and dates!" Jack shakes his head. "I doubt if we can use any of this terrible information in court because you obtained it illegally but at least I know who the players are."

"You should get a warrant for Frank Rizzo at the Happy Ranch. Aren't I a reliable source, enough for you to talk to a judge?"

"We'll see. We should be able to do that with this new information."

"Look at the last entry Jack. It shows my other client Eddy Winslow's daughter Janet was abducted Wednesday! While you ponder that I'll order some tacos. I haven't eaten in a while. You keep the copy. I'll keep the notebook in my office." Carey says.

"That is evidence, I should have the original Carey."

"My evidence, I made this copy for you."

Jack frowns as he folds the notes to stuff into his jacket. He eats chicken tacos and Coke with Carey and reminds her as they leave.

"I know Peggy Clarkson and Winslow's daughter may be there, but don't be foolish and go to the Happy Ranch. I will get a search warrant based on - as you said a reliable source."

"I will call you later."

"Yes, goodbye for now, and thanks for the info." Jack says and watches Carey wave goodbye. He walks to his car thinking. *I should think about dating again.*

Carey looks back and waves before she drives away. She smiles because she saw Jack still looking at her when she turned to wave. Carey drives to her office intent on putting the notebook that she left on her desk into her small safe.

Zach sees the purple Vespa approaching and dials Peter. He watches Carey park her motor scooter and enter her office. Ten minutes later Peter also parks near her office. Zach doubles up with Peter and goes to the entrance of Lange Investigations.

Before Carey picks up the notebook from her desk she calls Jack to tell him thanks for the early dinner. Then two men burst into her office. She hears Jack answer the phone, but she recognizes the two men and stuffs the phone in the back pocket of her slacks. Then she screams.

"Shut up!" Zach says pointing the barrel of his gun at her gut. "Where is the notebook you stole from Carl's apartment?" As he shouts he sees the notebook on her desk and grabs it. "This is it!" Zach exclaims after scanning through the pages. He examines Carey and exclaims. "Peter, she has blue eyes and brown hair. We need to take her!"

"Why should I go with you? You have the notebook now leave!"

"Sorry lady, you come with us." Zach pokes her ribs. He leads Carey to the car and holds a gun on her as Peter drives them to the Happy Ranch.

The Happy Ranch building sits at the edge of the road with no door or windows on the part facing Las Vegas Boulevard. The hot pink stucco exterior supports a huge Happy Ranch sign and a smaller sign stating parking is at the rear. A four feet high pink concrete wall surrounds the parking lot and conceals any cars parked inside.

Carey watches as Peter drives down the side street and through the gap in the wall behind the building. He parks close to the bright red entrance door that has heart-shaped red and white lights around it. As she gets out of the car with the two men, a man in a dark suit and tie comes out shielding his face. Peter smiles at the man who looks his way and gives him a weak thumb up before he gets in his car.

Carey steps inside the door and smells raspberry incense mixed in with marijuana smoke and other scents unknown to her. She hesitates at the entrance making mental notes and gives her best sheepish grin at the woman standing behind a podium.

The tall chalk-white woman in a bright purple gown smiles at Carey as she stands next to the dais that has a gray box and a credit card machine on top. The woman's purple dress stretches barely below her hips and the top is open below her belly button to a thin gold belt. She stands on purple high heels and appears to have on nothing else except large gold loop earrings partly covered by her auburn hair.

A small gold couch across from the woman has one black man and one white man, both clad only in briefs. Two young women in teddies are slinking on a long gold-colored couch on the other side from the men. One is an Asian girl and one perhaps a Mexican woman. The carpet is a light purple that almost matches the lighter purple walls. Hanging at eye level are several pictures of women and men in love scenes. Across from the entrance is a dark purple door that Carey knows must lead to the private rooms. The tall woman interrupts Carey's examination.

"Welcome to Happy Ranch." The woman in purple says and gives a smile as Carey is escorted past her.

"Help!" Carey shouts but she sees the hostess shrug her shoulders and turn away as do the tempters in the reception area.

Zach forces Carey across the entrance area and through the purple door. He shoves her down the hallway to the end and into Frank Rizzo's office and smiles at Frank still seated at his desk.

"Look what we have!" Zach exclaims. "We got the notebook and Miss blue eyes. I think we solved two problems."

Frank stands up and takes the notebook from Peter. He scans through the pages and smiles. Next, he examines Carey. He can tell she is under thirty, good complexion and blue eyes. He runs his hands over her body checking for muscle tone and just because he can.

"She will do fine indeed! You two get a bonus!" Frank sits down to look through the notebook more thoroughly.

"Thank you, boss!" Zach says.

"Put her with the other girl and give her a happy shot. I will call the buyer." Frank dials his phone as he watches Zach and Peter take Carey away.

"Yes?" A man answers.

"I have your package ready. Bring your van to the side door as usual." Frank says and hears his phone go dead. Then he sees Zach come into his office.

"We stripped the woman. Her cell phone was live. I don't know who she called. It's an unlisted number."

"Just ignore it. She must have butt phoned someone. Did you give her a shot?"

"Yeah, Peter just did that."

"Good. The buyer will be here in twenty minutes. Go sit with the girls and help load them when he gets here. After he leaves with the girls I will pay your bonus."

Frank waits for Zach to leave and then opens his safe and puts Carl's notebook inside. He counts out the bonus money for

Zach and Peter before closing the safe. Frank smiles and sits down at his desk, storing the money in his desk drawer. He is content to do nothing, then the side doorbell rings. He peeks out the peephole and sees his buyer Vern is there. Frank shuts off the alarm and opens the side door.

"Welcome my friend. We have what you requested, two beauties with blue eyes and brown hair. You have the cash?" Frank takes an attaché from Vern, sets it on his desk, and flips it open.

"You can count it but you know I wouldn't cheat you."

"I trust you Vern. The boys will help load the merchandise." Frank calls Zach and Peter. "Bring the women here!" Then he hears the alarm from his lobby host and hears sirens.

"What is this, a setup?" Vern shouts.

"No, I don't know. Maybe you should leave." Frank says and sees Vern grab his attaché and rush out the side door.

Chapter Thirty Nine

Police Detective Jack Foster follows behind two cruisers that speed into the Happy Ranch parking lot and stop next to the building entrance. Jack stops his car blocking a van that nearly crashes into his car trying to leave. He sees a policeman direct the driver out of the van as Jack runs through the commotion and sprints to the Happy Ranch entrance. He steps inside the cool building and into what seems like utter chaos. Policemen are corralling the screaming women and men in the lobby. He hears shouting voices as he moves further inside.

"Please don't hurt me!" The hostess Xenia cries. She steps away from the podium and points to the purple door.

Jack follows two policemen through the lobby, through the purple door, and into the hallway. It is dimly lit and his eyes adjust as he enters the hall with his gun drawn. He watches all the doors along the hall. Suddenly a man steps out a door near the end of the hall. The man runs across the hall.

"Stop or I shoot!" One of the officers shouts.

"Go ahead!" Zach yells and runs into Frank's office and out the side door.

"Was that Rizzo?" The cop asks Jack looking into the office.

"No, and our men will stop him outside. I need to find Miss Lange." Jack says. The first door he opens is across from Rizzo's office. He sees two girls in gray smocks on a bed. A man standing behind the bed fires a gun at him. Jack fires hitting the gunman in the chest and sees him collapse. He rushes in, kicks the gun away from the man. Then he feels pain, holsters his gun, and clutches his bloody left arm.

Jack sees Carey lying across a king-size bed next to another woman. Her clothes are piled on the floor in the corner of the room. Both women are tethered to a bed post by neck chains. He leans over Carey and sees her eyes rolling and a faint smile on her lips.

"We will get you out of here." Jack says and kisses her forehead. He smiles, thankful she is alive. Then the pain in his shoulder reminds him he is shot so he goes back to the door and leans against the frame. "Bring medics and a bolt cutter!" Jack shouts to one of the officers in the hallway.

More sirens cry outside and police cars and an ambulance pour into Happy Ranch with sirens winding down and adding to the spectacle of red and blue lights flashing. A swarm of officers invades the parking lot and building.

Frank Rizzo having run out his side door followed by Zach sees the officers coming toward him with guns drawn. He stretches his hands onto the van and waits while an officer cuffs him and Zach and Vern and leads them to a transport van.

Two paramedics rush inside Happy Ranch and are directed through the purple door. They see Jack waving at them and trot down the hallway to him.

The lead paramedic checks the man on the floor first and shakes his head. "He's deceased. Let's look at your arm."

"I hope he is the only fatality." Jack says.

"Only him so far," the man says. He wipes away the blood and determines the bullet only grazed Jack's arm so he preps the wound and bandages it.

"Now help these girls." Jack says. He gently lifts Carey to a sitting position.

"Howooo Jaah..." Carey whispers unable to speak normally or keep her eyes open.

"You're okay now." Jack whispers in her ear and sees her smile.

He wraps his arm around Carey while a paramedic checks her vitals. Jack feels her body lean into him and she tries unsuccessfully to flap an arm onto him. Jack has never seen her in a vulnerable state like this and for the first time he realizes how much he cares for her.

"Who needs a bolt cutter?" Officer Ron Clark shouts.

"In here Ron."

Jack watches Officer Clark cut the chains off the women. As the paramedics load Carey onto a gurney Jack pats Officer Clark on the shoulder.

"Ron, you go with the other woman. I have to go to the hospital with Miss Lange."

"Why?" Ron asks. "The paramedics think Lange will be okay, but this girl isn't doing so well. She may not survive."

"When Lange awakes she may have some vital information."

"I see but this girl won't. Okay, I'll go with this one. Do we know who she is?"

"She is Janet Winslow. Go with the medics. They may be able to get a response from her."

Jack waves at Ron and then he follows Carey and the gurney out of the building. He watches the medics making sure they treat Carey gently. After that Jack trots to his car and follows the ambulance to the hospital. He parks in the ER parking lot and waits in the lobby to hear how Carey is doing. A half-hour later a doctor calls for him.

"Detective Foster, I'm Doctor Patel. Miss Lange is resting peacefully."

"Thank you doctor, I would like to see her."

"You can wait in her room but she will sleep for many hours."

"Do you know what drug they gave her?"

"Yes, we found a used vile of Ketamine Hydrochloride by her."

"Isn't that used on animals?"

"Oh yes, it just deadened most of her non-essential muscles for a few hours depending on how big a dose she has. An overdose could kill her. Her blood pressure is okay and she is breathing on her own."

"So she will be alright?"

"Yes, unless some other problem shows up she will be fine."

"If it's alright with you doctor, I will stay with her."

"It may be hours before that will happen."

"I have all the time I need."

"Okay, come with me." The doctor slides his ID card to open the door to the emergency area. Doctor Patel walks to the back area and opens another door to a hallway. He steps into an elevator and waits for Jack to join him. Moments later he walks into a semiprivate room.

"Miss Lange is here. The Winslow woman has to stay in the ER. She is in much worse condition, apparently starved and dehydrated. She was doped up and they either didn't give her food and water or she refused it. Maybe she went into shock and couldn't eat or drink. She may not come out of her coma."

"I'm sure your staff will do whatever they can for Miss Winslow. I'm concerned about her, but I want to stay here."

"Okay, I have to leave now."

"Thanks for the info Doc."

Chapter Forty

Jack cozies up in the lounge chair next to Carey's bed, unwilling to go back to the Happy Ranch and help with the arrests. He watches her fitful sleep for a while thinking about the conversations with her that he felt were annoying at the time. Now he thinks back and smiles about all the subtle loving hints she gave him and he feels guilty. Jack makes a promise to himself that he will treat her better. He fantasizes about possibly dating her, and then he smiles and dozes off in a dead man's sleep. He wakes to hear Carey shouting.

"Whoa! Where am I! What are you doing here?" Carey shouts.

"Hey, you're awake." Jack mumbles shaking the sleep out of his brain. He checks his watch noting it is three in the morning.

"Where am I?" Carey stares at Jack trying to focus on his face.

"You are in Southern Hills Hospital. They moved you from the ER hours ago. Do you remember what happened to you?"

"Oh Jack, what are you doing here?"

"I'm watching you beautiful." Jack smiles.

"Thank you! I remember two guys kidnaped me." Carey grabs her head with her hands. "Yes, they took me to the Happy Ranch. They drugged me and chained me to a bed… and you rescued me!"

"It was your sharp thinking. You called me and all I heard was some muffled sounds and then you shouted help. I suspected you were in some kind of trouble. We tracked your phone to Happy Ranch and I got the warrant to search there so we went in force."

"What about Janet? I recognized her from her picture. How is she doing?"

"You mean Miss Winslow. She may not come to."

"I could tell she was comatose."

"Well now that I know you are okay, I can go home."

"You were here all night?"

"I wanted to see you come out of the sleep alright."

"That's sweet Jack. I thought you didn't care."

"Well, I do care. Now I'm going home."

"Yeah, just leave me here." Carey says dejected.

"I need some comfortable sleep. See me when you get out."

"Do you really want to see me after all this?"

"Definitely, I want to hear your pesky voice!"

"Okay, I'm going back to sleep and dream about that." Carey smiles and closes her eyes.

"Sleep well." Jack whispers. He pauses to stare at Carey for a moment and then walks out of the hospital room.

After a good sleep, Detective Jack Foster goes to his police station office early in the afternoon. Xenia, Frank Rizzo and the remaining goon Zach have been booked and interviewed. He sits down to look through their files and all that happened at Happy Ranch. After a brief scan Jack takes a moment to relax. He closes his eyes and leans back in his chair. Then his phone rings.

"Sergeant Downey here. We located the father of Janet Winslow, the girl missing since last Wednesday. He was at work. We told him his daughter is in Southern Hills Hospital."

"Thank you Sergeant."

"Yes, Mister Winslow is on his way to the hospital."

"Thanks again for the info." Jack hangs up and smiles.

Jack looks through his notes from the interviews. Rizzo claims his rival Arthur Cannon killed Carl Minion and wants him arrested.

It is late afternoon when he finishes going over his notes. His office and his stomach are empty. He feels empty inside too knowing he is divorced. He wants to talk to someone so he dials Carey Lange.

"Hello handsome." Carey sings.

"Hello Carey. You sound cheerful. How are you feeling?"

"I'm fully recovered, how about you?"

"A lot has happened today. Would you mind coming to the station? I think it would be easier to talk here."

"I'm with Eddy Winslow and his daughter. It took several bags of IVs to flush her system, but she finally woke up just minutes ago."

"Wow, that's great news that she is awake."

"She's a teenager Jack. Her young organs saved her. She's just too young to die."

"Congratulations on finding her."

"You know me, I get lucky sometimes."

"It helps to be good at what you do too."

"Thanks, I think that's a compliment from you. Are you okay?"

"No, did I tell you I got shot last night?"

"Oh no! What happened?"

"Just a flesh wound. It's okay. There is other news though, will you come here?"

"I'll be there in fifteen minutes." Carey rings off.

Jack busies himself with making more notes and tries to think of why he asked Carey Lange to come to his office. He could easily just talk over the phone. Then he admits he likes seeing Carey in spite of her being a nuisance at times. As he is thinking about her, he sees Carey walk into his office.

Carey is wearing tan slacks and a loose hanging tan blouse. She wraps her arms around his waist pressing her face into his shoulder.

"Thank you! I'm not letting go for a while." Carey mumbles.

"You're welcome, and I miss you too." He enjoys her embrace wrapping his arms around her, surprised at what he said.

"I'm glad you aren't hurt bad. Where are you shot?" Carey watches Jack step away, unbutton his shirt and show her the bandage on his upper arm.

"That's heart high! You could have been killed!"

"It's a hazard of my job Carey."

"I know, me too." She pats Jack's shoulder and then exhales noisily. "Now what about Rizzo, did he confess to anything?"

"Yes. We found out a lot about Happy Ranch today thanks to you leading us there. By the way, we had a search warrant in place when we found Carl Minion's notebook in Rizzo's safe. How did that happen?"

"The men took it from my office."

"However it got there, it's good evidence now. Happy Ranch will be shut down permanently. I would take you to dinner but you probably ate already. I still have to finish up on these reports."

"I've been too busy to eat, meeting Janet's father at the hospital and all. I can wait. I'm glad to be alive and I like to watch you work." Carey smiles and thinks *if you only knew how glad I'm to see you!*

"Actually, I haven't eaten anything all day and I'm hungry. I can do it all this Monday morning. I can celebrate that my divorce is final by having dinner with you. There is a quaint little Italian restaurant near my apartment. They have the best lasagna you'll ever taste. Do you want to go?"

"Are you asking me because you feel guilty for not helping more with Miss Winslow or just to tell me what happened at Happy Ranch? That's what this is right?" Carey teases.

"Yes, and do you want to go or not?"

"Lasagna and you, what more can I ask for? Let's go!" Carey jabs at Jack's arm.

"I guess that's a yes. Maybe we can think up a way to nab Carl Minion's killer."

"I'd like that and you can help me find Miss Clarkson. Should I follow you there?"

"Ride with me. You can get your scooter later, maybe much later!" Jack smiles at Carey and hooks arms with her to escort her out of his office.

Chapter Forty One

Late Monday morning Peggy and Ursula each give Brendan a thank you kiss before sliding into a taxi to return to the Stratosphere Hotel. Peggy hates to leave the Villa but when the taxi turns onto the strip, Peggy once again enjoys the array of displays and lights from the hotels along the way. Morning along the strip is awesome even in the daytime to Peggy and her enthusiasm for the strip is still rising.

She rides to the other end of Las Vegas Boulevard with Ursula. The taxi stops at the entrance of the hotel. At ten o'clock in the morning, she splits the taxi bill with Ursula and starts toward the hotel with Ursula.

"Well Peggy, think about my apartment. My ex-roommate got married and moved out. I'm going to drive home and freshen up. Do you want to take a look at my place now?" Ursula asks.

"I have to check in with Ann. Maybe I can see it later."

"Okay, I'll see you tonight with Barry and Brendan.

"See you later in the lobby." Peggy says and waves goodbye. She takes a deep breath before going inside the Stratosphere Hotel. She strolls through the lobby and steps into an elevator. As she waits for the elevator to ascend to the fifth floor she thinks. *I missed the sewing stuff but I had a blast! I wish I had remembered to take my phone to Reno. I did text Ann that I would be back today. I hope she's not too upset with me missing the classes.* Peggy goes to her room and uses her key to open the door.

"Peggy! This is great!" Ann rushes from the couch to greet her.

"It's good to be back!"

"Where were you? We've been searching for you for three days!"

"What's the problem? I sent you a text message that I would be back today. You answered with okay."

"I never got a text from you. I hired a private investigator and she's looking for you as we speak!"

"I'm sorry. You must have missed my text. I still have it on my phone. Look at this, oh no!" Peggy closes her eyes in dismay. "I sent it to our friend Ann Perry by mistake, and she answered okay! I was really tired when I sent this. I'm sorry Ann. I feel awful."

"It's okay Peggy. I'm glad you are alive and well. I must say you look great! Where did you get that beautiful green dress? It doesn't have a single thread of pink on it. I thought you only wore pink stuff."

"Yeah, well Brendan likes me in all different colors. He has a whole closet full of brand new clothes he got for his ex and they fit me fine. I wore a new navy blue dress too."

"That's not pink either. You always wear pink."

"I'm changing my ways Ann. This trip has opened my eyes!"

"Is this Brendan fellow rich?"

"He is, and Barry is too. His brother Barry lives year-round at the Luxor. And the Aurora Bar there looks like the Northern Lights. I had a bit of a problem there though. A guy named Carl attacked me. I got away and then he was murdered. I went with the party group to Brendan's Villa. That's where I made friends with Ursula and Brendan. Ursula is a good friend now and Brendan is a great guy. He and Barry took Ursula and me to Reno..."

"Wait, you were involved in a murder?"

"Well, I didn't kill him. I guess I had a more exciting time than sitting in sewing classes."

"You missed every class **and** both of the dinners!"

"I know but..."

"The goodbye dinner was awesome too. I had a Salmon steak to die for! You missed that too. This whole trip is a waste for you."

"No Ann, it wasn't. I learned about the real me. I'm not all that interested in sewing and I can make copies of your notes if I want. We still have several reservations for shows. I have a couple more days and nights of fun with Brendan before we fly out on Thursday morning. I never knew how good it feels to do what I want.

"Oh, Sam called me while you were in Reno. He said there is nothing to worry about there, even though the hurricane was still dumping rain on Lauderdale for an extra day. I didn't know if I should tell him you were lost. I told him I was having such a good time and that everything was going as expected here."

"Well, I couldn't talk to Max. My phone was in Vegas and I was in Reno."

"I almost told Sam you were missing! I was hoping the P I would find you, but I'd have Sam tell Max today if you were still missing."

"It's a good thing you didn't tell Sam. Max might have come out here to help find me. Okay, so the boys are fine. Let's do fun things from now on. What about you?"

"Well, I really enjoy 'normal things' as Sam does. But the whole group is going to Cirque du Soleil this afternoon. The tickets are part of the package so it is good you are back in time to go."

"I'm enjoying it so much out here! I wasn't going to tell anyone about this until I got home, but I want to stay in Las Vegas!"

"It is a fun city Peggy, but it's not for me; too artificial."

"But that's the charm of it Ann, like Brendan flying us to Reno just for fun to see his friend Harry Suave open at the Grand Theater. I get along well with Ursula Stein. I may share an apartment with her. She is a good gal to hang around with and I had fun with Brendan. I think he likes me. Ursula and I have another date with Brendan and Barry tonight. They want to take us casino hopping!"

"Will you talk to Max today and tell him what you are doing?"

"No, I want to keep it all a secret for now. I don't know how Max will react if I tell him his ex-fiancée went to Reno with a stranger the day after her breakup! Did you ever do anything wild and crazy Miss Goody-Two-Shoes?" Peggy asks.

"Hey, I'm not perfect either."

"You sure seem to be Missy."

"I have a secret too."

"Oh really?"

"I've been having dinner with Ralph!"

"Who is Ralph?"

"He's a guy I partnered with in classes, thanks to you!"

"You went to dinner with him?"

"Yes, so we shouldn't mention that either."

"Well did he kiss you or try anything?"

"No, I wouldn't have dined with him if I thought he would try anything. He is a perfect gentleman."

"Why would he dine with you?"

"He was deserted too."

"Sorry about that Ann. So what's the big secret then? Did you get drunk and lose your memory?"

"No I only drink tea for now, but he is so handsome and charming, it's a good thing I love Sam, or I might be tempted..., but I know that's not right."

"But you say he didn't do anything, right?"

"Of course not!"

"Then why was he hanging with you?"

"Because you weren't there and his sewing partner had to leave for a few days. We became friends. Whether you believe it or not, some women can have a male friend without having sex with him. We just talked and ate dinner together. He is good company."

"Well, let's leave the explanations until we get back home."

"I wonder if Max and Sam are still partying at Chet's house. I just hope they don't hook up with some of the cuties the band will surely have at the party."

"I'm glad Sam is with Max. He looks out for Max. You know Max tends to get in a jam sometimes."

"I know why." Peggy says. "It's because his pranks either turn into a problem or the bad Karma they create is a problem for Max. He has made me so mad at times!"

"I know you left him a few times but you always came back."

"Not this time Ann. I'm leaving, but not because I'm mad. We have different goals. I'm leaving because I love him. Can't you see?"

"Not really Peggy. I may never understand, but that's me. Anyway, Sam said it was raining there continuously. If I know Sam, he probably will drag Max away Monday so they can go back to work. I bet they will be working or maybe they will play hooky and watch some gross gory movies for an extra day or so. He said they will hunker down until Jezebel is history. What could go wrong there?"

"Oh, I wouldn't say nothing could happen." Ann blurts. "Look at the lovely time I had trying to find you. I have to call Ms. Lange now and tell her you returned. She did tell me late this morning that she and the police had closed down a bordello and she thought she would find you there but of course, she didn't."

"What, she thought I turned hooker!"

"No silly, the men used it for some kind of human trafficking. She said that guy Carl had apparently tried to abduct you."

"So that's why he isolated me from the crowd. I thought he was attracted to me."

"It looks like you had your first adventure in Las Vegas!"

"Yeah, well I hope Max is happy in his big house and isn't too upset with me having a ball here!"

"I haven't talked to Sam today. I bet life is dull for the guys compared to here. I miss Sam. I'll try calling him after I talk to Carey Lange. I wonder what the boys are doing." Ann says.

Chapter Forty Two

Sam shuffles his feet in the foyer and watches Charlotte saunter away from him. He considers his old feelings for her versus his great life with Ann.

Overwhelmed with emotion Sam feels both surprised and relieved that Charlotte took him off her bootie call. *I can't believe I turned down Charlotte, but Ann means the world to me. Ann would be proud of me too!* Sam stares at Charlotte as she disappears on the dance floor. He watches the dancers for a long time before he settles down enough to join the crowd. He wanders around the living room dancing with one woman or another until the music stops. The only thing still on Sam's mind is Charlotte and Ann and ensuring Charlotte doesn't try to compromise him again.

Sam wanders around still thinking about what happened until he spots Max at the edge of the living room sipping on a beer and talking to a man with long blonde hair. Sam sighs, trying to blank Charlotte from his mind as he saunters over to Max.

"Sam this is Bill Todd a producer for Todd Dell Pictures."

"Hello Bill." Sam shakes hands.

"Oh yeah, Bill this is my friend Sam Stormen."

"Hello Sam. Dan Batts invited me to this great party."

"Bill is planning a movie about the Danglebatts Band. He does action movies too. I've been telling him a wild story about politics, corruption, and murder. He thinks it would make a good movie.

"Well, did Max also mention a naked woman rescued at sea?"

"Funny, Max already said that. What would you do next Sam?"

"She goes to a party with the guys who rescued her not realizing her enemies are out to kill all of them, how's that?" Sam says sarcastically and wonders how much Max told Bill. Then Bill answers his suspicions.

"Yes, that's also what Max said. Did Max steal your story?"

"Well…"

"Of course," Bill interrupts, "a woman rescued from the ocean has been done before, but I'm not sure about a naked woman. You see Max says the woman wore a tight dress. I'm thinking maybe a uniform like a Playboy Bunny or a show dancer outfit with a built-in bra. When she is tossed in the ocean, she can't tread water with that on so she has to rip it off. So you see, she's practically naked already. I can see the scene unfolding in my head right now. This could make a great R-rated movie." Bill takes a sip of Jack Daniels Black. He makes a square with his hands and then closes his eyes.

"Max, can I have a word with you?" Sam says grabbing Max's arm. He pulls Max away from Bill and frowns.

"I'll see you later Bill! I want to watch the movie." Max shouts and pulls Sam toward the movie room.

"What are you doing Max? Are you going to tell him who the culprits are too and get more people at risk?" Sam says grabbing his shoulder and slowing Max.

"Sam, to him it's just a story that maybe he can sell as a movie. What can go wrong? I want to see the movie. Will you join me?" Max feels Sam grab his shoulder again and he stops.

"Do you realize what danger we are in? If Rose is right, that video will bring down several powerful people. I'm sure they are hunting us down as I speak."

"You always look at the negative side of things Sam. I want to see this movie." Max says as he leans toward the movie room.

"Go enjoy the movie while you can Max." Sam lets him go.

"Rose will turn in that video and be a hero. The good guys will put the bad guys away. I think nothing much will happen until all this hurricane threat is over."

"We need to be careful Max, because whether you believe it or not we are in another fine mess! Rose knows too much and so do we. They will find us. They will shut her up and us too!"

"How can they find us? Why would you say that?"

"Rose used your phone to call her boss, so they know the owner of the phone is you. By now they have your address and your phone GPS will lead them right to us!"

"You know I'm turning off the GPS app right now!" Max says and for the first time since rescuing Rose, Max worries as he walks into the movie room.

Before he starts his engine to go to Fort Lauderdale, Craig Benito slides off a lambskin glove and tilts the rear view mirror to make sure his disguise is still in place. He adjusts his blonde wig and checks his fake mole before putting his glove back on. Satisfied his disguise is still okay he smiles and re-aims the mirror.

"Damn good disguise." He says, knowing people tend to focus on a mole or tattoo to describe a stranger. He taps Max's address in the GPS app of his phone to get directions and then drives away from the Gatsby Apartments.

Craig goes to the Wal-Mart store in Coral Way and circles the parking lot before he parks his black van near a group of cars and trucks. Craig carries the construction bag full of Rose's stuff with him as he steps out of his van into the light rain. After trying a few door handles, he finds an older Explorer not locked and keys under the driver seat. Craig tosses the black bag inside and hops in pulling the door shut. Confident all will go well he plans to give the black bag and Rose's recorder to Matuso in Fort Lauderdale and get his cash.

Before Craig turns on the engine, he restarts his phone GPS. He weaves onto I-95 North toward Fort Lauderdale and Max's house.

Driving cautiously in the rain, Craig follows the GPS and finally aims the stolen Explorer through the open gates of Blue Lake Estates. An outer band of rain from the hurricane hits. His headlights shine on sheets of rain cascading down and swaying about in the gusty wind making it hard for Craig to read street signs. His eyes strain on the next sign and he is barely able to read Lux Lane. Craig feels the excitement of going on a kill as he mulls over taking out Rose Finley and Max Merchado. He knows several swampy areas suited for dumping bodies. *I will find them and have fun torturing Finley to get her recorder!* He smiles seeing 250 in large numbers on a mailbox.

He continues rolling past the house examining the area and all the shuttered houses. The yards are free of anything that may blow around and he sees a crowd of cars parked all over the yard and driveway of the neighbor's house and a banner sign flapping in the wind that reads 'Jezebel Hurricane Party'. Craig loops around at the end of the lane, comes back, and steers into Max's circular driveway. He stops under the stone canopy that shields the rain except what the wind gusts whip through the overhang.

Craig cinches up his raincoat against the wind and rain with one hand as he gets out of the Explorer. He holds his 9 mm Beretta with silencer under the raincoat as he trots to the front door, and rings the doorbell. Craig examines the door for weaknesses, tapping on the thick wood door to feel how solid it is. He notes the decorative metal plate that covers access to the latch and dead bolt area and sees the peephole has no light shining behind it. Craig tenses seeing a window curtain move to his right side, then relaxes again as a black cat stares at him from the exposed window pane. After a few minutes of no response and several rings, Craig runs back inside the shelter of the Explorer. He turns on his phone again and dials Matuso.

"Have you completed the job already?" Matuso's voice is gruff as if the phone call interrupted his activity.

"The subject isn't at home."

"His phone location indicates he is there. Check around."

"Yes sir." Craig says. He hears Matuso hang up.

Craig stares at the phone and curses. He looks through the windshield, and again notices all the parked cars filling the neighbor's driveway and yard. *They must be at the neighbor's party. It's worth a try.* Craig thinks.

He memorizes the pictures of Finley and Merchado on his phone before he turns his phone off. Craig closes his eyes for a moment and then looks through the windshield at the rain still coming in bursts across the manicured grass between the two houses. He steps out of the Explorer into the gusty wind and rain, cinches his raincoat closed and trots across the grass to the neighbor's house.

Chapter Forty Three

Katie starts the second movie 'The Lost World' and walks back into the living room still carrying her glass of orange juice. She looks around for Chet, but hears the doorbell ring and shuffles through the crowd to the front door. Looking through the peephole, she sees a man huddling against the wind. She smiles and opens the door.

"Come inside quick!" Katie draws him inside and lets him push the door closed. "May I help you?"

"I'm looking for Max Merchado. He said he'd be at a party. Is this the place?"

"Yes, Max is here. Welcome to the Ultimate Hurricane Jezebel Party. What is your name?"

"Paul Watson, just call me Paul. And you are?" Craig takes off his raincoat and hangs it on the coat rack. He uses his jacket to hide his shoulder holster and Beretta.

"Oh, I'm Katie Hatter, Chet's wife. You see all these people Paul. The more the merrier! I think I saw Max go into the movie room. We just started 'The Lost World' a minute ago. He said he wanted to see that. Come with me." Katie grabs his arm.

"No worries, I hope I'm not intruding."

"No problem Paul, I'll take you to him." Katie feels him pull his arm away.

"Please do what you were doing. I like to mingle. I just wanted to be sure I have the right place. I can see him after I socialize a little. Thank you so much Katie."

"Well okay then, welcome to the party. We are celebrating for two more days!" Katie bolts the door and starts swaying to the music as she leads Craig into the crowd.

"Great! I like that Danglebatts song. Are they here?"

"They're all here. This is our house. Let me take you to Chet."

"I think I see him over there. Let me go to the bar first and then I'll say hello."

"Help yourself then." Katie says and sways as she merges into the dancing crowd.

"No problem." Craig, says to a deaf ear. He sees Katie already talking to a short bald man. Craig surveys the room filled with dazzling lights flashing through the smoky air. He works his way through the crowd of people dancing to the rock and roll music and he finally stops at the bar.

Craig sees Rose across the dance floor in a corner of the living room, talking to a dark-haired man wearing a floral shirt and shorts. He sees a white cardboard sign taped to a closed door across from the bar with MOVIE ROOM neatly printed in giant black letters. Craig makes a mental note of everything. He grabs a Michelob beer, takes a sip, and starts toward the movie room.

"Hello handsome stranger! What's your name?" Charlotte slurs her words as she puts her hands on Craig's shoulders frustrated over Sam and searching for someone.

"Um... I'm Paul, Paul Watson." Craig says as Charlotte forces him to stop.

"Are you with someone?" She slides her hand onto his chest.

"No, I'm just a friend of Max. Who are you?"

"I'm Charlotte. I saw Max go into the movie room. I would take you to him but I know he doesn't want to be disturbed." She swings in front of him laying both hands back on his shoulders. She sways back and forth and bats her eyelashes at him.

"I can see him later Charlotte. Do you want to dance?" He sees her stagger into him, obviously drunk or high on something.

"Sure..." Charlotte dances for a moment but is still frustrated over the rejection by Sam. She feels Craig press his body against her and the only thing on her mind is sex! "I know there's a room over there that's not as loud as out here." Charlotte winks and points to an open door across the living room.

"I'd like that. Show me." Craig dances as he follows Charlotte into a bedroom.

"I like to slow dance." She says wrapping her hands around Craig's neck.

"Let's lie down." Craig sets his beer on a makeup desk near the door and slides out of his jacket, setting it next to the vanity. He puts his hands on her waist thinking. *This is great! I get to have sex and kill too!*

"Wow, you have a gun!" Charlotte blurts.

"I'm a plainclothes cop. Sorry, I forgot to leave it in the car."

"Yes! Even better!" Charlotte whispers. As she backs up coaxing him to the bed, she unbuttons his shirt and grabs his neck. She feels Craig undo her blouse revealing her bare chest and feels him caress her and hard kiss her lips as she backs against the bed. "It's time to lie down." Charlotte mumbles and falls onto the king-size bed, barely keeping her eyes open. She smiles as Craig lies down beside her.

Craig rolls on his side and pulls her to him, gently caressing her and kissing her lips. He hears her moan in response but then she goes limp. He sees her eyes open again and he attempts to kiss her but she makes a short grunting noise and passes out.

"Oh great! Goodnight Charlotte!" Craig says and slides off the bed. He slips on his jacket and eases out of the room.

Craig mixes with the crowd dancing his way across the floor. He stops at the entrance of the movie room and cracks the door open to look inside. Craig stares at the back of the viewer's heads. Of the eight people, only one fits the description of Max, a man sitting in the back row near the door. Craig smiles and gently closes the door. He steps back onto the dance floor and thinks. *The fly is in the spider's web!*

Craig dances and chats with some of the crowd. He learns all about the Danglebatts Band as he tries to conjure up a plan to take out Rose and Max. Finally, when Rose is alone, he sidles up to her and starts dancing. She smiles and starts to dance with him.

Craig enjoys her hips swaying to the music. He loves looking at her athletic body undulating to the beat of the music as he thinks. *It's a shame she has to die.*

"I'm Rose. You dance very well. I saw you came in late."

"Yeah, I had some business I had to do. Nice party, by the way I'm Paul a friend of Max." Craig says as a slow song starts.

"Well, I'm glad you came here. Let's slow dance Paul, my feet are killing me."

"I guess you've been dancing too much."

"Yeah, and it's the shoes."

"After this dance, let's find a place to sit for a while. Is there somewhere we can talk away from this noise?" Craig asks as he thinks. *How can I do you here? How can I get you out of here?*

"Just dance for now." Rose says. She presses against Craig and feels him embrace her with his warm arms. Rose closes her eyes and enjoys his slow dancing for the whole song, imagining she is slow dancing with Max. Her daydream is broken when the music goes back to fast rock and roll. She backs away from Craig.

"We could go in that bedroom." Rose points to a door.

"Well..." Craig says and follows Rose knowing he left Charlotte in that room.

"Oops! We can't go here. There's a semi-naked woman lying on the bed." Rose giggles seeing Charlotte on her back snoring.

"Let's go by the front door. I remember the foyer is somewhat isolated and it muffles the sounds. There's a small couch we can sit on." Rose wiggles through the crowd and Craig follows her to the entrance. "This is better. Thanks for the break."

"Relax and rest your sore feet." Craig says. He thinks of a great plan as he stands behind Rose, and massages her shoulders.

"It is a little quieter here. Oh, that does feel good! These sneakers are too big. I'm getting blisters." Rose says wincing and stretching her legs out. She turns and smiles at Craig.

"Why are your shoes too big?"

"I borrowed them. It's a long story."

"Let me fetch a drink for you and you can tell me all about it. What would you like?" Craig asks.

"A Michelob will do. I'll come with you."

"No, I can manage. Just sit and rest your feet, lady in pink."

"I normally don't wear pink."

"Okay, you can tell me why not and how your shoes got too big for you when I get back." Craig smiles at Rose and watches her frown at him as she slouches down to rest. He works his way through the crowd toward the movie room but sees Katie approach him and gently nudge him.

"Hello Paul. Did you find Max?"

"Yes, he is in the movie room and I wasn't going to disturb him, but I got a phone call. One I was waiting for. Max and I have to go take care of some business. We will be back in an hour or so."

"The rain is really bad right now Paul. It may let up in a while. Usually the rain is intermittent on the outskirts of a hurricane. So far we're only experiencing strong tropical conditions, but there's only one mile per hour difference between the two if the storm continues growing. I'm surprised the rain hasn't stopped by now. Do you have to do it right away?" Katie asks.

"Yes, nothing bad but we need to go handle it ASAP." Craig assures her.

"Hurry back. Oh, I hate for Max to miss the one movie he wants to see. He will have to wait until I reshow it tomorrow."

"Well, just go about whatever you were doing. We will be back before you can drink two beers. I'll go get him."

"I'm not drinking beers, the baby you know," she says pointing to her belly. "But you two be careful out there and hurry back!"

"Don't worry, enjoy your party!" Craig waves goodbye and sees Katie merge into the dance floor swaying to the beat of the music. "Max and Rose will worry for you!" He whispers and focuses on the movie room across the dance floor.

Chapter Forty Four

Craig hurries through the dancers to the movie room and steps inside. He stands by the door and taps Max on the shoulder motioning him to come to the door. Craig points the gun at Max when he stands up. "If you don't want your friends and you dead come with me right now!" Craig whispers motioning Max to come out of the movie room.

Craig leads Max across the living room to the foyer, hiding the gun under his jacket. He sees Rose stand up.

"Hey Paul, where is my beer?" Rose is dumbfounded.

"Shut up Rose! Open the door. We're leaving!" Craig shows her his gun, slips on his raincoat, carefully keeping aim on Max and Rose.

"What do you want? We don't have much money. It's pouring outside!" Max says.

"Put on your raincoats! Run for the car next door or I start shooting guests after I shoot you two!" Craig is careful to keep his voice and gun down and his distance from Rose knowing she might try to jump him. He tosses the only two raincoats at them and follows Rose and Max into the storm outside motioning them to run. The wind whips across his face as he runs. Once under the canopy, he orders them inside the Explorer.

Craig slides into the back seat. He shouts at Max.

"The key is in the ignition. Start driving!" Craig thinks about his first dumpsite.

"Are you kidnapping us?" Max asks.

"For now I'm unless Finley gives me the recorder."

"He wants us dead Max." Rose blurts.

"Start the car!" Craig snaps.

"You kill us and my camcorder goes to the police!" Rose shouts.

"I'll just take it from your dead body!"

"I don't have it on me. The camcorder is hidden."

"My boss thought your recorder went in the ocean with you, maybe it did."

"Not true. I hid it on the party boat in the quiet room. It has enough video on it to hang your boss and Sancho too!" Rose says.

"Is it still on the boat?"

"No, I hid it where you will never find it!"

"Okay, change of plans. Max, we go inside your house."

Craig follows Rose and Max out of the Explorer and into the house. He aims the gun at a movement but it is only the cat he saw in the window earlier who growls and jumps from the couch onto the fireplace mantel. The cat bares her teeth at him. He takes off his raincoat and watches as Max and Rose take off the raincoats. Craig sees Max reach for his raincoat but Craig backs away.

"Let me take the raincoats into the kitchen. You're dripping water all over the carpet." Max says but before Craig answers Max's phone rings.

"Don't answer that!" Craig shouts dropping his slicker on the floor.

"It's Sam. He must have seen us leave. He'll know something is wrong if I don't answer."

"Okay, answer it and make up a good story. Put on the speaker!"

"Hello, Sam. What do you want?"

"You are crazy going out in the rain. Who is that guy with you?"

"Yes, still crazy and a little wet you dumb ass. You know what I like to do and she is willing! I'm having a threesome with Rose and her friend, um?"

"Paul." Rose says.

"Yes, Paul. We are about to strip off our wet clothes. Leave us alone." Max is sure Sam will remember their secret code words 'dumb ass' for meaning they are in trouble. Not hearing from Sam for too long Max feels sweat ooze all over his body giving him a chill. Then Sam responds.

"Not my thing doing a threesome, and I don't want to know how you do a foursome! I should have guessed. I'm a dumb ass. You could have used one of the bedrooms here and stayed dry." Then Sam's mind paints a crazy picture about a stranger with Rose and Max in a threesome. He shakes that off, feeling nauseous as Max talks.

"No, the bedrooms were occupied and I like my own place."

"Okay, come back later. Have fun!"

"We will for sure!" Max says and rings off.

"You did okay." Craig admits. "So you like threesomes and foursomes! Well, maybe under different circumstances it could work. Now tie Rose's hands." Craig takes a tie wrap from his jacket, hands it to Max.

"I'll tie her in front in case she has to go potty or something."

"No tie her hands behind her. Just do it!" Craig watches him cinch up her wrists. He checks Rose's wrist tie-wrap. Satisfied, he shoves her onto the living room couch.

"What do I do now?" Max asks.

"Shut up and do your own hands." He tosses a tie wrap to Max and watches him tie up his own wrists in front. Craig cautiously tightens the loop on Max's wrists, sits him in his swivel rocker chair, and uses another tie-wrap to secure Max's ankles together.

"I won't give the video to you!" Rose states.

"I see no reason to keep you alive then. I just want to have a little fun first. If you are good, I'll keep you alive so you can walk to the car." Craig stuffs the gun in his waistband and opens his stiletto knife. He lays it against Rose's cheek.

"If you kill me that video goes right to the police." Rose says staring at the blade.

"That's interesting. Let's say I don't believe you. I just want to have some fun before I kill you." Craig smiles then looks at the distracting monitor flipping through different pictures of the perimeter of the house. He grabs his gun, fires a shot into the monitor. The screen sprays glass shards into the living room. It flashes, sparks, and goes dark oozing a curl of smoke toward the ceiling. Craig smiles as he rips open Rose's blouse and cuts her bra with his knife leaving a gash on her chest. He grabs her shorts and starts pulling them down.

"It was in the quiet room on the boat." Rose stares at Craig, hatred showing on her face. "It has video of Matuso's plan against Medina and him tossing me overboard. I don't think your boss wants that to get out."

"You know about Troutman!" Craig stops pulling on her shorts.

"Yes Paul. It is all on the video." Rose lies, not having seen the video yet.

"Okay, you went back and got the recorder off the boat?"

"Yes, thanks to Max."

"Where is it?"

"Let's bargain a little first."

"No bargaining, you will beg me to take it before I'm through." Craig shouts. He leans into Rose's face displaying near-perfect teeth in his smile. "I want that video Rose! You can avoid torture and pain by just giving it to me. Where is it?" He jumps back avoiding a dob of spit from Rose and leans back slapping Rose hard across her face.

"You will regret that!" Craig shouts.

"Why should I tell you? You're going to kill us anyway!" Rose shakes her head and spits at Craig again.

"The question is do you want to suffer immense pain before you die, or have an easy painless death? I'm going to look in the kitchen for some fun instruments of torture. I like forks and tongs and I love this house! You can scream all you want Rose and no one will hear you. Does Max know where the recorder is?"

"No, and it isn't here. We will have to go to where it is. Only one other person and I know where it is." Rose talks a convincing lie.

"Just tell me where it is Rose. I can kill you and Max right here, no pain or agony."

"You kill Max and I never talk!"

"Oh good, you care for him. I can cause both of you a lot of pain. That's more fun for me than just popping you in the head. Think about it while I'm gone. Wouldn't you rather have a quick death?" Craig smiles and turns toward the kitchen.

"I'm so sorry I got you involved in this Max." Rose says.

"He is going to kill us both, right?" Max stares at her wide-eyed.

"Yes. We know too much. Matuso must have sent him. He has to kill us but not until he gets the recorder. At least that buys us some time to think of a plan."

"Great! I got all this money, great friends, single, and now I'm going to die! There is no plan Rose!"

"How much is all that, Max?"

"I got a million. There's no point in keeping it a secret now."

"Wow, a million dollars?"

"Yeah, actually it's just under a mil. I used a couple chunks for down payments on a boat and this house."

"Paul is a dirt bag, maybe we can buy him!" Rose whispers.

Craig returns with an aluminum meat tenderizer mallet he heated on the stove.

"I like this mallet. Where do you want to be branded first Rose?"

He starts to set the forks and tongs on the coffee table but hears the cat growl at him so he throws a fork directly at her. Hera ducks the fork and bares her teeth at him growling louder and pacing back and forth on the mantel. Craig ignores the cat.

"Paul, we need to talk." Rose says.

"Fine, talk to me." Craig says frowning at the mallet in his hand wondering if Rose is giving in before he tortures her.

"Max has a wad of money. He wants to offer you a half million to walk away and let us go." Rose says. She sees a slight crack in his expression.

"It's not enough. The boss man has virtually unlimited resources to track me down and you want me to betray him?"

"How much is he paying you for this job?"

"Why should I tell you that? You're just delaying things." Craig steps in front of her and brings the hot mallet close to her face.

"You're going to kill us anyway, how much Paul?"

"Twenty thou each, let me hear you scream!" Craig looks at the mallet and then at Rose.

"What if we upped it to a million? That's fifty times what you get from Matuso? Ah!" Rose screams as Craig taps the hot mallet just above her left breast, then he backs off. She still feels the sting and smells her burnt flesh.

"I just had to give you a sample. The next burn will be longer! I may be interested, where is the cash?" Craig says admiring the burn spot on Rose's bare chest.

"In the morning when the bank opens Max can get all that money in cash." Rose says, but she moans seeing Craig's eyes haze over.

"You know Rose; I'm having too much fun. Forget the money! So tell me, where is the recorder?" Craig squeezes her right breast and brings the hot mallet toward her left breast. He smiles seeing the fear in her eyes and the blood oozing from the knife cut in the middle of her chest. Craig eases the mallet close to Rose's breast but stops when Max shouts at him

"Paul, stop and listen! That recorder is worth a lot more money! Matuso and Sancho will pay big bucks for it. Why settle for a mere twenty thou or even one million? That recorder is worth millions to Matuso and Sancho. You can get our cash, get their money and turn them in too. They won't get you if they're in jail." Max says.

"My job is to quiet you and Rose. Now you've complicated things with this recorder." Seeing Rose's bare chest excites Craig. "I'll call the boss after I have some fun." He smiles and tries to unbutton her shorts. Unable to undo it, he uses the knife to cut off the top button. He hears Rose grunt when he starts pulling down her shorts, but then the doorbell rings. Craig stares at Rose as he gets up. "Max will answer that and I'll be back!"

Chapter Forty Five

Sam Stormen listens as Bill Todd embellishes a scene about the Jamaica Jail adventure Max has told to Bill. As he listens he wonders. *How much more has Max said to this man! Did he tell him about our friend Byron? What about the shredded paper incident?* Then Sam sees Rose and Max go out the front door with a tall man. *What is that about?* Sam thinks as Bill Todd continues to talk excitedly about the story. Sam sets down his beer and starts toward the door.

"Excuse me Bill. I have to check on something."

"No listen! I just thought of a great idea for an ending!"

"Hey Bill, I have to do this. Excuse me."

Sam is deaf to words from Bill as he works his way through the crowd of dancers and finally gets to the front door. He opens it against the gusty wind and slips outside pulling the door closed. He sees the unfamiliar Explorer in Max's driveway and then sees Max and the others come out of the car and go inside the house. Sam is confused as he goes back inside. Katie taps his shoulder.

"What are you doing? Look at the rain you let in." Katie scowls.

"Max just left with um…"

"His name is Paul. He said he and Max will be back in an hour."

"Who is Paul?"

"He said he is a friend of Max. He just got here an hour or so ago. Then he had to leave. Some kind of business they have to take care of."

"I can't think of a friend named Paul, Paul who?"

"I think he said Paul Watson or Wilson."

"Oh, maybe it was Max's boat friend." Sam lies to Katie.

"He could be. Maybe it is about his boat. It must be serious to go out in this rain."

"I'll call Max." Sam says.

"Paul said it was a minor thing. What minor thing makes him go out now?" Katie asks but sees Sam dialing Max.

The first words he recognizes from Max are calling him a 'dumb ass'. Sam barely keeps his composure. He fakes understanding about the threesome and ends the call.

Sam stands inside the door staring at his phone. Then as he goes for the doorknob he feels Katie tap his shoulder again.

"That was a strange call Sam. What's going on?"

"Oh, I have to go help Max and um..."

"Paul Wilson you said. Did Rose go with them?"

"Oh, I guess she did."

"Why, and you sure you know Paul?"

"I'm not sure, but I think I will know him very soon!" Sam says. He waves goodbye to a frowning Katie, opens the door, and steps out under the canopy.

Sam runs from Chet's house into the swirling rain slipping on the wet grass, regaining his balance, bracing against the wind and rain, and skids to a stop under Max's canopy. Sam looks at the unfamiliar Ford Explorer. He shakes rain from his hair and peeks through the window next to the door. Sam sees barechested Rose tied up and sprawled onto the couch. The tall man tosses a fork at the cat. Sam backs away from the window, stunned for a second. He cups his phone against the wind and dials his boss Mark Goodman. The phone rings five times before Mark answers.

"Hello Sam. Wow, you sound like you're out in the storm!"

"I'm. The thing is... I need help. We are in trouble."

"Not again! What trouble are you in now?"

"It looks like we have another hostage situation, in a different house, and a different gunman. I thought we would tell you all about our adventure after the news got out." Sam briefly unloads about fishing Rose from the ocean and her troubles.

"I think he plans to kill all of us." Sam concludes.

"Okay Sam. Jeez, I could make a movie about all the strange situations you two get into. Once again, I will call Captain Holland. You know the rain is really bad right now. You couldn't pick a worse time to call."

"A worse time is if that guy kills them before we stop him."

"Okay, I'll call you when they are on the way."

"No, don't call me. I'm going in. I can delay him killing them or maybe stop him."

"That's crazy Sam! Stand clear. Let us handle this."

"You may be too late, Mark. I have to go in! You know you would too."

"Sam!"

Sam rings off and tucks his phone back in his pocket. As Sam goes to the front door, Dan Batts' words come back to him. *"Someday you will see how strong your bond with Max really is and it may surprise you."*

"Okay, I'm surprised!" Sam mumbles. He steps to the door feeling a little unsteady. *I wish I hadn't drunk so much. Lord, help me make it through this! Maybe I can jump in, surprise him, and disarm him!* Sam whispers to himself. He rings the doorbell and hides behind the Explorer.

Craig grunts when the doorbell rings. Upset, he cuts the ankle tie-wrap on Max and when Max stands up Craig pokes Max in the ribs with his gun barrel.

"Answer the door. Get rid of whoever it is and keep your hands hidden." Craig orders and pushes Max toward the door.

Max looks through the peep hole and sees nothing. He pulls the door slightly open, leans his head into the opening and sees Sam peek from behind the SUV. Then Sam ducks down. Max goes back inside.

"There's nobody out here. Maybe some flying debris hit the doorbell or it rang for no good reason. I got to get that dumb ass thing fixed." Max starts to close the door hoping to leave it unlocked but Craig pushes him aside.

"Let me look!" Craig shouts. He reaches for the door.

Sam springs forward, uses the side of the Explorer for a springboard and slams the front door into Craig and Max. He shoves the door wide-open knocking Craig and Max backward. Sam lunges and Craig fires the gun just before he falls backward. The bullet hits Sam in the upper chest as they roll onto the floor. Craig's gun bounces on the carpet a few feet away. Sam leaps over Craig and grabs the gun. Sam fires a round into Craig's side as the man leaps for Sam.

"Stay back!" Sam shouts as Craig drops to the floor moaning.

"Wow, Sam my Judo man!" Max shouts.

"Hurry Max!" Sam shouts. He can feel his strength failing with each gush of blood pumping out of his chest. He forces himself to grab the knife and cut the tie-wrap on Max's wrists. Seeing Max is free Sam slumps back on the floor drained of his energy. All he can think about is sleeping. He closes his eyes.

"Sam, what's wrong? Oh no, you're shot!" Max shouts seeing Sam's flowery shirt turning blood red.

"Cut Rose loose and tie up that guy. Just let me lie here Max. Tell Ann I love her. I think I'm going to die!" Sam whispers barely able to speak.

Max frees Rose and grabs the gun. He kneels next to Craig and watches Rose frisk the man pulling some tie wraps from his pocket.

"If he dies, you die!" Max says pointing the gun at Craig's nose.

Rose flips Craig on his stomach and forces his arms behind him. "I'm going to hog-tie this creep!" She shouts.

"Rose, you're bloody too." Max says seeing the cut on her chest.

"Hey, I'm all right, how is Sam?"

"Not good, I think he's hurt bad!"

"Oh Lord, please don't let him die!" Rose blurts. "Call 911 please." Rose looks down at her chest. She pulls the blouse together.

"I will call 911 and stay with Sam. Go in the bathroom and dab that bloody cut. Use some Band-Aids and help yourself to some more of Peggy's clothes." Max says. He watches her turn toward the master bedroom as he sets the gun on the floor and dials 911. Max keeps pressing his hand on Sam's wound keeping more blood from spewing out. He sees Sam open his eyes briefly gasping for air.

"Call Mark, we don't need him now. Will you really kill him if I die Max?"

"Yes I will! You say you called Mark?"

"The police would take too long. Oh!" Sam winces in pain.

"Sam, don't talk anymore. We'll get you to a hospital."

"You know Dan says I'm the wind beneath..." Sam whispers but then his eyes close.

"Hey Sam! Sam don't die!" Max shouts feeling Sam go limp. Max weeps uncontrollably. He presses his head onto Sam's shoulder as Rose comes into the room wearing another pink blouse.

"The rain is coming in." Rose says. She closes the front door.

"Yeah, I'm not sure what to do Rose. It looks like he killed Sam. I think I should kill him right now." Max points the gun at Craig squirming on the floor.

"Give me the gun Max!"

"I really need to kill him!" Max sobs tears pour out blurring his vision, his hand is shaking. He points the gun at Craig and keeps the other hand pressing on Sam's chest.

"Please calm down. Killing him will only make things worse." Rose says. She squeezes his shoulder in sympathy.

"I promised I would kill this creep if Sam dies. I need to kill him!"

"We don't know that Sam is dead. Give me the gun." Rose says trying to ease the gun from Max. As she reaches for the gun Max swings it toward the couch and fires. "Good, you killed the couch!" Rose takes the gun and sees Max bow his head and weep.

"You kill him then!" Max sobs, feeling Rose kneel beside him and hug him. He sits in silence with Rose until she breaks the silence.

"I have to contact Donna Grant's boss." Rose says.

"You know his name?" Max asks regaining his composure.

"Yeah, but I have to get into my apartment. I have a file of names and numbers encrypted on my laptop." She hears Craig cough.

"The rain is pretty bad. Sam is dying or dead. Can it wait?"

"This could be a life or death situation, Max. I remember they mentioned Sara Troutman. I think Medina's girl Friday may be in danger. Donna Grant has to be in on it so I can't call her. I have to call the director to help us. Maybe I can take that Ford in the driveway. I have to go to my apartment. The keys are in the ignition, right?"

"Just cool it Rose. Let's bandage Sam as best we can. We need to stop the bleeding. Go in the kitchen and get the first aid kit."

Max grabs a pillow off the couch as he kneels beside Sam. He props up Sam's head but Sam is limp and his eyes are closed.

"You **will** make it Sam!" Max mumbles, but he has his doubts. Max rips open Sam's shirt. Rose hands him a large gauze pad and he tapes it on Sam's chest. The bleeding doesn't stop so Max presses his hand on the wound.

Rose rolls Craig onto his side. She pulls open his shirt and presses the gauze pad on the wound and tapes the pad in place. Then she kicks him in the groin.

"That's for the cut and the burn mark!" Rose glares at Craig, then turns to Max. "He deserved that! Are you okay Max?"

"This is too much for me Rose!"

"He will live Max." Rose wraps her arms around him.

"I think he's dead!" Max begins sobbing again. He holds pressure on the wound.

"Max, he's not dead if he's still pulsing out blood."

"I need to step away. I'm going outside. Please keep pressure on his wound." Max whispers to Rose. He stands up wipes his eyes and pauses at the front door nearly passing out from the thought of losing his hero Sam.

"He will be okay Max. Go calm down. I'll stay with Sam and the creep." Rose says. She sees Max give a weak wave as he opens the door but he steps from one chaos into another one.

Chapter Forty Six

Max is oblivious to the blast of wet air that hits him as he steps outside wondering what life will be like without Sam. Before he can close the door a man in black wrestles him to the ground. Max tries to talk, but the man has him on his stomach about to cuff him while two armed men rush inside his house.

"Who is inside?" The man shouts at Max.

"Hey, I'm the good guy! The bad guy is tied up inside. Check my wallet." Max feels the man pull out his wallet.

"Oh yeah Mister Merchado, I'm sorry about this, Captain Fred Holland here. We were about to scope through the window, evaluate the situation and break in." Fred says and flashes his badge for Max.

"Hello Captain. I remember you from Clifton Street. This time my friend Sam overpowered the gunman but they shot each other. We tied up the bad guy."

"Clear!" A man shouts from inside.

"The gunman is tied up?"

"Yes, he's hog-tied and wounded. My friend Sam needs emergency help pronto!" Max says. A siren starts whining in the distance. A moment later, an ambulance stops next to the Explorer.

"The paramedics are here. What do you need Max?"

"Get inside! My friend needs help!" Max directs the paramedics and then turns to Captain Holland. "You need to talk to Rose." Max tells Fred and leads the paramedics inside the open door to Sam.

"Tend to this man first!" Max shouts to the paramedics pointing at Sam who he sees is covered with blood and still unresponsive. He watches a medic start an IV for Sam while one man checks his vitals. Max helps lift Sam onto a gurney and pats Sam's shoulder as a medic covers him with a blanket and a waterproof sheet. Max follows as they roll Sam out the door into the rain. He watches them slide Sam into the ambulance.

"Will he live?" Max asks the man closing the ambulance doors.

"He lost a lot of blood. It looks bad. He could possibly make it if we stop the bleeding and nothing major is damaged. We must get him to the hospital!"

Max stands in the rain watching them take Sam away with sirens blaring. Hatred wells up in Max. He feels helpless to fix things, and angry he is losing his best friend.

He goes back inside and sees Craig Benito, alias Paul Watson, standing up with his tie-wraps off, handcuffs on and a smile on his face. Max watches a paramedic finish re-bandaging Craig's wound. Unable to control his rage, Max steps in front of the paramedic who is finishing his patch job on Craig.

"You killed my friend!" Max shouts and delivers a right cross to Craig's jaw. Bleary-eyed and livid, Max grits his teeth seeing Craig drop unconscious to the floor. An officer pulls him away from Craig.

"No Sir!" The officer shouts. "Oh, did he hurt you?"

Max is stunned by his own violent action. Then as a paramedic wraps Max in a blanket, he rubs his sore fist and murmurs. "Yes."

Max answers questions as best he can all the time thinking about how life will be if Sam dies because of this gunman. He thinks about all the great adventures he enjoyed with Sam and how much fun he had catching fish just this morning. *Please God let him live! If Sam dies, this guy dies!* Max whispers to himself as they carry Craig Bonito out of his house. He starts conjuring up ways to torture and kill the man.

Rose fidgets with her hands answering questions about the gunman and acting as ignorant as she can. She is committed to watching all the video and contacting Langston before the police get involved with why a man would try to kill them. It is eight o'clock by the time the questioning is over and she waves good-bye to the police.

Max notices his wet clothes and he feels his body reacting to Rose as he wraps an arm around her and she snuggles closer to him.

"You know this isn't over Max. Matuso will send someone else. I think it's time I watch the videos. I want to see what else I recorded."

"I want to watch the video too."

"It's confidential Max. You shouldn't." Rose looks up at him.

"I'm as deep in this as you are. Let me watch it." Max stares into her green eyes.

Rose feels her heart pounding. She melts. "Okay Max." She says and follows Max into the garage. She climbs the ladder again. She retrieves the recorder from the attic and stuffs it in her bra before easing back down to the floor.

Back in the living room, Max turns on his laptop and holds out his hand toward Rose. He smiles as she takes out the micro-camcorder and gives it to him. Max plugs a USB cable into the camcorder, opens a file, and turns up the volume.

The first image he sees is Rose's face full in the camera and then a view of the couch. He watches the men enter the room noting how big Matuso is and how clear the images are for such a small camera. Max watches Matuso start talking to Sancho and then the door opens. He sees Victor come in before the tussle with Rose and Matuso tossing her overboard. However, then he sees another bazaar scene. After the window is closed Rafael Matuso calls Donna Grant and tells her what he did! Then he tells her details of his plan.

"He plans to murder Sara Troutman this weekend!" Max blurts.

"That's why Donna thought I was dead!" Rose shouts. "Matuso told her he killed me! Also, I didn't think he would mur-der Troutman! Donna said she is in Atlanta meeting with our leader Walter Langston. I have to talk with him. There is a contacts file encrypted on my computer. I have to go home!"

"It's nasty outside Rose. The storm is bound to be worse in Miami. I mean the wind gusts could be dangerous. If your boss is with her boss, you should wait until they are alone. We shouldn't go out in this rain."

"Max, you can stay here but I have to go. I have to talk to her boss. Remember the kill is for this weekend. I'd use the SUV but the cops took it away."

"It was a stolen vehicle. They towed it."

"Well I must go, please call a taxi for me."

"No, let the cops handle it now. You told them everything right?"

"No, if I told them about this they would arrest Matuso and he would cancel his plan. I want them caught as someone tries to kill Troutman so there is no doubt. I give this to the cops and all we get is maybe Matuso for attempted murder. Some liberal lawyer can argue I recorded them without their consent and get the video thrown out of court. Then it is their word against mine and he gets off. No, I have a better plan Max. I need to get the number for Langston and talk to him first. I have to get home."

"You have no money or ID Rose. How will you manage?"

"When I frisked that guy, I found a wad of money in his pocket. I counted several hundred. I figure I earned it from him."

"You stole his money?" Max shakes his head.

"I borrowed it. He can't use it in jail. Please call a cab Max."

"I'll take you." Max blurts.

"That's crazy Max. You want to go to Sam. Your car might get beat up if stuff flies around. We need cabs!"

"I've been thinking Rose and timing is important. Maybe we can save a life. I want to take down these bastards as much as you do! I'm ready for a new car anyhow. The Corvette is much lower to the ground. I doubt if the wind affects it at all. I'll take my .45 gun along. We'll be alright Rose. Let's do it!" Max says.

"Max, these guys are nasty and they play for keeps. You think you can handle that?" She sees Max nod yes. "Then bring a flashlight. Let's go!" Rose says bouncing with excitement.

"I swear you look like a cute Energizer Bunny hopping up and down." Max smirks. Even in his grief and anger, Max manages a smile for Rose.

"Very funny Max. Can we go now?"

"Let's hide the camcorder back in the attic first."

"Why?"

"In case something happens to us, Sam will look for it there."

"What if he…"

"Dies? That's a chance we have to take. We could all die and then it wouldn't matter. I pray we all live Rose."

"Okay, same place right?"

"Yup, let's stuff it and go."

After hiding the camcorder Max grabs two of the raincoats and gives one to Rose before they slide in his Corvette. Even with the windows up, Max hears the garage door open and creak in protest as a gust of wind swirls inside the garage. Max backs the car out and says a silent 'thank you' seeing the garage door go all the way down. He drives with wipers on, headlights, and fog lights illuminating sheets of rain beating on his windshield as he eases away from his house onto Lux Lane. Max turns onto Blue Lake Boulevard, through the open gates of Blue Lake Estates zigzagging to avoid some small debris in the street, and turns onto Federal Highway southbound.

The tropical storm wind gusts buffet the side of the car as it glides along the roadway. Driving slower than normal, it is nine in the evening when Max arrives at the Gatsby Apartments on 12th Street. He sees the black van is gone and the power is off. The dark parking lot is only half-full of cars.

Max parks in front of the building entrance and shuts down the Corvette. The sky is black. In the darkness, he sees some trash and rain swirl around in the wind each time lightning illuminates the area. The rain, the lightning, and the constant rumble of thunder makes Max think. *This place gives me the creeps!*

Chapter Forty Seven

Rose taps Max on his shoulder to get his attention. "May I have your gun and flashlight?" She slips an arm into the raincoat and pokes an open hand toward Max. She wiggles into the rest of the raincoat and then takes the gun from Max. Then he hands her his flashlight.

"This is an LED flashlight. It should shine for hours. Surely you want me to go too?" He says after he gives her the flashlight.

"No, you've taken enough risks, and just like the Captain said in the 'Airplane' movie, don't call me Shirley!" She gives a weak laugh.

"I protest." Max says not laughing with her.

"If someone is still waiting for me, they should only shoot at me." Rose checks that the gun is properly loaded before stuffing it in her waistband.

"Okay, but if you're not out in ten minutes..."

"You'll do what, come to help without a gun or anything?"

"Okay, but if someone suspicious goes in I will blow my horn."

"Thanks please watch my back from here. I can handle myself. The power is off so my internet will be down too. Maybe when I get back you can drive me to my car. I'll look at the video on my laptop and find a WIFI somewhere. Hang in here." She says forgetting the camera is in Fort Lauderdale. She kisses Max's cheek before leaving.

Rose buttons up the slicker, and takes a deep breath before she opens the door and runs across the sidewalk. She leans into a gust of wind that tries to push her sideways. Her face and hands sting from sudden hard rain. After dashing inside the apartment building Rose leans against a wall and sighs.

She readies the .45 Smith & Wesson and scans the dimly lit stairway. Most of the old emergency batteries are drained and the incandescent lights are out, so she stands still in the semi-darkness. The outside door closes shutting out most of the noise from the gusty wind and rain. Rose listens for any noises. Only one dim light is on in the first-floor hallway. The second-floor stairway has one newer LED light shining bright. Hearing and seeing nothing, she starts up the stairs to the third floor.

One hall light on the third floor is still on but dim, lighting the passageway that is as long as a football field. She sees no one in the hallway so she heads for her apartment midway along the right side. All the apartment doors are recessed and Rose treks by one recess to the next. As she gets closer to her door, she stops to listen intently. She hears the faint howling of the wind and rain bouncing on the windows at the end of the hallway.

Rose sees her apartment door isn't completely closed. She cocks the gun hammer and reaches out, swings the door wide open, and points the gun and the light beam inside. The beam first lights up an empty couch. With the windows shuttered for the possible hurricane and no lights, her apartment is pitch-black. Rose sweeps the flashlight beam around but sees no one.

After making sure she is alone, Rose closes her door and flips on the deadbolt. She slides a metal trash can against the front door knowing it will make a racket if anyone picks the lock and tries to come in. She scans her once neat apartment. A flash of lightning stabs through slats in the shutters, revealing books and knickknacks strewn about on the floor. The most obvious thing missing is her laptop from her metal desk, and she sees the desk drawers open and her backup thumb drives are gone along with some of her files.

"Damn! I'll have to get my extra backups."

She uncocks the gun and stuffs it in her waist. She opens a step stool in the kitchen, climbs on it, and lifts the third ceiling tile from the pantry corner. Rose reaches on top of the next tile and smiles feeling the small Ziploc bag of thumb drives and her 9 mm Glock pistol. She temporarily stuffs the bag and the Glock in her waist and takes a quick breath when the cold steel of her gun touches her abdomen. Rose replaces the tile and puts away the step stool.

Using the flashlight to guide her, Rose walks to her bedroom. She sheds the raincoat and strips off everything. Rose selects some shear powder blue underwear, a light blue cotton blouse and denim shorts, puts on her own clothes and laces up her black sneakers. Next, Rose takes out her spare keys from the Ziploc bag and stuffs them in her pants pocket along with the thumb drives and the wad of money from the gunman. She shoves the .45 pistol and the 9 mm Glock in her waistband and drapes her blouse over them. Her shorts struggle to stay up with the weight of the two guns.

Rose leaves the bedroom shining the flashlight ahead of her. "What a mess I have to clean up!" Rose whispers then as she approaches the door to leave she hears a car horn honking but not in the usual way a triggered alarm would sound. Rose peers through a gap in the window shutter and sees Max frantically waving through his car windshield. "Someone is coming inside! I knew we shouldn't have talked about going to my apartment in front of Paul! I bet he called Matuso!" She whispers and rushes to her door to leave.

She turns off the flashlight, stuffs it in her pocket, and peeks outside her apartment. The hallway is dark and silent. The only illumination is from the weak emergency light close to her door. Rose checks both directions listening to the wind howl from the stairwells at each end before she eases out of her apartment, closes her door, and starts toward the stairs a hundred feet away. Then she hears a loud pop and the emergency light goes out. *Was that a gunshot?* Rose wonders. With no more lights, Rose is plunged into darkness. For a second, all she sees is black.

Rose instinctively flattens into a neighbor's door recess along the wall and draws out her Glock. She stands still letting her eyes adjust to the dark and listens intently. The only sound is the wind and rain pounding on the distant windows. *Is someone already here? Did I hear something move when that light went out?* She thinks. Her eyes adjust to the pitch-blackness so she can see shadows of doorways and the faint light coming from the stairwell. She starts to edge toward the stairs when a door opens ahead of her, spewing a beam of light into the hallway and she hears shuffling. She hides in another door recess and sees the light beam sweep past her. When she peeks out, she sees a man standing maybe thirty feet in front of her shining a light away from her toward the stairs. A woman limps out behind the man and closes a door. Rose swings the gun flat against the wall still keeping her finger next to the trigger. The couple seems unaware of her as they walk toward the stairwell swinging the light beam back and forth ahead of them.

"I've never used the stairs before. I hope I can manage." The woman says as she holds onto the man and hobbles.

"I will help you Marge. We have to get to the hospital right now!" The man says.

Rose creeps behind them tiptoeing from one door recess to the next. Watching them walk to the stairs and open the exit door. Then a man passes them as they try to enter the stairwell door.

"Hello mister. Too bad the power is off isn't it?" The woman says. She waits for comment but gets none from the man. "Well, good luck finding your way."

Rose waits for the stairwell door to close but she sees the man come into the hallway shining a beam of light nearly catching her in sight. She ducks into a recess before he sweeps his light beam by her. Her heart pounds heavy in her chest as she hides in the recess waiting. She can tell the man is approaching by the angle of the light beam he swings back and forth and his footsteps grow louder. He steps alongside her before he realizes

Rose is standing in a door recess. The man starts to swing his gun toward her.

Rose chops at his arm with her fist forcing him to drop the gun onto the walkway. He swings the flashlight at Rose but she ducks and lands a punch in his stomach. She sees his flashlight fly out of his hand and rattle onto the floor. In the semi-darkness, Rose swings the butt of her Glock hard-hitting the man on his skull. She watches him crumble to the floor.

"I've got to get out of here!" Rose says. She reaches for her flashlight but it fell out of her pocket in the tussle. Rose feels around the floor where she saw his gun land, she finds it and takes the gun with her. Not wanting to waste time she feels her way along the wall in the darkness finally reaching the stairs. Rose cracks open the stairwell door and watches the couple ease out the exit below. She feels the air whoosh until the door slams shut. Rose uses light from the second-floor emergency light to help her see the way as she rushes down the stairs.

Chapter Forty Eight

Max sits in the car in the dark, feeling the wind occasionally rock the car and the rain pelt the windshield as he waits for Rose to come out. He checks his Jaeger-LeCoultre watch seeing it is after nine. Sitting in the dark, Max tries talking to himself about fishing to ease his mind but he reverts to thinking about fishing Rose out of the ocean. He tries to garner some comfort from talking to himself, but he only makes himself more anxious.

"So what do you think about our main catch for the day Max? Oh, she's a lot prettier than any fish, and she's strong as an ox. I saw the way she wrestled with that Matuso guy in the video. She must work out a lot, nice body! I think I have a crush on her. The trouble is Rose works for the FBI and I'm in more trouble than I want. Now I understand why Sam is leery of redheads. I remember his girlfriend Jessica in Denver. She hurt him when she dumped him." Max rambles on continuing to reminisce.

"I remember trying to fix a non-problem in Jamaica and almost got shot. Then, the bad guys shot at us when we returned that big diamond. Now I'm trying to expose some bad guys and Sam is shot again. This is like strike three and yes I'm worried about what will happen next."

Max is about to recall more adventures when he sees a black car speed in the parking area. He ducks down and watches the car park near his car. Then a tall man gets out and rushes to the apartment door, stops to check a hand gun, and slips inside the building. Max panics and starts pressing his horn over and over and waving through his windshield hoping Rose will see his warning.

A horrendous bang of thunder and a blinding flash of lightning makes Max jump in his seat. He gasps and turns toward the boom to see the giant oak tree at the entrance make a crackling noise, uproot, and crash on top of two cars. The tree bounces once and settles across the only exit for the parking lot.

"Oh no!" Max shouts. He stares at the tree wondering how he will get out. Then he sees the exit door open.

"I hope this is Rose!" Max says thinking she is coming out but he sees an older couple rush out and hobble through the rain to a small sedan. The car aims for the exit and then stops. After a pause, the car turns around and drives away from the tree.

"Who are these people? Where are you Rose? Did you get my warning?" Max tenses up.

He watches the sedan drive off the pavement and onto the grass. It edges its way onto the grass strip between the building and the parking lot. The car drives all the way across the strip, around the top of the tree, and onto the street.

Max can wait no longer. He reaches for the door handle but stops. *You're not trying to go after Rose are you?* Max remembers Rose's warning. *I have no gun or anything but I must help her.* In spite of all the reasons not to go, Max jumps out of his car. He starts toward the building and then sees Rose come out.

"Thank God!" Max says seeing her red hair whip about in the wind. He turns around and hustles back inside the car.

Max reaches across and opens the door for Rose.

"What happened in there? You have three guns."

"Yes, one is from the gunman, one is mine. Let's get the Hell out of here!"

Max backs out of his parking slot and drives away from the exit.

"Thanks for the horn warning. What are you doing?" Rose shouts then sees the downed tree. "Oh no!"

"I have a plan to get out."

"I hope so." She opens the raincoat revealing her new clothes.

"I guess you were tired of pink." Max chuckles.

"What the Hell were you doing out of the car?"

"I was coming to your rescue."

"That could have been suicide Max!"

"I was worried about you."

"I appreciate the thought, but to quote you guys, that was a dumb ass idea. Do you think I'm so inept that I can't handle myself? You could have compromised my position. I may have had to rescue you! That's why I work alone Max, you civilians screw up things. You could have been killed!" Rose tries to convince herself with talk that Max is bad for her, but in her mind Rose thinks. *I love him for trying! No Rose! You can't love this guy!*

"It's a chance I was willing to take. I'm sorry Rose." He sees her anger subside.

"Okay, that was brave and stupid Max, but it was a sweet thing to do." Rose leans over and kisses his cheek.

"Thanks! So what took so long? Did you find your laptop?"

"No, my apartment is ransacked. Most of the emergency lights are off too."

"That must have been the van guy that messed up your place."

"Yeah, he took my laptop and my backup discs Max, but he didn't get my extra backup discs. I will have to use some other computer to see the list. If you take me to my car at the marina, this mess will be over for you. I have my own clothes, spare keys, and my own gun and stuff. Once I find a computer and contact Grant's boss my job is over. Langston can set up a sting." Rose says. She takes the 9 mm Beretta from her waist and sets it on the floorboard. Then she gives the Smith & Wesson .45 back to Max.

"You do remember your video recorder is in my attic?"

"Damn! We should have taken that with us!"

"I'm glad we left it at my house."

"You could have been free of me Max."

"I thought by now you would know I want to be with you."

"I will do fine by myself but then... I'm worried about you."

"And me of you." Max says. They stare at each other for an awkward long time before Max asks. "Do you always backup stuff more than once?"

"Yes, I rotate through the backups. Doesn't everyone?" Rose looks confused.

"I don't think so." Max pauses before he continues. "Also, I have a great laptop at my house and the power is on there. You can get Mr. Langston's number and call from there, even send the video to him. Your car might be too dangerous. Grant or Matuso may have someone watching it. They want to find you at any cost! I can take you to get your car after the bad guys are caught."

"I know but I should leave you. I've already put Sam in the hospital and you in grave danger. I just hope Sam is alive. I work better alone Max and you need to see Sam. Oh, but..."

"But what?"

"The problem is Matuso is aware by now that you know too much so he will send another hit man after you. I guess we both should hide somewhere until the lid blows off this thing."

"Yes, we are better off staying together. I think he will definitely go after all of us, including Sam." Max says.

"You told that creep Paul that Sam was dead when you punched him. I'm sure he will tell Matuso that Sam is dead. So for now he will only be after us."

"Oh, I hope Sam is alive!" Max bows his head and feels Rose squeeze his shoulder.

"He will live Max." Rose forces confidence in her voice.

"We are better off staying together. You know, two heads are better than one..."

"That makes it easier for someone to knock us off all at once, but it's your call." Rose stares at Max. She talks tough but inside she melts when Max looks at her.

"I say we stay together and we go back to my house, you make your call and then we go to the hospital." Max says.

"Yes!" Rose flashes a smile.
"So we go to my place?" Max asks.
"Yes." Rose nods.

Chapter Forty Nine

"I can use your laptop, get the phone list, call the director and give him the bombshell to handle. Then I want to go with you to see Sam." Rose says.

"Next stop is 250 Lux Lane. That tree got hit by lightning. The only way out is the same way that car went a while ago."

Max looks at the narrow strip of grass between the parking slots and the building that the sedan just drove across. It looks wide enough to drive his car through to the open road past the top of the tree.

"Those oaks are beautiful but deadly." Rose says. "You never know when one will topple over just like that one did and kill someone. You think you can go around it?"

"That sedan drove over that strip of grass next to the building. I think I can too."

"If they can do it, you can Max."

"This car is awful low to the ground but we have to try."

Max drives into the rain across the parking lot. With his wipers on full speed, he aims for the narrow strip of grass at the end of the lot away from the tree. He drives onto the grass following the fence line and turns in front of the grass strip between the parking lot concrete barrier strips and the building. Max can see two deep furrows the sedan made going across the soft grass.

"I have to straddle one of those ruts." Max says.

Building up as much speed as he can without spinning his tires he drives onto the grass. Max picks the rut closest to the building to straddle thinking the ground will be more solid there. He senses his wheels sinking and hears the bottom intermittently scraping on the waterlogged grass. Still a long way off, his car continues to slide along the soft grass jerking forward, then slowing down. Max spins the tires and backs off the gas to let the tires grip again. A strong gust of wind bumps the side of his car. Max keeps rolling feeling the car slowing with each foot closer to the road. The car is barely at a crawl when it reaches the end of the grassy patch. Max edges the car onto the more solid yard between the top branches of the tree and the corner of the building and maneuvers the car through the exit area. He reaches the tar road and leaves the Gatsby Apartments.

"We made it, good job Max!" Rose cheers. She looks back at the building and sees the gunman stager outside and run to a car.

"Thanks, now let's go home!"

On the trek from Miami, Max dodges bits of debris across some of the streets. A small plastic garbage can skids in front of the car and flies off in a gust of wind as Max turns into his subdivision. The black road contrasts the bright Blue Lake Estates sign. Max drives through the open gates onto Blue Lake Boulevard toward Lux Lane only three blocks to go.

"I guess they are leaving the gates open in case the hurricane shifts direction and we lose power. Thank God we made it and we do have power here!" Max exhales in relief.

"You did a great job Max."

"Yeah, we nearly got hit by a flying trash can. I thought by now everything would have found somewhere to lodge."

"Okay Max, let's get to your computer."

"My super laptop is still in the living room."

"Oh no keep going straight! There is a black SUV parked along the curb by your house with a man inside!"

Max stays on Blue Lake Boulevard. He sees the man in the SUV who appears to be talking on a cell phone.

"What do we do now?" Max asks.

"Get out of here! I'll have to find a computer somewhere else!"

"Whoa Rose, we have a problem."

"What now?"

"Well your camcorder is in my attic!"

"Oh yeah, 'leave it in the attic' you said. That was a brilliant idea, not!"

"Sorry Rose. Well that SUV is actually next to Chet's house. Maybe he just stopped to make a call. We have to get the camcorder!" Then his phone rings with a blocked caller ID. Max answers in speaker mode.

"Hello, is this Mister Merchado?" Max feels a chill run up his spine realizing this is the woman wanting to kill them.

"That's Donna Grant!" Rose whispers and grabs for the phone.

Max is barely able to fend off Rose with the limited space in the Corvette. He raises a stiff arm to defend the phone and takes a deep breath before speaking.

"Yes, this is Max, what do you want?"

"Mister Merchado is Rose Finley with you?"

"Who is this? Ow!" Max says feeling his hair pulled by Rose. He grabs her arm to stop her.

"This is Florida FBI Director Donna Grant. I need to talk to Rose Finley now!"

"Just a minute..." Max says and mutes the phone so he can wrestle with Rose who is frantically pestering him. "I know you're mad at Donna Grant but..."

"Yes, I want to blast her!" Rose grumbles, her fists clenched and her face distraught.

"Whoa! Calm down. Think first Rose. Don't get mad. She can't have us killed until she secures the video recorder. Tell her you are willing to talk but she has to call off the Troutman thing or you will take the recorder to the police. It could buy us some precious time. What do you think, can you do that?" Max waits with his arm raised and ready to fend off another attack. He watches Rose change from wild anger to a more calm control, her rapid breathing slows down.

Rose takes several deep breaths and finally relaxes. Her face lightens up. "I'm okay now. I can do this. Yes, give me the phone."

"Here she is." Max unmutes the phone and hands it to Rose.

"Hello boss. I'm still alive and your man is in jail!"

"My man? I had no say in that. What do you want Rose?"

"Oh I think maybe the police will be interested in a video I have. They would love to see Matuso tossing me in the ocean and then talk to you about his plan for Troutman."

"You know I was just playing along with Matuso. I'm not really on his side. You saved that recorder somehow, and I know you didn't give it to the police, that's good. The FBI should handle this. I'm trying to uncover these guys too. Let me have it and I can use it against them. Let the forces of the FBI handle this Rose."

"I want to give it to the police in Fort Lauderdale because I don't trust you or the Miami cops! The police I give it to in Miami may be on your side!"

"That's unfair Rose. Listen, Sancho and Matuso were out of line with what they did. I never would order them to kill you, believe me. I'm trying to nail Sancho just like you are."

"I saw him tell you that he planned to kill Troutman. Have you ordered the arrest of Sancho or Matuso?"

"No."

"I told you he tried to kill me and you did nothing! You're as corrupt as they are!"

"I have to wait until I have the recorder for evidence. Rose, you have to give me that recorder. I promise nothing will happen to you, just turn it in."

"You expect me to believe you?"

"You can't survive out there Rose. Matuso's people will find you and your friend and you know what he is capable of doing."

"Well, I can give the video to the police right now. You can explain it to them."

"What do you want?"

"I want you to stop the hit on Troutman, and then call me!"

"That's impossible Rose! Give me what I want and I guarantee no one will harm you. Hell, you're one of my best agents Finley. Don't let this spoil a great career."

"Call off the hit Ms. Grant. Then call me within 24 hours or the video goes to the cops. Understand?"

"I'm not sure I can do that." Donna Grant stops talking to think.

"Talk to Matuso, find a way!" Rose shouts into the phone.

"I'll see what I can do."

"Stop it, or I go public." Rose disconnects. She laughs aloud at the phone and then sees Max's worried face.

"Okay we can't stay at my house. What do we do now?"

"We have to get the recorder!"

"How can we get it?"

"If I don't have it there is no sense calling Langston. Maybe I can go in the back side of your house."

"Yes, I have a rear door into the kitchen."

"That will do. Let's hope the SUV guy isn't looking for us. Drop me off on the street behind your house. I can slip in your house. What is the alarm code?"

"I forgot to set it when we left. I'm not sure I even locked the front door. I want to go with you this time."

"Max, you'd get drenched again and possibly killed if that guy comes in the house. Besides, I like to work alone!"

"What's one more drenching? You need me to watch your back. You're alone too much already Rose. I want to be with you and I have my .45 now. I'm going!"

"You should stay with the car."

"I can park on Falcon Lane behind my house. The car will be out of sight. I know you would be better off with Sam and his black belt Judo thing but I can handle myself too. You may need help. I'm going with you."

"Max, please let's not both run out in the rain. No offense Max, it really would be better if Mister Judo were here."

"Sam may be dead." Max turns away shocked by his own words.

"He will live Max. He is strong." Rose leans on his shoulder until he speaks.

"I say we just get inside as soon as we can, get the recorder and watch the video. That guy in the van may not even be a problem."

"Okay, okay just park behind your house somewhere."

Chapter Fifty

When Matuso heard from his number two man who failed to capture Rose at her apartment, he directed his last hope the ax-man to wait at Max's house in case Max and Rose came back there.

Jose Xavier nicknamed the Axe-man sits in his SUV along the curb parked on Lux Lane near Max's house facing Blue Lake Boulevard. He has already looked inside Max's house, found no one, and noted the Corvette was missing from the garage.

Jose is tuned to his favorite Seventies channel on XM radio. His attention diverts from listening and watching the rain pelt his windshield when he sees a red Corvette go by on Blue Lake Boulevard. He thinks maybe it is Max, but it glides past Lux Lane going somewhere else. After listening to the end of Eric Clapton's 'Layla' he turns up the volume on the Eagles "Hotel California". He closes his eyes to enjoy the song.

Max parks his red Corvette on the street behind Max's house.

"You go first" Rose shouts. "I'll follow you. Go!" Rose waits for Max to run into the rain and follows Max. A wind gust nearly tips her over as she sprints across the yard of 251 Falcon Lane and into the back yard of Max's house. Another gust of wind flips open her unbuttoned raincoat as she runs to the door. The rain pelts her front side and she joins Max in the kitchen sopping wet.

"Good grief! It looks like your raincoat was open too!" Max shouts shaking water off as best he can. He sees Rose is soaked also, dripping rainwater onto the floor. Her drenched blouse and denim shorts cling to her body like spandex.

"Shush! Someone may have heard us come in." Rose peeks from the kitchen into the dining room and living room listening for noises. Then she nods okay to Max.

"We should shed some water before we go through the living room." Max says.

Rose nods and removes her raincoat revealing her soaked blouse. She wrings out some of the water from the bottom of her blouse and considers removing it.

"You can strip off everything and borrow some more clothes from Peggy." Max jokes admiring Rose as he removes his shirt.

"I'm not taking off any clothes Max!" Rose giggles.

"It's just a suggestion." Max laughs. He suddenly feels an uncontrollable attraction to Rose. Max tries to brush it off but flexes his muscles as he wrings out his shirt in the kitchen sink. "Let's get the recorder and get out of here."

"God, you're gorgeous!" Rose blurts and immediately stretches her arms out toward Max. "I'm sorry! I shouldn't say that sort of..."

Rose feels Max grab her arms and pull her to him, and without a word, she feels his arms around her and his lips press on hers. Her hands reach out and cradle his back. She clings to a long tender kiss with Max. Her mind is full of joy. She tilts her head back when Max sweeps her off her feet. Rose smiles as Max carries her through the kitchen, the living room, the hall, and into the master bedroom, paying no attention to anything else.

"Are you sure this is okay with Hera?" Rose whispers as Hera jumps off the bed and runs out of the room.

"She would be growling at you if it wasn't." Max gently lets Rose stand up.

"I was kidding Max but I'm glad she isn't mad at me."

Rose touches Max's arms, looks into his eyes, and kisses him on the lips. Then she unbuttons her blouse and shorts and drops them to the floor thinking. *What are you doing Girl?* She impulsively backs away but then she strips off the rest of her clothes and watches Max do the same. Rose stretches across the king-size bed and sees Max lie down alongside her. She feels his lips on her again and feels him caress her eager body. Rose pulls him on top of her and feels him inside her. All her expectations of making love to Max come true. She laughs with joy working with Max until she knows they are both satisfied. Rose smiles as Max rolls next to her breathing harder than normal. She rolls partly onto him, kisses him on the cheek, and stares into his brown eyes.

Max is lost in the world of Rose. He knows Rose is beautiful and yet dangerous! The excitement in the kitchen of seeing her soaking wet and her crazy comment was too much for Max to ignore. *Peggy split up with me*. Max admits to himself as he deals with his attraction to Rose. He rests a few minutes before re-membering what they need to do. Max starts to remind Rose about the micro-camcorder but she gets up and rushes into the bathroom. He hears the shower run. As if some force directs him, Max trots into the bathroom and joins Rose in the shower. He sees her eyes close and her head tip up as he caresses her and kisses her under the spray. Then she pulls away.

"We have to stop. Someone may still be watching your house. We have to get to the camcorder and call Langston!" Rose whis-pers as she kisses him on the neck. Then she leaves him in the shower. He finishes washing and dries off. In the bedroom, he watches Rose put on more of Peggy's clothes.

Rose slips on her own sneakers after dressing in some dry clothes and stuffs her Glock handgun in her waistband. She waits for Max and follows him to the garage.

"Rose, I tried not to do anything but you overwhelm me. I know being with you isn't what you want but would this happen if you had no feelings for me?" Max asks stepping into the gar-age.

"I don't know Max. All I know is what we did is foolish. We should have used protection for one thing."

"I don't have any STDs, do you?"

"No, it's not that. I controlled my urges for a long time, if you can call many hours a long time. I seem to have totally lost my brain. I think it is the dip in the ocean when I thought I would die that messed me up. It changed me but I still think I'm better off alone. I will only put you in danger like now. Please stay away from me!"

"I get it Rose, but that doesn't mean I don't want you. My brain was fried when I thought that guy was going to kill us. I'm okay with whatever we did and whatever we do because I think I love you."

"That must not happen Max. You love Peggy."

"I agree, but I love you too."

"Promise me you won't tell her about what happened no matter what. This will be our secret. Let's get the camcorder and laptop and do what we have to do."

"Right you are ma'am! But if you ever get tired of being alone call me." Max leads her through the living room to the garage door.

"You are a civilian. I will never endanger you again Max."

"Never say never, Rose."

Max grabs the ladder and sets it up under the attic access hole. He enjoys his view of her tight pink shorts that cling to her like a coat of pink paint as she climbs.

Rose slides the cover back and retrieves the micro-camcorder and stuffs it in her bra. She replaces the cover but as she steps down, her wet sneaker slips off a rung.

Max sees her falling and catches her in his arms as if he were planning to carry her away. His mind freezes as he holds her with her eyes and lips inches away from his.

"Wow, you saved my life again!" Rose says. Without asking, she opens her mouth and presses her lips to his. She feels Max devour her kiss as he eases her onto her feet and embraces her. Rose wraps her arms around Max feeling her passion explode again. She presses hard against him and she can tell Max is excited too.

Chapter Fifty One

After his favorite song ends the Axe-man scans the area once more. He sees a red Corvette parked on the street behind Max's house. *I think they snuck inside!* Axe-man rushes out of his SUV. He takes out his gun before he pushes the front door open.

Rose backs away starting to unbutton her blouse when she feels the air whoosh like a door opening. She changes to defense and forces herself to deal with the new situation.

"I think someone came in!" Rose whispers, buttoning her blouse.

"I know!" Max says as he tiptoes behind Rose to the open door.

"You flatten against the wall. I'll go see who's there."

"No, I have a gun too. Let me go!" Max whispers.

"You stay. I go." Rose whispers as she grabs her 9 mm Glock and slides the safety off.

Rose knows they must cross the living room and the dining room to get to the kitchen and the rear door. Rose slinks into the living room listening and looking for any motions. Hearing nothing, she starts across the floor heading for the kitchen exposing her to the hallway. From the edge of her vision, she detects motion from the hallway and ducks just in time to hear two pops from a gun. The bullets bang into the wall behind her. She instinctively rolls and fires toward the sound. Rose leaps sideways as another bullet grazes her side and hits the wall. She sees a man peek from a bedroom door, and fires toward him.

"All I want is the recorder! Give me that and I will leave!" Ax-man shouts.

"Ah!" Rose shouts feeling the hot sting from her wound. She presses her hand over the wound and fires another shot at the bedroom before swinging back into the garage. Rose sinks to the floor against the wall, blood oozing onto her hand and blouse.

"You're shot!" Max shouts seeing the blood as she sits with her gun in her lap. He crouches next to her wanting to do something, but she waves him off.

"It's just a flesh wound. I think the bullet went through clean. We need to get out of here! The man is hiding in a bedroom for now. We have the recorder. If we stay here he will come after us!" Rose says.

"Wait a minute!" Max takes some gauze and tape from a first aid kit by the door. He feels her head press onto his chest.

"What are you doing?" Rose says feeling Max lift up her blouse.

He closes his eyes for a second imagining what it would be like to make love to her right now, but he suppresses the urge.

"Let me look. The bullet just clipped your side." He dabs some alcohol on the cut that is already trying to seal up the oozing blood. He wipes away the blood and presses a bandage over the wound.

"Ouch! Thank you Max. Oh my!" Rose blurts covering her mouth with a hand.

"What? Did I hurt you?"

"It's okay Max, but what if that guy came in a little earlier!"

"We'd be dead!" Max says and stares into her eyes in awe.

"We must have a guardian angel looking out for us Max." Rose whispers. She peeks into the living room. The man is easing out of a bedroom and coming toward her in the hallway. Rose fires hitting him in the shoulder. He falls, and Rose seizes the chance to get away.

"Max come now!" She waves at Max and starts across the living room. As the intruder crawls toward his dropped gun, Rose hears Max fire several rounds. She runs behind Max across the open area firing again toward where she saw the man as she crosses the dining room and glances into the hallway. Rose isn't sure where the man is because she sees Max fire a shaky shot at the living room hitting the couch. *Did the guy run behind the couch?* She wonders as she scurries into the kitchen behind Max.

"Let's go!" Rose shouts. She bumps into Max, gives him a quick kiss on the cheek, and pushes him toward the rear door.

"You shouldn't kiss me anymore!" Max says as he rushes across the kitchen. He follows Rose outside running into the rain. Max waits until Rose closes her car door before he enters to prevent the rain from blowing through the car. As he starts the car, he looks at Rose and laughs. "We forgot our raincoats. We are both sopping wet again!"

Max sees a man lean out the side of his house and point a gun at him. He shifts into gear and spins the tires speeding away. He races onto Blue Lake Boulevard and out of Blue Lake Estates, his mind worries about the gunman as he stops for a red light. Max also worries about what he will tell Peggy. Then Rose interrupts his thinking.

"Are you okay Max?"

"Yeah, I was just thinking about how this will all end."

"Whatever happens, it was meant to be."

"You mean like Kismet?" Max asks as he turns toward her.

"Sort of, or maybe fate brought us together."

"You think meeting you wasn't an accident?"

"Yes, but I don't know why. Oh, that kiss before we left was just a thank you for helping me and patching me up." Rose says as she adjusts her gun in her waistband. She feels her passion swell up barely able to hide the glow she feels all over.

"You know if things were different Rose...Why am I waiting for this red light?" Max shouts seeing the streets are deserted. He speeds through the intersection.

"And you know when I fell from the ladder and kissed you, you kissed me back Max. We can't be doing that anymore." Rose says as she flaps the blouse over her Glock and shrugs implying the kiss was nothing. In her gut though, she wishes she could jump his bones again right now!

"You are right. I have to be careful Rose. You are so close and so beautiful and sexy… and passionate! I want to love you, but I need to know what Peggy wants."

"Hey to paraphrase a Vegas ad, what happens in Max's house, stays in Max's house. Peggy will never know of our secret tryst. So what do we do now?"

Rose puts on a blank face trying to act calm. Inside her heart is still pounding and her mind is reeling from his kisses. *If only I could be with him, but you know you aren't right for him. But, we could mess around forever! If only…* Then Max interrupts her.

"You know, I either forgot to lock that front door or that man found my spare key under a fake rock out front. I wanted to change the key locks for combo locks ever since I bought that house. I think I'll do that as soon as I can."

"Maybe when you forgot to set the alarm, you forgot to lock the door too."

"I'll check the fake rock after the storm. I'm going to Sam's apartment. You can use his laptop."

"Great! I hope you can get in."

"No problem. I have the combo lock code and the alarm code."

"Really?"

"Yes, Sam told me the codes in case I have an emergency and need to get in when no one is home. We'll be there in five minutes."

"That's trusting of him."

"Like I said, we are soul brothers. That's what trust is about Rose." Max says and squeezes her thigh. Then a small hole cracks in the rear window. Max feels his seat thump and hears a distant pop.

"Hey, he's shooting at us!" Rose yells.

"Let's see if his SUV can keep up!" Max swerves onto Commercial Boulevard and seeing no other vehicles on the road, he stomps the gas. The tires spin a little and catch and he feels the acceleration press him into the seat as it shifts through gears racing along the boulevard. Max passes a few stoplights before he slows down to veer onto Powerline Road. As he turns he sees the SUV fade far behind. Then he turns onto a side road and works his way through a quiet neighborhood finally reaching the Bridgestone Apartments with no sign of the SUV. He parks in Sam's covered parking slot and runs through the rain into the building with Rose.

The elevator takes them to the third floor and Sam's apartment #303. As soon as Max goes inside, he puts on the deadbolt and plops down on Sam's couch. He sighs in relief as Rose flops beside him.

"I felt that bullet hit the back of my seat." Max says.

"Now you see why being around me is unsafe. That bullet could have killed you."

"Our guardian angel is helping us Rose."

"Well, you did a perfect getaway Max. I'm proud of you for that!" She says, but then Rose ruins the celebration. "We can't stay here long either, just enough to use the laptop. The SUV guy will check this place as our possible destination. They know where Sam's apartment is by now and obviously about your red Corvette too."

"Good grief, your right! We may have company soon."

"Let me get the number for Langston. I just need to talk to him and send him the file. Then we can go hide somewhere and wait to hear what happens."

Max brings out Sam's laptop to the living room game table before speaking.

"Is there any chance Donna's boss is in cahoots with her?"

Chapter Fifty Two

"There is no way that could happen." Rose stares at Max, her face flushed and stunned for a second before dismissing the idea.

"I know it's highly unlikely but possible."

"Max please! You make this more difficult for me! I have to rat on my boss! I hate this! I'm only so strong!" Her eyes tear up. She feels Max embrace her and the warmth soothes her as if he possesses some magic touch. Then she feels him stroke her hair pressing her head against his shoulder. Her confidence comes back to her and she breaks away from Max forcing a hold on her passion again.

"I'm sorry but you said to trust no one."

"I'm okay now." She says patting Max on the chest.

Rose decrypts her phone number file on Sam's laptop and dials the emergency number for Walter Langston, the FBI Special Agent in charge. After four rings, Langston's voice mail picks up. She closes her eyes curses. After the beep, she speaks.

"Mister Langston, this is special agent Rose Finley Number 3234137 with vital information. I need to send a file to you that will explain everything..." A voice comes on the line and interrupts Rose.

"This is Langston, Finley. Where are you? Grant is looking for you. Why are you calling me?"

"Sir, I have a video you need to see. Please listen to me. I'm not the bad one here. Will you at least let me send this file to you?"

"I was told you stole a video recorder from Grant. Her agents are looking for you. Why should I believe you?"

"Did she tell you why she wants this recorder from me?"

"No, she didn't say why, just that you stole a top secret video."

"That's odd sir, because it has some incriminating evidence against her. Please hear me out sir. Donna Grant is trying whatever she can to stop me from sending this video to the police, let alone to you. My apartment is trashed and Matuso has tried to kill us twice so far. This video shows the attempt to murder me on the party boat, and a murder plan Rafael Matuso explains in detail to Sancho and Grant! You need to see this!"

"Grant is here in Atlanta, she couldn't have been with Matuso. I'm guessing you mean Rafael Matuso?"

"Yes, Matuso called her directly from the boat. Check her incoming phone calls with the carrier."

"I will do that."

"Matuso realized I must have been spying on him. I was thrown into the Atlantic Ocean five miles offshore! He wanted me to drown a horrible death and Sancho helped! Then he called Donna. I was lucky two fishing men rescued me. Please let me send this file to you. It will convince you I'm telling the truth."

"Donna said you'll claim you were on a boat with Sancho and Matuso and they tossed you overboard. You realize you are making serious accusations against Sancho, Matuso, and Grant, about attempted murder?"

"Yes, let me explain." Rose tells Walter about the micro-camcorder and what happened that forces her to call him.

"This is hard to believe Finley. Send the file. I will play it."

"Yes sir, and thank you! If you will verify your email address, I can send it now."

"Tell me what you have." Langston verifies the address. "Okay Finley, let's say you are telling the truth. Grant told me she has all her agents searching for you. Is this the phone you used to call Grant?"

"Yes, I know she can locate it. I will turn it off sir."

"It's twenty-three hundred hours here. Find a secure place and call me in two hours. That gives me time to evaluate the video."

"Yes sir. Thank you for listening. I'm sending the file now."

Rose types in Langston's email address. She plugs in the micro-camcorder and hesitates knowing the gravity of what she is doing. After taking a deep breath, she clicks the send button.

"The file is on the way sir."

"Call in two hours." Langston rings off.

"Okay Rose, why did you say 'vital information'?" Max asks.

"I just used vital information, no secret code or anything special about it. We do have some codes we memorize for certain problems. If we fit the code into a talk or text it to someone, they know there is a certain type of problem."

"Oh yeah, like when I called Sam a dumb ass."

"See Max, that's secret agent stuff. Oh, turn off your cell phone."

"Okay, but no thanks on being a spy. I have enough excitement just falling into this type of thing. I admit this is thrilling being with you, but it's scary too."

"I apologize for getting you into this, but I'm glad you saved me. Together we will make a difference. If we had let Matuso carry out his plan Hubert Sancho will be re-elected."

"I'm amazed at how corrupt Sancho is."

"Yes, and now we need to find a secure place to hide."

"I'm happy here." Max says.

"They know where Sam lives. Do you have another suggestion?"

"I like the luxury of the Pier 66 Hotel. At least we'll be comfy."

"They'd get your credit card and find us, and think of the cost!"

"Trust me, the money is no problem."

"I could pay with this cash, but I think they would still want an ID." Rose waves the cash from Craig Benito at him.

"Okay, a long time ago I stayed at a dingy motel called Griffin's Rooms. Do you remember the song Secret Agent Man?"

"It's my motto Max." She sings. "Swinging on the Riviera one day, and then lying in a Bombay Alley the next day!" Then Rose asks. "What about it?"

"Nice job singing Rose. Well, Griffin's Rooms is like the Bombay Alley of motels. It's nasty. I don't think they ever change the bed sheets, but the clerk takes cash and no questions asked."

"It can't be that bad. We can ask for clean sheets. Let's do that! Can you think of a better plan?"

Chapter Fifty Three

"I remember feeling creepy and dirty in that motel room. I vote to stay here at least until you talk to Langston again. It's clean and safe and dry here." Max says.

"No, we need to leave. At least we are only dealing with rain and not Hurricane Jezebel on top of us Max. It's foolhardy to stay here."

"There is one thing we have to do." Max says.

"What?"

"We got wet again and look at your blouse." Max points to the blood stains.

"Oh yeah, but we are almost dry now."

"Well, see if you can find a non-bloody blouse in Ann's closet that fits." Max walks Rose into the master bedroom. He grabs one of Sam's blue shirts and some trousers to borrow and watches Rose pick out a tan blouse and shorts.

"At least these aren't pink, and the shorts should fit. Are you sure this is okay? Can I please wear them?" Rose waves them at Max.

"I'm reading Ann's mind and she says of course you can."

"Oh good, I'm starting to hate pink."

"How long will it take to round up the bad guys?"

"I bet he starts tonight." Rose drops the pink clothes and puts on Ann's clothes.

"How do I look?" She says posing for Max.

"I must say you look stunning!" Max smiles admiring Rose. "Anyway, if Langston believes you and does start tonight, we have to protect ourselves until he gives us the all-clear. If we go to Griffin's Rooms, I'll bring some bug spray and Lysol."

"Can we just go back to the party? We can leave your car here and take a cab back to the Danglebatts party. I kind of like that idea."

"If we can leave before they find us that may work." Max says.

"I think I will keep the camcorder with me though. Let's go now!" Rose says.

"That is too dangerous. What if Langston is in bed with Grant and kills the video? You would have the only copy on you if they catch you. Let's hide it here. I have a hiding place that no one will ever find except Sam and me."

"Really? We almost were killed hiding it at your house!"

"That was different. We needed to get it right away to talk to Langston. Now that is done we can hide it for a while."

"Okay, show me."

"Come with me." Max leads Rose into the kitchen. He pries off the front cover of the microwave oven that Sam once showed him. "This area is big enough to hide your camcorder."

"You want me to store it in there?" Rose is skeptical.

"Yes. It's perfectly safe here and only you and I will know where it is. I will leave a note for Sam so he will know in case something happens to us." He watches Rose think and stare at the opening. Then as if a switch turns on, she stuffs the micro-camcorder in the opening.

"What a neat place. Now let's get out of here!" Rose says watching Max snap the cover back in place.

"I'll leave a note for Sam. He will know where the camcorder is if I just say, 'check your special hiding place.' Let's nix Griffin's rooms. I'll reserve a room at the Pier 66 Hotel and we take the Corvette there." Max says as he dials his phone.

"We can't do that Max. Grant will find us if we rent a room."

"They will be checking everywhere. If they think we are at the Pier 66 Hotel, they may not bother with Chet's house."

"Okay, so go to the hotel, then what?"

"We go to the hotel, check in using my credit card, and go to the room. You call Langston from the hotel. Then we fake staying there, leave the TV on the news channel. I turn on the GPS and leave my phone in the room and we take a taxi to the party. They will find the signal coming from the hotel and think we are still in the room. How is that for a plan?"

"I like it. Let's go!" Rose shouts and hugs Max.

"First let me check your wound." He lifts up her blouse. "You need a new patch and that's all I'm doing." Max smiles, winks at her, and goes to find a bandage.

At eleven thirty Max locks Sam's apartment and takes a roll of duct tape with him. He trots to the elevator with Rose. Downstairs they rush through the rain to the Corvette. Max slaps a piece of duct tape over the bullet hole in the rear window before he slides inside with Rose. As he starts the car he sees the black SUV coming into the parking area. Max believes the driver saw them when the SUV follows him out of the Bridgestone Apartments.

"We are being followed again." Max says.

He loops onto Andrews Avenue, then makes a sharp turn onto 26th street and zigzags through an older section of town called Wilton Manors. He continues to speed the sports car through side streets. Some of the streets purposely have barriers making them dead ends to help channel traffic and help police stop runaway criminals. Max knows which streets to avoid. He finally drives onto the beach road and south to the Pier 66 Hotel. The SUV is history long before he stops in front of the entrance.

"That was an exciting ride." Rose says getting out of the car.

Max smiles and accepts a valet ticket before he follows Rose into the lobby. He registers, gets the keycard and leads the way to the elevators and into their room.

Rose goes to the king-size bed, and hand thumps the springs.

"Nice action." Rose teases.

"Very tempting!" Max closes his eyes and shakes his head. He feels Rose wrap her arms around his waist.

"When this is over we may never meet again." Rose whispers.

"We have an hour to kill." Max flops onto the bed with Rose in his arms.

Max is awakened from a dead man's sleep by his phone's alarm he set for a quarter to one in the morning. He rolls over and kisses Rose. Max sits up and stretches before he stands up from the rumpled bed and checks his watch.

"I'm going to take a quick shower to wake up." Max says.

"Me too!" Rose follows Max into the bathroom stripping clothes as she goes. *What is wrong with your brain? Are you in love with this man?* She thinks and pauses before she steps into the shower after Max. Inside the shower feels warm and yet refreshing. She hugs Max from behind and hums with joy.

"This is exactly what we shouldn't be doing." Max says. Then he turns around, gives Rose a quick kiss, and steps out of the shower. Max dries with a bath towel, uses deodorant from the welcome pack, and starts to dress.

Rose towels off, uses the same deodorant from the welcome pack, and slips into her clothes. She feels the same want again when she looks at Max but she controls her emotions. Rose sees Max check his watch as she walks from the bathroom.

"It's time to call." Max says. He hands his cell phone to Rose.

"Okay Max, here goes!" Rose kisses Max, sits on the edge of the bed, takes a deep breath, and dials Langston.

Chapter Fifty Four

Walter Langston sits in his leather swivel chair in the bedroom he converted into an office. The walls are neutral beige like all the other walls in his four-bedroom home. Unlike the other rooms, plaques and awards cover most of the available wall space. Being a pragmatic man, he also has a loaded gun and other special devices hidden somewhere in every room. He stares across his array of flat screen monitors that continually display various cameras and information of ongoing investigations. Walter focuses on the middle screen that is ready to display the video he received from Rose Finley at twenty-three hundred hours.

He has mixed emotions having had a dinner meeting with Donna Grant hours ago and impressed by her charm. The woman seemed dedicated to serving her country. Later she called and told him about a top-secret video Rose Finley allegedly stole from her office. Grant declared Finley is a rogue agent and an irresponsible goof-up. Walter scanned through Finley's employee records and recent entries seemed to confirm what Grant said. Now this supposed goof-up agent is saying Donna is the rogue. *Whom should I believe?* Walter mumbles to himself. He is tempted to just delete the file and believe Donna's tale that Finley is a thief and is compromising the investigation of Sancho. But, his gut feeling tells him to watch the video. *What the Hell, it checks clean for viruses.* He thinks and opens the file.

Walter starts the video and watches the struggle between Matuso and Rose and her being tossed out the window. Before the video ends, Walter calls Fort Lauderdale.

"Fred Holland."

"Fred I'm glad I got you, it's Walter Langston."

"Hi Walter, what can I do for you."

"Fred, I have a situation and I need your help. What's your situation there with the storm and all?"

"It's fine, nothing major is going on. If you're calling me for help, it must be important, so what's up?"

"Fred, I need you to handle a sensitive situation. One of my agents in Miami discovered a murder plan against candidate Medina. I don't believe the culprits know we found this out so we have a time advantage."

"Someone plans to assassinate Bill Medina!"

"No, their plan is to assassinate Medina's assistant Troutman and blame it on him."

"What do you need me to do Walter?"

"You need to safeguard her immediately. It's going to take me some time to get agents in place though so I may need more help from you.

"Whatever you need, I'll take care of it Walter."

"I know you will, that's why I called you. Look Fred, there are some big names involved here."

"Who are we talking about?"

"As far as I know right now, Rafael Matuso, and Senator Hubert Sancho!"

"You're kidding! Why would Sancho deal with Matuso? Hubert Sancho is supposed to be a good guy."

"Well he's not. I suspect my head agent from Miami Donna Grant is working with Matuso. I can't use the FBI agents in Miami or Fort Lauderdale which means I need to pull agents from out of the area and that takes time. I know I'm asking a lot of you, but your people may need to handle this until I get my people to you. Grant is here in Atlanta but I don't know who else is working with her down there. Troutman lives in Fort Lauderdale and I know I can trust you. I hope you and your crew can prevent the assassination before the woman is killed."

"I'm sorry to hear you have a bad agent."

"Yes, I'm going to keep Grant busy here until this shakes out. I know you have a trusted friend with Miami police in case you need help outside your area. We need to stop them ASAP, however, I need your people to remain behind the scenes. As much as preventing this woman's murder is critical, we don't want to scare anyone off. We have an advantage as no one knows we're onto their plans so we have an opportunity to prevent a murder while collecting solid evidence needed to prosecute those involved."

"So you need us to handle this quietly, will do. I do have a close friend in Miami, Captain Martinez. I will give this case top priority!"

"Thank you, but only use your best officers. If possible, try not to alert Miami unless it's absolutely necessary. I want to keep this information to as few people as possible so don't call Martinez yet. The murder is supposed to take place this weekend! Can you pull together a small covert team who can guard her and collect evidence until I get someone there?"

"I have a couple of people I trust who I can put on this. Let me know who your contact will be once you get your crew together. I'll coordinate with them when they get here. In the meantime, I'll get on this and keep you informed."

"Make it happen Fred. I'm counting on you."

"No problem Walter." Fred Holland hangs up. He remembers fondly how he and Walter became close friends in college and how they've worked together previously on a case.

Walter dials his right-hand man Paul Nichols. Like every agent, Walter trusts very few people, but he does have nearly complete trust in Fred Holland and Paul Nichols. As he waits for Paul to answer, he thinks about all the conversations he has had with Agent Grant. He remembers Donna telling him Agent Finley is a bumbling agent, always seeming to arrive too late to catch a culprit. Now he wonders if Donna has been giving warnings to the very perpetrators Finley was trying to apprehend. It all seems to fit into place if Grant is the rogue agent.

"Hello sir."

"Hello Paul. I know it is late but this is urgent. I need you to come here as soon as you can."

"It must be important if you're calling this late?"

"It is. I don't want to get into it over the phone, how soon can you meet me at my house?

"I'll be over in ten minutes sir."

"Good." Walter says and hangs up. While he waits for Paul to get there, he wastes no time running checks on phone numbers to and from Grant's cell phone first and acquiring necessary search warrants to expand outward to other numbers encountered. He knows, Grant's phone logs aren't protected as a government agent, but by getting the appropriate search warrants, he is able to ensure he can follow any evidence he finds. Fortunately, it doesn't take long to get the necessary paperwork in place by the time Paul arrives."

Chapter Fifty Five

Walter quickly fills Paul in on what's happening and plays the video for Paul before discussing how to handle the situation in Florida. They form a plan and Paul leaves for Florida immediately to meet up with Fred Holland.

Fred Holland quickly looks to see who's on duty and pulls a couple guys in for a meeting. After explaining the situation based upon the information he received from Walter Langston, he has his team work up a plan to prevent the murder of Sara Troutman without alerting the assassins that the authorities are onto them. Fred makes it clear, the FBI is on the way to handle the takedown, so they are only tasked with preventing Troutman's murder.

It's after one o'clock. As if on cue, his phone rings.

"Hello Agent Finley. I have already started acting on what you sent. I suggest you and your friend become unavailable to everyone until this is over." Walter says.

"Thank you for believing in me sir." Rose says sighing in relief.

"Thank you for your outstanding work Agent Finley. I'm curious. Why go on the boat when Grant said not to do that?"

"I had a gut feeling about it. It's like a sixth sense sir."

"I know Finley, I have that too. Follow that sense. It may save a life someday."

"Thank you, sir. What are you doing about Sancho and Matuso?"

"It's confidential Finley, you know that. Trust me this is going to happen fast and may get messy. I need you to stay out of the picture, while we try to arrest Matuso and Sancho. Do you know what I'm saying Finley?"

"You mean you want someone else to be the big celebrity?"

"Yes that, but also I don't want you getting in the middle of things that could undo the measures we're taking on this. You've done a lot, but now it's time to leave it to me. You are more valuable staying out of the public eye. My order for you is to disappear unless something critical comes up. Then call me between thirteen hundred and fifteen hundred hours on Tuesday. This will be a busy time for me. Goodbye for now."

"Yes sir." Rose hears Walter disconnect. She stares at the phone awe struck. "Wow, he believes me! Did you hear what he said Max!"

"Yes that's terrific! You are terrific Rose! Now it's time to exit. I need to get a cab and see how Sam is doing." Max turns on the GPS on his cell phone, turns the TV on loud, and leaves with Rose hanging a 'Do Not Disturb' sign on the door.

Max enters the Pier 66 lobby with Rose trailing behind him. Outside he sees a taxi dropping off a couple at the doorway. Max hustles through the door.

"Just a minute sir!" Max shouts seeing the cabby getting back in his car. He waits until the man stands up. "Thanks we need a ride."

"No can do. It's after one and I'm shut down for tonight."

"Will an extra hundred in cash make it worthwhile?" Max waits while the driver thinks.

"We have a deal!" He laughs and starts to leave.

"Just a minute." Max searches the area for someone watching him. Seeing nothing, he hails Rose and slides in the back seat with her.

"You people know it is pouring rain again? Okay, where to?" The driver grumps.

"Take us to Holy Cross Hospital."

"That's way up on North Federal Highway."

"Are you able?" Max frowns at the man.

"Yeah, I can. It's just a lot of time."

Max sits with Rose and remains silent during most of the ride. After looking behind for a few minutes as the taxi drives along, Max is convinced no one is following them. He watches the taxi driver avoid some minor debris in the road. Then the gravity of the situation with Sam hits Max like a steam train. He leans over cupping his hands on his face and moans.

"Sam is alright Max." Rose says laying her arm on his back.

"Sam is my best friend ever. He's family to me. I don't know what I will do if he dies. What will Ann do? He is her whole world."

"You need to calm down. You have no idea how serious he is."

"Oh I saw how serious he is."

"Looks can be deceiving Max."

"He was shot before. He almost died then."

"No! When was that?"

"We were held at gunpoint in a limo that crashed. The man's shotgun went off and hit Sam. He was lucky he survived."

"Why were you being held at gunpoint, oh never mind. Tell me later. Let's just pray that Sam is conscious by now."

The driver stops under the overhang at Holy Cross Hospital. Max has Rose pay the man from her wad of money and then rushes inside with Rose. The waiting room clock shows nearly two o'clock.

The information desk is vacant. Max doesn't know what to do when a nurse comes in from behind a locking door.

"Please, we need to see Samuel Stormen." Max says.

"Just a moment sir, I can look up Mister Stormen." After checking, she frowns. "Oh."

"Where is he?" Max asks the blood draining from his face.

"He's in ICU, no visitors allowed at this hour. Are you family?"

"Yes. Can we talk to the doctor treating him?" Max slowly regains composure knowing Sam is at least not dead.

"Doctor Allison is on duty. I'll see if he is free."

"Max!" An angry voice shouts from the far side of the lobby. Max is surprised to hear Dale Stormen and see him and Fay Stormen. He never realized Sam's parents were already at the hospital.

"Wow, what are you two doing here?" Max walks across the room to where Dale is standing. He tries to shake hands but Dale glares at Max crossing his arms on his chest.

"What do you think! We are waiting for some news about our son! The doctor says Sam may not live." Dale says glaring at Max.

"You know he saved our lives sir." Max says. He sees Fay dab at her eyes.

"What the Hell trouble are you in now Max. You're supposed to be his best friend and you let him get shot again. This time is worse than last time! We can't reach Ann. She needs to be contacted!"

"I will call her. I didn't ask Sam to burst in and tackle the gunman. I'm sorry this happened. Where exactly is he shot?"

"I don't know, and I blame you for this!" His face is angry red.

"You can't blame Max sir!" Rose butts in.

"Who the Hell are you? What are you doing with Max while Peggy is away?"

"It's not what you think sir. I'm an FBI agent. Max and Sam rescued me from a situation and inadvertently were pulled into a sensitive matter that caused this."

"Why are you still with Max then?"

"My boss has taken over the case and I wanted to see how Sam is and to say thanks, but it looks like that will have to wait."

Max stares at Dale, causing an awkward pause. Then Max starts pacing back and forth in the lobby. Dale blows some air and sits down. Doctor Allison comes out from behind the locked door.

"Stormen?" He calls.

"Yes Doc, how is my son doing?" Dale shouts. Fay and Dale rush to the doctor. He sees Max and Rose move closer to the doctor.

"His upper chest was hit with the bullet. The bullet fragments only tore some muscle tissue but one piece cut a critical blood vessel. That was the most serious damage that had to be repaired immediately. Fortunately he survived the surgery. With so much blood lost initially, I'm not sure if he will suffer any brain damage. So far there is no change in your son's condition."

"Is he going to live?"

"No change is a good sign. His chances improve with every minute he lives. He is breathing on his own. We are monitoring his vital signs continuously. I have seen this type of injury before. I don't expect him to wake for hours yet. It's after two now. I suggest you go home and get some sleep. Check back in the afternoon."

"Can I stay with him?" Fay Stormen asks.

"He is in the ICU. For the safety of all the patients, we don't allow anyone to stay there more than a few minutes. You can camp out here in the lobby, but I suggest you go home and get some needed rest. There is nothing you can do except wait for now. We will monitor him tonight and hopefully have better news later in the day."

"Thank you doctor, I guess we will leave now." Dale turns to Max. "See what your foolishness did for him Max!" Without another word to Max or the doctor, Dale and Fay leave the hospital.

Max watches, as Sam's parents storm out of the lobby, frustrated about how they feel. He thinks about all the good times he had with Sam and how sad he will be if Sam should pass. He jerks out of his nightmare when Rose taps his shoulder.

"Hey big guy, let's go to the Danglebatts party. It will take your mind off of Sam."

"I feel so bad Rose. It's like I caused all this trouble."

"If you blame anyone it should be me. I got you guys into this mess but I know it is worth doing for the good of the people Max. I just pray Sam comes to okay."

"You are right Rose. If not for you the police would arrest the wrong murderer and those bad guys would be home free. I hope Sam is having a great dream while he sleeps. Let's go to the party."

"You think Sam is dreaming?"

"Yes I do. I hope it isn't another nightmare!"

"He has nightmares?"

"Sometimes."

Chapter Fifty Six

Max and Rose step outside of Holy Cross Hospital and see a taxi parked at the edge of the overhang. Max waves at the cab but gets no response so he rushes to the cab, taps on the window and shouts.

"Hey mister!" He waits for the cabby to drop the window.

"What's the matter?" The man says.

"We need a ride." Max says.

"Great! Where to?"

"Can you just drive toward Federal Highway for now."

"You don't have an address?"

"We...I'm a bit frazzled. My friend was injured during a break-in at my house earlier. I'm worried he might not live and I guess I'm not thinking clearly. Something so unexpected like this has us a bit shaken." Max says.

"I understand, I'm sorry about your friend."

"What's your name sir?"

"Raul." He points at the sun visor where his license sits.

"Okay Raul, Take us to 246 Lux Lane. Do you know it?"

"Yeah, I know it. That's a ritzy place in Blue Lake Estates."

"You could say that about our friend. How long to get there?"

"I guess twenty minutes."

Max feels the cab occasionally tilt from a gust of wind. He constantly scans behind, checking for any vehicle that may be tailing them and sees Rose looking too. A few cars come near them but not one follows them.

"Don't worry sir. If I felt the weather was too unsafe to drive in, I wouldn't be out here. As long as I drive safely with the rain and wind gusts, I'll get you to your destination."

Max has a confused look on his face at first about what the cabby just said and then realized he noticed him looking around to see if they were being followed. "I'm sorry, I meant no offense about your driving. If it weren't for my friend being injured this evening, I wouldn't be out in this weather. I guess in my current state, the wind gusts and debris have me on edge."

"I fully understand sir. I'll have you at your location in a jiffy safe and sound."

"Thank you Raul."

Max continues to scan the area as the cab turns onto Lux Lane. He doesn't see the SUV or any vehicle that looks suspicious near his house or Chet's house. The same cars cover the driveway and most of the yard at Chet's house so he directs the cabby to stop on the street next to the driveway. Before he gets out, he digs out the last of his mad money handing it to the driver.

"Thanks Raul, have an extra treat on us. You did great. I hope you have a safe time the rest of the night." Max says as he hands the money to the driver.

"Thank you! You made my night." Raul says and smiles at Max.

"Drive careful Raul." Max says and jumps out of the cab.

The storm is mostly a light wind with a few gusts here and there and cold rain that hits his back and face as Max runs behind Rose. A large blast of rain pours on him and Rose just before they get under the stone canopy. Max shakes off the rain and watches Raul drive away in the new flurry of rain. He rings the doorbell and feels a gust of wind whip through the canopy. Finally Katie answers the door.

"Hello, you two. I was napping. Where were you? I'll get some dry clothes. You two are sopping wet!" Katie ushers them inside.

"We had a mission to do and we did it. We will dry in time."

"The party is winding down. It's after three. Where are Paul and Sam?" Katie says accepting Max's face only hug.

"Sam and Paul went other places. I don't expect them back to the party. Rose damaged the other clothes so she changed."

"That's too bad. Paul seems a little shy. I kind of like him."

"Yeah, he's a real cutup." Max says and hears Rose groan at him.

"Wait, when did Rose leave and where did she get tan clothes?"

"Too many questions for now Katie."

"Yes but…"

"I'm kind of tired Katie. Where can we crash?" Rose asks.

"Are you sure you're okay Max?"

"Yes dear. I will explain everything later."

"Well, Chet has some air mattresses set up in the garage."

"Great. We may not want to venture out for a day or so."

"Well… Oh the mattresses may be claimed by now. Max, you are shivering. You had a raincoat on when you left. Let me get some dry clothes for both of you." Katie leaves and returns with Danglebatts T-shirts and other clothing.

"You didn't have to do this Katie." Rose says.

"You two could catch a cold. That would be awful in the middle of the summer."

"It's not that cold in here." Max says but Katie ignores him.

"Max, I got some of Chet's clothes for you. Rose, I know my bra won't fit you. I did the best I could for you. Just use one of the bathrooms to towel off and change."

"Thanks Katie." Rose says as she heads for a vacant bathroom.

Max does the same and meets Rose in the living room. He sees Rose has on a grossly oversized Danglebatts T-shirt and tan short-shorts. He smiles at the no bra look. Max is wearing a Danglebatts T-shirt and a pair of baggy green shorts.

"I'm ready to party!" Max shouts.

Chapter Fifty Seven

"Her bras are too small." Rose folds her arms on her chest.

"Hey, you look fine just as you are!" Max says as Katie joins them again.

"My bust will never be that big even being pregnant." Katie laughs.

"This is fine Katie. Thanks again for the clothes."

"Where is Chet?" Max asks.

"He's crazy! He's out by the pool quote 'enjoying the sound of the wind and rain', smoking a cigar with Dan and some buddies. I forbid cigar smoke in here. He and Dan just had to have their cigars."

"Do you think he has an extra one?"

"There's a humidor on a table near the pool door. Knock yourself out."

"Thanks Katie." Max says as he dances around the few diehard dancing fools on his way toward the pool. He finds the cigars and takes one. Max bites off the end of his cigar as he goes through the open glass doors to the screened in pool. Rain beats loud on the metal pool roof and wind whooshes through the screens around the pool. Max hears Dan Batts shout at him.

"Hello stranger! I got a lighter over here. Where have you been?" Dan says seeing Max with a cigar.

"Well Dan, I just can't tell you right yet. We did some bizarre things and now it's time to wait and see." Max says. He sets his cigar plug in an ashtray and accepts the lighter to puff his cigar to life. His first curl of smoke wisps away in a gust of wind that sweeps through the pool area. After Max hands the lighter back, he eases down in the last vacant lounge chair. The power goes off for a moment and Max nervously scans the pool area but then the lights come back on.

"Boy you're jumpy Max. Are you okay? I heard you found a naked woman in the ocean. Talk about hard to believe stories Max. Was she a mermaid? What the Hell?" Dan says and puffs on his cigar.

"I guess Chet told you all about her."

"Well he started to but he can't. I think he's dead." Dan jokingly points his cigar at Chet, passed out in a lounge chair snoring and his cigar lying on the flat stone deck.

"I thought he was drinking pretty heavy earlier. I guess it caught up with him."

"You think? I've never seen him drunk! He usually goes to his room after a concert and the rest of us try to run a local bar out of booze. He'll recover in a few hours."

"You guys get along pretty good then?"

"Yeah, we do a group hug after a great performance, usually after an encore and after we bow to the audience."

"Oh, Sam and I never hug."

"Sam said you did."

"Well rarely, once or twice when things look really bleak."

"I think something bleak is going on right now Max. Are you in trouble with the law?"

"No, I can't talk about it Dan, it might endanger you."

"Then I don't want to know. It sounds serious."

"I love this cigar. Where did you get this?" Max says changing the subject.

"Italy Max, we did some shopping after a concert in Barcelona."

"No kidding, is this a Toscano?"

"Yes, these are some of Italy's finest."

"I wanted to buy some when we were in Italy but never got to do that. I read the cigar company is over a hundred years old."

"Hey, no wonder they taste like this!"

Max chats with Dan until four in the morning without telling Dan about all the adventures with Rose. He finishes his cigar and beer and feels his eyes closing.

"I think I'll find a place to crash." Max says. He starts to get up but his legs are wobbly. He drops down again and resolves to rest his head for a moment.

"Suit yourself. I'm going to stay here and enjoy the sound of the rain hitting the roof." Dan says but he realizes he is talking to deaf ears. Max is already out like Chet.

Rose is walking toward the bar when a thin muscular man steps in front of her. She sees him puff on his reefer. Rose looks into his sleepy brown eyes that are barely able to focus. She tries to go around the man but he blocks her retreat again.

"Let's dance!" He says smiling and gently grabbing Rose's arm. He escorts Rose onto the dance area and begins swaying to the music. Rose starts dancing with him.

"Don't you guys ever sleep? It's after three in the morning!"

"Hey it's the hurricane party of all times. Why sleep when I can dance with you?"

"What's your name?" Rose asks ignoring his inane attempt at flirting. However, she feels a slight attraction to the perfectly tanned man even though he is shorter than she is. She wants to get Max out of her thoughts. She thinks she needs to connect with some other humans.

"I'm Chris. What is your name beautiful?"

"I'm Rose. You're pretty handsome too Chris."

"I'm rescuing you Rose. I like to cheer up sad people."

"Thanks. I've got a lot on my mind Chris. I was planning to get drunk for a few days and forget all my troubles."

"What can bother such a lovely lady?"

"It's private. I can't talk about it."

"It's not good to keep things bottled up. You should get it off your chest, and I mean really, get it off that lovely chest!"

"Thanks, your chest is lovely too. Let's just dance."

Rose sees him shrug and smile at her. She feels the steady boom of the bass in the music as she dances and enjoys watching the man undulate. His hips rotate and his hands slide up and down his sides as he dances. She notices he seems to focus on her chest often. Then she remembers she is braless and wearing a Danglebatts T-shirt and she smiles. *Of course! I hope you enjoy the view!* She thinks and laughs forgetting about Max for the moment.

Since Chris is looking at her chest, she stares at his. His loose yellow shirt is unbuttoned halfway down and his tan chest has a fair patch of dark brown hair on it and a gold chain hanging below his neck. Rose smiles and gyrates to the music and feels excited looking at his face. She is oblivious to her worries and the whole world as she dances and enjoys the music. Her spell is broken when the music shifts to a slow song. She feels Chris reach around her waist gently squeezing her body.

"I like you a lot Rose. Let's dance to this." Chris says pressing himself into Rose.

"I can do that." She enjoys his musky odor dancing close to him.

"Maybe we can do more than dance." Chris suggests. He slides his hands down onto her buttocks, elated that Rose doesn't flinch.

"I'm curious. What do you do Chris? You seemed to like it when I stared all over your body." She says with her arms around his neck.

"I'm a stripper. I like women staring at my body. I mainly work in Miami at a Just for Women Club. I went to high school with Dan Batts. He asked my guy and me to come here. I mean like how could we refuse? All the booze, food and pot we want, but Pat passed out. No worries he won't see me with a hot chick like you. I love it!"

"Dan is a generous person. I have to go now." Rose says. She gives a false smile to Chris, pushes away and waves goodbye. Any hot's she had for Chris sunk like a cockroach stuck to a lead sinker in the ocean and she is upset thinking. *The man tried to hook up with me, with his partner asleep at the same party!*

Rose walks to the bar and pops open a beer. She surveys the crowd feeling a little frustrated and maybe horny and she absolutely blames Max for stirring up her hormones. Rose scans the living room with bleary eyes and wants to check out what she sees.

Chapter Fifty Eight

Rose ambles toward a man sitting on the floor at the edge of the dance area picking on a dark blue acoustic guitar. She recognizes John Fret and is attracted to the thin man because of his long reddish-brown hair and mustache. Her eyes are a little blurry but she focuses on the Danglebatts rhythm guitarist. Curious to know more about the man, she stands in front of him and listens to him pick the melody of the rock music that is blaring. After no recognition from him, Rose turns to walk away but hears him stop picking.

"Hello carrot top." He says smiling up at Rose.

"I thought you were ignoring me and carrot top yourself!"

"I noticed you right off. I was trying to think of what to say."

"Calling me carrot top isn't the best line I ever heard."

"I'm sorry my love. I'm carrot top John, what's your name?"

"My name is Rose. I know who you are, carrot top John Fret."

"Ah Rose, like the beautiful flower you are. I saw you earlier. Where have you been? I'm like a carrot top too and know you want to hang with another carrot top. I think that's why you came over here."

"I love hearing you play but why are you sitting on the floor?"

"I can't get up. I'm too stoned. Come and sit." He pats the floor.

"I can tell you're stoned John, even with my tired eyes."

"Do you know I'm the Danglebatts rhythm man?"

"Yes, and I met your buddies earlier. I think you were hiding somewhere in the smoke. The smoke is too strong in here. I can get high just breathing. You know it's after three in the morning.

I can't believe how many people are still awake and dancing. Don't you people ever sleep?"

"We got all day to sleep love. I've been sitting here since, oh I can't remember. I'm getting even higher just looking at you. Hey, I got a couple joints in my shirt pocket. I would really like it if you would sit down and partake with me. Do you want to hear a song?" John slaps the floor next to him again and smiles at Rose.

"I'll pass on joint, but I'd love to listen to you play. Would you play a song just for me?" Rose asks and squats down beside John.

"Absolutely I will no problem! I can still do that as stoned as I'm even."

"Can you play *Black Spider Woman?*"

"Does a donkey have an ass? Oh yeah..." John starts to sing the song, but the blaring music overpowers his guitar and voice."

"I can barely hear you!" Rose shouts.

"We should go to a quieter place."

"What do you have in mind John?"

"I have my bedroom down that hallway. I sing you a song and maybe we make out, if you are interested." John points a limp finger past Rose.

"You have a bedroom? How many bedrooms are here?"

"Chet I think said eight, yeah eight but I only use one."

"Are you single, unattached?"

"Tweet, tweet, I'm as free as a bird tweet, tweet!" John slurs.

"Let's go tweeter!" Rose helps John get off the floor and staggers along to his bedroom. She smiles seeing him sit on the bed with his guitar. She closes the bedroom door, sits on the bed next to John and thinks. *This is crazy. Why are you doing this Rose!* But she smiles as he starts playing a love song.

"Here I'm with a beautiful Rose..." John starts to sing and then flops on his back. His guitar slides off his lap onto the carpet.

"Hey, at least finish the song!" Rose complains, but John is in dreamland.

"Some company you are! Here, make out with this!" She picks up the guitar, lays it across John, and puts his arms on top of the strings before she gets up.

She walks back to the living room looking for Max. Although the music is still on, everyone is gone. Rose finds Max sleeping on a lounge chair in the pool area. All the chairs are occupied. She remembers Katie saying there are air mattresses in the garage so she goes there. As expected, all the air mattresses are occupied.

She remembers the small couch next to the front door. She goes there but sees a woman in shorts sleeping on her back with one foot on the floor and the other foot propped up on the end of the couch. She looks for an unoccupied bedroom but all the doors are closed. Frustrated and tired, Rose goes back to the bedroom with John Fret. She lies down next to him and falls into a deep sleep until morning.

Rose wakes up lying on her back. She focuses her blurry eyes on her own image with disheveled hair reflected from the mirror on the ceiling. *Funny I didn't notice that before.* She thinks and looks at her watch. It reads ten in the morning. Her mouth feels like it is full of cotton. Rose works her jaw trying to get saliva in her mouth as she looks around the room and then looks at John Fret still passed out lying parallel to her, his arms still embracing the guitar.

"I have to find a bathroom!" Rose says to deaf ears. She dashes to a smaller door and is happy it leads into a bathroom. After relieving herself, she checks on John to be sure he is still breathing. After that, she traipses out of the bedroom and aims for the kitchen. She can smell bacon cooking as she nears and sees Katie and a few others at the kitchen dining table.

"Get a plate and have some breakfast Rose." Katie says.

"Thanks. I need some food." Rose takes some scrambled eggs and bacon from the serving trays and sits down next to Dan Batts.

"I saw Max by the pool." Katie says. "Where were you?"

"I hate to admit it but I slept with John Fret."

"Really, he was wasted early in the evening." Dan interjects.

"I meant I only slept next to him. He's still passed out."

"Oh I think that happens often with John." Katie says.

"You say you saw Max?" Rose asks.

"Check the pool. After you eat, I'll loan a bathing suit to you. All I have is Bikini suits left over from before I was pregnant. I don't think the Bikini top will fit you but the bottom will and clothing is optional in the pool. However, you may want to keep the T-shirt on. You can jump in the pool with Max and the others." Katie says.

"Sounds like fun. I've never seen Max in a bathing suit."

"I have. He looks really fine."

"I just met him Thursday, but I'm learning a lot about him."

"I see the way you look at Max. Just how friendly are you with him? Do you know his fiancée Peggy?"

"No, he said she broke up with him."

"Yes, I know she was about to split. I like you Rose, but I like Peggy too. If there is a chance Max and Peggy can be together again then I want that to happen."

"According to Max, they have different goals and Peggy initiated the split. I have different goals too Katie. I prefer to live alone like a free spirit. I will never butt into his life after this problem is over."

"Never is a strong word Rose, but thank you. Now explain the problem to me. What is going on? Where did Paul and Sam go? You act like it is some kind of secret mission going on."

"That's one way to put it."

"Put what?"

"Just trust us for now. Then good things will happen."

"Good things... Okay, forget it! You are as bad as Max about this secret thing whatever it is."

"I'm sorry Katie."

"Okay whatever... I think we will all be in the pool most of today. I cleaned up the cigars and ash trays. This is pool party day."

After breakfast, Rose puts on the Bikini bottom Katie loans her. As Katie said, the top is too small so Rose keeps on the T-shirt. As she nears the pool, she sees six women and five men already in the pool. Two of the couples appear to be completely nude. She sees Max relaxing along the edge of the pool staring at the women. She steps into the pool feeling the warm water embrace her body as she wades over to Max.

"Hello Rose." Max says turning his focus toward her smile.

"Hi. This must be a heated pool."

"Indeed, it is and very comfortable."

"I suppose you are enjoying all the scenery?"

"Absolutely, but you'd win a wet T-shirt contest hands down!"

"Thanks but I meant about all the other scantily dressed women."

"There are men for you to ogle too."

"Oh yes but most of them have their trousers on."

"I could take mine off."

"You would take off your shorts for me?"

"Sure! You go first!"

"I think you have enough to ogle."

"Yes, it's tough but someone has to do this."

"We have at least another day of this luxury to suffer through."

"It's a tough life Rose."

"I just thought, what about your cat?"

"Oh Hera has plenty of food. She only eats dry cat food and she has plenty of water. She'll be okay for days."

"I hope Mister Langston helps us go back to normal."

"I have no normal anymore Rose. Everything is changed."

"Well Max, I believe change happens for a purpose. Like you fishing me out of the ocean, and all the events since. Those bad guys need to be caught and I hope Chief Langston is able to save Troutman. It's his show time now."

"Yeah, my first show time is tomorrow when you call him."

"You have another show time?"

"Yes, when Peggy comes home."

Chapter Fifty Nine

Fred Holland looks up the South Lauderdale address for Medina's secretary Sara Troutman before placing his call.

"Walter, I wanted to update you on things here. I've assembled a small team and a plan to get to Troutman under the radar if possible. We're nearly ready to head out. I'll be calling Judge Mackey immediately after I hang up with you to obtain warrants in the event we need them."

"That's good Fred. I've got my guy Paul Nichols on the road to you already, but it'll be hours until he can get there and you need to get to Troutman ASAP!"

"Understood."

"As much as I'd prefer my guys to handle this, your guys need to do it instead. I wish we'd learned of this earlier, but I trust you Fred and I know you'll get this done."

"Thanks Walter. I'll keep you updated." Fred says ringing off.

"Dunsford, get to Judge Mackey to get the warrants and meet us onscene." Fred says.

"Clark, since you're green team, I want you to take lead."

"Yes Captain." Clark states.

"Remember, we're going in quiet. Kehoe, when we get there, you go around to the back stairwell to prevent anyone slipping out that way. Pitkins, you'll support Clark. Ideally, we can get there before the perpetrators get to Troutman, so all we have to do is keep her safe. The problem is as you all know, we came to this information late, so there's no telling what we'll walk into or how many perpetrators there'll be, so stay alert and watch your backs." Fred says as a final pep talk as they all head out.

Fred grabs his vest as he rushes to his Mustang and races through the rain toward Sara Troutman's apartment. Fortunately, the streets are empty as he speeds along without the siren on.

He calls Sara but gets her voice mail. "I hope she's asleep and just turned off her phone." Fred mumbles.

Fred parks in an empty spot at the Coral Reef Apartment Complex in the empty security guard parking spot. Fred follows Clark and the officers as they move through the light rain into the drab gray building after scoping the area.

The men hustle quietly up the stairwell to the fifth floor. They move down the well-lit hall to apartment 518. Clark leads the way to her apartment with Pitkins and Fred lagging intentionally behind. Prepared to knock on the door, Clark finds the door has already been forced open. He signals to the others and cautiously using his gun, slowly pushes the door open wide and pausing before peeking inside. He ducks back instantly seeing a man's gun pointing toward the open door. Two shots blast through the door hitting the opposite building wall. Clark fires a blind shot inside and takes a quick glance inside but the shooter is no longer there. Clark and Pitkins carefully move through the apartment door. Clark moves carefully foot after foot with both hands supporting his gun while Pitkins follows behind taking a low posture to prevent the gunman from having two targets to shoot at. Once inside the living room, each officer takes up a position of cover while searching the darkness of the apartment for the perp and Troutman careful to know who they would be firing at if a target presents itself.

"Police, come out with your hands up!" Clark shouts toward the bedroom. Hearing no answer, Clark moves carefully to the bedroom door. Peeking inside he sees a man leaning out an opened window and motions to Pitkins what's happening.

"Stop or I'll shoot. Get back inside with your hands up!" Clark shouts.

"No shoot!" Rocky Mara shouts and ceases his window escape reentering purposefully with both arms raised over his head still holding his gun.

"Drop the gun now!" Clark shouts.

He sees Rocky jerk the gun down to shoot and fires first planting a bullet in Rocky's upper chest and another in his shoulder. He keeps his gun trained on the man as Rocky slumps to the floor the gun falling from his hand. Pitkins who had taken up a position outside the bedroom door rushes in to the man after receiving an all safe nod from Clark and quickly kicks the gun away from the suspect to prevent it's access while Clark keeps a steady aim on the suspect waiting for an inappropriate movement. Once the gun has been kicked away, Pitkins immediately pats down the perp for any other weapons before cuffing him and assessing his medical status.

Kehoe and Fred enter the apartment while Clark and Pitkins are in the bedroom searching to make sure there are no other perps in the apartment. Entering the bedroom, Kehoe moves to the bathroom door as Clark takes up a defensive position in case anyone is hiding in there now the Rocky has been secured. Rapping on the door with his gun, Kehoe gets no response and opens the door ready to shoot. He hears Sara Troutman scream from her crouched position in the tub behind the sliding shower doors. He kneels down and touches her shoulder.

"It's okay Miss Troutman. You're safe now."

"Clear!" Clark shouts alerting Fred that its safe to enter the bedroom.

"Miss Troutman is shaken up, but okay. The perp is still alive. It looks like we missed his vital organs."

"Get some paramedics here." Fred says.

After Fred sees Sara Troutman come out of the bathroom Dunsford hands him an envelope.

"What's next?" Clark asks.

"Good work guys. Get Miss Troutman out to the living room. We have to work fast before Matuso gets wind what happened here. Dunsford call it in. When the ambulances arrive, get Trout-man to the hospital to get checked out along with the suspect, you'll ride with the suspect to the hospital, and Kehoe, you'll ride with Troutman. Stay with her at the hospital and I'll get more guys for security. Clark, you're with me after you secure the apartment and instruct an Officer, we'll process it later. We need to get to Rafael Matuso before he has a chance to get wind that his plan has failed!" Fred says.

Rafael Matuso paces around in his North Lauderdale mansion enjoying all his possessions. He looks at his pricey paintings on the Navaho white walls, a porcelain statue of Saint Mary on a small table facing the leather furniture. Everything he owns was acquired through his drug dealing and controlling government interference. Instead of enjoying his wealth and ill got gains to-night however, he's worried that everything could come crash-ing down for him.

Matuso checks his Rolex watch again as he finishes packing a small contingency suitcase. It's nearly three in the morning. He paces the floor in his living room waiting for his phone to ring. Matuso left voice mail hours ago for his hit man Rocky Mara to cancel the hit on Sara Troutman. He knows Rocky normally calls after he completes a job and that he likes to work in the wee hours of the morning, the same as Rafael. He hopes Rocky got the message before he shut off his phone. Rafael watches his right-hand man Frank refill scotch and water drinks and hand one to him then sit on the plush leather sofa.

"I called Rocky hours ago. We need to find that agent and the recorder before she passes it to someone else." Matuso says.

"Perhaps Rocky is taking care of business. He would have his phone off."

"I should call Mister Ruiz." Rafael sips his drink and contin-ues to pace the floor, nervous and upset. He knows he will have to leave his luxury home if the recorder gets to the authorities.

"It isn't wise to call Mister Ruiz at this hour."

"It's a simple thing for Rocky to answer me by now no? We should exit. We will be arrested if that recorder information gets out."

"Mister Ruiz is already upset with you and now you want to hide. Maybe the agent is lying about a recorder."

"No she knows too much. We lost control to that bitch agent. We have to leave here and set up somewhere else. Mister Ruiz will be okay with that."

"Perhaps Rocky is doing the job. It was to happen before dawn. He has never failed to perform." Frank offers as he hears Matuso's phone ring.

"This may be him." Matuso smiles as he answers. "Yes?"

"Mister M, they hold me at hospital. They shoot me. I need lawyer."

"Say nothing! Understand?" Matuso's smile fades away.

"Yes but the cops, they catch me. They know I would be there!"

"They what! Don't worry. I will send someone." Matuso hangs up and stares at his phone. He hates what he must do next.

"That was Rocky?" Frank asks.

"Yes. Craig fails, Jose fails and now Rocky fails. We need to cut our losses Frank. Rocky says the police knew about the hit. If they know that, they know everything! The police obviously have the recorder."

"What do you want to do boss?"

"Get the guns. We leave before they come for us! I will call Don as soon as we are in a safe place. Pack up, we must go now!"

"Yes sir." Frank says and joins Rafael to finish packing.

Matuso goes to the wall safe. He retrieves a bag of money and a small journal. He stuffs the items in a valise and waits for Frank to carry the suitcases to the car.

Frank opens the trunk, stuffs in the suitcases and goes back into the house. He retrieves two Uzi 9 mm machine guns from a gun safe. He checks the magazines and the safeties as he trots back into the living room. Frank rushes out the door. Then flashing red and blue lights sweep across the yard.

"They're here already!" Frank shouts.

"Give me a gun!" Matuso shouts taking an Uzi from Frank.

"We are too late to go. We need to surrender! Mister Ruiz will help with legal stuff. They catch us aiming guns at them we're dead!"

"We are dead either way! Contrary to what you think, Ruiz will not help us. He will have us killed before we go to trial!"

"You want to shoot it out with the police?"

"Yes. We have no option. Mister Ruiz is already upset with us. Get behind the Cadillac!"

"I think we should surrender. Let's take our chances."

"No I only see two cars. There aren't many cops." Rafael sprays a burst of shots into the first squad car shattering the windshield. He sees the car stop and the doors open. He showers the second vehicle with bullets. Then Rafael shoots into the radiators of the two cars. Before any return fire starts he shouts. "Get in the car and drive!"

Frank jumps in the Cadillac with Rafael and tries to drive by the police cars. A hail of return fire cracks through the side windows hitting both Rafael and Frank in the head. The Cadillac veers off the path and crashes into a palm tree. The horn blares.

Officer Clark races to the Cadillac gun aimed at the window. He gets no response from the car so he opens the passenger door and sees Rafael Matuso fall out onto the ground, his head a bloody mess. Looking into the car he sees Frank Carver slumped over the steering wheel dripping blood from his face. Clark lifts the man off the steering wheel horn.

"We don't need to cuff anyone here." Officer Clark says as Fred Holland approaches him.

"I'll call the coroner. I wanted to interview Matuso. Are any of our men wounded?" Fred asks.

"One bullet grazed John's ear. He didn't duck quickly enough."

"That's not bad. The biggest loss is the car radiators."

"Yes we can leave these for the tow trucks. It's time to do the paperwork." Officer Clark holsters his gun and checks to verify Rafael and Frank are dead. Neither man has a pulse, but he secures the weapons from their car anyway.

Fred Holland sees two more squad cars stop. An officer rushes out of one car and comes to Fred.

"Jones here, I brought the warrants sir."

"Good, we have other business. Jones, secure the scene here, we'll process it later." Fred says.

"Fred, is there anything else to do?" Officer Clark asks.

"Yes! I was waiting for these warrants. Next is the big Kahuna himself, Hubert Sancho!"

"Okay! The good Miami Senator turned out to be not so good."

"Officer Clark, your shift is over, you can go get some sleep. I don't need heavy firepower for this. Just two officers will do."

"Oh but I want to do this! I want to see him squirm!"

"Well, you're welcome to come along."

"Officer Jones can handle this. Do you want to do any more before we go?"

"No, let's commandeer a squad car. I want to get Sancho this morning before he has a chance to run. He is the last one for now. I have the warrant. Follow me." Fred says as he walks to a squad car.

"This is going to hit the news hard." Officer Clark says walking to the car with Fred.

"Yeah, this is better news than the hurricane! I want to get Sancho this morning before the report of Matuso gets out. We'll give the media some more exciting news!"

Chapter Sixty

Fred Holland drives the squad car to Hubert Sancho's residence with Officer Clark. Another squad car follows him. He yawns and checks his watch noting it's nearly five in the morning. The sun will be popping up soon. As he approaches Sancho's home on Bay Lane, he sees mostly bright streetlights, huge estates and manicured lawns along a wet but pristine road in a pricier area of Fort Lauderdale. Most of the mansions are dark or have on marginal lights.

Fred pulls to a stop in the circular driveway of Sancho's massive home. The boarded windows show no lights from inside. A minimal rain is still dropping on Fred as he exits his car and joins Officer Clark walking to the front door. He stops on a large welcome rug under the deep overhang and waits for two other policemen to join them. He shades his eyes as a bright proximity light comes on. Fred rings the doorbell. Unlike the Matuso situation, Fred doesn't expect any gunplay here. He rings the doorbell a second time and waits for lights to come on inside.

Hubert Sancho awakes from his sound sleep. He feels his wife Joanna nudging him. He ignores the nudging but she persists and he breaks out of his dreamland.

"What is it Joanna?" He mumbles somewhat annoyed.

"The doorbell is ringing. Who would call at this hour? You need to see who it is."

Hubert stares at the alarm clock with blurry eyes. He focuses and sees it is five something. "There is no one I want to talk to at this hour. I'm not answering."

"It may be important." She says when the doorbell rings again.

"It could be a bum who lost his way or wants something."

"Please!"

"Yeah... okay." Hubert Sancho sits up in bed. He rubs his eyes, puts on a robe over his underwear, grabs his .38 revolver from a drawer in his night table and walks into the living room. He jumps when he hears pounding on his door and shouting.

"Police! Open up Hubert Sancho!" Fred shouts.

Sancho freezes for a second before flipping on the living room lights. He stumbles across the living room and looks out the peephole in the front door. Hubert sees two men dressed in black with bullet proof vests on standing under the overhang and two more policemen behind them.

"All right, all right I want to see your badges!" Sancho shouts holding his gun at ready. Looking through the peephole, he sees their badges flash in the porch light.

"Okay, just a minute." Sancho trots back to the bedroom to put down his gun.

"Who is it Hubert?" Joanna asks.

"Just some police business. Go back to sleep." Sancho says. He ties the sash on his robe and walks back in the living room to open his front door.

"We need to come inside Senator." Fred says.

"Sure, come in and sit down men. I hope you have a good reason for waking us up at this hour. What's this about?" He steps aside as Fred Holland, Ron Clark and two other police officers enter.

"No need to sit down Mister Sancho. We need you to get dressed. You have to come to the police station right now." Fred says.

"Why would I need to do that?"

"We are arresting you sir."

"That's ridiculous! What for?"

"Conspiracy to commit murder of an FBI agent and aiding in the attempted murder of your opponent's secretary. I'm sure the DA can think of some other charges to add on." Fred says and reads Sancho his rights.

"This is crazy! Have you got a warrant?"

"Matter of fact I do sir. I had to wake up Judge Mackey to get it but we felt it couldn't wait." Fred says.

"Whoever gave you your information to arrest me is lying! I would never conspire to kill anyone. I'm innocent! This isn't right!" Sancho shouts.

"We have video of you helping Rafael Matuso toss an FBI agent into the ocean. You also discussed a plan to kill Sara Troutman and blame it on Medina. We have no record of you reporting any of that." Fred waits but Sancho is silent, his lips pressed together.

"I'm through with you. I want my lawyer." Sancho motions the men to leave, but he sees an officer pull out handcuffs.

"Will you come peaceably or do we have to cuff you?" Fred asks. He sees a woman in a robe enter the living room.

"What's going on?" The woman asks cinching up her robe.

"Who are you ma'am?" Fred asks.

"Who do you think I'm? I'm Joanna Sancho, the Senator's wife!"

"I'm sorry Ms. Sancho. We have to take your husband to the police station."

"In the middle of the night, what is so important that it can't wait until daylight?"

"We are arresting him ma'am."

"There is no reason in the world to arrest Hubert! He is the most honest and trustworthy man I know. Something is wrong officer!"

"I'm sorry ma'am but your husband is involved in conspiracy and attempted murder. He can call his lawyer from the police station."

"That can't be true! Hubert, tell them this can't be true!" As she pleads with Hubert, tears well up in Joanna's eyes. She sees Hubert give a weak nod and bow his head. Joanna is shocked and freezes in place.

"Let me at least get dressed. Let's get this nonsense over with!" Sancho interrupts. Then without making eye contact with Joanna, he stomps past her into his bedroom.

His legs are unsteady so he sits on the edge of his bed. Sancho covers his face with his hands and starts weeping. *Oh, what will happen to me? What will my daughter think if I'm in prison? How can I face Joanna now? I hate you Matuso! Everything is wrong!*

Sancho starts sweating profusely but as he wipes his forehead, calmness comes over him. *I have the answer right here!* He grabs his gun from the night table and stares at it. Then he nods his head. Sancho cocks the hammer, points the barrel to his temple and pulls the trigger. The pop from the gun echoes through the house like a shock wave. In an instant Sancho's worries are gone. His world goes dark.

"Crap! I should have gone with him." Officer Clark shouts. He draws his gun and races across the living room and into the bedroom.

Fred gently grabs Joanna's arm as she tries to follow Officer Clark. "Stay here Ms. Sancho." He walks Joanna back to a chair.

"Oh no, didn't he shoot at you? You won't shoot him?" She asks, fear in her eyes.

"I can't say. Officer Clark will tell us what happened. Please sit down." Then Fred sees Officer Clark come out alone.

"Hubert, are you okay!" Joanna shouts.

"I'm sorry Ms. Sancho. Your husband is deceased."

"No!" Joanna tries to run to the bedroom but Fred holds her.

"I don't think you want to look in there now."

"I want to see what happened!" Joanna wrenches free and rushes into the bedroom. She screams when she sees Hubert lying on the floor, blood still oozing out of his head.

"Come with me. There is nothing you can do here." Fred says gently aiming her back into the living room.

"We'll call this in." Officer Clark says dialing his phone.

Fred nods and motions Joanna to sit in a chair.

"This is so awful!" Joanna sobs. "I know he has been troubled ever since the boat party. Something is going on. Hubert did a mysterious run out in the rain before dinner too. I thought he was doing some undercover work."

Joanna drops into a chair and buries her face in her hands as Fred pats her on the shoulder. After a while she hears an officer answer the knock on the door and watches as more police pass going into the bedroom.

"Try to stay calm Ms. Sancho." Fred Holland says. "The coroner and his forensic team are here to take care of your husband, and psychiatrist Doctor Klein just arrived. I want you to talk to him. He will help you with the grief you are feeling. You have our condolences." Fred starts to walk to the door and sees a small girl in pajamas come in the living room.

"Mommy, I heard noises and I got scared! Why are all these men here?" The girl says shielding her eyes from the lights.

"Go back to bed Cynthia." Joanna tells her daughter. She walks Cynthia to her bedroom and then returns to sit next to Doctor Klein.

"Why would he do this?" She weeps with her hands on her face.

"Maybe he was depressed." Fred Holland offers.

"He was just on another fund-raiser party boat. He was with all his friends and supporters. That usually cheers him up."

Fred turns back to her. "That party was different Ms. Sancho. I suspect what happened was too much for him to handle since you know him as an honest man."

"You think he did something he is ashamed of?"

"It's not for me to say Ms. Sancho." Fred says. Then Officer Clark interrupts him.

"What now sir?"

"Doctor Klein is here, the coroner, detectives and officers are here, let's let everyone do their jobs. We'll give our statements and leave. I need to tackle the paperwork and make calls."

"Yeah, I'm ready to go now that's its over." Officer Clark says as they walk out.

"I want to get through the paperwork and calls so I can crash for a couple hours." Fred Holland says.

Chapter Sixty One

Late Tuesday morning Max sits in a lounge chair by the shady edge of the pool that isn't immersed in sunlight. He stares at the crowd splashing around, especially two of the women in Bikinis. Max is enjoying the view and doesn't notice Rose approach until she taps his shoulder.

"We waited here long enough Max. The sky is clear. Hurricane Jezebel is history headed for Central America. I'm really tired of dancing, swimming, eating, drinking, watching movies, sleeping, and mingling. I've gathered up all my stuff and the clothes we shed. I have a perpetual headache. I think it's from all of the strange smoke in the air and maybe lack of a good night's sleep. Ugh!" Rose says waving a hand by her nose when she smells the stink of cigar butts again.

"I'm not used to all this partying either." Max says.

"Chet is listening to the noon news now. The band specifically nixed the TV's until now so no bad news would dampen the party. Now the party is over. Apparently Matuso lost a gunfight and Sancho is dead too. They didn't say how Sancho died, but I'm sure it is safe to go home."

"Yeah, most of the people have already left." Max adds.

"I want to go home and I need to call Walter Langston at one o'clock. Let's hope he gives us an all clear sign. I want to hear it from Mister Langston that all the bad guys are in jail and you are safe."

"Yes, I want to check on Sam and I really want to get back to work. I bet my boss is trying to reach me on my cell phone. I need to retrieve it from Pier 66 and call the tour company in Colorado for a sale of a whole group of helicopters."

"You think they will buy?"

"Yes if I can call them and tell them our facility is still standing. You know what non-Floridians think about hurricanes even if they just come close. Anyway, I want to get this big sale." Max says and sees Chet come to him.

"Max, Senator Sancho is dead! I know you are rooting for Bill Medina but this is crazy! Sancho's party will have to scramble to find a new candidate."

"I think the news has hit the fan." Max says.

"There was a shootout with a man named Rafael Matuso too. I bet it's connected to Sancho. Boy, leave the TV's off a few days and all Hell breaks out. That's exactly why I'm glad we left the TVs off!" Chet says. He walks back into the living room with Max and Rose to watch the noon news. Then Rose speaks.

"It's twelve-fifteen Max. We should leave. You need to get your phone. I need to get my camcorder. We need to visit Sam. We both want to get back to normal. Let's go!" Rose says.

"I'm ready after we say our goodbyes." Max pats Chet on the shoulder. "Thanks for the amazing party Chet."

"Thanks for everything." Rose adds giving Chet a gentle hug.

"I'm glad you could make it." Chet says and smiles at Rose. "I know the guys enjoyed seeing you dance and especially in the Bikini Katie loaned you with the T-shirt top. You were the life of the party on the dance floor." Chet admits.

"Thanks, and it was nice to have something on when I went swimming!" Rose chuckles with Chet and Max.

"Oh what are all the secrets about Max?" Chet asks.

"I will explain the mysteries after we talk to Ann and Peggy."

"That's fair. Are you going to run away with Rose?"

"Absolutely not!" Rose butts in. "But I thought about running off with John Fret. He flirted with me even if he didn't do anything."

"You certainly are tempting, Rose." Max adds.

"Okay, I will wait for your explanation with anticipation. It's too bad that Sam and the other fellow didn't come back. That must be part of the problem."

"Well, I didn't want to spoil your party Chet, but Sam is in Holy Cross Hospital with a serious gunshot wound. Paul is in jail."

"That's incredible Max! A guy named Paul shot Sam?"

"Yes, though I'm not sure that's his real name."

"Will Sam be all right?"

"I don't know yet. I will explain everything soon. You got a hint of things from the news today. Anyway, thanks for the party Chet. We'll say goodbye to the rest of the gang and head out. Rose has business she must take care of and I need to visit with Sam and make a few calls." Max says. He works his way through a few guests to say goodbye to the rest of the band members and Katie before leaving.

"Wow! The sky is blue and the air is fresh and clean. Look at this wonderful day!" Rose shouts as she walks outside.

"We go to Pier 66 first to get my phone." Max says as he traipses across the lawns toward his house with Rose. The sun is shining and Max feels the heat of the near ninety degree breeze.

"Yes. I need to get my recorder too." Rose says. "I want to visit Sam and then go to Miami and clean up my apartment. I'm sure you want to be free of me."

"That's not really true Rose. Anyway, we can use Sam's van."

Max smiles and scans the area for any out of ordinary vehicles or persons while he walks across the lawns with Rose. He breathes easy seeing only a few birds flitting around. Max goes inside his house noting his front door is unlocked. He sees the bullet holes in the walls and in his torn up couch. Rose stops him inside the door.

"Let me check out everything." Rose says waving Max to wait in the foyer. She readies her Glock and searches every room. The rest of the house is empty, but in the master bedroom she picks up the clothes she shed there. The only movement she sees is Hera on the bed. Rose comes back to Max, not noticing Hera follows her. She tucks the gun in her waist and shouts "Clear."

"Great, even the master bedroom?" Max asks embracing her.

"Yes, please don't tempt me Max. You need to talk to Peggy."

"I'm sorry Rose."

"You need to see what Peggy wants. Oh yes, I'll take Peggy's clothes to wash them before I return them later, and I'm keeping on the T-shirt. It's better than another pink blouse." Rose says backing away from Max and nearly tripping over Hera.

"You look good in anything Rose."

"Max, you live in a la-la world. Don't you understand? I would only keep you in danger all the time. Stay safe with Peggy."

"Maybe." Max says. He picks up Hera and she purrs when Rose pets her.

"Thank you Hera for not growling at me." Rose smiles.

"It's time." Max eases Hera down and walks to the garage.

"Yes, I want to hear what Langston says."

"We'll take Sam's Caravan. A moving target is harder to hit." Max retrieves a key fob from a drawer and slips inside the minivan to start the engine. He opens the garage door and drives onto Lux Lane and to the Pier 66 Hotel.

Max goes to their room and retrieves his cell phone from the cabinet. He stops at the front desk and checks out of the room before having the valet retrieve his Corvette. He tips the valet gets in the car.

"My phone is almost dead Rose. I'm glad I have a charger here." Max says. He plugs his phone into a charger cable and hands the phone to Rose.

Rose dials Langston. The car's wireless speakers kick on.

"Hello Mister Langston, this is Rose."

"Hello Agent Finley. I've been waiting for your call. I have all good news for you."

"Oh thank you. How is that sir?"

"Hubert Sancho, Rafael Matuso and his main man Frank Carver are dead. Thanks to you Sara Troutman is alive. We got to her just in time and we did catch the shooter."

"This is great news! What about Donna Grant?"

"We took her into custody here. She is cooperating with us. She named who was working with her in Miami. They are in custody too." Langston continues telling Rose the details of what happened. He pauses at the end and Rose replies.

"Was Agent Cooper arrested?"

"Yes."

"Great, so we can come out of hiding?"

"Yes. This is a total success. I know you lost your cell phone in the Atlantic Ocean. You can get another one in Miami or you can pick up a new phone in Atlanta with a bump in pay. I have a position here for you if you are interested."

"Yes sir I'm interested! I grew up in Atlanta."

"I know that. Good, take a few days to pack and get things in order. I will email details and your instructions today. By the way, I'm removing all the recent derogatory comments Grant put in your file. It seems she intentionally made you look like a fool."

"Thank you, sir!"

"Excellent work Finley. I expect you to do the same here."

"Yes sir!" Rose says goodbye and stares at the phone smiling.

"So we are safe to go wherever we want." Max says.

"Well, let's go to Sam's place to get my recorder."

"You follow me, and park in Sam's space." Max hands the minivan fob to Rose. He stops the car next to the Caravan.

"We are on the way!" Rose says as she gets out of Max's car.

Chapter Sixty Two

The traffic is light and soon Max parks at the Bridgestone apartments. He leads the way to Sam's place and taps in the door code. Max looks around. Everything is as he left it. He retrieves the camcorder from the microwave and hands it to Rose.

"What do I do with this?" She says holding the fob for the Caravan toward Max and stuffing the camcorder in her pocket.

"I'll take the fob." Max says as he follows Rose out and locks the door. "Next stop is Holy Cross Hospital."

"Shouldn't you leave the fob in the apartment?"

"No, it's an extra one for the minivan. I've got to remember to put it back in that drawer when I get home."

"Okay, let me gather up the clothes I shed here and then we can go."

"I'll get a trash bag for you."

Max starts the Corvette and drives to Holy Cross Hospital. He rushes across the parking area and into the Hospital with Rose trailing behind him. Max leads Rose directly to ICU but finds Sam isn't there.

"You should check at the information desk." A nurse says.

"What happened to him?" Max asks. His legs are suddenly weak.

"We moved him to a private room today. He is doing better."

"Bless you! Can you tell me what room he is in?"

Max rushes ahead of Rose to the elevators. When the doors open on the fourth floor, Max speed walks to Sam's room. He smiles seeing Sam is sitting up reading a dinner menu. "Sam!"

Max shouts and rushes to him. He shakes Sam's outreached hand.

"This is one of those moments!" Max leans over and hugs Sam. "Hello brother!"

"What are you doing Max!" Sam grunts in pain from the hug.

"I know, but this warrants a hug."

"That was painful! Where have you two been?"

"Langston told us to hide while he took care of business. We snuck back to Chet's party." Max says backing away from Sam. He notices Dale and Fay Stormen sitting across the room. He avoids looking at them concentrating on Sam.

"So while I'm shot up in the hospital eating hospital food you and Rose are having King Crab legs and caviar at Chet's?" Sam winces and smiles as Rose gently hugs him.

"Well, it wasn't that wonderful Sam. We were worried about you and other things."

"Mom and dad know what happened. I told them everything." Sam says. His dad extends a hand toward Max.

"I apologize for what I said to you Max. I was upset. I know you're Sam's best friend even though you tend to get him into jams." Dale Stormen says.

"Thanks Mr. Stormen. Sam is more than my best friend he is my soul brother. You know that Sancho and Matuso are dead then. I want you to know I was going to kill the gunman if Sam died."

Max and Rose chat with the Stormen's for nearly an hour until the nurse orders everyone out so Sam can rest. Max and Rose say goodbye to Sam's parents as they walk out of the hospital. Max sits in his car and holds Rose's hand. Finally Rose speaks.

"Max, take me to my car now. You need to be free of me."

"I don't want to be free." Max says.

"I know we have feelings for each other but you don't need trouble like me. You have your job and Peggy and a normal life to think of. Everything will work out."

Max is silent. He has mixed emotions about Rose. He drives along thinking. *Rose is the most exciting woman I have ever met but she is also the most dangerous one. But who cares about danger when you are in love? Am I in love with two women?* Max drives slowly, wanting this time together to last forever. He finally pulls into the parking area at the small marina in Miami and slows to a stop.

"That's Bertha over there." Rose points at the gray Chrysler parked among other newer shinier cars. The car next to Bertha leaves. The entire strip of stores is humming with activity.

"You drive that big old thing?" Max asks.

"Bertha is a most forgettable car. I like a car that doesn't stand out, and I keep Bertha in excellent shape under the hood."

"So Bertha only looks like she belongs in the junk yard."

"That's the idea Max. I look like a poor nobody in that."

"I believe anyone would." Max says and parks next to Bertha. He hurries to help Rose out and gives her a big hug.

"Okay Rose, no more kissing on the lips or I'm liable to carry you off and have my way with you, and Bertha has a large back seat!" Max says kissing her cheek. He continues to hug Rose for a long time and feels her not wanting to let go either. Finally, he trades kisses on the cheek again and releases her.

"You are the greatest!" Rose says. She rests her hands on Max's shoulders.

"Speaking for Sam and me, we will miss you Agent Finley."

"I'm thankful for all that you have done for me. I love you and I love Sam, but I 'love-love' you Max. You got more than you bargained for on that fishing trip and Sam too. I hope you only catch fish from now on."

"I think that is an official I love you Rose. The fact is I love you too. But I guess you want that exciting life in Atlanta, doing surveillance, catching the bad guys and all. You want me to work out something safe and comfortable with Peggy." Max says.

"There's always another hill to climb. I'm still climbing. You already have your life together and I like working alone. I think you'll get back to normal."

"As a matter of fact, I'll go back to work this afternoon, and glad of it. I'm not sure about Sam, but I actually love my job." Max says.

"I remember a line from an old song that goes, 'Do what you do do best!' We are doing what we do best." Rose says backing away.

"Yes." Max says. He stares at Rose during an awkward pause. Then Rose looks into his eyes and speaks.

"Max, I want you to know the other day in your house... I know it was foolish, but that was the most wonderful time for me."

"It was for me too Rose. I thought I would be miserable without Peggy but I'm thankful you came into my life and now you're going away." Max gives Rose another hug.

"I will get a burner phone and call you. Maybe I'll see you one more time."

"Well, I'm not sure I could stand saying goodbye again Rose." Max watches Rose turn and walk to her car admiring her hourglass figure. He feels his eyes water as Rose slips inside Bertha and starts the engine. Max waves goodbye as Rose drives away.

"Well, back to normal. I wish I could act like all this time with Rose didn't happen." Max says wiping his eyes before he gets back in his Corvette. His mind is still buzzing. *Think of it as another adventure where we stepped in poop and came out smelling like a rose – a rose flower I mean. Oh, bad humor Max. Except this time, my heart aches! This will be an awkward welcome home. Oh well... Next stop is back to the hospital.* Max sighs. He drives away from the marina heading to Holy Cross Hospital.

It's late afternoon when Max parks at the hospital. He goes to Sam who is alone in the semiprivate room.

"Hello Max party animal! The doctor says I'm going to live."

"Well, I knew that all along." Max lies. "You have to quit getting shot though."

"I've had two strikes now."

"Well, the first one the guy was pointing the gun at me just before the crash."

"I thought I was dying then, and this time too."

"You can't be killed with just one shot. You're like the Super Judo man!"

"Believe it or not the doctor did say because I have such a healthy body, I bounced back faster than he expected. Even with all the blood loss, I have no memory loss, and I'm healing fast."

"That's the best news I've heard, even better than talking to Langston."

"Now tell me all about Langston and especially about Rose since mom and dad are gone. All I heard is what you told my parents."

"I didn't say this earlier Sam, but I love Rose. I love her Sam!"

"That's crazy Max! You see what happens in her world."

"I know, I know, but I can't help it!" Max sobs covering his face with his hands.

"Then go to her Max."

"She doesn't want me. She said goodbye and she means forever!"

"I guess it's not like the old days when you would be happy an affair is over, and glad to look for a new challenge. Now you have to lick your wounds and start over. I'm sorry you feel so bad. Just remember we survived. That has to make you feel better."

"Not this time Sam." Max laments. He pauses and asks. "When will you be out?"

"Doctor Allison says I might be released Thursday, in time to meet the girls. He wants to be sure that the patches are good, and I have no leaks or infections. You know they kick you out as soon as possible to avoid you catching something."

"Wow, that's fast. Are you very sore?"

"I hurt the most where the stitches are."

"What do we tell the girls?"

"It looks like we must fess up. I can't hide the gunshot wound."

"I have to tell about Rose?"

"Yup, I don't see how we can avoid it. We told people at the party. Chet and Katie are bound to mention her."

"I think Thursday evening will be interesting." Max states.

Max orders a hospital dinner and stays with Sam until late evening, chatting about various things including when they might go fishing again. He avoids telling his best friend again how sad he is about losing Rose. Inside he wishes he could be with Rose but knows it is over. Max leaves at ten and drives home to an empty house.

He sits alone in his favorite swivel rocker chair at 250 Lux Lane. Hera hops in his lap purring and Max pets her affectionately. The emptiness sinks in that Peggy is no longer with him. "Hera, do you think she will change her mind and want to stay with me?" He waits for an answer but Hera just tilts her head not indicating yes or no.

"What do you know, you're just a cat! Well, we will have to wait to see what happens." He leans back and closes his eyes. He pets Hera and dozes off.

Chapter Sixty Three

Wednesday evening Peggy packs her pink roll-around suitcase stuffing clothes with no concern about folding or neatness. Her mind is on worrying about what she will say to Max. Between the attempted abduction and the trip to Reno, she missed all of the sewing lessons. However, she feels great, since she hasn't heard any more from Detective Foster after his brief questioning about Mister Carl Minion.

"You could have had a lot more fun Ann." Peggy says zipping up her roll-around.

"I'm not a big party goer."

"What did you do the last two nights?"

"Oh, I read through some of the material. I did a little gambling with our friend Ralph before his partner returned. You know Ralph sat with me in most of the classes."

"I know and he's a chatty fellow."

"What about you? What did you and party animal Ursula do?"

"Ursula and I had a blast. We bar hopped along the strip with Brendan and Barry. Let me think. We went in the 107 Sky Lounge, the Carnival Court, the X S Nightclub, and the Bellagio. We had a blast with those guys!"

"You hung out with the guys from the Luxor?"

"Yes. We were in the Petrossian Bar last night. They are fun to be with, and I felt more alive than I have in a year."

"I can tell you loved it, but do you miss Max? I miss Sam terribly."

"It's crazy, but I didn't think about Max until I started packing. I'm staying here Ann. This is where I should be. Ursula has a nice apartment here and says she needs a roommate. Her old roommate got married. I think I made a good friend. I just have to find a way to tell Max all this."

"So this is what you want?"

"I split up with Max so we could do our own things. Yeah, there is something missing in my life. I talked to Ralph about it. He barhopped with us last night and his mate Sheridan is a fun guy too."

"So you are sure about leaving a hunk like Max?"

"I think so... No, I know so, I'm okay with it Ann! Max is a wonderful man but I feel trapped with him. I want a more exciting life. Max is settling down and wants kids."

"Sam and I want kids too. I guess you will know soon enough, but I'm pregnant. That's why I didn't want to go drinking with you."

"Holy cow Ann, I'm so happy for you! When are you due?" Peggy gives Ann a hug.

"In seven months and Sam is elated. He didn't want me to go off in my condition."

"And I thought you were mad at me."

"No, I just like the idea of kids and stability Peggy."

"Stability is too dull for me Ann."

"This trip wasn't about sewing, you wanted to test the waters."

"Exactly, and I like the waters! I want to live here."

"That's crazy talk Peggy! You mean not go home at all?"

"No, I have to go back to explain all this to Max in person. I was going to rent an apartment here until Ursula offered her place. That way I can travel and not worry about having the yard mowed or feeding a cat or anything. I love all the glitter and bigness of this place. I want to be a part of this crazy town."

"Wow that sounds serious. Oh, do you know if Ralph is dining with us tonight?"

"We are on our own. Ralph is dining with Sheridan tonight. He said they want to dine alone tonight."

"To celebrate no doubt, the last dinner and he ducks out on us." Ann says thinking about not seeing Ralph anymore. She has dined with him every evening since she met him, although the last day he talked more about Sheridan returning than anything else.

"I have his phone number. I will call him when I get back here."

"I think Ralph helped us a lot. He indirectly saved some lives too. For someone who doesn't date women, he sure was nice to me. He got me Carey Lange to hire to search for you."

"Miss Lange said Detective Foster captured some bad guys and rescued a woman named Janet Winslow." Peggy states.

"They saved her bacon for sure. I like him but his voice gets on my nerves."

"I sort of got used to his voice. Well, let's have a relaxing dinner and sack out early. I'm glad they finally brought us single beds."

"Yes, I'm tired of sleeping with you."

"Me too, you kick your legs around in your sleep." Ann says.

"I never noticed it, but Max says that too."

"I'm ready to leave tomorrow. Are you ready?"

"I hate leaving even for a little while, but I must talk to Max."

"I hope everything works out Peg. Let's go eat."

"I hope to move here right away." Peggy says.

"I still find it hard to believe you want to do that."

"It's just me. I did like being with Max. I felt alive with Carl but I felt guilty too. I got over that with Brendan. Once I talk to Max I will feel totally free."

"Peggy, Carl was murdered! You would have been killed too if you hadn't left when you did!"

"You're kidding! Well, maybe so with Carl, but I have friends here that will help me be more careful. I have all this money and I want to celebrate while I can. Max just wants to have kids. We have different mindsets. Do you understand that?"

"Maybe," Ann says. She zips up her suitcase and follows Peggy out the door to go eat dinner.

The plane lifts off early Thursday morning from Las Vegas, Nevada. Peggy still struggles with what to tell Max. She frets as the silver bird races non-stop toward Fort Lauderdale, Florida. She knew what to say to Max two days ago but now she is unsure. Her brain keeps mulling over things. *How can I tell Max about partying with Carl and what about Brendan? I would never have encouraged Carl if I wasn't free of Max and wasted on rum and Coke. I love being free again. How do I tell him I missed every sewing class, and the dinners! I hope Max isn't hurt too bad and can be happy for me.* She leans back succumbing to the drone of the engines and dozes off. Hours later the plane touches down at Fort Lauderdale-Hollywood International Airport. The tire bump and the air breaking of the engines pull her forward, awakening her. The plane stops and Peggy feels a tension headache coming on.

"Look, the sky is blue Peggy. It's like the storm never happened. The boys should be waiting for us. I'm so glad we're back. I miss Sam so much!" Ann says staring out the window at the afternoon sky.

"Great. Remember don't tell any secrets until we are home!"

"Mum's the word. I still think you should stay with Max. You know he loves you. He's a good man Peggy."

"We love each other. That's why we are separating, so we can each be happy."

"I still don't see the logic there, but I will try to keep quiet about this until I hear from you. Don't mention about me and Ralph. I don't know how Sam will react to me going to dinners and classes with another man, even if he is gay."

"So you don't want to tell Sam you spent time with Ralph? You told me you enjoyed his company!"

"Hey quiet!"

"Then he had dinner with you every night. I saw him rub your back one time. What about that?"

"He was trying to encourage me about something."

"What else did you do with him?"

"I talked to him about how God loves us no matter what, and that we are all sinners."

"Yesterday you told him he was good looking."

"I see no reason to mention that one bit!"

"I told Max before I left, what happens in Vegas stays in Vegas. Right now I wish I had stayed there."

"So we don't talk about Carl, Brendan or Ralph."

"Not until we each get home. That's the plan." Peggy says. Then she hears a chime and the seat belt sign goes off. She gets up wishing she were back in Las Vegas as she undoes her seat belt.

Ann says a brief prayer before she gets out of her seat.

Chapter Sixty Four

Max fidgets as he sits with Sam waiting at the gate for Peggy and Ann. His mind is racing thinking about what to say. *I hope Peggy wants kids now. That would help me forget Rose. How am I going to tell her about rescuing a naked woman from the ocean? I can't tell her about Rose dropping the raincoat when we were in the closet, or that I made love to her? I definitely did more than just make friends with Rose!* He frowns at Sam sitting next to him. *Sam can play the sympathy act. He got shot and only I know about Charlotte trying to entice him. He really has no problems with Ann.* Max is annoyed when Sam mumbles at him.

"What?" Max snaps at Sam.

"Whoa! Why are you so testy? You were deep in thought."

"Sorry, I was thinking about how to explain things to Peggy."

"I think she will be okay Max. I on the other hand am not sure I should tell Ann about Charlotte. We were lovers once you know."

"Yes, Eliza and I were in the cabana next to you and Charlotte's cabana that night on the beach, remember?"

"Oh yes Eliza, the girl who didn't like pranks. Anyway, all those feelings came back to me Max. I tried to stay with her and watch the movie, but all I could think about was being with her back then, but I couldn't hurt Ann if I gave in."

"Hey, you backed off."

"Yes. I thought about Ann, and how much I love her, she is everything to me and I knew how much it would hurt her if I did anything with Charlotte. I'm not sure I should tell Ann about her."

"You don't have to tell her anything, Sam. If you hadn't been shot, maybe we could've just said nothing happened!"

"Yes, but Ann will see the wound."

"That's tough to ignore. What will you say?"

"We have to tell the whole story Max."

"If you can avoid grunting in pain until you get home, we should wait until then to tell them some version of the truth, agreed?" Max says and Sam nods.

"Yes, we'll each tell them in private. Oh, here they come." Sam says feeling some pain as he rises from his seat.

Ann follows Peggy into the concourse. She sees how Peggy stands out in the crowd, a tall brunette with bright blue eyes, wearing all pink with her bright pink blouse and pink shorts. Ann walks along following Peggy and the crowd from the plane. She feels a rush of anticipation as the crowd thins and Ann looks ahead. Excitement floods her body when she sees Sam stand up a hundred feet away. Out of control, she runs to him and wraps her arms around Sam feeling him embrace her and grunt. She hardly notices Peggy and Max embracing too. After the hug and a few kisses, she talks.

"I missed you so much!" Ann says nearly in tears.

"I missed you too. Did you lose all your money? How did you and Peggy do?" Sam asks jokingly as he releases her and they trek toward baggage claim.

"Well, we survived just fine. How did you two do?" Ann says.

"We muddled through the rain alive." Sam says.

Max follows Sam and Ann to the baggage claim area. He looks at Peggy walking next to him and wonders what is bothering her.

"Are you okay Peggy? You look worried."

"Remember what happens in Vegas stays in Vegas!" Peggy giggles nervously.

"Well then, what happens while you're away stays away, except I finally replaced the house locks with combo locks."

"Something happened. Why did you change the locks? What kind of prank did you do Max?" Peggy giggles again.

"I asked you first Peg. Anyway, I got a big contract with Colorado Guided Tours Company yesterday after they realized our company didn't get hit by the hurricane. They already had the specifications on the helicopters and wired the initial money to purchase the first one. If they like it, and I'm sure they will, they will buy copters for all their other locations around the world!"

"That's great Max. There is a reason you are the number one salesman!" Peggy says and then is silent until her luggage rides around on the carousel. "Let's get our bags and get out of here."

"Yes, I want to go home." Ann sees her bag on the conveyer belt.

"We have some catching up to do." Sam says and winks at Ann.

"Sam, we are ready whenever you are." Max says grabbing Peggy's bag and Ann's bag from the conveyor belt.

"Thanks Max." Sam says.

"You're hurt! I heard you grunt when I hugged you." Ann says.

"Yes. It happened a few days ago."

"What did you do?"

"I'll tell you all about it when we get home."

"Does this involve Max again?"

"In a way, but not really."

Sam hums barely saying anything as he lets Max load the luggage in the minivan. He drives out of the airport noticing everyone is quiet. Sam feels like he's in the quiet before a tornado hits!

Chapter Sixty Five

Ann stays silent looking out the window as they leave the airport. At the Blue Lake Estates, she sees even the streets seem cleaner than usual. Still maintaining her silence, she watches Sam swing the minivan onto Lux Lane and stop under the stone canopy of Max's house.

"You want to come in for a beer or something?" Max asks half-heartedly as he unloads Peggy's travel bag.

"I really want to go home." Ann says looking at Sam.

"Come over in the morning about ten-ish. Sam and I are taking the day off. I'm going to grill a bunch of those fish Sam and I caught last week."

"That sounds nice." Ann says.

"See you about ten." Sam says before the sliding door closes.

Sam drives onto Lux Lane before Ann breaks the silence.

"Are you going to tell me what crazy thing happened?"

"Why do you think something crazy happened?"

"I can read you like a book Sam. You're hurt and something weird happened."

"Well, something happened in Vegas too. What was that?"

"I can't tell you!"

"Then something did happen!" Sam stops for a red light and stares at Ann.

"Promise you won't get upset." Ann bows her head.

"Oh no, you lost all your money?" Sam's stitches hurt as he turns to stare at Ann.

"No Sam and I love you more than ever! I just feel guilty."

"Just exactly what did you do in Vegas?"

"I can't keep this secret from you. I had dinners with a man who helped me!"

"Did you have sex with him?"

"Heavens no, he's gay!" Embarrassed, Ann covers her face.

"Okay let me see if I got this right. A gay man helped you do something and you had dinner with him to thank him. Is that it?"

"No, I had the first dinner with him before he helped me. Then I had dinner every night except last night."

"Why did you do that?"

"His partner was away until last night. He didn't want to eat alone and neither did I."

"Where was Peggy? Did she dine with you too?"

"Um…, yes once."

"Let's go home. I want to hear the whole story!"

"Then you'll forgive me?"

"Well, first I think you should tell me what this guy did that is so great!" Sam says as he drives to the Bridgestone apartments.

"Well, he helped me search for Peggy."

"Where was Peggy? You had dinner with this guy instead of with your group because Peggy was off somewhere?"

"Yes, well he was part of the group."

"Well I can guess why he took you to dinner!" Sam says as he parks the minivan.

"He isn't like that Sam! I can't tell you about it yet. Now, what happened while I was gone? You seem to be harboring something."

"Why should I tell you if you won't tell me what happened in Vegas?" Sam says pulling her suitcase out of the minivan with a painful grunt.

"Sam! Tell me! I promised Peggy I wouldn't talk about what happened yet."

"So this is about Peggy? Did both of you go out with him? Is the law after you?" Sam teases as he walks with Ann to the elevator.

"No, did you two do something awful?" Ann asks.

"No, I think I discovered how much I really love you."

"Then let's forget about talking. I'm so happy to be home." Ann smiles as the elevator doors open on the third floor.

"Prepare yourself, I have a surprise inside." Sam opens the door.

"Oh my! Sam!" Ann gushes admiring the trail of red paper rose petals leading to their bedroom, and a welcome home sign above the bedroom door.

"What do you think?"

"This is really tacky Sam! Bolt the door, I love it!"

Max rolls Peggy's suitcase inside still wondering how to tell her what happened while she was in Las Vegas. He follows her into the bedroom to help her unload her travel bag. To his surprise, Peggy starts to undress.

"How were the classes? Did you learn a lot?" Max asks.

"Oh, yes..., I learned a lot out there." Peggy says tossing her blouse on the bed. She seductively strips out of her shorts, stares at Max. She turns away, unhooks her bra and tosses it at him as she glances over her shoulder.

"Oh, tell me all about it." Max unbuttons his shirt.

"I'm going to shower Max. Join me?" Peggy asks as she provocatively slides her underwear onto the floor. She poses for Max and then dashes into the bathroom.

"That's a silly question!" Max dumps his clothes near hers, and follows her into the bathroom. He eases under the spray with her. Max can feel the tension in Peggy as he massages her back.

"I need to tell you about something Max." Peggy bows her head.

"It can wait for a while. I just want to not talk right now."

"Max, I do love you!"

Peggy turns and embraces Max. She begins kissing him and feels her body turn on as she presses fully against him. All her pent up desires are bursting out. She presses her arms onto his back. As she wraps her legs around him, she feels Max hold her and carry her out of the shower into the bedroom. She sinks onto the bed and feels Max caress and kiss her. Her body writhes with desire as she feels him bond with her. Peggy works her body with him until her longings are satisfied. She feels Max roll away from her and she enjoys the afterglow for a few minutes before speaking.

"We left the shower on, didn't we?" She says, knowing the answer.

"Yes. I think we need to go back." Max rolls off the bed and trots into the bathroom. They only smile as they bathe together.

Max towels off and puts on shorts and another flowery shirt. He leaves the bedroom, slogs into the living room, and leans back in his swivel rocker chair. Hera jumps in his lap and starts purring.

"Okay Hera, do you really want me to tell her everything?" Max whispers. He feels Hera purr as she looks up at him and tilts her head. "Oh, what do you know, you're just a cat." Max pets her lovingly.

He sees Peggy come out of the bedroom and go to the kitchen. The idea of telling Peggy about Rose bothers him. Then Max hears her bang the refrigerator door closed and come into the living room. She faces him with her hands on her hips.

Chapter Sixty Six

"I'm hungry and there's nothing I want to eat in the refrigerator. You know all the food I left for you is still there!"

"Well Sam and I mostly ate at Chet's house or we got take out."

"Did you ever open the refrigerator?"

"Of course, we have our beer and wine in there."

"I'll go shopping tomorrow after I clean out the old food. Would you mind ordering a pizza for us tonight? I don't feel like going out."

"That sounds good Peg. I'll do it right now."

"No wait Max, I need to tell you what happened in Vegas." Peggy is distressed. She turns away from Max and folds her arms across her chest.

"I thought we were going to keep everything secret."

"I can't do that."

"I will order the pizza later."

"This is hanging over my head. I hope you will understand."

"This sounds serious Peg, what happened?"

Peggy tells Max about Carl, the murder, and everything.

"I wish you hadn't gone to Las Vegas at all."

"Why? I needed to get away. I had the time of my life there."

"So this is it? I should cancel the wedding ideas for sure?"

"Yes, I'm sorry Max. Okay, what happened here? I can tell something happened."

"It's nothing much Peggy. I'd rather go back in the bedroom."

"Oh yeah, tell me about the bedroom! Some of my clothes are missing, more specifically, underwear, shorts, blouses, and even my pink sneakers! Why do we have a new couch and why does it smell like fresh paint in here? Please explain."

"You keep track of every little thing?"

"Yes, I keep a very orderly house including my closet and drawers. Now things are a mess. Did you give my clothes away? If you say you started cross-dressing, I won't believe you!"

"It isn't that simple. I had to paint to cover up the patches…

"Patches, what patches?"

"From the bullet holes."

"Bullet holes! My God, you shotguns in the living room!"

"There was an altercation here, shots were fired, but that's not how Sam got shot."

"Sam was shot! I thought he was just sore from something. Will Sam be all right?"

"He's recovering nicely."

"Harrumph. I suppose our old couch was shot too. This one is different… darker."

"Matter of fact, a stray bullet ripped a huge gap in it, but it had a little blood stain on it anyway. I matched the color as best I could."

"The couch had a blood stain? How did that happen?"

"I'm not sure who the blood was from."

"You're not sure who… And what did you do with my clothes?"

"Oh well, here goes. I loaned some of your clothes to Rose."

"You did what! Who is Rose?"

"She's FBI agent Rose Finley."

"You loaned my clothes to an FBI woman?"

"This may take some time."

"I've got lots of time, what happened Max?" Peggy blurts.

Max tells almost everything; how he and Sam saved Rose from the Atlantic, the Sancho-Matuso events and the rogue FBI agent, only keeping his romps with Rose a secret.

"I want my stuff back! You kissed Rose! What else did you do?"

"Don't ask, and she kissed me!"

"How old is Rose? Is she good looking?" Peggy feels a twinge of jealousy.

"She looks a lot like you, except she has red hair. I guess she's in her late twenties. Peggy, I have feelings for her, but I'm a one-woman man. I wanted us to be together. Also, she's a dedicated FBI agent, which means she doesn't want a liability like me hanging around to give an advantage to a criminal."

"I want to see her. Did you take any nude pictures of her?"

"No, no pictures of her. I don't think Sam did either."

"You say she is moving from Miami to Atlanta?"

"Yes, she got a promotion." Max says. Then his phone rings.

"Hi Max, this is Rose. I'm calling from my new burner phone."

"Hello! Well this is awkward."

"You must be with Peggy."

"Yes, I'll make a note of this number for sure."

"Good, I'm all packed. Everything is happening so fast. I flew to Atlanta Tuesday night and found an apartment right away. I flew back Wednesday evening. The movers are coming Friday morning to load all my stuff. I leave tomorrow night. I want you to know I love you Max, but..."

"Me too." Max pauses. "Well Peggy is back. I hope you have a nice flight."

"No, I'm driving Bertha to Atlanta tomorrow night."

"Oh yeah Bertha, but why travel at night?"

"There is less traffic at night. Bertha is ready to go. Well, goodbye Max."

"Goodbye." Max rings off. He sees Peggy staring at him.

"Who is Bertha and what was that 'me too' about?"

"Rose named her car Bertha and she is driving to Atlanta tomorrow night. Um...she is getting back to normal. I said me too."

"We need to have a going away dinner for her. That way she can bring back my stuff."

"Really? She's leaving tomorrow night. You want us to have dinner with her?"

"Yes, you told me she lives in Miami, right? She can dine here on the way to Atlanta! Catch her before she makes other plans. Tell her to bring back my stuff!"

"How about tomorrow night at Café Del Mar?"

"Okay, see if you can get a reservation there."

"You know I can." Max says.

"I'm going to clean up all the towels and stuff in our bathroom. You left a mess there too. Let me know what she says."

As he dials Rose, he thinks. *I'll tell her not to doll up. There is no need to stir the pot!*

Chapter Sixty Seven

By calling in a favor, Max manages to reserve a table at the Café Del Mar. They leave for the restaurant at quarter to five. Max wears a pale blue shirt, a gray and blue tie and a black striped suit. Peggy is wearing a black dress with a sexy lacey hem and pink vertical stripes. She wears shiny black shoes and black sapphire earrings. Sam and Ann dress semi-formal too, but now he is worried about telling Rose to dress casually. Max makes idle chitchat as he rides to the restaurant with Sam and Ann. A valet takes the minivan. The foursome goes into the restaurant.

Max sees Rose standing inside the entrance and shakes his head in disbelief. Contrary to what he expected for Peggy's sake, Rose is wearing a short dark maroon dress with a very sexy lacey hem similar to the hem on Peggy's dress. Her flaming red hair in a pageboy style looks as if she just stepped out of a beauty parlor, much nicer than the tangled mess he saw when she came out of the ocean. As he gets closer to her he smells a hint of cinnamon. He sees her shiny amber earrings that enhance her impish and perfect smile. *Drop dead gorgeous!* Max thinks.

"Hello Rose, you look exceptional. I like the dress and earrings." Max says frowning at her as he shakes her hand.

"Hello Max and thank you. I called Sam to see how he was doing and he told me what to wear. I even wore lipstick tonight just for this occasion."

"Oh, right, you talked to Sam."

"Yes and Max you clean up nice too. Oh, you must be Peggy, I love your dress. I have some of your stuff in my car all clean and neat. I didn't want to bring it in here. Hello Sam, I guess this is Ann." Rose smiles and shakes hands with Peggy and Ann.

"Peggy had to meet the super-woman who survived in the ocean." Max says.

"I managed to stay afloat until you guys rescued me."

Peggy mumbles to herself. "Nice floats slut!"

"What honey?" Max asks not quite hearing Peggy.

"What guts you have… I mean to live through all that. Lucky for you Max came along and rescued you." Peggy says aloud feeling a twinge of jealousy about Rose.

"Yes, let's get our table." Max says seeing Rose feign a smile.

Max sits down with the others and enjoys a great meal along with some red wine. By eight in the evening, he is ready to leave. While they wait for Rose's car and the Caravan, he says goodbye to Rose giving her a hug and a peck on her cheek. He works hard to hide his feelings for her.

"Goodbye Max." Rose says holding him just a second longer than she should.

"Goodbye and stay safe in Atlanta." Max says.

"It's getting late Rose. You should stay at our house until morning." Peggy offers.

"No thanks, I like driving at night. It's quieter and less traffic."

"Well, goodbye then." Peggy says as Rose's car stops near them.

Max waves with the others as Rose drives away. He follows Peggy to the minivan and settles inside before he speaks.

"How about playing Hearts at the house tonight?" Max says.

"What about that, Ann?" Sam asks.

"That sounds good. We need to unwind and get back to normal."

"Great, after some wine we can play strip poker." Max jests.

"One of these days we might say yes Max, but for now it's still no." Ann says.

"Wait until I get some booze in you! Women seem to do strange things when they get tanked up. It seems we all have secrets don't we?" Max smirks at Peggy.

Sam chitchats with the others as he drives back to Blue Lake Estates. When he turns onto Lux Lane, he notices a dark grey Camaro parked along the curb at Chet's house. He knows Chet said parking on the curb especially overnight is against the homeowner's rules and he had an exception for his hurricane party that expired several days ago. All the cars for Chet's party are long gone. He waits until he stops under the canopy before commenting on the parked car.

"It's awful late for a car to be parked on the curb. Does the association allow cars to stay parked on the curb overnight now?" Sam asks pointing to the rogue car.

"Maybe the car died there. If it isn't gone in the morning I'm sure someone will complain." Max opens the house door by tapping in the code on his new combo lock. He waves everyone inside. After the undoing of the preparation for Hurricane Jezebel everything in the house is back to normal. Max with the help from some workers patched and painted the bullet holes in the walls, the shutters are open, the rug has been cleaned of the bloodstains, a new monitor is in place and the old shot up couch was replaced with a new darker tan couch. Hera is on her usual place perched on the back of the new couch in the living room. Max removes his jacket and heads for the kitchen.

"Beer or wine everyone?" Max asks.

"Let's stick with wine." Sam says stripping off his jacket.

"Just water for me." Ann says.

"No wine for you?" Max asks.

"Right, I guess Sam didn't tell you I'm pregnant."

"Wow, Ann, that is wonderful! No the rascal didn't. I thought it was strange you had tea with dinner."

"Enough fanfare, let's play cards." Ann says.

"Peggy, if you'll get out the cards and stuff I'll pour the wine and get a bottle of water for the pregnant one."

"I'm going to take off this dress first." Peggy says.

"Go ahead!" Max laughs.

"Not here Max, I'm going to the bedroom to change into shorts. Ann, do you want to borrow some comfy clothes?"

"No thanks, I'm fine in this."

"Okay everyone." Max brings glasses and wine to the table and waits for Peggy to return before he sits down. Max starts to deal the cards when the doorbell rings.

"I'll get it." Peggy says. She walks to the door. When she opens it, she screams seeing a man point a gun at her head. He pushes her back and steps inside.

"Get over there with your pals!" Victor Campbell says.

"What do you want? We don't have much money!" Peggy says.

"You two ruined my life, now I'm gonna ruin yours!" The man shouts as he steps into the light and aims his gun at Max.

Max recognizes Victor Campbell the campaign director for Hubert Sancho. He saw the man several times on TV with the Senator, and in the video when Matuso tossed Rose overboard.

"Why aren't you in jail?" Max shouts.

"I got out on bail. I knew it was coming. My job is gone. My wife is divorcing me. My life is gone! I'm going to make it worthwhile going to prison."

"I watched the video sir. I thought you were as shocked as Sancho was about what happened. Why make things worse? You can plead that you didn't know what he was going to do. You could get a lighter sentence..." Max offers.

"No, I saw Sancho open the window, I watched and I did nothing, nothing! I was shocked, but she's just an agent. I was okay with her dying. Then you had to save her! You ruined everything! I lost my career and my family!"

"Surely you didn't want her to die."

"No, but she was a spy. She was caught and dealt with. Everything would have worked out."

"You just made it worse for yourself coming here sir. So you are okay with drowning a human being?"

"It can't get worse! All my plans are ruined!"

"You know she had to strip off the dress to stay afloat!"

"I heard Finley was naked when you found her? I bet you had a good look! My boss is dead so I think I need to make you dead too."

"What are you going to do, kill all of us? You can't kill four people in cold blood!" Max says.

"Maybe I can Max. They say it gets easier the more you kill. Call Finley, I know you must have her number. Tell her to come here or I start killing people."

"Rose is in Atlanta. She can't come here." Max lies.

"Call anyway. I hope seeing her naked was worth it. I know I'd like to see her naked too. Hey, instead of Rose, let's see you strip!" Victor points to Peggy.

"Are you crazy? Peggy, don't strip for this lunatic!" Max shouts.

"Take off your clothes now or I shoot your man!" Victor shouts.

"Don't shoot anyone! I can do that!" Peggy yells. She stands up and begins unbuttoning her blouse hoping she distracts Victor enough so Max or Sam can disarm Victor before she takes off everything.

Chapter Sixty Eight

Rose drives away from the restaurant wiping away tears as she works her way onto I-95 North heading for Atlanta. All her worldly possessions except for what she loaded in Bertha are already en route to her new apartment and scheduled for delivery in the morning. She smiles thinking about how everything worked out with Matuso and Sancho dead, and Donna Grant in custody about to go down in flames. She talked to Langston again and found out Grant never called Agent Cooper to meet her. Grant made several calls to Matuso though, so Grant had no intentions of Cooper meeting her at her apartment. Rose thinks the video may not be admissible as evidence, but she heard the man who was going to shoot Bill Medina's secretary is talking his head off trying to bargain his way into a lighter sentence. *All is right except for this one thing, leaving Max. If fate brought us together, why are we not together? I have a great job, so why are my eyes watering?* She feels sad wondering if Atlanta is what she really wants. She believes Peggy will reconcile with Max and have kids. She still likes working alone which make it hard to have a relationship, especially with someone like Max. She adjusts her rearview mirror down to check her eyes and sees the bag of Peggy's stuff on top of her belongings in the back seat.

"Oh crap, I meant to return that at the restaurant. I'll just mail it from Atlanta." She says, but she seesaws between wanting to see Max again and having to backtrack many miles. She needs the closure of giving back Peggy's clothes and pink sneakers. Her sixth sense tells her she must go back. Rose groans but then she smiles remembering her special time with Max. She makes a U-turn at Boca Raton.

Rose takes I-95 South to Commercial Boulevard. She zig-zags her way to Blue Lake Estates. As she turns onto Lux Lane, she sees the familiar dark gray Camaro of Victor Campbell parked along the curb near Max's house. *This can't be good!* Rose thinks as she turns off her headlights and rolls to a stop behind Sam's Caravan.

She kills her engine, grabs Peggy's bag of stuff and tucks her Glock in her waistband before heading for the house. Instead of ringing the doorbell, Rose eases next to a front window that has the curtain slightly open and peers inside. She sees Peggy drop her blouse to the floor in front of Victor Campbell, who is aiming a gun at Max.

Rose drops Peggy's stuff, draws her gun out and gives the front door knob a twist. To her surprise, she feels the door start to open. *No one locked the door. Here we go!* Rose thinks to herself and swings the door wide open.

"Drop the gun Victor!" Rose shouts. She sees Victor turn his gun toward her. Rose fires first and Victor jerks back, grabs his shoulder and drops his gun.

"No!" Victor shouts. He scrambles for his gun but Max picks up the weapon and points it at Victor.

"Someone call 9 1 1!" Max shouts. "Hello Rose!"

"I'm glad I came back."

"You had a premonition?"

"No, I forgot to give Peggy her stuff." Rose trots outside and brings in a big bag that she hands to Peggy.

"It looks like you saved our lives this time Rose." Max says.

"I wasn't keeping score, just trying to do the right thing."

"Well thank you for not returning Peggy's clothes earlier. Sometimes forgetfulness can be a good thing." Max joshes wondering how he will ever forget Rose.

"I have the police and paramedics on the way." Peggy says buttoning her blouse. She sees Victor sitting on the couch holding his bloody shoulder and weeping.

Max asks out of curiosity. "Why did you stay with Sancho when you found out what a scumbag he was?"

"I needed the job, and I thought Matuso was just making a generous contribution." Victor cringes as he eyes his shoulder seeping blood onto his hand. He hears a siren taper off and red and blue lights flash across the windows.

Two officers and two paramedics enter the house. They patch up Victor, handcuff him and take him away. The officers take notes for their report and within an hour are gone.

"I guess the party is over." Rose says. "By the way Max, Captain Holland returned my laptop and the other stuff to me. It was in a bag in the front seat of the Ford Explorer right in your driveway. We could have saved a trip to Miami!" Rose says.

"Enjoy the 'Journey' I say." Max shakes his head.

"I guess you should leave again." Peggy says giving Rose a hug.

"Yes, it's time. I'll have to be in Atlanta by morning when they deliver my stuff. You all have seen enough of me, and quite literally for you two." She points at Max and Sam.

"Well, hugs all around." Peggy says. She gives Rose another quick hug.

Rose hugs everyone and once again holding Max a little longer than the others before she says goodbye. She slips into her car and as she drives away and waves, tears stream down her face again. "Goodbye forever my love!" She sobs as she leaves Lux Lane.

Max waves at Rose driving away. He smiles for Peggy but inside he hurts. *If only she could be with me.* Max thinks. Then Sam speaks.

"I think we have Guardian Angels watching over us Max."

"Yeah, I've heard that before. I think we are blessed."

"I wonder what will happen to Victor."

"He will have a new job at the Graybar Hotel."

"Yeah he's going back to jail and we can get back to normal. I like normal." Sam says.

"Me too, Sam. Hey, Peg can you finish that striptease act?"
"Just finish dealing the cards Max." Peggy blurts.
"Yes dear. Now that's back to normal!"

Chapter Sixty Nine

Max sits in his swivel rocker chair in the living room with Hera purring in his lap watching the election returns on the first Tuesday in November. Clad only in his boxer shorts and T-shirt he's watching the eleven o'clock news. Max has already earned a huge commission check from the sale of five more helicopters to the sightseeing company in Colorado, with more orders to come. He also has the ear of his Army General friend about a contract for a load of military drones. In his own way Max is happy. He sips some Livingston Rose' wine and pets Hera, not thinking of going to bed.

"It's just you and me Hera now that Peggy has totally moved to Vegas. I miss her and Rose too. I think it's time to get over feeling sorry for myself. I've been too busy at work. I should start dating again." Max says trying to be cheerful. He pets Hera and feels her loud purring. "Do you think I should sell this house and move somewhere more efficient when I start dating again?" Max asks but Hera shakes her head no.

"What do you know, you're just a cat." Max scratches behind her ears. "You know Alan Duncan isn't doing as well as the media predicted. It looks like a landslide for Bill Medina. Even with all the hype, the biased media made for Duncan, Medina is winning easily. It was crazy to predict Duncan could win over Medina starting out with less than three months before the election, especially after the Sancho-Matuso scandal that never got the TV time it deserved." He sees Hera gently nod perhaps in agreement.

"Let's hope Medina doesn't get trashed by the media once he gets in office. All the mainstream news seems controlled by

Duncan's party and they're sore losers. I see you are nodding in agreement Hera." Max still thinks his cat is psychic.

"I'm not sleepy tonight. Maybe we can watch a movie. Would you like that?" Max hears Hera purr louder. He changes to a movie channel on the TV and then mutes the volume when his phone rings. He smiles when he sees the caller ID.

"Hello Sam. Are you watching our man win? What a land-slide!"

"Well yes, but that's not why I'm calling. I thought you ought to know Rose called us just a while ago."

Max feels his heart skip a beat. A painful longing stirs in-side him just when he vowed to be over her. He remembers their passionate lovemaking when they worried they might be killed. Max thinks about what she said about no ties that could be a weakness for an FBI agent. His casual voice changes to a sad and serious response.

"How's she doing Sam?"

"She's fine Max and still in Atlanta. Rose only wanted me to know. She said not to tell you she called, but I disagree. I know how you feel about her Max. I could tell she's troubled. She's not sure what to do. She said not to bother you, but you should know what's going on."

"You know I miss her a lot, but she doesn't want me. That's why she called you instead of me. She said it's too painful for us to communicate. Is she in trouble? Does she need help?"

"Well, maybe Max. She wanted me to keep her secret for a long time."

"What secret, and how long?"

"Maybe eighteen years until her twins grow up. She just confirmed that she is pregnant and she knows it's by you. She says she will raise them on her own. I couldn't keep that from you brother." Sam waits a long time. "Max, are you still there?"

"She told you I'm going to be a father!"

"Yes the doctor thinks he sees two babies. She didn't know Peggy is long gone. I told her but it seemed to upset her more. Why haven't you told her that Max?"

"We haven't talked since she left. I tried her burner phone but it is disconnected. I guessed she wanted it that way."

"What are you going to do?"

"I want to go to Atlanta to be with her right now Sam!"

"Maybe you should call, see how she feels first instead of just surprising her. Are you sure you want to go there?"

"I don't have her number and I don't care if I surprise her. I want to see her."

"You told me you have a meeting with your General friend Wednesday morning. What about that?"

"The General will understand, there is a romantic under that tough skin. The meeting will have to wait. Did Rose give you her address?"

"Yes, I will text it to you."

"I must see her Sam. I can't go on like this. Thank you Sam, thank you!"

Chapter Seventy

Max ends the call and rushes into his bedroom to dress and pack a small bag of essentials. He sees Hera jump on his bed and stare at him. "You'll have to get by without me for a while Hera. I have to go to Rose!" He sees Hera nod at him. "I swear you're psychic!"

Max waves goodbye and sprints to the garage, tosses his bag in, and fires up his Corvette. He thumps the steering wheel while he waits for the garage door to open. Within minutes, he is on I-95 driving north. He stops at a rest area, gases up and buys a cup of coffee. Max sets the cruise control to five miles over the limit and fights the urge to stomp on the gas pedal.

The traffic is bunching up at six in the morning when he enters the outskirts of Atlanta. His GPS directs him to Peoples Town, an area of southern Atlanta, and a fairly decent neighborhood. Many of the buildings are red brick and look like typical middle-class houses. Max follows the GPS to where Rose lives at the Columbia Apartments and parks next to the middle building thinking. *Rose is right. It is quieter to travel at night.*

Max feels a chill in the air as he exits his Corvette. A weak fog hugs the ground in the early morning hours. The parking lot is still sprayed with rays of metallic light. Max trots across the concrete walkway and rushes inside the middle building. As he nears her apartment, he remembers Sam saying that maybe he should call her first. He panics wondering if she is seeing someone. *Maybe she has a friend with her now! Am I wrong just barging in on her? I hope this trip isn't a fool's errand!*

Rose gets up feeling tired after sleeping in short naps tossing about in her bed and thinking how foolish she was to call Sam.

She settles down with her morning cup of coffee in her favorite kitchen chair wondering how a pregnant woman can be a strong FBI agent. Trying to do a good job for Langston and trying to learn the city again, she hasn't tried to hook up with anyone.

She also tried to blank out the memory of Max, so she put all her energy into the job, and ignored the fact that she missed her period in September. At times the job became intense working with the DEA. She remembers how she ran down one suspect and had to defend herself two times already from drug-high crazies. When she missed her period again in October, she remembered missing September and got concerned. Rose recalls checking herself with a pregnancy stick. To confirm the positive test result she saw Doctor Martin.

"The Sonogram confirms it Miss Finley. I think there are two fetuses in this image. How do you feel about that?" The Doctor asks.

"I don't know, two? I didn't plan to even get pregnant, my job you know…"

"There are options. You don't have to keep the babies."

"No, I want the baby, or babies. They are very special to me."

Rose sits in her kitchen sipping coffee and remembers feeling frightened and joyful at the same time when the doctor confirmed her pregnancy. She knows it has to be from the unprotected sex with Max and losing her purse and her pills when she was tossed into the ocean. Rose remembers how wonderful that slice of her life was. She still yearns to be with Max since she just found out he's not with Peggy. *He must not want me or he would have called and told me. I won't burden him with this.* Rose recalls how she urged Max to stay with Peggy. She still remembers how she told Max she works alone. That used to be how she felt but now things are different.

The confirmation from the doctor kept filling her mind until last night she called Sam to avoid upsetting Max, but at least she let Sam know. What kept her up all night was how she seems to have lost the thrill of being an FBI agent, chasing criminals, and dodging bullets. Would that be safe for the babies? The job lost all of its glory when she found out she's pregnant.

A pounding on her door and the doorbell ringing several times interrupts her thoughts. She rubs her eyes and draws her robe together as she goes to the door to see who is there this early in the morning.

"Oh my God!" Rose whispers shocked to see Max through the peephole. She turns away and leans against the door. Tears well up in her eyes and Rose isn't sure what to do. She hears the doorbell ring again several times. She cracks open the door.

"You're here!" Rose cries. Her heart melts seeing Max reaching for her. She lets him wrap his arms around her.

"Why didn't you call me?" Max utters.

"Why are you here? I told Sam not to tell you! Peggy is gone and you didn't call me."

"She moved to Vegas, and you should have called me."

"I didn't want to upset you again."

"She moved in September, but you didn't want me to call you."

"Really Max? You could have broken the rule for that! Why didn't you tell me?"

"I thought you wanted to forget me. I tried calling your burner phone but it's dead. I believed you didn't give me your new phone number on purpose."

"Oh no, I really tried to forget you but I miss you so much!"

"Sam called me, told me you are pregnant. I know you want to be alone, but I had to see you."

"I should have called you instead of Sam. All that stuff I said about working alone and being alone, well I was wrong! The truth is it all changed when I met you. All I want is to be with you. I mean I don't know what... What are you doing?"

Max sweeps her off her feet, shuffles inside and kicks her door shut before he sets her on her feet again. "Look Rose, no more secrets. I love you and I miss you. You once said you want to have lots of kids. I want that too. I got a big house. I want you to come back to Fort Lauderdale with me. What do you think about that?" Max states and stares into her teary green eyes.

"Oh Max, you may need a bigger house!" Rose wraps her arms around him.

"Thank you! That sounds like a yes!"

-0-

About the Author

 Rob has become an avid writer of action and suspense novels. He enjoys writing books that include some of his exciting life events.

Rob is living his dream writing stories he's always wanted to do, but time did not allow. Previously he wrote non-fiction writing related to his real estate career, like his eBook on property management called *The Landlord Way.* He began adapting stories based loosely on his early experiences visualizing many more adventures happening in future stories to come.

His first fiction novel *Deadly Plans* was inspired by a visit to an orange bauxite lake in Jamaica. His next book *Deadly Diamond: A Diamond to Die for* centers around South Florida and Italy leading to his current book *Secrets: Murder, Lies, and Politics* which is the final storyline for the group of friends Max, Sam, Ann and Peggy whom he developed based upon close friends from his past. Currently he his working on his new book with new characters to fall in love with.

Follow me at www.facebook.com/Author.Rob.Davis, www.authorrobdavis.com or email me at: author.rob.davis@gmail.com

If you enjoyed this book, please check out my other two books with these same lovable characters.

A simple day at work becomes a race for his life as loyal and patriotic Max discovers sensitive information that's he not supposed to find. Thinking his friend and boss Mark is working with terrorists developing a new form of chemical weapons for mass destruction, Max enlists the help of his best friend Sam to foil the plans he discovered. Quickly Max is hiding out in FT Lauderdale before he and Sam fly to Jamaica where he discovers the truth. The US Government working with Mark has set a trap to stop a major terrorist group working in Afghanistan. Things don't go quite as planned and Max and Sam learn their good life living in sunny Ft Lauderdale takes some serious turns as they become the hunted by both Jake a deranged psycho and the terrorists whose weapons supply, they intended to stop.

An Italian Mafia Mogul purchases a rare diamond and dies before the unveiling. His murderers flee to America, Fort Lauderdale, Florida after stealing the diamond and a sum of cash. Before they get to enjoy their new life, more killing occurs. Years later on his prison deathbed, a father tells his sons where he's hidden this rare stone starting the diamond's curse all over again. For Maximillian Merchado and his friends, they once again find themselves in the middle of a murderous rampage spanning two continents. Invited to Italy, they nearly lose their lives. After returning home and putting the ordeal behind them, they discover they are not safe. The question becomes as news of this rare diamond and its immense value driving people's greed; can Max and his friends escape this time?

www.ingramcontent.com/pod-product-compliance
Lightning Source LLC
Chambersburg PA
CBHW061101210726
48294CB00001B/243